AGED OUT

Patrice Nussbaum

Copyright © 2021 Patrice Nussbaum
All rights reserved
First Edition

PAGE PUBLISHING, INC.
Conneaut Lake, PA

First originally published by Page Publishing 2021

ISBN 978-1-6624-4136-3 (pbk)
ISBN 978-1-6624-4137-0 (digital)

Printed in the United States of America

To my husband, Stephen, who has always believed in me. He chased me until I caught him…

The First Reminder

May 30, 2525, 2:30 a.m.

Ding! Ding! Ding!

Whaaa? My eyes pop wide open. After I immediately sat up in bed, the first thing I noticed was the sharp pain between my eyes. Then remembering how much I had to drink last night at my birthday party, I was not so surprised. I should have known better. But what woke me? Glancing at the nightstand beside my bed, I noticed my mensa tablet blinking bright red. Who would be trying to contact me at this hour?

I reached over, grabbed the tablet and opened my messenger. What I found there was terrifying! It was from the government of the United Quadrants!

> Naia Gold, greetings from your most benevolent government. We wish you a very happy birthday! Now that you've reached your milestone sixty-ninth birthday, we will be sending you information throughout your last year to assist you in preparing for your upcoming aging out, which is to occur on June 29, 2526. Your loving government wants this to be a wonderful and worry-free year for you! You will soon be receiving a list of all the exciting opportunities that await you in your last year. Enjoy it all!

I sat, eyes dazed over, thinking about this for almost an hour. There would be no more sleep for me tonight. I didn't know why

I was so surprised by this. Most of my friends my age had gotten similar birthday messages, and I'd commiserated with each one of them. I got up and made myself a cup of tea. Sitting in my tiny living space on my worn sofa, I tried to remember the little I'd been told about how all this started centuries ago. I wondered how much of it was true.

The History

It seemed that it was back in the mid-twentieth century when things began to change. I was not completely certain if this was true or just a tale. By the time I was old enough to learn of such things, all history had been deemed pretty much irrelevant and was very rarely passed along. Back in the twentieth century, some president came up with the idea that the government should help all the young girls who had babies they couldn't afford to raise and care for.

My great-great-grandmother had passed this piece of information through the family history as if this was somehow immoral and unusual. The way I understood it, this promise of a monthly income just for giving birth caused quite a spike in households with no fathers in the home.

Now many would laugh at such a narrow-minded notion because that was frequently the norm. Rarely did anyone marry anymore, and many women were somewhat unsure who the father of their child might actually be. Before the guaranteed yearly income that the government began paying in the late twenty-first century, there was great income disparity. The poor hated the rich, and eventually, a president was elected who campaigned on equality among races, among sexes, among the entire population. Social mores changed dramatically as well. Sexual intercourse became more of a party game, and sexually transmitted diseases became rampant. Fortunately, vaccines and cures had been developed so that by the time I began engaging in sexual activities, they were no longer a threat.

President Haddad, who was considered the god of good social thinking, made many inroads into making sure that all had equal access to everything considered must-haves for daily living. Food was free, what schooling that existed was free, everyone had equal access to health care, and all had similar dwellings determined by family size. The old adage that the more children you had, the more the government would give you was still true to this day.

About twenty-five years into this wonderful new society, things began to go terribly wrong. There were so many people collecting their yearly stipend that the taxes taken from them to fund all this equality became too onerous to tolerate. People were having as many children as possible to up their incomes. About this time, many people worldwide were becoming addicted to mind-altering drugs. Babies were being born addicted and damaged. Crime and easy access to handguns made the streets a battle zone. Many United Quadrant women of childbearing age were increasingly becoming addicted. Habitually drugged moms did not take good care of their children, and many young children came into the world and were so traumatized by their home life that most schools became more like counseling centers than institutions of learning.

Finally, the government stepped in and passed laws that any man or woman of childbearing age with a drug offense against them, no matter how minor, must immediately have surgery to prevent reproduction. Tubal ligation for women and vasectomies for men became very common. My oldest daughter, René, would never be able to give me grandchildren, even though she'd been clean for many years now. There were no second chances.

When tax levels reached 85 percent, brutal protests began. The unrest that followed was so vicious that many cities were destroyed. There was a huge uprising of people who demanded to know why the great new society wasn't working. They paid higher and higher taxes each year to fund it all and demanded the government take action to stop this equal impoverishment.

I believe my grandparents were still children when lawmakers began to bandy about the idea of using the "aging out" method to combat overpopulation and the growing drain on society, which was perceived to be caused by the elderly. At first, it was met with horror and incredulity, but as younger generations had to pay more and more of their income as taxes to provide care for those deemed to have had enough birthdays, it became a talking point for consideration from prospective politicians seeking election.

In 2389, both the House of Representatives and the Senate voted in favor of the bill and sent it to the president of the United Quadrants, who, at age twenty-seven, had campaigned in its favor and was pleased to sign it into law. Long before this became legislation, the government mandated that every person should be identified and kept account of. It wanted to be completely knowledgeable about the citizenship status and whereabouts of every person who lived in this country. At birth, each child, without exception, had an identifying chip inserted with all pertinent information and a GPS tracking device implanted in their backs an inch to the right of their spine. Devices had been invented by then that made this a very minor procedure that only required a few days of Band-Aid use. It was a completely forgettable operation with no significance—until it became an essential tool for the Aged Out Program.

The Aged Out Law was a death sentence that became routine. When a person turned sixty-nine, they would begin to get electronic messages from the government urging them to start preparing for their upcoming euthanasia. This was to take place exactly one month after they turned seventy years old.

This was a very hotly contested issue for the first twenty years or so, but as the people's taxes began to drop, more and more young people favored the idea of "aging out" senior citizens. Presently, the average age of all citizens was around thirty-seven years old. It had also become common practice for anyone over the age of fifty-five to not be given medical attention during a medical emergency, letting death happen naturally. This had considerably thinned out the group approaching seventy.

For many years, people tried to stay under the radar about their age by having extensive cosmetic surgery to look younger than they were, but the chip always gave them away. A cottage industry boomed for almost a decade where those reaching their final years paid to have their chips replaced with a false one. This was usually done in a back room of someone with little medical experience and less-than-sanitary conditions. It worked for those who managed to recover from this homegrown surgery! All government and municipal readers that were in place in every public area were fooled! It worked for about ten years until the invention of a special alloy chip. These special chips had to be highly accounted for by those who had access to them. They were impossible to forge or duplicate. In time, all false chips were found and replaced.

Many tried to escape this fate by going off the grid. I'd been told that my great-aunt and great-uncle ran for the hills and lived completely off the land for four or five years. But as years passed, the grid grew ever bigger until there was no place left to hide. Many tried to flee to those countries in other parts of the world that still revered their elderly, but much too soon, that option was also closed. These countries became so saturated by older Americans and Europeans seeking asylum that none of them would accept immigrants from countries where aging out the elderly was standard practice.

This was history of the Aged Out Program.

Now I had just received my first government message to start preparing for my death, which was to occur exactly thirteen months from my sixty-ninth birthday. I turned sixty-nine on May 29.

I was angry and scared. I did not want to die!

Chapter 1

May 31, 2525

On my sixty-ninth birthday, those friends who were still here gathered together to give me the party of a lifetime. We sang and danced for almost two days straight. We played games, and I received many gifts and pretty trinkets. Even though no mention was made of this being my last full year to live, it was not forgotten. My husband, Stephen, had been through this same farewell three years earlier. It was strange. When we thought of *years passing*, we would think of them being far off into the future. My time had seemed so far away, but three years seemed to pass by overnight.

Stephen accepted his fate with little to no opposition. In our youth, we'd both been proponents of the aging out movement. Back then, age seventy seemed a thousand years away. As we both aged, we knew what was coming and had come to terms with the notion that if we both lived long enough, this would be our fate.

One month after he turned seventy, a limousine arrived at our home at 8:00 a.m. to take him for his last ride. I was not allowed to accompany him, and his destination was secret. As I held him close for the last time, I did what we discussed I would never do. I began to cry and beg him not to go. Those who came to get him restrained me, and the last thing I saw of him was his look of sadness and disappointment that I had lost my composure.

It took about six months for his ashes to be returned to me. There were so many laws about the disposal of ashes that I was not sure what to do with his. For over two years now, his ashes had been sitting on the kitchen table. It wasn't long into my widowhood that I started talking to the urn as if he were still here. It was not nearly so lonely if he was here to listen. At times, I felt as if he answered me, but I didn't tell anyone about that. All cemeteries had been emptied long ago, and mass cremations of the remains were held all over the country. The land was needed for new construction and served no useful purpose for the dead.

All of us who reached the age of sixty-nine were to be treated royally in our last year of life. Stephen's wishes had been granted. I was determined that my last year was going to be nothing but mindless fun, at least to those who looked on. In reality, I was thinking and plotting of ways not to die.

Chapter 2

My best friend, Wilda, came to visit. It had been a while since we'd seen each other. Wilda, a January baby, had even less time than me. I thought that perhaps between the two of us, we could come up with a plan to save us both. After a glass or two of wine, I whispered this notion into her ear.

Wilda physically jumped and exclaimed, "Are you crazy? That's against the law! What would everyone think if we attempted something so bizarre? We'd never get away with it either! You know what happens to people who try to do something stupid like that!"

I did indeed know. If anyone was caught trying to escape during their last year, they spent that last year in unpleasant confinement. It only took a few rebels being apprehended to create the notion that it couldn't be done and that the attempt was not worth it.

I countered, "Are you just going to sit around and wait until they come for you?"

Sadly, she answered me, "Yes, what else can I do?"

Just as sadly, I had no answer…yet.

At dinner that night, we met up with a few friends. When older women went out and congregated in public at bars and restaurants, younger men were in abundance to fawn all over us. It was not at all unusual to be approached by many during the evening.

The first twentysomething sauntered to our table just as we were sitting down. "Hey, beautiful ladies! Can I buy you a round of drinks?"

Depending on our mood in the moment, sometimes we allowed them to. If we allowed that first step, we would soon be treated to extreme romantic gestures and a free dinner. Before the evening was over, each of us could have a young fellow profusely gushing over us.

Our appearance, age, or weight was not important to these young men. They knew they would be coming home with us, and we all looked the same in the dark. We'd all had multiple lovers throughout the years, and we wanted our needs for sex and human touch met just as much as anyone else.

Tonight I turned them down, as did Wilda, Lakeisha, Lynn, and Sally. We had a lot to talk about, but that would have to wait till later when we could find a place with no listening devices. Stephen and I had spent a fortune installing an alarm in our home to detect listening devices since, at any time, the government could listen to our conversations. We had to get approval from Homeland Security to have it installed. Since we both were considered low risk, our request was granted. All of us were allowed the alarm except Sally. She had been something of a rebel her entire life, and the government did not quite trust her. But we did!

I'd moved Stephen off the kitchen table before we gathered at my house. I always gave his urn a little pat whenever I moved him. He'd be back on the table before the night was over.

As the wine was poured, Wilda blurted out, "Has Naia told you about her harebrained idea?"

I kicked her under the table because I didn't want anyone else to know of my plans.

She looked at me in surprise and asked, "Was it supposed to be a secret?"

I couldn't believe her naiveté and that she'd gotten my other friends curious. Lakeisha, Lynn, and Sally looked at me with expectation for what I was about to disclose. I quickly came up with a lie that I was considering a six-month world tour. They looked at me rather grimly.

Lynn asked, "That's not what you really want to do with your last twelve months, is it?"

"It was just a thought," I replied while giving Wilda the "Shut the hell" up look, which she thoroughly understood.

We gossiped for hours about the so-called government celebrities and engaged in the usual bragging about our children till almost eleven. I called a car service to take everyone home. I had that privilege because I was in my last year. I put Stephen back in his rightful place and told him good night. I played a few games on my mensa tablet as I lay in bed. I began to wish I'd let one of those young men buy me that drink.

Chapter 3

June 29, 2525

I decided I'd better really get down to the business of finding my way out of my death sentence. I began to write down idea after idea, whether they were feasible or not. Hide in a cave? Nope, caves had readers installed now, and I was not an outdoorsy person. I wondered if I could stow away on a plane or ship. I wish I were so much more independent than I was. Stephen had babied and spoiled me so much throughout our lives together that I wasn't really sure what steps were safe for me to take. I could not afford to arouse any suspicions by being careless with my searches.

Since all knowledge was on the Pipeline now, I suppose I could look up the schematics for a ship bound for foreign lands. Ships were only used now for tourist entertainment. Transportation of goods had evolved into instant molecular delivery. Perhaps I could be lucky enough to see a hiding place that would get me out of the country. I'd have to be very careful to get on a vessel that was going to a country that didn't practice a form of the Aged Out Program. But if I did manage to make it to one, what would I do? I would have to depend on a translator assist app to talk to people. I would really stick out in China and Japan, which were two of the few countries that still let the elderly live. Africa still had places where one could hide, but I would certainly be easily noticed in a city. It was doubtful that I could manage to stay alive in the jungle, even though most exotic animals were extinct now. It would be a very primitive existence.

I became more and more depressed from my lack of a workable idea. I couldn't ask Know Everything on the Pipeline how to escape from the country without law enforcement showing up immediately at my front door. I wondered if they'd believe me if I told them I was just doing it for fun.

"Always curious about everything," I'd claim. I wished Stephen were here to tell me.

After a short cry and pity party, I was determined to get over my fear. If I was so afraid of staying here and dying, then I was going to have to get over my fear of leaving and being on my own.

I decided to try new things over the next few weeks. I would make myself try things I was scared to death to try. My first thought was skydiving. So before I could talk myself out of it, I called an instructor and made an appointment for a tandem jump for the next week. What else scared me? Perhaps bungee jumping off a bridge? Swimming with sharks or wrestling a grizzly bear? I was starting to get loopy and distracted now.

Perhaps I'll go out to dinner. Maybe I'll choose not to be alone tonight.

After what's-his-name left very early the next morning, I lay in bed in something of a pleasant stupor. Then I heard the bell on my computer ping, telling me I had a message. Despite hating to move, I reached over for my mensa tablet to see what it was. I lay there in disbelief at my second notification from the government, which had a list of what I should be doing to prepare for my death.

I was to designate who would receive my ashes and what funeral incinerator I preferred to cremate me. If I had any possessions I wanted to leave for anyone, I should have their name permanently etched on them so there would be no doubt among my children and heirs what my intentions were. I would also need to make arrangements to have my small government-owned home thoroughly cleaned, repaired, and updated for the next person who would occupy it after my demise.

Stephen and I had been relocated several times during our lives. Single people stayed with their family until they decided to couple. Then after a long application process, when a small dwelling became available, the couple could live in it together. It was possible to be put in a dwelling far from where you wanted to live. Stephen and I were fortunate to be placed in one within two hundred miles of our families. While it was unusual, Stephen and I decided to marry a few years after we met. The instant attraction that drew us together for a night of incredible sex had never waned. So after living together for a couple of years, we decided this was probably a forever thing.

When our children began to arrive, we were moved two more times into larger dwellings. Surprisingly, all four of my children eventually coupled and left. We were then moved into this much smaller house that I still live in today.

The exterior of these dwellings could not be altered. No add-ons or plantings or anything that would distinguish one house from another was allowed. This made sure the dwellings looked all alike so no animosity could arise that would make inequality an issue. The only thing that did distinguish one house from another was the government-generated black house numbers that were to be placed precisely above the front door. All exteriors were painted the same color that I laughingly called dung brown. It had an official name, but I couldn't remember what it was. All interiors were furnished with government-issued furniture, but here we had some leeway to add some personality to what was given to us. I liked to think of myself as quite crafty, so many of our belongings had been bedazzled or in some way touched by me and my hot glue gun.

I would have to rid the house of my personal belongings and my personality before my death. A few days before my final day, an official trash truck would be dispatched to go through my dwelling to return it to its basic look. By then, I should have given away everything I wanted to pass along, but my kids didn't particularly care for my things anyway. They might take something for the sentimentality of it, but I had little of value. As far as I knew, no one did.

Chapter 4

Well, I did it! I actually made myself go the airport for my skydiving appointment. Since this was such a frightening event for me, I thought I would certainly chicken out. But I did get on the plane after rudimentary instructions on how to land with my partner. I figured I could always change my mind at the last minute.

But as my turn approached, I thought, *Why not?*

I was going to die anyway. Could this be any worse than calmly waiting for my executioners? As we were strapped together for our descent, my instructor told me to relax and enjoy the fall! About the time I thought about enjoying the fall, he'd pushed us through the open door of the plane.

I knew that I was going to die! This was it!

But almost immediately I opened my eyes after the jerk of his opening the parachute. I loved that rush of air! Interestingly, I did not feel terror. As we floated through the air, I watched the ground slowly approaching. For a second or two, I thought this must be what a bird felt as it glided through the air. I did close my eyes right before we touched ground, though. It wasn't as hard a hit as I had dreaded. My instructor, Glen, took the brunt of the landing. After a few seconds of making sure all my limbs were still intact, I was able to get up on my feet.

I wanted to do it again! I began to wonder if being able to do this on my own might somehow aid in my escape. I signed up for skydiving lessons. If I could face something like this, what else might I be able to do?

I had invited Sally to come over to dinner and had preordered prime rib substitute for the two of us to be delivered around eight o'clock. She was to be here at my house around six thirty for pre-dinner cocktails. I had always admired Sally's knowledge about the world and her ability not to give a shit about much of anything that she considered trivial. She was born earlier in May of the same year as I was, and it was hard for me to believe this rebel would sit idly by as her death date approached.

She was one of the most totally unique people I'd ever met. She was fierce in her beliefs but able to accept others who did not see the world through her eyes. She was probably one of the few people I'd ever known who truly and simply just loved. Her approach seemed to always be "live and let live." Just by her being here, I was comforted and felt a lightness to my step.

She arrived closer to seven o'clock, as I knew she would, because Sally was always fashionably late. I'd made a huge pitcher of margaritas for us, and we got down to enjoying them right away. I was wary of asking her if she was going to try to do something to get away from her upcoming date with death. It was scary to even broach the subject because despite how well you thought you knew your friends, you would never know who might turn you in. There were certain perks that came with turning in someone else, but I would never do it. And my gut told me Sally never would either.

I tried to be subtle as I asked about her plans for her last months. I even made the statement that I wished things could be different for us. She looked carefully at me and agreed. I thought we were both a little scared to actually say out loud what was on our minds. I wasn't surprised, though, when Sally came right out and asked me if I was thinking of doing something out of the ordinary. We played around the subject for a few more seconds.

Then I said, "Sally, I am not going to sit quietly by and let them kill me! I'm trying to plan an escape!"

She nodded and quietly said, "So am I."

I told her of my skydiving exploits and that I was doing that to become less fearful. Then I wondered out loud if having that skill might help me get away. She was doubtful about that, but becoming more fearless and confident could only be helpful and would work to my benefit. She was careful in her queries about getting away. Her home was definitely bugged. Every move she made within the listening and observational scope of the government was known and entered into her life file. This was a huge detriment to her search, but unfortunately, she'd brought it on to herself many, many years ago. As I said, Sally never liked the rules, and frequently in her youth, she had bent them almost to a breaking point. Fortunately, her father was a low-level government official, and that helped her out a little bit—but not enough to be completely trusted.

When dinner arrived, we quietly agreed to let the subject rest for a day when we hadn't had so many margaritas and could think a little more clearly. Even in our tipsy state, we both realized this was something we could not cavalierly talk about. We decided to get together in an open place in two days. As Sally left, she embraced me. We both knew we were entrusting each other with our lives. Sleep didn't come easily that night. I could not seem to think of any feasible way to avoid my fate and thought about that almost all night.

Two days later, Sally and I met in a public garden. Among the artificial trees, we whispered. Sally was much more advanced in her planning than I. I was totally amazed at her scheme to live! She had a web of people who were all planning the same thing! Together they had thrashed out so many things that had never occurred to me to even think about. I wanted so much to be a part of this group and begged Sally to let me in. She warned me I would have to be fully vetted before I could learn another thing. I would be investigated thoroughly to make sure I wasn't a secret agent for the government trying for extra perks for turning in the group. Sally knew I wasn't, but her say-so would not be enough. The secrecy of this group was what kept them alive. If I received the okay, I would be allowed to have access to a special location. This location was not the place where they met. But I would be watched to make sure I was not followed or a government mole.

Now I had real hope!

Sally went home that night with every hope and idea that she would help Naia escape her upcoming death. She had hopes that the group she'd helped form would embrace Naia as one of them. Sally and Naia were lifetime friends. The older they'd gotten, the better friends they became. It was on her slate to get as many people away to safely live out the rest of their lives as possible. There were a few people whom she'd gladly wave goodbye to as they took their last ride, but Naia wasn't one of them. She planned on encouraging her group to agree to bring Naia along to safety and felt there would be no hesitation in accepting her.

Chapter 5

July 29, 2525

I didn't have a lot of money. No one did anymore. Taxes were very high on our guaranteed incomes, and with Stephen gone, I was only getting half the amount we'd gotten together. The "last-year perks" and equality laws didn't leave me any needs that weren't met. With the Aged Out Program, things had gotten better in that respect. Money was not really needed much anyway. All our basic needs were met. Everyone got food, housing, and health care. But anything beyond the norm had to be paid for in one way or another. "One way or another" could mean many different things.

Food production had undergone tremendous changes over the past two hundred years or so. There were no longer farms and gardens or real meats and vegetables. Food was produced in large warehouses run completely by automation and robots under government supervision. There were no animals or plants used in our food sources. That ancient method of food production took up far too much land needed for housing, and gases produced by animals contributed greatly to world warming. With our earth-saving means of food production, chemical concoctions made up the bulk of the food that the government allotted to everyone according to family size. The vitamins and minerals the government deemed sufficient were added into each and every food offering. Different flavorings and colors made these concoctions tolerable to our human palates. If I ordered chicken, I'd get a square of a chicken-flavored chewy product. Usually, this item had a slight yellow color, which I assumed was the color of chicken. Our vegetables were also molded into squares and colored to represent their original hue. The flavorings taste good for those of us who've never tasted real food.

In our last year, we no longer needed to abide by any constraints. We could order as much chem food as we wanted. That was supposed to be a great perk in the year before we were killed. "Last-year folks" were granted much largess from "our most benevolent government" for the last 365 days and 1 month of life left to us. Stephen's wishes had been to be with me and his virtual dog, Buddy. He never cared for travel, and all his wishes for extravagant food and wine and endless talk on the Pipeline were honored.

I was determined that my last year was going to be nothing but mindless fun, at least to those who looked on. In reality, I was thinking of ways not to die.

Chapter 6

I think it was almost ninety years ago when it was announced that we'd finally reached that long sought-after goal—equity and equality. I hadn't been born yet when the great Equality Law became the most important law in the land. Because of it, we were all to be equally poor, had to wait months to be seen by a doctor, and subjected to limited food supplies. But the great experiment had seemed to work to everyone's satisfaction until taxes on everyone's guaranteed income had become high once again.

There were talks in the works of trying another approach to eliminate other sources of high-maintenance government costs, but I wasn't sure who or what the next savings plan might entail. I only hoped it wouldn't lower the Aged Out Program's limit of life. I had an uneasy feeling it would be either children or education that might feel the brunt of the new legislation. There had been great consternation over birth regulations years ago when it was decided that babies born with any kind of defect were "helped" to die quickly. If something was detected before birth, an abortion was immediately performed. If some traumatic brain injury happened at any age, that person, no matter how young or old, was quickly dispatched before they could be a drain on society. In fact, anyone who couldn't realistically take care of themselves by adulthood was ripe for extermination!

It was hard to know what or whom to believe about what was really happening in the world today. What was true was only true through the eyes of the person who was reporting it. There were conflicting views on every media outlet. But most people paid little attention anymore because truth didn't seem to be the objective of the news. More and more, it seemed like it was just about who could talk the longest and loudest.

Chapter 7

I got another message from the government yesterday, asking me if there was anything that officials could do to help me prepare or any things I might like to see or do in the next few months. I would have to think about that. I wished I had more of a plan. Then what I would ask for might help me along with my escape.

On this, I was waiting for Sally and her group to let me be one of them. Then I'd know more of what to ask for. I could say I wanted to visit a country that did not have any policy similar to the Aged Out Program, and I was sure they'd let me take the trip. The only problem was, those countries wouldn't welcome me as anything but a short-term tourist, and they all had a strict and fast-moving extradition exchange with the United Quadrants. If I wanted to try that, I'd have a government escort. I'd have to get away from them and then set out on my own. Perhaps I'd better start learning an Asian language. I should sign up for Chinese lessons at my local continuing-education program tomorrow. I had to make absolutely sure I was prepared for anything!

My Chinese language classes started two weeks later. The professor was a tiny Chinese woman with the blackest hair and eyes I'd ever seen. The first class began in English with basic Chinese names for everyday objects. I was surprised to see so many people about my age here to learn Chinese.

Who does this at our age? I wondered. But all sixteen of us seemed very intent on learning. This made me wonder, *Do some of these people have a plan to escape?*

I wondered if I was feeling the same sense of desperation from these other people that I was feeling myself. Could any one of these people be a part of Sally's escape group? At the end of the class, everyone hurried out quickly and went their separate ways. No one seemed to want to hang around and socialize. If these people were contemplating the same ideas as I was, they would not talk to a stranger about it. But how I wished I knew! Perhaps if we could trust one another, we could plan together. But trust was in very short supply since no one had any privacy anymore. I trusted that my home was not wired for government intrusion, but I really didn't know for sure.

After our next lesson, I asked the instructor if she'd like to go out for a drink after class. To my surprise, she agreed. She spoke English very well but had a distinct Chinese accent. After a vodka and cranberry for me and a martini for her, we both had relaxed a little bit with each other. I told her a little bit about my husband and children, but at thirty-seven, she had not yet coupled and still lived with her parents. I asked how old her parents were, and she responded that they were sixty-four and sixty-eight. I felt sorrow for her because, in the next few years, she'd be losing them both. When I expressed my sympathy to her about her soon-to-be loss, she informed me that, even though her parents were United Quadrant citizens, they still had family in China who would take them in when the time came. She'd eventually follow them back to China as she aged.

"You must feel a great sigh of relief knowing that your folks will get to live out their lives for many years to come," I said to her.

"Oh, yes," she replied. "I love my parents very much, and I would fight to the death if they had to be aged out."

I thought of my own children, who seemed to have little regard for what was to become my fate. This had gone on for so many years that it was just a normal part of getting older to them. They knew it would happen to them too. There was much more independence for children now. There was really nothing to want and very little to aspire to. Real life seemed to have become a more and more tortuous time for them to get though. They were easily bored and had little incentive to do much of anything, especially if it was difficult. Most never had any desire to work or contribute anything that didn't directly gratify them. There were still a few young adults who had the ambition to make something of themselves for the good of their communities. That was where we got the few doctors and educators we had.

Chapter 8

The scream of sirens woke me about two in the morning. I could see flashes of light and the smell of smoke in the air. Then I heard the people! I peeped out my window and saw that the streets were full of people, angry people, who were fighting with one another, carrying torches, setting fires, and running toward the center of town. Then the sound of gunfire erupted! The *pop, pop, pop* of machine gun fire bounced against the close walls of my neighbors and became a continuous echo. I was petrified with fright. I had no idea what this was all about, and I didn't know if all these people were running from something or to somewhere that I might also need to go! I got my small handgun out of my nightstand and loaded it, just in case I needed it. Every citizen was armed now. I had never had to use mine yet, but I'd just been lucky. There were very few people who had not had to kill in self-defense.

As the crowd began to thin out, I stuck my head out the door and asked one of the passersby what had happened.

A young girl slowed down long enough to yell to me, "They aren't gonna get away with this!"

I screamed after her, "Who's *they?*" But she kept on going.

I turned on my central news system to see if I could find out what was happening. One or two stations were blacked out, which was never a good sign. It made me wonder if there were some kind of localized outages or if the rioters might have burned or torn down the central system headquarters.

I finally found a station on air. As I've said, no one really trusted the news anymore, and I rarely listened to it. From what I could learn from this channel, it seemed a new law had been passed without the people's knowledge or consent. That wasn't so unusual, but this time, it was big! It was very serious and would affect many people's lives. To attempt to lower taxes again, the government had apparently implemented a new law.

A lottery would become the standard tool of birth control! From what I gathered from the news, a bill had been signed into law that only women between the ages of twenty and thirty could have a child, and those who would be allowed to do so were chosen from a lottery with their personal chip number! Only they would be allowed to give birth!

If your number wasn't chosen, you would be sterilized at ten years old. This would go into effect immediately according to the news. Picking lottery numbers among ten-year-olds now would be in preparation for the ten-year period they would be allowed to breed. I guessed it would make sense that those allowed to be the child bearers would be among the brightest and best. But that would definitely be against the law. From all walks of life, the lottery would be totally random—equal opportunity for all! There didn't seem to be much more information about what would happen if someone couldn't or didn't want to have a child. But this riot, like all the others that had come before, would cause neighborhoods to be destroyed and people to be killed. This was a terrifying and tragic night for everyone. I imagined it would be this way for a while. Until this action was accepted, it would continue to cause unrest and trouble.

After the first batch of children whose chip numbers weren't drawn were sterilized, people would get used to this new normal. It would be just another ugly story in our history books, if history books were still written anymore.

I knew that there were a few chosen from each quadrant who were tasked to be the record keepers and journal writers for a certain allotment of square miles. History, unfortunately, was in the eye of the journalist and was rarely recorded objectively. I believed people's reactions had been similar every time the government made laws that were unpopular. After the initial and often-violent opposition and protests, people eventually became comfortable with it over time and accepted it, especially if taxes went down.

This happened with the Aged Out Law, and now "most" of us were used to it. Since all my kids were all over thirty, this might cause immense sadness for my youngest son, Jack, who had only recently coupled with a woman over thirty. I believed he would have been a great dad. He was sort of like his own father. Stephen was very intelligent but very impatient. He was a good father, though, and the children had benefited greatly by his being their dad. Jack was very smart, too, and seemed a good deal more comfortable with himself than his father had ever been.

Chapter 9

August 29, 2525

Oh my god! Oh my god! I got the news early this morning that Jack had died in the gunfire last night!

A little after dawn, a hard pounding woke me up from a troubled sleep. Glancing out the window before unlocking the five locks on my door, I was immediately terrified! There were two government officers at my front door. They never came to tell anyone good news, so I knew something awful had happened. And it had! They informed me in a cold, harsh voice that Jack had been among the rioters last night and had charged toward a government official. He'd been shot down immediately!

All I could think was *Why had he done something so stupid? He knew better than that! You never threaten a government official, or you die!*

I fell to my knees, sobbing. How could he do this? He was so smart! How COULD HE DO THIS? After briefly telling me where his body was taken to be cremated, they asked if I wanted his ashes turned over to me or to the young woman he was coupled with? I didn't know Robin all that well, so I filled out the form to have them returned to me.

There was no sympathy for anyone who was killed by the government. So I had to fill out the cremation form sitting there on the floor. Tears and snot were running down my face as they stood over me. When I'd completed the form, I handed them back a tear-stained piece of paper. They turned and walked away, leaving me to lie there on the cold floor all alone with my grief.

Eventually, I made myself stand when I realized I had to get to Robin! Was she aware of what had happened? Had anyone told her yet? I needed to get to her quickly! I hadn't used my fly pack in a very long time. I rarely traveled any distance anymore, so I usually used the car service. Most people flew by molecular distribution now, but I didn't like to. I always felt sick after the fewer than dozen times I'd tried it. Calling the car service would be so much easier for me. I'd enter my destination into the car's GPS, and the driverless car would go. Today I did not have time for that. I quickly dressed and went to the attic to get my fly pack. Thank goodness Stephen had always stressed to keep the thing plugged in, so mine had plenty of energy to get to Robin and Jack's house.

As Jack's widow, Robin normally would be allowed to stay in the house, but since Jack had died from an assault on government personnel, she would have to move back with her family. They might give her three days to move out, but I wasn't sure.

I strapped on my pack and attempted to start it. It sputtered and smoked, and I worried a little if it was air worthy. I truly didn't care what happened to me now. I shakily lifted off from my backyard in my one-person pack and took off. Mine was not the newest model, but its GPS still worked, and it coordinated all the data and started me on to my destination. I had the oxygen nose plugs in and was able to go higher than I could without them, which made me get there quicker. I traversed the distance in about thirty-five minutes. It was not a particularly smooth landing, but damn it, I survived it!

I knocked on the front door. Momentarily, I could hear the multiple locks being opened and then saw Robin's astonished face when she opened the door and saw me. Since I'd never visited before, what started out as a grin quickly turned into horror. She realized that I was not the bearer of good news.

She threw herself into my arms and screamed into my ear, "Is Jack dead?" She stepped back, saw my face, and then she knew.

I stepped into their sparse but comfortable small living area. It was almost a mirror image of mine. We sat together on the well-worn, two-person sofa. I sat there quietly as she cried.

Eventually, she said, "I told him not to go! I told him!"

She continued to howl like a wounded animal, and I held her until she was as dried out as I'd been this morning. She sat up slowly and looked at me. I spoke softly to her and asked why he'd been there. Almost hypnotically, she started to tell me all that had happened the day before.

"We were so happy with each other," she said. "We'd been talking for a few months about starting a family. I've been off birth control for almost two months now, and for all I know, I might already be pregnant. We'd started to get so excited by the prospect. Then this news broke about this new law. Jack just went crazy! He slammed out of the house and took off running with a crowd who seemed just as angry as he was. I tried to stop him, but he kept on running."

This was all spoken in a voice so monotone that I wondered if it would ever seem alive again.

"How did you find out about it?" I asked her.

She looked up at me as if she was surprised I was there. "What?" she asked.

"How did you find out about the law?" I asked again.

She drew in a long breath and told me how he'd come home from a walk, screaming about it. "I couldn't make any sense of it for the longest time. He was so upset. I'd never seen him that upset by anything before," she said. "It was frightening. He began to holler that they could not do this do us! I still wasn't sure who was doing what to us. He was almost incoherent!

"Then he heard the crowd, opened the door, and heard them chanting just what he said, and he ran after them. I yelled for him to come back, but he never even looked back. He just kept on running. After he left, I turned on news center and learned about the new law. I couldn't believe that this country would deny us children, but what could I do? I was somewhat worried when he didn't come home last night but reasoned he was out getting plastered or screwing some woman in his drunken sorrow. But never this!"

Later on that afternoon, a government spokesperson came to her door and told her she must be out of the house within two days.

"Where will I go?" she cried. "I have no place to go."

"You'll go back and live with your parents like you did before," I gently told her.

"No! You don't understand. My mother and father are dead! I've lived with my sister and her partner for the last five years before Jack and I coupled!" she said.

"Then you'll go back there," I told her.

"No! I can't go back there. They didn't want me there as it was, and they did not treat me very well. They won't let me go back, especially if I might be pregnant."

"They have to take you back," I stated firmly.

"They might legally have to take me back, but they don't want me. I'm scared they might hurt me and potentially my baby!" Her eyes began to well up again, and big huge tears rolled down her face.

"Robin, you don't know if you're pregnant or not yet, do you?" I asked gently. "I got a pregnancy test yesterday at the Pharma Depository. I was going use it last night when Jack got home. I'm two and a half weeks late. I'd thought we'd have something to celebrate," she choked out through her tears. "What do you think will happen if I am? Will they make me abort it?"

"I don't know, honey. I honestly don't know," I sadly answered.

Robin got the pregnancy test and went into the bathroom. A few minutes later, she called me in to see the results. We met each other's eyes; the test was positive. She sat down on the toilet, and I perched on the edge of the tub. We didn't speak for a while, both of us lost in our own thoughts.

The next morning, I helped her pack up the few possessions that she and Jack had managed to collect. It didn't take much time to get her completely ready to leave. She still had another day allowed in the house, but then what? As I said, I didn't know Robin very well. I'd only met her once when Jack brought her home to meet me. I knew that she wanted me to invite her to live with me, but I was not sure I really wanted to do that. I had less than a year left myself. Would having another person in the house hamper my plans to escape? Would we even get along?

Then I thought about the last essence of Jack in her belly, and I blurted out, "Come home with me. Yes, come live with me!" She dropped to her knees and grabbed me around the legs.

"Thank you, thank you," she croaked through great, gaping sobs.

Knowing we had much to do and plans to make, I grasped her by the arms and pulled her onto her feet. I spoke to her rather gruffly, "Get ahold of yourself. We don't have time to cry. We have to get information and then plot our course."

We had to get the car service to get us back to my house. I only had the one flight pack, and Robin didn't own one. Molecular distribution was discouraged for anyone pregnant, and we couldn't give away the fact that she'd need a belly guard. When the car arrived, I programmed in my address, and we settled in for the long ride back. It would take us twelve hours to get back by car. The sun was on its ascent as we pulled in front of my house. I had five locks to unlock before we could enter. Walking through that door was such a relief! But the relief was short-lived. We had so little time, and so much to do!

Chapter 10

September 29, 2525

I was four months into my final year. I was still lightly sleeping and very weary from yesterday's long car trip when the ping on the computer made itself heard. I was pretty sure I knew who it was from. To my surprise, it was Sally asking what I was up to.

I replied to her email by typing, "Oh, the same old thing."

We could not say anything of substance by email because it was all monitored and analyzed. Artificial intelligence could ferret out even the tiniest bit of subversive language, and we'd be in trouble.

"Why don't we take a walk later on after the day cools down?" she suggested in her response.

I had a Chinese class that night, and I asked her to meet me after class. She agreed. I hoped so much that this meeting would be about the escape group and their willingness to let me join them.

I made myself get completely out of bed and get myself dressed. As I was leaving my sleeping area, the computer bell pinged again. This time, it wasn't a friend. It was my monthly message from the government. This time, it was quite a pleasant little missive asking if I'd made any plans for travel and pleasure yet. It was asking if there was anything the government could provide for me to make my remaining time more pleasant.

I responded, "No, not yet, but I'll let you know if anything strikes my fancy."

I woke Robin up to eat breakfast. She must have been crying most of the night because her eyes were so red and swollen she was looking at me from sad little slits. I did not yet feel I could trust Robin enough to take a chance on confiding in her about much of anything. I did tell her before we became unnecessarily upset that we needed to find out everything about the childbearing law. We must know every code and codicil.

Life for her might not be easy now. By attacking a government official, Jack might have ruined her chances for much of the government's largess. If it became known that she was carrying his child, both might conveniently disappear. Using my computer, I went to the site Know Everything. I asked for information on the new childbearing lottery law. I asked that it be explained to me in laymen's terms and in great detail. The main thing we must know was if a woman who was already pregnant would be allowed to bring the child to term.

The law, as it was deciphered to me, was 193 pages long. I carefully read each and every word. I almost fainted with happiness when I read that women currently pregnant would not be forced to abort, even if they were over the age limit of thirty. As I read this information word-for-word to Robin, the sobbing started up again, but this time, it was because of relief and gratitude. I warned her how important it was that no one ever knew that this was Jack's child. The baby would be chipped as "father unknown," which was extremely common these days.

Robin ate a few bites of the freeze-dried breakfast I had rehydrated for her. Suddenly, she stood up, shoved her hand to her mouth, and ran for the bathroom. I heard the sound of violent retching and went to the bathroom to see if I could be of any help. As I held her hair back from her sweating brow, she completely emptied what little food had been in her stomach. She started to cry again, and I wondered if this crying stuff was going to keep up the entire nine months. I helped her to wash off her face and gave her some water to rinse her mouth. I was somewhat impatient with her for nothing she had done. I was pissed that, in my process to save my life, I had to attempt to save hers as well. Right now, I felt too damned old for this!

Chapter 11

Later on that evening, as I was preparing to go to class, Robin began to cry again and begged me not to go and leave her alone. It was so difficult not to yell at her and let her know that I was not going to change anything in my life because she was in my house! I tried my best to explain that I had plans tonight that I couldn't change—actually, *wouldn't* change. The rest of my existence might depend on what I learned tonight. I got downright aggressive, and she finally sat as the sniffling slowed down. I did feel some sympathy for her as I knew how I felt the night after they took Stephen away. I had never been in a house all alone before, not in my entire life! I didn't want to ask her and get the crying going again, but I could imagine that she'd spent little time alone either.

I repeated my directions from earlier to engage all the locks on the door and draw the shades. She pitifully sat there, nodding her head, as I walked out the door.

When I didn't hear the locks locking, I knocked hard on the door and hollered, "Lock the door!"

I didn't move from the doorstep until I heard the click of all five locks. Satisfied, I climbed into the car and programmed the school's address into its GPS.

That night, we all had partners and tried to speak a rudimentary version of Chinese to one another. I could understand my partner, a very gentlemanly man, DeQuan, quite well, as he could me. Then we were tasked to write down what the professor said to us in Chinese, and that had a totally different outcome for most of us. Her Chinese was spoken so rapidly that I could make out very few of her words. Her spoken language wasn't bastardized by an American accent. I was quite upset along with others that we'd done so poorly.

The professor was quite comforting, though, and said that we were doing well for our first attempt. At this point, she gave us a recording of her speaking about a particular subject in Chinese. We were to take them home and practice translating what she said. We were told that there would be a new one for us every week. None of us was learning to write in Chinese. But we would eventually get a recording of her asking us questions, and we must record and bring back to her our answers in Chinese. I had devoted an hour or so every day to studying, but it appeared now that I was going to have to lengthen my study time.

Leaving class around dusk, I was in a hurry to meet with Sally. I was stopped by a man in my class who seemed to want to chat. At any other time, I would have welcomed this, but I needed to get to Sally now! When I tried to excuse myself, he told me that it was he that I was to meet tonight. His persistence was uncomfortable, and I felt around in my pocket for my small pistol. Of course, I had no reason to doubt that he wasn't carrying, too, but I wanted to be ready in case I needed to shoot first.

Then he stopped me in my tracks by saying, "I'm a friend of Sally's, and she thought we would get along."

I stammered back loudly, "Are you…are you part of her group?"

My exuberance was a big mistake! He gave me a disgusted look, turned abruptly, and started to walk away. I quickened my pace to try to keep up with him, realizing I must have made a terrible blunder by greeting him this way. He kept on walking and never looked back. I could not keep up with him, and before long, the darkness swallowed him up.

Oh, no! What have I done? I've ruined my chances! I berated myself for speaking without thinking first.

This had gotten me in trouble before. At this moment, for the first time in my life, I thought of taking that gun out of my pocket and ending this right here and now, on my own terms. Then I thought of Robin back at home, waiting for me. I had not grown much attachment to her yet, and I wasn't sure if I even liked her or not. But right now she needed me, even though I told myself very firmly that I did not need her! I climbed back into the car, programmed in my address, and rode home. I'd never felt so alone in my life.

I emailed Sally later on that night and told her I was sorry I was late for our appointment and hoped we could plan another walk soon. I waited and waited, but I never heard from Sally again, at least not directly.

I looked in the mirror at myself and wondered how I could have compromised myself and the group so easily. Now I was truly on my own. I noticed my long black hair had gone gray about half an inch from the roots. I was really quite vain and wondered how I could have let this occur. I studied myself in the mirror and thought I looked pretty good for a woman who was about to be aged out. My skin was a light caramel from my Middle Eastern heritage. My eyes were still very dark and my wrinkles were few. Stephen was from German Jewish decent, and between the two of us, we managed to turn out four very handsome children.

Long before I was born, my family had been devoutly Muslim, as his had been in their Jewish faith. It was hard to imagine that many years ago, it would have been unheard of for us to be together. Nobody paid much attention to ethnicity anymore—or religion at all. I once unearthed an old Koran in the basement of a relative's house. I attempted to skim through it but found it was in some obscure language that I could not read. Stephen had told me what he knew about some sacred scrolls that his great-grandfather had once told him about, but he knew nothing more about them than I did my own supposed holy book. There was no law that you couldn't be religious. If anyone practiced any kind of religion these days, I was not aware of it.

Robin was sick again this morning. This had become something of an unpleasant ritual. She looked so tired, as if she had no energy at all. I asked her if there was any food that appealed to her and told her that I would order it, but she sadly shook her head no.

I rummaged around and found a few restaurant-packaged crackers. I urged her to eat them to see if that would calm her stomach, but they quickly came back up too. I was growing more and more impatient with her. I knew that she was ill and couldn't help it, but the more I had to take care of her, the less time I had to try to save myself. I wondered to myself if that was even possible now.

I tried a few times to teleathought Sally. But if I managed to get through, she never answered back. There was nothing but blackness in return.

Chapter 12

Wilda had emailed me asking if she could come for a visit tonight. I didn't know if I felt up for a visitor, but she might cheer up both Robin and me. We both sure could use it. I had ordered a light meal and some white wine for the two of us. I ordered some bland chicken broth and ginger soda for Robin in the hope that it would stay down and give her some strength back. She had done nothing but lie on the guest cot all day, staring at the ceiling. I encouraged her to get up and bathe.

"I know that will make you feel better," I said.

She turned her head in my direction and stared blankly back at me. This listlessness caused me a wee bit of concern. So I pulled her to her feet and literally undressed us both. I climbed into the shower with her and washed her hair and bathed her. Seeing her naked concerned me even more. She looked so thin, and maybe it was just my imagination, but I thought I saw a tiny bit of swelling in her belly area. It seemed far too early for that. As I ran the soapy washcloth over her, I could feel her begin to relax. She stood completely still in the warm water, never moving until I turned her in a different direction. I was sorry when I had to turn the water off, but I could feel that the water was starting to cool, and I didn't want her to catch a chill. I dried her off and rubbed her legs, arms, and hands with lotion. Robin had short hair, so I was able to towel-dry it. It dried in tiny little ringlets all over her head. Even though she was over thirty years old, she looked so child-like and vulnerable. I helped her dress into some comfortable clean clothes. She lay back down again, comfortable, but it was as if the shower had completely exhausted her.

I straightened myself up a little as well because we were having a visitor. I hadn't told any of my close friends about Jack's death because he had died in such a scandalous manner. I would tell Wilda, of course, but she'd probably be the only one of my friends I would confide in. Robin and I had already planned the story that she was the daughter of a friend who was staying with me till her pregnancy came to term. It was just far better for Robin and her child's future not to be associated with Jack's name. I probably couldn't fool Wilda even if I tried. She was very intuitive, and she'd guess I wasn't telling the truth. She would not call me on it, but she'd know. Wilda was a great stickler for the rules. She would not give our secret away, but I doubt if she would approve of it either.

Wilda arrived about five minutes before the food did. She liked to eat earlier than I usually did, but she was the guest, so we ate early. I did not tell her about Jack right away, even though I knew she was curious about this young girl in my house. I thought I'd wait for Robin to eat, and I'd get her to bed before I said anything about Jack. The story might bring tears to my eyes, but it would bring hysterical wailing from Robin.

Wilda was very polite, as she always was, when she met Robin. Robin sat at the table with us and tried to spoon a little broth into her mouth. A few seconds later, she was up running to the bathroom again to throw it up. Once again, I helped her to get herself cleaned up. Afterward she went to the guest area and lay down on her cot. When I returned to my small kitchen, Wilda looked at me with concern and lots of questions. I sat with her there and told her everything. It was such a relief to be able to share this with someone, and without Wilda, I wouldn't have anyone I felt this close to.

When I got to the pregnancy part, that was when she became truly worried. Wilda had always had a gift for doctoring and caring for sick people.

"Has that girl been able to eat anything since she's been here with you?" she asked.

"No," I replied, "She can keep nothing down."

Wilda exclaimed, "That child needs to be in a hospital! She is bound to be dehydrated and weak. Conditions like that are sure not good for a baby!"

I agreed with her and wondered aloud what questions they might ask me at the hospital.

"I'm on record as being Jack's mother," I said. "It's surely known that she was coupled with him. It would not take too much information fed into a computer to confirm that connection. Her chip and mine will give them more than enough data to let them assume this child is Jack's. Any suspicions will make them run a DNA test, and then what?"

Wilda shook her head. "I don't know what will happen. But I know that both that girl and her child will die if this continues much longer!"

Under any other circumstances, Wilda would have been right at my side, but she was only five months from her own execution, and she couldn't be around anyone who might get her confined for her last months. She still volunteered to go with me, but there was no way on earth that I was going to let her chance it. I called for two cars—one to take Wilda home and one to take Robin and me to the nearest hospital.

Chapter 13

Just as I suspected, our chips were read the moment we stepped over the hospital threshold. Approaching the robotic intake cube, I could hear the *ping, ping, ping* of the computer, which sounded as if it was warning someone about something. I had a pretty good idea what the warning was about, so I would not be able to lie our way out of this. A robotic voice told us to sit in the black circle in the back of the room. We were the only ones sitting here, even though the room was crowded. Was this to designate that we were unsavory people? We did get a few disgusted looks in our direction. Normally, I would have been upset by the looks of disapproval, but not today. I looked back at the haters, then blew them a kiss. This would make them turn away!

I knew this would be a two- or three-day ordeal because there were so few doctors to treat the ill anymore. I wish I'd been taught some basic medical procedures, such as starting an IV drip. But needles always made me queasy, so I avoided that class and took basic first aid. By now, Robin was so weak she collapsed on my shoulder as we sat on the hard wooden chairs. I held her in my arms to keep her from falling onto the floor. A little later on, I noticed that I was sitting there, absentmindedly stroking her hair. I stopped immediately. She was *not my child*! I refused to get any more involved than I already was!

To my surprise, late the next afternoon, I heard her name called. We'd gotten in much quicker than I expected. They had to get a gurney to get her to the exam room. At some point last night, she must have fallen into unconsciousness. As the robot scanned her body, I could see it making all kinds of calculations on its screen. The calculations were then transferred to a screen right above her head. Most of what it said was gibberish to me, but when I got to the area related to pregnancy, the *yes* light was lit. I wondered what would happen next. There were twelve other people in this exam room, and apparently, we were the last in line. I hoped that Robin would live long enough to be treated, and I told every robot and every human that walked into that room how sick she was. That did not move her any closer to the front of the line. I wondered if that was because of who we were or if this was just how things worked now. I guessed the most urgent patient had to wait in line behind the sprained wrists and the broken toes these days.

It took us six more hours to reach the front of the line. I had carefully been watching Robin's chest to make sure she was still breathing. She was, but the movement of her chest had become much shallower as we waited. As the medical technician stood at her side, examining her, I told her how ill she'd been and unable to keep even a sip of water down. When they asked me if she'd peed much in the last twenty-four hours, it occurred to me that I hadn't taken her to the bathroom at all! She pinched the back of her hand, and it stayed pinched. It did not spring back!

"Classic signs of dehydration," said the tech. "She has a form of extreme morning sickness called hyperemesis gravidarum. It may be too late to help her, and that baby of hers will probably miscarry as well. Let's get her on an IV drip and see if there will be any improvement. I've noted whose child this is. If she lives, do you think she would prefer for us to abort it?"

"No!" I yelled back. "Everything that can possibly be done to save this woman and child must be done!" The tech gave a condescending "Eh…" and then called for someone to roll Robin to a room and ordered an IV. As I expected, there were at least thirty other men and women lying in this room in various stages of treatment for a variety of illnesses. I had grabbed a mask for both Robin and me as she was wheeled in. There could really be some very contagious illnesses floating around in here, and this might offer us little protection.

After Robin's IV was inserted, I sat on the floor at the side of her bed. By this time, my back was killing me, but there was no place else to sit. As the bag slowly dripped into her veins, I waited to see if she would start to wake up and feel a little better. But there was no discernible change that I could see. After two more bags of saline solution, they put a tube down her nose into her stomach and started giving her food. She didn't even gag as they inserted it. These bags had a mixture of what looked like a melted greenish milkshake in them. I knew they were going to ask me to leave as nighttime approached, but I hated to leave not knowing if she'd be alive tomorrow when I came back. It was with a heavy heart that I left that treatment room and took the car back home.

After unlocking my front door and stepping inside, the house felt especially lonely and quiet. Robin had been with me only a few days, and I resisted the idea that I might miss her a little bit. Walking into the kitchen, I was startled to see Stephen's urn still sitting on the shelf. He hadn't been on the kitchen table since Robin's arrival! I apologized to him and put him back in his rightful place. I was amazed I hadn't noticed until now!

Exhausted, I fell into a restless sleep the moment I lay down. I dreamed I could hear one of my babies crying, but I could not get to them to see what they needed. I seemed paralyzed, and the crying intensified. I wanted so badly to reach my baby, but I was unable to move! The crying suddenly stopped, and I jerked awake. It was four thirty in the morning, but I knew I would never be able to fall back to sleep. I grabbed my mensa tablet and started playing my games. When I looked up, it was almost seven. I ate a bite and cleaned up to return to the hospital so I could be there by nine when visiting hours began.

When I got to Robin's bedside, I noticed her color was better. When I touched her arm and said her name, she slowly opened her eyes. They still seemed glazed over, and she did not speak, but I spent the biggest part of the day talking to her as if she could understand every word I said.

Later on that night, she turned to me and said, "Mama?"

I fought myself very hard for a moment, then gave in, and answered back, "Yes, baby, it's Mama."

She closed her eyes again, but her lips had formed the tiniest of smiles.

Chapter 14

Robin was hospitalized for two more days, and I was beside her the entire time. By the time she was discharged, she looked and felt so much better. They had loaded us up with medicines of all kinds, and she was told to eat lightly for the next two weeks. Even though we were shown no compassion at all, I was pleasantly surprised that she'd gotten such good care. I was pleasantly surprised that she was still alive!

I called and canceled my skydiving lessons. It seemed more important to stay home with Robin. I rationalized all this by telling myself I would have more time to research and plan if I stayed home. I still planned to continue with my Chinese lessons. I was picking it up reasonably well, and there might be a chance to make a better impression with my fellow student, Sally's *friend*. I had kept up with my homework during Robin's hospital stay, studying and translating for hours on the floor as I sat by her bed.

My evenings out with my lady friends seemed to have come to an end since Jack's death. Sally was out of my life, and I couldn't seem to find a time that was convenient for Lynn and LaKeisha to meet me for dinner. Despite not telling anyone but Wilda the story of Jack's death, it would have been very easy for them to find out. The list of dissidents killed during the last protest was listed on the Pipeline. Anyone who hung out with me would be more closely monitored, and that certainly was not desirable. If the tails were turned, I would probably try to avoid them too. There were no personal relationships that stood a chance if the government had reason to notice you in a less-than-favorable light. I would cast a long shadow that friends and acquaintances would also be shaded by if they continued to associate with me. It made me sad, but I totally understood.

I spent the next few days searching the Pipeline for any hint of an idea of how to save myself. I did it as innocuously as possible so that I would arouse no suspicion. I knew I'd be watched more closely now than ever before. Nothing stood out to me as a possibility. I would have been painfully depressed if Robin hadn't been here. I tried very hard to remain positive around her. In doing so, for no discernible reason, I felt my spirits rise as well. She really was warm and quite funny, and we enjoyed each other's company. I understood now why Jack was so attracted to her. I could genuinely say now without hesitation that I liked her a lot.

I had a Chinese class later on that night, and Robin no longer begged me not to go. She trusted me to come back. I knew I might have to betray that trust someday if I could find a way to stave off my murder, but that certainly wasn't a concern at the moment with the luck I'd been having. I wondered if Robin remembered this was my last year. We had never broached the subject, and I hesitated to do so. Things had been going so well. I didn't want to start another torrent of crying and sorrow, so I said nothing.

I was so disappointed that the man who claimed to be Sally's friend was not in class tonight. I did well on my homework translations and did better taking the notes on what the professor said to us in her language.

As class broke up, I stood and casually wondered aloud, "Where's Jesse tonight?" A few people mumbled they didn't know, and a few more turned away with no answer at all.

Okay, that started me thinking, *Are the people who didn't answer and would not meet my eyes afraid of something? Do they all have something in common? Hmmmm...*

Beyond curious, I made a note to myself to be prepared to get to know a few of these people. If Jesse wanted nothing to do with me, perhaps I could find someone else who would give me a little hope. I hummed a little tune in the car as I headed back home.

When I got back home, Robin was so happy to tell me she'd felt a little tickle inside her. She was beginning to get noticeably rounder in the tummy. I thought both of these occurrences were happening much sooner than I remembered them happening to me. But that was so long ago. I probably had forgotten. We celebrated that night with cake and ice cream. Normally, I celebrated with vodka, but since Robin could not drink alcohol, I made merry her way. It was a good night!

I slept well that night for the first time in a long time. I was in that last blissful state right before I fully awakened when that damned computer pinged again. To my surprise, it was from another student in the Chinese language class. I had to stop a moment and put a face to this name. Which one was DeQuan? Then I remembered that he was the man I had first practiced talking to in class. We had never partnered again, so this truly was strange for him to contact me! Ever mindful that he could be part of the group I longed to join, I said yes to his invitation for drinks and dinner.

When I told Robin I was going out later that night, a momentary cloud crossed her face. I knew she didn't want me to be out two nights in a row, but I left her with no doubt in the knowledge I was going to go. She recovered quickly, smiled, and said she hoped I'd have a good time.

I had ordered the car service to pick me up so I would be a little late to the restaurant. I did that in hopes that he'd already be there, and I wouldn't have to deal with a gaggle of young men bothering me. I was very pleased to see he was waiting for me to arrive and escort me inside. I remembered now that my first impression of him had been that he was a very courtly gentleman. I was right! He pulled my chair out for me to sit down; in doing so, he leaned down and whispered in my ear that we had much to talk about.

I was excited beyond belief! I was completely convinced that I was being given a second chance! I drank very lightly with a small glass of really good wine. I didn't want to take a chance that I might get too tipsy and miss something important he had to tell me. He, on the other hand, had three straight shots of bourbon before we'd even ordered! This bothered me a little bit because I figured he was either a heavy drinker who could handle all this alcohol or he really had nothing of substance to tell me and we were out on a date. If I had misread all this and made up a fantasy in my head, I was going to be sorely disappointed. Normally, I would have enjoyed going out with this man, but I had hoped that tonight would be so much more!

After we'd ordered and before dinner came, he had another shot, and I drank another glass of wine. I was having a very hard time masking my disappointment about what I thought this night would hold. I knew he sensed a change in my demeanor, but he did not question me about it. I ate my food very slowly, my appetite nonexistent. We left the restaurant, and he suggested we take a short walk to continue the evening a little longer. As we walked along, he grasped my hand and tucked it into the crook of his elbow. This was not unpleasant, but I was ready for this night to be over.

As we stepped into the street, he quietly commented, "I heard you asking about Jesse last night in class. Is he a friend of yours?"

"No, not really," I replied carefully. Maybe there was more to this than I thought.

"Did he try to speak to you after class a few weeks ago?" he queried.

"Yes, he did." I replied. "He introduced himself as a friend of a good friend of mine."

"And who was this friend?" he queried.

I almost automatically answered with Sally's name, but something about this line of inquiry didn't feel right. I immediately answered, "Diane. My friend Diane."

"Does Diane have a last name?" he asked.

I stopped immediately and pulled my hand from his arm. "Of course, Diane has a last name, but why all the questions?"

"Just carrying on a conversation, my dear." He grabbed my hand again.

This made my blood run cold. Who was DeQuan, and why was he so interested in Jesse and the names of my friends? I really didn't know anyone named Diane, but DeQuan seemed far more interested in whom I knew than was necessary. Since he held me captive again, I turned the tables and started asking him questions.

"Do you work outside the home, DeQuan?"

We walked along for at least ten steps before he answered me. "Why, no, Naia, what made you think that?"

I answered him back, "Just trying to make conversation, DeQuan."

Soon after this, we turned back toward the restaurant. Reaching the car, he kissed my hand and cordially bid me good night. Feeling like my hand was dirty, I wiped the back of it on my black pants. I rode home in apprehension about what I might have told him. I would need to be far more careful in what I said and did from here on out. If I was already on the government's radar, I could never take things casually ever again. I'd have to be suspicious of everyone!

What a way to spend my last year!

Chapter 15

October 29, 2525

The next morning, as I was preparing breakfast for Robin, she was wearing a plain gray T-shirt that was much too tight. I was amazed at how pregnant she looked in such a short time.

"Robin," I asked, "are you sure you're just two months pregnant? Your belly is really growing."

"Oh, yes," she said emphatically. "Just two months, I'm sure!"

"We need to get you to a midwife and have you checked out. You may be having twins!" I exclaimed. "Wouldn't that be somethin'?"

Thinking about the prospect of two babies wasn't something I really wanted to contemplate. By the time Robin had this child, my time would be almost over if I hadn't managed to save myself by then. One baby would be hard for her to raise on her own; she seemed barely capable of taking care of herself. But two? She surely would have to go back to her sister's house if that was the case. She would have to have some kind of help! I didn't blame her for not wanting to go back there if they were abusive, but she might have no other choice. I didn't know what she'd do. They might give her a house of her own if the government did not suspect the child was Jack's. With our trip to the hospital and our chip readings there, the government could already know.

"We need to go down to the clothes exchange and get you some larger clothes," I told her. No one had a large number or variety of clothes. When clothes were needed, there were huge warehouses dotted all over the country where clothes could be picked up. Many were preworn but were usually in good shape. Everyone was allowed seven gray shirts for everyday wear, three pairs of black pants, and a limited supply of underwear and socks. We were given two pairs of brand-new running shoes per year. Shoes were always new. Children were allowed three pairs because they were more likely to outgrow their shoes. If needed, one could get a dressier pair of the grays and blacks, but these were just loaned to you and could not be kept for the long term. I had gotten the dress versions of the uniform-like clothes on two occasions in my life. The first was when I married Stephen; the second time was when I picked up his ashes from the crematory.

Since we would be going out together, I suggested this would be an excellent time to engage a midwife. The most trusted midwives usually had long lines outside their homes with women in various stages of pregnancy in queues.

"It is a very pretty day, and we can take a blanket to sit on and some water to drink. It should be very pleasant," I coaxed.

"Oh, I don't need to do that," she said. "I can go when the baby is about to be born, but no need to go ahead of time."

I wondered why she wasn't more eager. Yes, it would be a long, tiring day, but she'd get to see her child during the ultrasound exam.

"Robin," I said, "I'm going to insist we go for the sake of your health and that of your child. You need to be checked on and have certain tests run. I have a certain type of blood where I had to have injections throughout my pregnancy. If Jack inherited that and has passed along this trait to your child, you may need them too!"

"No!" she exclaimed. "I don't want to, and I'm not going!"

I was really surprised by her emphatic refusal. I didn't think I'd ever heard her raise her voice before and never to me. "What's wrong?" I questioned. "Are you upset about something?"

She turned her back on me and proclaimed, "I just want to be left alone. Is that okay? Am I allowed?" She stomped off to her guest space and left me standing there in shock! This was a side of Robin I'd never seen before and one I didn't want to see again.

All right! I thought to myself. *She has certainly gotten her point across to me!*

Maybe I'd been worrying too much about Robin and lost my focus on finding a way to cheat death. No more! I was only going to be thinking about my life now. If she wanted or needed anything, I'd let her tell me. I had to keep reminding myself that she was *not my child*!

The sweetness seemed to leave my house after this exchange. She became quite reserved with me, and I left her alone as she requested. She began to take the food that I prepared for her and ate alone in her guest space. For a few days, I puzzled over what I might have said or done to bring out this stranger. But within a week, this was the new normal, and I quit thinking about it. I gradually stopped fixing her meals. Whether she ate or not was no longer my responsibility. We stayed out of each other's way.

Chapter 16

It was now mid-October. Very early in the morning, I heard the ping of my computer. I wondered who this might be. To my surprise, it was another government message.

> From now until your euthanasia, we will be sending you messages more frequently to remind you of your responsibilities. There is still time to honor a special request from you, but your time is growing more limited.

What? I never remembered this kind of government harassment in Stephen's last year. I remembered him getting the occasional message. His special request had been exquisite chem food, wine, and privacy; but I couldn't remember any type of veiled threat, nothing about limited time. Instead of developing a plan, I was becoming more and more confused. My head was just too full!

At exactly 6:30 a.m., the expected bell pinged. I had gotten one other message from the government a week ago. The messages were becoming more frequent, and less and less cordial. This one was a review of the laws referring to the allowed method of disposing of my ashes. I guessed the government wasn't too concerned that Stephen was sitting here on my kitchen table! Since I ate there alone now, he had regained his rightful spot.

Robin and I rarely addressed each other anymore. I could hear her in the house, but we did not linger in the same room. She was continuing to grow bigger and bigger, but I said nothing. She pulled on the same tight T-shirts every day, though I noticed that she'd begun cutting a slit up the back a little bit to ease the tightness around her belly. I supposed she'd keep nipping the back until she reached the neckline of the shirt. But that was no longer my concern, and I didn't care.

I'd also noticed that she left the house a couple of times a week at two in the morning. I assumed she thought I slept through her comings and goings, but sleep for me was in short supply. I awakened at the slightest noise, so I knew when she left and when she came back. I had no idea where she went or if she met someone else, and while I told myself I could not care less, I was extremely curious. I worried about her being out at night and all the trouble she could find or the trouble that might find her!

Chapter 17

At my next Chinese lesson, the professor suggested that now that autumn had arrived, we should do something as a class. I was doing very well in the class and no longer had much difficulty having a conversation in Chinese with the professor and my fellow classmates. She frequently complimented us as a class for how hard we worked and how much progress we'd made. At the suggestion of a get-together, no one uttered a word. We all sat quietly, giving one another sideways glances to see if anyone had anything to say and, if so, who would speak first. For as much time as we'd spent together in class, we really didn't know much about one another. I felt as if we had to be suspicious of each other; it was just much safer that way.

"Does anyone have any suggestions of what we might do?" asked the professor, and again, there was only silence. "Well, if no one has an idea, please allow me to suggest a small dinner party. At the party, we will speak no other language but Chinese. We will immerse ourselves into the Chinese culture and language as we socialize. How does that sound to everyone?" she asked.

At this, there were some low mumblings among us, but no one objected. So the party was on. Since none of us had a home large enough for the sixteen of us, it was decided that we'd have the party at school. We were all asked to bring a Chinese meal item to share, and the professor would bring her wok and fix the main course for all of us. It had been so long since I'd had any kind of social life. I was excited by the thought of a party!

When I returned home, Robin had some young man visiting her. She did not bother to introduce him to me, so I introduced myself.

Hand outstretched, I said, "Hi, I'm Naia, Robin's friend."

AGED OUT

He hesitated before he reached out and gave my hand a weak little shake. He did not tell me his name and only said hello in a voice slightly above a whisper. Soon thereafter, he stood and left. He never attempted to acknowledge me on his way out. I was so tempted to question her, but things had gotten so tense between us that I didn't feel up for any kind of confrontation tonight. I wanted to try to stay in the pleasant mood that thoughts of the party had given me.

Chapter 18

The next morning, Robin appeared in the kitchen and was in a much larger T-shirt than before. I guessed nipping the back to enlarge the much smaller one had ceased to work. Robin's belly was getting so big, so much bigger than I remembered being at this stage of pregnancy. I made no comment on it. I wondered if she'd ever seen a midwife, but I did not ask. I got a thoughtcall from Wilda asking if I'd like to come and visit this afternoon. Longing to leave this house that had become so gloomy with the issues Robin and I were having, I immediately thoughtcalled back: "Yes!"

Thoughtcalling or thoughtchatting was something all of us tried to learn as young adults. Being able to harness our thoughts directly to another person took a lot of practice. I didn't use it as often as I should. It took so much concentration and focus that, usually, I didn't bother. There was a finite number of people that one could do this with because there were just so many brain boosts that could make it possible to send and receive. Overdoing it could produce a terrible headache, and there had been some unfortunate souls who'd stroked out in the process. Some seemed to have a greater capacity to hold on to many contacts, but I only had a limited number. If the government had any capacity to intercept thoughtcalls, I'd never heard of it. My best girl friends, my children, and Stephen were about all I could ever handle. Now the calls between most of us had stopped—Stephen because he was dead, and most of my friends because they knew I was under what I thought was a limited amount of government scrutiny. Like Sally, when I tried to thoughtcall any of them, all I got in return was blackness and silence. Wilda kept the line open, though, and I was certain that she always would.

AGED OUT

Arriving at her house around two thirty in the afternoon, I was a little surprised by her demeanor. She always had something homemade to snack on and something lovely to drink. She had the snacks and drink as usual, but she seemed troubled about something. She suggested we go out into her tiny little garden she'd fashioned from a spot on top of a utility unit directly out her back door. She had two small chairs and a cloth draped over the big rectangular metal box. She had some small pots with flowers sitting on top of the pretty cover. She had a tarp hung to shield this small area off from prying eyes.

No one had flowers or gardens outside. They were banned years ago because people had the tendency to try to outdo one another and make their houses look different. That broke the Law of Equality, so it was forbidden. You had to know Wilda to know how much she loved her few flowers because going against any rule was something she never ever did!

It was a little warm inside the tarp, and the hum of the utility unit was ever present; but she had turned the mundane and ugly space into her own little oasis. Since she was in her last year, the government might turn a blind eye to this infraction if it became known, but who could say for sure? No one around her had turned her in. Wilda had good neighbors because she was such a good neighbor to those around her.

After beckoning me into her miniscule secret garden, she invited me to have a seat. We ate some of the beer cheese she'd made and drunk a small glass of the wine her mother had made before she was aged out. We talked about frivolous things, and then she motioned for me to lean in closer to her. Curious about what she was about to tell or show me, I leaned in till I was only about five inches from her face. She reached and pulled me by my head in position to whisper something in my ear.

I jerked away and looked at her, wide-eyed and in disbelief about what I thought she'd said! She looked me straight in the eye, nodded in the affirmative, and once again pulled me to whisper more. Surely this must be some crazy fantasy. She whispered her information for a long time, and my ear became damp from the moisture in her breath. I understood now why she'd wanted to talk out here in her garden. She wanted to take no chances that her supposedly listening-device-free home really was.

We went back inside and made a little more small talk in case there was anyone listening. We didn't want to arouse any suspicion. Leaving shortly thereafter, I had much to ponder.

Chapter 19

Arriving home, I found Robin puttering around in the kitchen. With her back to me, I could see that she was nothing but skin and bones. When she turned to face me, she was almost nothing but belly. We had avoided each other so much that I had failed to notice how pale she was and how sunken her eyes appeared. Then I noticed that her hair seemed to be thinning as well. Those curls I'd found so sweet at one time had disappeared, and now her hair hung in dry straight hunks. This girl was desperately ill right here in the same house with me, and I didn't realize it!

"Robin," I asked, "what has happened to you? You look so unwell. How are you feeling?"

She tried to brush past me, muttering, "I'm fine."

I grabbed her arm and stepped in front of her so she could not go around me. "No, you're not!"

Armed with what Wilda had told me earlier, I insisted she sit down. I was not going to take any bullshit from her anymore! I could easily ask her to leave my house, and as loathe as I was to do that, she had to talk to me! She perched sullenly on the edge of my small couch, but she would not raise her head and look me in the eye.

In a firm yet gentle voice I asked her again, "How are you feeling, and have you been to see the midwife yet? You look very ill, and I want to know what is going on with you. I insist that you talk to me." I watched and saw her small shoulders sag until she was almost resting her chin on her huge stomach. Then just as quickly, she straightened her spine and sat up as if she were readying herself to take me on! She looked at me in defiance and said nothing.

This time, I stated facts to her. "Look, Robin, whatever is going on with you is going on in my house. I have avoided confronting you up until this point, but that is changing right now! Have you been to a midwife?"

She nodded her head. "Yes."

"You are so thin and pale. What has she said about that? You surely aren't gaining the proper amount of weight for a pregnant woman. I want the midwife's name, and I plan on going to her for answers. You will be going with me on that little trip too!"

At that, she stood up to leave the room. I could stand much quicker, so I blocked her way. "Sit down!" I said in a menacing tone. "You will sit there until you answer every question I have."

She sat back down but would not answer me at all. She would not speak. I was becoming more and more angry at her, and with each question, my voice rose louder in pitch. She sat there and totally ignored me. Now I was furious!

"I will not stand for this insolence any longer," I said threateningly. "We got along so well for the first few weeks. What happened? We are both grown women, and you've been skulking around here for weeks like a sullen teenager! I lived with four legitimate sullen teenagers in my life, and I will not live with a thirtysomething one! You aren't my child, and I will not spend my last months like this!"

With this, she jerked her head around and looked me in the eye for the first time. This time, there was no defiance or anger in her look.

"Why are you saying *last months*? What's going to happen to you?" she asked in a fearful voice.

"Robin, I will be aged out in about six months. Surely you know that. Surely Jack had told you my age and my fate."

"No!" she moaned long and low. At that, she threw herself into my arms. Her tears dampened the front of my shirt. For the second time that day, I was completely shocked! Eventually, I put my arms around her as well and held her for what seemed like hours as she cried. Her crying finally started to abate and dissolve into what sounded like hiccups.

When I felt she was calming down, I pushed her away from me, picked up her chin, and looked her directly in the eye.

"Now are you ready?" I queried. With that, her face crumpled again, and she was back in my arms. *What the hell is happening?* I wondered to myself, but I did not ask any more questions. I was as emotionally exhausted as Robin appeared to be. *The questions will be answered very soon,* I told myself.

My face was resting on her head, and soon we were both sound asleep. When she started to stir in my arms, I slowly woke up. We both tried to gather our composure, but both of us were a little embarrassed by the hour-long episode. I got up and fixed us both a freeze-dried veggie burger. By the time it was done, I was starving. We both sat at the table, while Stephen, in his urn, watched us from the shelf.

I was ravenous and ate very quickly, but Robin only picked at her plate. I wanted to urge her to eat, but I didn't. She wasn't a child, and she wasn't my child, I reminded myself. I didn't want to have any more drama tonight, and frankly, I did not know what to do to get any answers from Robin. After cleaning up and putting Stephen back on the table, we went to bed on somewhat better terms, but nothing was settled in my mind.

The next morning, when I woke up, I found Robin had left the house. All her belongings were gone. She left no note, and I had no idea where she'd gone and what would happen to her. I took my shower, ate a bit, and planned to sit down to think about everything that had happened in the last twenty-four hours. It was amazing how such a short amount of time could bring about so many changes.

I realized I was grieving because Robin was gone. I could not even think about that child in her belly as being my grandchild. That would have devastated me if I had grown any attachment to the baby. For a short period in the beginning, I had a daughter again. I'd felt this loss before. I was stunned by the losses I'd had since I began my last year. I needed to get out of my own head, so I decided to go out to dinner tonight all by myself. I doubted very seriously if I would come home the same way.

By midmorning the next day, Bryan had gone, and I was feeling adrift. There was nothing I wanted to do, nor was there anyone I had a desire to see. What was wrong with me? I had thought to have a plan in place to save myself by this time when I began my journey six months ago. I had intended to have lots of good times in the time I had left, but neither was happening.

    I had accomplished nothing.

Chapter 20

I have decided what I want to take to the Chinese class party. I wanted it to be quite exotic, so I put in my order to arrive at the school just in time for the party. For the first time since Robin left, I ventured into the guest space. There had been little in here to begin with, and except for the sheets on the cot, it was much the way it had been before she got here.

Ripping off the sheets, I decided to take its small mattress off and air it out on a chair by the front stoop. Throwing the linens into the dry screener to be hit and sanitized by the low-level laser lights would really refresh them. After getting that process started, I took a kitchen chair and put it right out beside my front steps. I went back in to haul the mattress out, and something fell to the floor. I took the mattress out and lay it over the chair. I would have to sit near a window so I could watch that no one would steal it. Before I sat down, I went to pick up what had fallen out of Robin's bed. Reaching for my glasses, I sat down in front of the window and started to look over the folded stash of papers. It was hard for me to imagine Robin writing anything on real paper because real paper was so precious and expensive.

As I started to read, I understood why she didn't want it on her government-monitored mensa tablet. The writings here were clearly subversive in nature and would get her in so much trouble if they fell into the wrong hands. It took me most of the day to read through this journal-like mishmash of writing. It seemed to start long before Jack was killed, and it appeared that whatever was being planned, Jack was a big part of it! I was seeing names of prominent government officials, words like *overthrow*, *protest*, and *assassinate*. While there were many very scary thoughts on this paper, there didn't seem to be concrete plans for any kind of an insurrection or coup. I couldn't imagine Jack being involved in anything like this.

A few clues jumped out at me. There was a street name and a number, but there was no city listed. There were numbers that could be chip numbers, lock combinations, or any number of other things.

I could easily look to see if these were chip numbers. Government databases had numerical and alphabetical listings of what chip number was assigned to each person. I could enter the address into my city's database to see if that street and address existed in my quadrant. If it wasn't here, then I could do a countrywide search to see what cities might have this address, but hunting down the exact place would be a daunting task.

The address was 1953 Pearl Street. I had no doubt that Pearl Street was quite a common street name in many towns.

Sitting down at my computer, I pulled up the government chip records to see if this string of numbers actually was a chip number. Typing in 285-47-6599 did bring up a name—Kentura Bing. I didn't know anyone by that name, but I entered it in the Know Everything search window. My computer immediately died and went black.

What the...? I thought.

I turned the power off, waited a few seconds, and then turned it back on. It slowly rebooted itself and came back online. After trying it a second time, I had the same results! I tried rebooting and trying it one more time and again I got a black screen. I had never had my computer react to anything in this way before. I needed to do a more exhaustive search but obviously not from my home computer.

The only supercomputers I knew of were all in government facilities. Whom did I know who might let me look this up or, better yet, do this for me? The only person I could think of who might be high enough up the ladder to have access to a computer like this was my acquaintance Tracy. I had not seen her in a very long time, but we'd gotten along okay when we were together. She was a pragmatic woman who, unlike many other public works people, did not fall to her knees and worship the government at every opportunity. I'd heard her make a few disparaging remarks in my presence that startled me a little bit. Maybe if you actually worked for the bureaucracy, it might be a little bit safer to banter about it.

How could I approach her? It was probably almost three years since we'd communicated. I knew it would be strange if I just happened to pop back up into her life. If I was not mistaken, the last time I saw her was a few weeks after Stephen died. She stopped by to offer me her sympathy.

I knew where she'd lived the last time I'd seen her, but I didn't know if she was still there. She was in her midforties, and her two children might have coupled by now. If so, they would have been moved into a smaller house. It was a little after 2:00 p.m. Government work hours were 10:00 a.m. to 1:00 p.m. with an hour off for a meal. She could possibly be home. If I did go to see her, I would have to tell her a reason for asking about this individual… Um, what could I say? Maybe I could say something close to the truth, but not exactly true. Anyway, I sent her an email asking when I could come to visit so we could get caught up. I didn't hear from her that day; perhaps she had enough acquaintances and was not in the mood to rekindle an old one with me.

For the heck of it, I walked to the house of the courts the next morning to see if I could find a Kentura Bing in any of the old paper records. When I asked, the clerk looked at me strangely and said they never let anyone into the old paper record journals. They were too fragile to even see the light of day. Then the clerk told me that everything on paper had been entered into the database years ago and that all I had to do was look it up.

I smiled sardonically at him and said, "Thank you." Then I walked away.

I had been around computers all of my life. They had been a fact of life for centuries. I had usually been able to navigate myself around the Pipeline independently with anything I'd needed to find. But I was *not a maven* on the machine! I hated it when some little snot told me to go look things up!

Returning home, I checked my email to see if there was any reply from Tracy, and there wasn't. So my next inquiry was to the records of the cities in the entire country. I went to the search engine and typed in "1953 Pearl Street." I was surprised when only two listings showed up. I guessed having the street number really honed in on the search. One was in the northwest thirty-first quadrant in a city called New Falls, all the way across the country; the other was in the eastern middle of the fourteenth quadrant in a city called Bishop Town. I had heard of Bishop Town. It was one of the larger cities in the fourteenth quadrant. I lived in the twelfth quadrant, so it was really only about two hundred miles away.

I tried to do a reverse listing on both places to see if I could get information about who lived at these addresses. The one in the thirty-first quadrant popped up right away as Lloyd Martin and Jody Ramerez. When I entered the one in Bishop Town, it listed a K. Bing. I jumped up, whooping and high-fived myself! Now I was on to something. Then I noticed the chip number of Bing. It was different than the one from my first chip search. It definitely was not the number on Robin's paper! That really had me stumped. Everyone had their correct chip number now. How could Kentura Bing have two different numbers and live at the same address?

Oh, Stephen, how I wish you and your analytical brain were here to give me your thoughts. I know what usually baffles the illogical me comes easily to you.

It was three days later that I received an email from Tracy, inviting me over for appetizers later that same day. With a fresh shower, newly washed hair, and a clean pair of the gray and blacks, I ordered a car to take me to her house.

She still lived in the same place, so I assumed her children were still living with her. She welcomed me with a brief hug and ushered me into her living area. With her larger house, she had room for a full size couch and a small side chair. We did not have to sit side by side but could sit facing each other. She expressed her surprise to hear from me after all these years. I told her I was trying to reconnect with old friends while I still had time. I didn't know if she bought that or not since technically we'd never really been friends. I decided to confide a few salient facts to her and see how she reacted.

When I told her about Jack's death, as I figured, she already knew. Government killings were usually well publicized by the media.

While I knew she probably thought Jack got just what he deserved for attacking a public official, I knew she felt sympathy for me as a mother. She could only imagine how it would be to lose a child and didn't wish me the pain that went with that.

I told her about Jack leaving a pregnant partner behind and that I'd lost touch with her. I told her I really wanted to see my grandchild before I died but could not locate her. I told her I'd checked with the only family she had left, and they had not seen her. The only thing I could imagine was she lived with a friend.

I told her that the name Kentura Bing had come up as one of her possible acquaintances. I even had an address for him, but I could not find any more information about him. I played my scaredy-cat role and said I was really afraid to go to his home without knowing anything about him. I could play the poor elderly widow very well when it suited my purpose.

"I was wondering, as a favor to me"—*sniff, sniff*—"if you could look on your big computer and find out more about him before I show up at his door." It was at this point that I lowered my head and dabbed at my eyes a little bit. "I just want to see my grandchild before I die," I said sadly.

Tracy fell right into my theatrical web. She rose and sat beside me and patted my knee. "Sure, Naia, I'll see what I can find out for you."

After wiping my eyes again, I looked up and told her how grateful I would be if she could help me locate Robin.

After a cup of tea and a few cookies, I rose to leave. "How long do you think it will take to get some answers for me?" I asked.

"I'll try to do it tomorrow and email any information I can get," she responded.

Again, I thanked her and left in the car.

Returning home again, I was surprised to see Wilda sitting on the step, waiting for me. Was I supposed to meet her and had forgotten? Climbing out of the car, I hit the return car button.

I said to her, "Hi, there. Did I forget you were coming over?"

"No, you didn't," she replied. "I thought I'd take my chances to see if you were here."

"Have you been waiting for a long time?" I inquired.

It really bothered me that she might have been sitting out here in the cold for any length of time.

"I've been here about thirty minutes," she said. "If you hadn't come soon, I was going to head back home."

I looked around for her car but did not see one.

"Did you walk over here all the way from your house?" I asked, somewhat exasperated.

"Yes," she said. "It did not take all that long, and you know I like to stay active. But I'm sure ready for something warm to drink now."

Coming into the house, I got water to heat some tea for her. We sat for a moment and talked about nothing of substance because we both were afraid to do that anymore.

After a while, I called for a car and we went out to dinner. We ended up at a club full of younger people dancing and yelling to each other to be heard above the loud music. This was not one of our regular haunts, so no one looked familiar. After turning down numerous offers to buy us drinks, we sat closely together on a small sofa. My acting abilities came in handy when I put my arm around her and whispered in her ear as if we were lovers. This was the only way we could speak candidly to one another inside an establishment. We could have taken a walk, but it was twenty-five degrees outside at 10:00 p.m.

"Have you thought about what I told you the other day?" she shouted into my ear.

"Not much yet," I replied, then told her what I had found and been researching the past two days.

She looked at me quizzically, then said, "The name, Kentura Bing, that is familiar to me for some reason."

I told her of my ruse to get "government Tracy" to find out more information for me. I told her about the one name with two different chip numbers too. She looked more surprised by that than anything. That just did not happen in our world anymore. We both were about to go deaf from the loud music and the necessity of yelling into each other's ears to have a conversation. We agreed to meet at her house in three days to discuss this more. We agreed to write down all conversations so that no one would be able to access them. Normally, I would have used my tablet, but I didn't feel quite as safe with that anymore.

The next afternoon, around two thirty, there was a knock on my door. To my surprise, it was Tracy!

She looked around my living room warily and whispered, "Is the house guarded by listening devices?"

This stopped me in my tracks. What could she possibly have to tell me?

I grabbed the tablet of precious paper and wrote down, "It's supposed to be, but I have my doubts."

She proceeded to say out loud, "It was great to see you the other day and talk about old times." While she was speaking, she was writing furiously on the paper that Robin could be in a lot of trouble.

"Yes, we had such a lot to catch up on. It was great to see you too," I responded out loud, secretly writing, "How? Why?"

She shouted, "Have you got any of the good wine you used to serve?" And she again was writing. "I got into trouble at work today for even trying to search for Kentura Bing. Apparently, that name set off some kind of alarm, and my supervisor immediately came and started asking questions."

"Of course, I have that wine," I said out loud. "I always make sure I have a bottle of it." I wrote, "What did the supervisor say? Why did the name Kentura Bing set off alarms?"

"Oh, that's great," she said out loud while writing, "My supervisor didn't go into any details other than to say that I was making inquiries about a person who was wanted by the government for treasonous activities!"

I wrote back, "I guess I gave them all they needed to get him then by giving them an address?"

She said aloud, "Tell me again about what your son is up to these days." She wrote, "No, apparently, that address is a safe house for witnesses who are reporting unsavory people and activities against the government."

"My son Arvin has coupled and has two children," I said.

This time, I wrote nothing because I didn't have any idea why Robin would have anything to do with reporting dissidents.

Then thinking of a question, I wrote, "Did they ask you about why you were asking about Bing?"

"Two children, you say? Wow, nothing like grandchildren!"

She wrote back, "Yes, they did, and I told them the truth. I care about you, but I'm not going to take a bullet for you."

I looked her in the eye and said into the air, "That's right. They are certainly precious."

That ended the candid conversation because she thought a grandchild was my reason to be searching in the first place.

"More wine?" I asked.

"Oh, no," she replied, "I really need to be getting home."

As she walked out the door, I said, "It was great to see you. Let's do this again soon." She looked at me worriedly without saying anything. I knew I probably would never see Tracy again.

Who in the world is this two-chip Bing character? I wondered to myself. *Why did Robin have his name and address? What had they to do with each other?*

Chapter 21

I had been faithfully studying Chinese. I felt that I certainly spoke with an English accent, but I thought if I spent the rest of my days in China, I would easily be able to communicate with the locals. On the other hand, they would have to speak slowly for me to understand them. I believed I would eventually be able to understand at a normal pace, but I was not there yet.

The classroom party was tonight, and I was dressing the part. I doubt if anyone else would, but that would make it more fun, I believed. I always liked to be the one in costume or the one dancing out in the rain. I guessed you could say I used to be, and apparently still was, a closet exhibitionist. I loved the attention! It was my way to stand out without breaking any laws. Now I felt as if I mustn't draw any more attention to myself than necessary, but no one would see me tonight except my classmates.

I wanted to put extra eyeliner on to appear to have that oriental eye, but I knew better than that. I might offend someone! Offending anyone's ethnicity, culture, or sexual orientation could draw a huge fine and black mark on one's character that was not easily shed. I had heard that back when almost everyone worked, a person could lose their livelihoods over one misspoken word. So serious an offense was this considered that no one seemed to be able to apologize enough or attempt to make reparations, and no forgiveness or second chances were given. I couldn't imagine a time like that, or what words were used to make this such a firm part of the Equality Law?

At this point, there was no real difference in anyone, and there was no need to try to be superior to anyone. We all had exactly the same incomes, homes, foods, and access to health care; no one existed who was superior. No one was very wealthy. No one was very poor. As I said, equal impoverishment.

I had picked up an old black and gray from the street and brought it home, gave it a good washing, and tried to turn it into what I thought a Chinese person would wear. The Chinese people I actually knew were dressed just the same as me, but I got on Know Everything and saw some historical pictures and tried to emulate them. I did pull my hair back into a long low ponytail, the way I saw the women in the pictures wore their hair, but I just used my regular makeup.

I had reserved the car service for exactly seven thirty, which would get me there fashionably late. I wanted to make the tiniest of entrances. "Hehehe…" I giggled to myself.

I got there around eight fifteen. I opened the door to the room and loudly cleared my throat so everyone would look up and see me enter the room. A few people laughed when they saw me, a few people shook their heads, but one man, DeQuan, noticeably scowled at me. When he realized I was looking directly at him, he quickly turned his head. The next time I encountered him, he greeted me pleasantly enough.

The catering company had delivered my contribution to the evening meal, and I was determined to have a good time! Just as the professor had directed us, we were trying to talk solely in Chinese. I had reached the level of proficiency where I could carry on a conversation with only a short pause between words. A few people were amazing at it, while others struggled to say anything comprehensible.

We had a full bar, and everyone seemed in a good mood as we tried to communicate with one another. When one of us was trying to ask where the bathroom was and it ended up sounding like a completely different place, we all had a good-hearted laugh. The person who'd made the mistake laughed along with us. Thank goodness!

Jokes and laughter at someone else's expense were frowned upon. This was almost as frowned upon as saying or mocking someone's ethnicity. Luckily, this lady could take a joke! Almost anything comical was considered racist, no matter how innocuous one tried to make it.

Our professor had set up her wok and was cooking something that smelled wonderful! We all were getting a little punchy because of the liquor. I walked into the lady's room and smelled a peculiar smell that I didn't recognize. There was smoke coming from one of the stalls, but it certainly wasn't odorless vape smoke. Soon the commode flushed, and out walked one of my classmates. She had a slightly dazed expression on her face, and I asked what she was smoking.

She slurred the answer but said, "High-quality Mexican brown."

Okay, now I understood. She was smoking marijuana. That used to be legal a long time ago, but it caused so much trouble for everyone it went the way of most other drugs that people once used. I did not say anything, but she immediately let me know hers was medical grade and that it helped with her social anxiety.

"Does it really help?" I asked.

"Oh, yes," she replied. "I would have been unable to be here tonight if I didn't have it. Wanna try some?"

I knew I shouldn't, but what the heck? I was out to have a good time, and I might as well try anything at this stage.

"Okay," I answered her, "but you've got to tell me how to do it."

She lit one up and instructed me to inhale as large a puff as I could and hold it in for as long as I could. I did the best I could even though it burned my throat and made me gag. I couldn't hold it all that long because I started coughing.

"Here, try it again," she said, holding it out to me once more.

I put my lips around it again and sucked in as hard as I was able to. It still choked me, but I was able to hold it a little longer before I started coughing again. She pinched off the burning end and washed it down the drain.

Patting me on the arm, she encouraged me. "Have a good time." Then she left the bathroom.

I immediately started to feel very dizzy, and I began to feel sick to my stomach as well.

Well, that's what I get for mixing alcohol and marijuana, I thought to myself.

I sat down on the small chair there in the ladies room to wait for the dizziness and nausea to pass. Holding my head in my hands,

I seemed to lose all track of time and place. I didn't know how long I sat there, but it seemed like quite awhile. Forcing myself to stand, I walked over to the sink and looked at myself in the mirror. To my surprise, my hair was a mess, and my makeup was smeared all over my face! I bent over the sink and splashed some cold water over my face.

How long have I been here? I wondered, *Why hasn't someone else come into the bathroom to find me?*

Still groggy, I inched my feet across the floor, trying to reach the door. Pulling it open, I held on to it for a few seconds, trying to clear my head enough to walk out and join the others. What? There was no one else here! All the lights had been turned off, and I was completely alone here in the dark! I was instantly afraid!

Still too lightheaded to walk across the floor, I decided to scoot and crawl my way to the exit door. This took almost an hour because I had to pause and peer through the blackness to see where I was in relation to the door. When I finally got to the door, it was hard to stand and pull it open. Standing up, I pulled hard on the handle, but it wouldn't budge.

It was locked, and I could not get out! Pure, unadulterated terror made its way into my alcohol and marijuana-impaired brain. I didn't understand this at all! I pulled and beat on the door and yelled to be let out, but help never came. Finally, I sat down by the door. I tried my best to thoughtcall Wilda, but my brain would not boost enough for me to do it. I had no choice but to wait here. Eventually, I lay down and fell asleep.

I woke with a start when the door was pushed open and it banged the wall behind it. A thundering of feet came pounding in as I lay there on the floor in shock! It stopped abruptly when the group of children saw me lying there. A few giggled and pointed, but one young girl came up to me and asked if I was okay.

I slowly sat up and told her, "No, I am not okay. Where is your watcher?"

"She's coming. She's coming!" she insisted.

I knew what this group of children was. Since anyone rarely worked anymore, parents were always at home. In order to give them a break from their children on a regular basis, the kids were taken to these Parent R and Rs (rest and relaxation) centers for care during much of the day. They all were standard issue. All were the same, had the same advantages, and had a certain curriculum to be followed throughout the day. I believed it even had a name, *common curriculum*—or *com course* for short. Soon a teenager came in and started to direct the children to the big screen on the opposite wall. Then she saw me.

"Lady, what are you doing in here?" she demanded. "You aren't supposed to be in here!"

I explained that I was at an event held here last night, had become ill, and was left behind in the bathroom by the other people in attendance.

She looked at me skeptically and then asked, "What do you need?"

"First, I need help getting up off the floor," I said. "Then I need to order a car. May I borrow your mensa tablet?" I asked.

I never brought my mensa tablet out with me. Mine was full size, and I would have to hold on to it everywhere I went. Most kids were given a miniature one as soon as they were old enough to carry one around. I sure wished I'd had one with me last night. I was going to order a small version as soon as I could get myself home!

"I need to order a car," I told her.

She reluctantly handed over her tablet, and I made arrangements to be picked up immediately. I thanked the young woman for her assistance. She yanked the tablet out of my hand, helped me stand, and then sort of shoved me out the door. My senses still felt dull after my cocktail of liquor and marijuana. I'd never have guessed that it would hit me so hard!

Chapter 22

The car soon came. I entered my address and sat back with tremendous gratitude that I was on my way home. Exiting the car, I dug around in my small carryall for my keys. They weren't there! I poured out the entire contents of my bag there on the street, and there were no keys! I was ready to cry. I had no way to call for help and no way to get into the house. The only thing I could think of was to break a window and try not to rip myself on the ragged glass pane. I saw nothing to break it with. I wondered if I could kick high enough to smash it with my foot.

Walking by my front door to get to the window, I took a chance and turned the doorknob. My door opened! It was not locked! I always, without fail, locked all five locks on my door!

Have I been robbed? I wondered?

Who'd had access to my keys and used them to get into my house? The door was not splintered, so whoever got in had used my keys! Now I was afraid. I opened the door an inch or so and peeked inside. All was quiet and still. Then I opened it enough to step through the door. No noise. Nothing looked out of place. I left the door wide open in case I needed to escape something or someone. I walked as silently as possible throughout the house. I saw nothing amiss. I checked behind everything and into every closet. After a while, my heartbeat was no longer pounding in my ears, and I felt certain there was no one in my house but me. Cautiously, I took one last look behind me as I shut my door and locked every lock.

I poured myself a glass of wine and tried to understand what had happened to me last night. I knew there was much more to it than the combo of vodka and pot. Why was I left like that? Everyone knew I was there. As hard as it was for me to fathom, I became more and more convinced that I was set up. But by whom, and for what purpose?

I drained my wine glass. I felt so dirty and yucky that all I wanted to do was get clean and go to bed. My shower was so soothing and warm. I stayed in it until the water began to cool. The ache in my muscles had abated with the warm water, and I felt hungry. It occurred to me that I hadn't gotten any of the professor's stir-fry last night.

Why didn't the professor wonder where I was? I thought to myself. None of this made sense to me. Someone had definitely known I was impaired in that bathroom because someone had taken my keys out of my bag and been through my house!

I need to have my locks changed and get new keys right away! I went to my mensa tablet, looked in Know Everything to search for a locksmith. I found one fairly close by and emailed her and told her my situation and that I needed help immediately. Quickly she responded that she was on her way. I ate a bite to quell that emptiness in my stomach. Then I sat to wait for the locksmith. As I waited, I wondered if I'd ever feel safe in my home again. Even with new locks, my security and peace of mind had been violated.

Letting the locksmith out the door after she finished, I quickly locked every lock behind her. It had taken her about two hours to get the job done, and it was five in the afternoon. As tired as I had been then was how awake I was now. I did not want to go to bed this early, yet I had the whole evening to sit here alone, think too much, and scare myself over and over again. Except for Wilda, all my friends have distanced themselves from me for their own protection. You just didn't hang out with someone who the government was surely watching.

I was not surprised at all, though, that Wilda still came around. Wilda had accepted her fate and loved me enough to want me in her life for her last six months. I sent her an email to see if she wanted to come over for supper. I hoped that she hadn't already eaten. When she responded, she told me she'd gotten her supper almost prepared and asked if I want to come to her house. I really, really did not want to leave the house! More than that, though, I did not want to sit here alone with my own thoughts.

I responded yes to her invitation and ordered a car. This time, I took my tablet and held it tightly to my chest. Until I got a miniature one, I was not leaving home without it!

Chapter 23

When I arrived at Wilda's, she offered me a shot of tequila. I wasn't into shots very much, so I added mine in with a mixer. Wilda, though, was the queen of tequila shots. She downed the tequila, salt and lime, and then she made the face that everyone seemed to make when they drank alcohol straight. I nursed my drink, and we talked.

I deliberately had my mensa tablet offline so that I could tell her all that happened to me last night without saying it out loud. She told me some story as she watched me type frantically. When I'd gotten the story all out, she looked horrified! At this point, I started telling her a story about my word game I'd become addicted to while she typed her thoughts and questions back to me.

"Remember what I told you?" she typed. "I told you I had heard it whispered around that you weren't safe. That's why everyone is staying away from you! They don't want to get caught up in whatever might befall you. With the death of Jack and Robin's pregnancy and your strange behavior, you are on the government's radar. They've probably gotten wind of your activities about trying to escape your Aged Out date too!"

I sat there dumbfounded. I thought I was being so slick and cautious. I appeared to be drawing an arrow straight to my door.

"What should I do?" I typed back.

Wilda sadly shook her head and typed back to me. "Do what I'm doing. Accept your fate, as many have before you. Live the rest of your time doing what pleases you, and when the end arrives, go with dignity."

I was so depressed by her answer, but I nodded my head in the affirmative and appeared to accept her advice. For the first time ever, I was going to have to keep secrets from Wilda. Getting home around 10:00 p.m., I was determined to lie in bed and think of something to do next. I was asleep the moment I lay my head on my pillow.

Chapter 24

The next morning, I awoke to the ping of my computer again. I had been getting government messages almost every week now. Most of the time, they were fairly innocuous, but today's seemed to have a strong sense of menace about it that I had not received before. It said:

> This is a warning from your kind, benevolent government. You may be involved with characters that do not have your best interests at heart. The government will grant you a small leeway to mend your ways. Be aware that we will be coming for you on June 29, 2526. Don't abuse the largess we are giving you. Enjoy your time.

I sat there and read this missive over and over. Now I had confirmation that I was truly on the government's radar. They knew things about me that I didn't think they knew! I wondered if whoever came in my house the other night had somehow scanned everything on my tablet and computer. I wondered if I'd hidden my paper writings well enough.

Oh, no, I thought. *I never thought to see if my secret paper conversations had been found!*

Running up the stairs into the attic, I moved several storage boxes, removed a floor board, and saw…nothing! My written conversations were gone! I thought I'd hidden them so well! How did they know?

Now I began to wonder if there might be hidden cameras in my house. How else would they have known my hiding place unless they saw me hide it there? I realized that I had no privacy at all any longer. Everything I said or did was being recorded.

I was woefully depressed now. Feeling no hope at all, I sat and played games on my mensa tablet for two days. I only stopped to eat, sleep, and pee. At least, I had the soothing sense that whoever or whatever was watching me wasn't getting much excitement from my actions now. I hoped I appeared to have listened and followed their directions, and sadly that might be just what I'm doing. I did this for about a week, and it was killing me! I had to have something to do and somewhere to go.

I'd gone to what was supposed to be my last Chinese class of the semester last night, but there wasn't another soul there. It was as if the classes had never happened at all! Had I dreamed it? If so, it was strange. I could speak a rudimentary version of Chinese.

I decided it was time to tell the government something I'd like to do in my remaining months. But I had one last thing to do first. I arranged for a car to take me to 1953 Pearl Street in Bishop Town. I might be dooming myself, but I had to satisfy my curiosity. Did Kentura Bing live there? Was Robin there? Before I left home, perhaps forever, I needed to know.

Arriving there two hours later, I was surprised to see that it was a very big house. It wasn't brown. It wasn't stucco, and it had a yard! There were flowers blooming in every hue and bushes loaded with exotic blossoms perfuming the air with their sweetness. Why hadn't the Equality Law been enforced here? I had never seen anything like this before in my life! I walked up to the big mahogany front door that was gilded with multiple flourishes. I could actually hear voices coming from the back of the house! This house had a backyard! I suddenly felt very small, but I reached out and knocked on the door. I knocked hard on that big door! No one answered my knock. I decided to walk around to the back and see if I could speak to someone. The back was surrounded by a very high white-painted fence, and I could only see through little slits into what appeared to be a very lush large backyard.

There appeared to be children playing happily together. Squeals of laughter rang out like the tinkle of a bell. Was this place a huge Parent R and R? But then I saw slivers of adults, too, standing in groups, seemingly enjoying each other. R and Rs usually had some older children in charge. These looked like families enjoying themselves! I saw what I believe are older adults that looked as if they had long passed their aging out dates! Could this be the group that Sally had told me about? Had they found their way out of their predestined fate? I was completely confused by the wonders I was seeing here! What fantastic place had I found? But more importantly, why had the government allowed it? Why was it allowed to stand here and seem to make its own rules? I wanted in!

I started speaking in a loud voice, "Helloooo there, everyone! I'm over here on the other side of the fence. May I come in?" Not a single soul looked in my direction. This time, I yelled, "I'd like to come in! Will someone please let me in?"

I knew I was heard. I had to be as loudly as I was yelling. But no one even raised their heads to turn in my direction! Then I started pounding on the fence, screaming, "Someone please talk to me! Acknowledge my existence! I'm right here less than ten feet away!" Then I started to sob. "Let me in. I want to be in there with all of you! I'm not going away until you talk to me and let me come in!"

Suddenly I felt a tremendous stinging pain in the side of my arm! Before I could turn to see what had happened, the world went completely dark, and I started falling. When I woke up, I was sitting in the car, parked in front of my house! I sat for a long period completely dazed by what I'd seen and the confusion I felt at being inexplicably back home. Judging by the sun, a lot of time had passed, and dusk was rapidly approaching. My arm was sore. I reached to rub it. It really hurt! When I brought my hand back and looked at it, there was dried blood on my fingers.

What had happened to me? I wondered. *Had I been bitten or stung and had some sort of allergic reaction? If so, how did I get back home?*

I knew I saw what I thought I saw today. I had not dreamed or imagined it! Right now, though, I just wanted to go inside, have a glass of wine, and try to figure out what happened today. I would investigate again tomorrow. I pushed the home button on the car so it could return to its home lot. I unlocked my door and wearily went inside. It was so good to be back home. Even after the break-in, it still was my safe place. I didn't care if anyone was listening or watching me tonight. I was home.

Chapter 25

After a restless night with little sleep, I began to have doubts about what I thought I'd seen yesterday. I could swear I saw the big house and all the happy people, but if it had been real, why did no one acknowledge my presence? I had never heard anyone speak of such a place as this, and if it was real, there would have been much talk and probably many protests about these people living in such a large beautiful house with trees, flowers, and bushes. This broke the Equality Law in every way possible, and that just didn't happen. If you could get in trouble for even having your house number above your door askew, then this would never have been allowed!

I had no one to talk to about this now. Wilda thought me docile now and adhering to all the rules. She thought I had accepted my fate, and I had to let her continue to believe that. I would never rest until I validated what I'd seen yesterday. I ate breakfast and ordered another car. I was going back!

Once again, I entered "1953 Pearl Street, Bishop Town," into the car's GPS. I settled down for another two-hour ride. I tried to relax, but I could not reach that level of calm. Eventually, I managed to doze off. Maybe the lack of sleep last night finally caught up with me. I awoke to the feeling that the car was no longer moving. We were parked in front a brown stucco house with no yard, no flowers, and the house number 1953 above the door.

"What?" I said out loud. "This can't be right! This has got to be a mistake. The car has taken me to the wrong address. I'm in some other neighborhood in front of a house with the same street number!" I punched in "Bishop Town, 1953 Pearl Street" into the GPS once again.

Its robotic voice said, "Calculating." Then to my astonishment, it announced that I'd reached my destination!

I climbed out of the car and marched myself up to the front door. I knocked, and it was shortly answered by a middle-aged man. I told him that I was there looking for Kentura Bing and would like to come in and speak with him.

The man looked at me strangely and said, "That was my father's name, but he was aged out almost ten years ago. My name is Simon Bing." He invited me in and offered me tea, which I gladly accepted.

The house was nicely appointed and much larger than it looked from the street. It seemed almost an optical illusion. It appeared much grander from the inside than it did the exterior. I was curious, but I had more important things on my mind today.

I sat with him and told him my story of Robin and finding this address in what she'd left behind. I thought she might be here. I did not tell him about my experience of yesterday. I wanted him to think of me as being of sound mind.

"No, I'm sorry," he said. "The only other person who lives here is my husband, José. I don't know why your friend would have this address in her possession since Dad's been gone for so long now."

"Did he live here for a long time?" I questioned.

"We lived here as a family for many years. When Mom got sick, she was above the age for medical treatment, so she passed away from pneumonia," he said. "We were allowed to stay here because there were two of us. I coupled with José two years before Dad's death, and we were allowed to stay here as well."

None of this made sense to me. I never knew of anyone getting to keep a house as large as this one for only two people. These, though, were questions for another time.

"So you have no idea why my friend Robin might have had this address in her room?" I asked again.

He replied, "None whatsoever. We stay very close to home and rarely have guests. I'm afraid I can think of nothing that will be able to help you."

I was sorely disappointed but thanked him for his kindness and hospitality. Then I left. Climbing into my car, the only thought that came to me was that I was losing my mind! I must be so stressed by my impending death that it had rendered me incapable of rational thought. I began to wonder if I had imagined the last three or four months of my life. Had my brain shut down in my terror of dying? I was no longer sure of my sanity!

Arriving back home in early evening, I could not stand the idea of staying cooped up here alone for the rest of the night. I again ordered a car and went to an upscale restaurant that I wanted to try. I had gotten dressed up in my best black and grays and punched in the address to the restaurant. It looked like a nice place. A high-functioning robot was standing outside to open the door for me. The maître d' robot greeted me and asked if I'd rather be seated in the quiet section or the social section. In other words, did I want to be left alone, or did I want to be bombarded by young men?

If I'd wanted to eat all alone, I should have just stayed home, I thought. Aloud I said, "I'd like to be in the social section, please."

"Very well, madam," he responded in that monotone robotic voice. He led me to a small table at the periphery of the room. That was fine with me. I wasn't sure if I wanted to be fawned over and taken home that night. But from this vantage point, I could watch the shenanigans of the young men and watch the women my age lead them on. I had something cheerful and fun to watch as I ate. I was offered a drink three times by a wannabe Lothario as I sat there, but I never accepted.

I managed to sleep well that night. It was amazing what strong medicine, a little entertainment, and good vodka could do.

Chapter 26

Today I was determined not to let myself stress over anything. I read, ate, and napped for most of the day. I closed my eyes that night and suddenly sat straight up in bed!

"Why hadn't I thought of that?" I wondered out loud. At this point, anything was possible. I immediately got up and went to my computer, where I'd looked up 1953 Pearl Street before. What about the 1953 Pearl Street address in the thirty-first quadrant of Lloyd Martin and Jody Ramerez? It was a stretch, but perhaps that was the answer! I had been knocking on the wrong door.

As far as that vision I had of the big white house on the large lush lot, I'd almost convinced myself that I had hallucinated the entire thing. Too much stress and anxiety, I reasoned. It was remarkable what the human brain could imagine when placed under so much stress.

I looked up the thirty-first quadrant on Know Everything to see what might pass as a tourist spot that I could feasibly ask to visit.

Well, let's see, there are mountains. Okay.

Then I honed in on New Falls to see if I would have any solid reason to request to go anywhere near there. Wow! New Falls was almost on the Pacific Ocean! That seemed like a reasonable thing to want to see. New Falls was also best known as the steepest city built in the UQ! Better and better! I went to the New Falls website to see what could be had in the way of accommodations. I searched through the limited selection of what was available.

"Oh my god!" I exclaimed. One of the few places was 1953 Pearl Street! It appeared that Lloyd and Jody had a small tourist business. That surely must mean something, shouldn't it?

I had a feeling I should try to do this on my own. The government would know that I was traveling, but it wouldn't find my exact location until I was there. Hopefully, if they came for me, I would have had enough time to get some answers before they took me in. I could not fool around with this.

I got on the Pipeline and ordered a much better grade of flight pack than the one I had. It was to be delivered later this morning. I got dressed here in the middle of the night and started making plans about what I could take with me. It must be carefully picked but limited to a few things. I could strap a small bag to my chest, and it would need to have the essentials in it. I would only take two pairs of black and grays. I could wash them out when needed. I had already purchased a miniature mensa tablet and added it to my bag.

Let's see—two pair of clothes, tablet, and a few toiletries.

I was ready to take off the moment the flight pack came, and I read the directions on how to fly the damned thing! Going back to bed, I fell asleep quickly.

When my eyes opened the next morning, I was startled that I'd slept so late. I thought I'd wake up at the crack of dawn as I usually did. It was almost nine in morning! I had hoped to be up in the air by now. Hopefully, my flight pack had been delivered and no one had stolen it off my front porch! I ran to the front door and hurriedly opened all five of my locks. There it was, sitting right at my doorstep! My brand-new, prime-grade flight pack!

I brought the box in so carefully as if I were carrying in an exquisite glass ornament. I sat down on the floor with it and was in sort of a daze—the kind of daze one got in when something really big and exciting and frightening was about to happen. Right now, I was just plain old Naia. When I opened this box to examine its contents, my life as I knew it might never be the same again! Ever so slowly I started to open the seams of the box. One flap opened, then the next, and the next. I stared down into the box, ogling its contents. Wow! It looked pretty fancy to me!

I carefully lifted the backpack object from its organically grown cardboard box. It was much lighter than I expected. I thought something this serious for which I'd spent so much money would be more substantial. Looking for the instructions on how to fly it, I hoped I would be able to figure it out. It was not like I could ask anyone for help. I was extremely relieved that I did not have to put anything together. I did need to charge it, though. I couldn't believe I didn't think of that! I plugged it in and kept on reading.

Apparently, when it is fully charged, all I'd need to do before I took off was program in my destination and adjust the straps so it was secure and comfortable for me. I used the hour it had to charge and checked over the things I planned to bring with me. I ate a small breakfast. I was so nervous that I was a little afraid what I ate might come back up. Fortunately, it did stay down.

My new flight pack had a running time of sixteen hours, so I'd be able to make it there easily before the sun goes down, especially since I'd be heading west. I knew I'd have to set it down at some point during the trip to use the restroom and get more to eat. But I would not linger in one spot very long.

When it was fully charged, I programmed in 1953 Pearl Street in New Falls, thirty-first quadrant. I strapped my front bag securely to my chest, made sure I had my oxygen nose plugs in an easy to reach location on my person, and then lifted the flight pack to my shoulders. I put my arms through the straps and fastened the three front buckles. I was ready! I looked around one last time, wondering if I'd ever see my house again. I kissed Stephen's urn, turned quickly, and walked out my back door. I never looked back.

My takeoff was swift and smooth! Its motor purred almost soundlessly. I was startled by my rate of assent! I was at my cruising altitude before I had time to get my oxygen in. I quickly attached it and could tell the oxygen was pouring into my bloodstream. All seemed well. About two hours into my flight, I started to run into wind and very dark clouds. I needed to get above these clouds before lightning struck. I had to go up quite slowly. I did not want to take a chance of running headlong into someone else flying in the opposite direction.

Suddenly, a boom of thunder sounded! Lightning struck so closely nearby I could feel every hair on my body stand on end! Just as I began to get truly frightened, I burst through the very darkest cloud into the bright blue sky and sunshine! I had gotten wet going through the rain clouds, so the sun shining on me felt wonderful! I stayed at that higher altitude until the clouds below me were white and fluffy and I could see the ground in between them. Then I lowered myself carefully to my previous level.

After another three hours had passed, I needed to go to the bathroom and was getting hungry. I checked the location monitor on the screen on my pack, and it said I was in the twenty-third quadrant. After being aloft for almost six hours, I was a little more than a third of the way to my destination. I landed very smoothly onto a patch of concrete in the center of the area. I got a bite to eat and used the universal facilities that dotted almost every other corner. Feeling better now, I took off again, very pleased with my progress thus far.

The altitude I was flying at allowed me to see the ground quite clearly. I could see large metropolitan areas long before I reached them, so it was easy to avoid flying directly over them. The stench from highly populated areas was horrible, and I tried to avoid them.

I really enjoyed all the suburban areas. There were even some grassy areas that had not been built on yet. Those were especially pleasing to see. My pack was equipped with a radar function that kept birds at least twenty feet away from me in all directions. I'd enjoy actually getting to see one, but bird sightings were rare. Most birds had died out long ago during the officially named Destruction Days. It took many years for people, especially people in the United Quadrants, to begin to conserve and turn to renewable energy. Much land mass and many animal species were lost during this period of rising earth temperatures.

Out of necessity, people finally realized that if the human race was to have a future, changes would have to be made. From what I understood, the coastlines of many landmasses changed drastically during these times. Shrinking land masses made overpopulation especially pronounced. But until this latest law was passed about who could and could not bear children, no means of strict birth control had ever been enforced. Some people had many children, and many had none at all. With the passage of the new law, two positive things could happen. People's taxes would go down and the population would eventually stabilize. It was just a shame that the choice to bear children had been taken out of private hands and was now a random government-issued mandate. A lot of great people who would have been wonderful parents would never be given the chance to have a child. It was also very possible that some awfully unfit, mentally deficient, unstable people would be the chosen ones to pass along their DNA. It seemed like there should be some kind of test to find the very best people to bear and raise children. But that would smash the Equity Law, and that would never be tolerated.

About three hours later, I began to feel very tired and sleepy. *Oh, shoot*, I thought. *I was making such great progress.*

I knew that this fancy flight pack had a sleep mode, where it would fly completely on autopilot, but I was leery of trying something like that in my first flight in this pack. I was determined to keep on going. Soon, though, I jumped with a start! I had fallen asleep, and the stench of Chicago woke me up! I was flying directly over it! I sat down on a flat roof of some large building and perched there for a much-needed short nap.

I set the alarm on my mensa tablet to wake me up an hour later, but when the alarm sounded, I raised my head groggily and realized I was not rested enough to continue. Disappointed, I lay back down and gave in to my tiredness. I awoke a little before dawn. I had certainly been ambitious yesterday, thinking I could make the trip all in one day.

I probably could have made it if I'd been well rested before starting. All those nights of little sleep had caught up with me. Heading into one of the public bathrooms, I removed my helmet and goggles and looked at myself in the mirror. I was surprised by my appearance. My eyes looked haunted, and my complexion was much paler than my usual caramel color. I didn't look like a vacationer at all. I'd really need to clean and perk myself up before I got to the inn. I certainly didn't want to arrive looking like a fugitive! I washed my face, brushed my hair, and tied it up. I put a touch of color on my cheeks and lips. I looked a little better but not much. Taking off from the rooftop went smoothly, and I was on my way again.

I was now within spitting distance of my destination. New Falls was located very high in the Rocky Mountains. The Pacific Ocean backed up to the very first rise of the mountains. There was no beach here, just a steep mountainside dropping off into the sea. I hadn't expected this. The only experience I might have with the ocean could be looking down on it from the mountaintop. New Falls seemed to be fittingly named. It was a few centuries old on the mountain that had originally been an unpopulated, inaccessible part of the Rockies. When the oceans rose, only the mountains could hold it back, and this was the land people had to adjust to. I had never been in such a mountainous setting before. I was amazed at the tapering done along the steep cliffs to make building spaces and roads possible. There were many high fenced areas that protected one from falling straight down into the sea! It was a little scary but very beautiful!

It was a little harder to find a universal restroom here. They weren't located all over the place as they were in eastern quadrants. I really wanted to improve my appearance before showing up at the inn. I washed myself as thoroughly as possible standing at the sink. The lighting was so dim it was impossible to see if I was getting any semblance of makeup on my face, but I did the best I could. I rented a public locker in the town square to stow my flight pack. I was as ready as I'd ever be to head to the inn.

I called for a car, and a robotic voice said I would have about a forty-five-minute wait before one became available. I guessed they didn't have that many driverless lots in small towns like this. I spent my time walking around and around the town square. There was nothing to see but rows of lockers and one or two restaurants on the periphery. I bet I walked that square at least twenty times before the car finally came into view. Climbing in, I punched in "1953 Pearl Street." I felt myself getting more apprehensive as the car lurched away. The trip was short, and I tried to calm myself down in the few moments I had to myself. I hoped I, at least, looked a little calmer.

The car came to a stop at a fairly nondescript medium-sized dwelling. Like all the other houses in the country, it had nothing to distinguish it from every other house but the number above the door: 1953. I got out of the car, retrieved my bag, and walked the two steps to the front door. I wasn't sure if I should knock or just walk right in. My reasoning was if this was a business, then the front door would be unlocked and open. To be prudent, though, I lightly knocked on the door. No answer. I just about screamed at how often lately I had knocked on doors that never opened.

I knocked again, loudly this time. Within seconds, I heard a click, and I could tell the door had been unlocked. This house was actually much more spacious than most. When I stepped inside, I was in a real entrance hall! I didn't know that I'd ever been in a house with an entrance hall before. They were considered wasted space in the houses built during the last century. The only thing I could figure was this house was very old and somehow had escaped with its original footprint.

From the vestibule, I looked into a good-sized seating area. Not only did it have a full-sized sofa but two chairs and a bench. I was amazed to see a replica of a fireplace in the far wall. No one had them anymore! Burning any kind of fossil fuel had been outlawed many years ago, and I was surprised that an example of an old-fashioned fireplace was still allowed. I crossed into that room and soon heard the sound of footsteps on the stairs coming from the floor above. When I looked up, there was a very old lady headed my way. Now I knew something was really wrong! No way could someone this old still be alive! She looked many years past the Aged Out limit!

Was I having another hallucination? I slowly approached her, and she smiled at me. I could see the empty spaces where teeth should be, but she jovially welcomed me to the Pearl Street Inn.

"Are you alright, lady?" she asked. "You don't look well!"

I felt very lightheaded and sat down quickly on one of the chairs.

"Oh, dear," she said as she shuffled to my side. "Can I get you something?" she asked. "A glass of water, a shot of bourbon? I have some pills that will help if you need them."

I sat there openmouthed, once again doubting my sanity. Finally, I told her I was all right, that I just needed a moment. She sat there patiently until she was sure I was feeling better.

"Just sit still for a little while," she said. "I'll get my great-great-great-granddaughter to come and get you checked in to your room. We all share a bathroom here. I hope you don't mind."

Great-great-great-granddaughter! I thought. *Who lives long enough to see a great-great-great-grandchild?*

I scooted and leaned back into the chair, totally at odds with what I was seeing. This was like the big white house hallucination I'd had. This could not possibly be real! I sat there for what seemed like an hour, and finally, a young woman came down the steps and seemed very surprised to see me.

"Oh," she said. "May I help you with something?" She looked at me very quizzically and then asked, "How did you get in?"

At this point, I was so confused; it seemed impossible to come up with a coherent answer. She continued to stare at me, and I finally was able to say, "Your great-great-great-grandmother let me in."

"What? Who did you say?" she demanded in a much louder voice.

"The older woman told me she was your great-great-great-grandmother," I replied.

"Ma'am," she stated, "you must be mistaken. My great-great-great-grandmother was aged out many years ago. Who are you, and why are you here?"

Feeling totally insane by now, I answered in a small voice, "I have a reservation."

She seemed satisfied with that reply and got on her computer. She brought her small scanner to where I was and ran it just above my chip in my lower back.

"Okay. Yes, now I see who you are. Are you feeling well enough to go to your room?" I nodded yes. If she'd asked me if I was well enough to walk on the ceiling, by now I thought I would have nodded yes.

The room was an actual room! It was not a curtained-off area like every other house I'd been in. It had a door that could be shut! As whacked out as I felt, I could not help but marvel at the secrets this house contained. I became very curious. Could there be even more secrets? If I had enough time before I was discovered, I was going to find out.

The next day, I heard the ding on my mensa tablet, letting me know I had a message. It was from the government! In the subject line, it asked, "Where are you?"

Wait a minute, I thought. *Why are they asking me where I am? They should know exactly where I am!*

For some reason, they were not able to read my location from my chip! I was not about to open this email. It must surely have some sort of tracking device embedded in it. If I opened it, they'd know immediately where I was. I hoped this was the right thing to do. I deleted it!

I hoped I was not fooling myself that for the first time in my life, my whereabouts were unknown! I was not sure what was happening in this place, but I felt a sense of freedom here I'd never felt before! If this was what insanity felt like, then please let me stay this way!

Chapter 27

I felt so good and energetic I dressed and went downstairs. The young woman was there and said, "Good morning. How did you sleep?"

How did I sleep? I thought to myself. I went to sleep the moment my head touched the pillow. I didn't lie for hours and think of anything! I wasn't worried about a thing in this world! I was *free*! I tamped down my enthusiasm before answering her.

I responded, "I slept very well, thank you."

She smiled and said, "Most people who come here usually have a good night's sleep." I looked at her curiously. "It must be the mountain air," she replied in a teasing voice.

I did not feel as if I was in on the joke yet, but I didn't care. I didn't have a care in the world anymore!

As the weeks went by, I felt better and stronger than I ever had in my life! I walked for miles up the mountain paths and byways. I took off my shoes and socks and stepped into the freezing cold mountain streams. I'd scream in delight as the chilled water took my breath away. Even with Stephen, even with my children, I'd never had so much fun and been as contented in my entire life as I was now!

At least once a week, I'd get a government missive asking me where I was in the subject line. Delete, delete, and delete!

On my walk one day, I ran into the first person I'd ever met out here on the mountain's edge. He was quite handsome and looked to be about my age. I thought perhaps we'd just pass each other with a nod, but he stopped and waited for me to reach where he was. I guessed I should have been wary of a stranger, but I wasn't. He didn't look like a killer/rapist, and that notion was enough to satisfy me.

He introduced himself, "Hi, my name is Steve. What's yours?"

Momentarily shocked at him being a Steve, I replied "Naia" in a timid little voice.

"What?" he asked.

"Naia," I said in a much stronger voice. "My name is Naia."

He looked at me thoughtfully but said nothing.

I spoke and asked, "Are you from New Falls, or are you like me—on vacation?"

He answered my question, quietly saying, "Vacation."

It started to feel awkward when he didn't say anything else, so I passed around him quickly and hollered back, "It was nice to meet you!" After a few dozen yards or so, I looked back, and he was still in the same spot, looking at me. I stopped where I was and looked at him too. After a few seconds of this, he started walking toward me again. I waited for him to catch up.

"I'm sorry," he said. "It was when you said your name was Naia. My wife's name was Naia too."

Now I was completely taken aback. Steve or Stephen wasn't that much of an unusual name, but I'd only run into one other Naia in my life!

What are the odds? I wondered to myself. I sat down on a rock ledge and let my legs dangle over the edge. Steve did the same.

"When you told me your name I was a little shocked too," I said. "My husband's name was Stephen."

We looked at each other for a few moments. Then he jumped up, offered me a hand, and off we took, laughing and getting to know each other.

As the rosy blush of evening started to turn the mountains to gold, he said, "I don't want today to end. Let's go have dinner."

Over dinner, we talked a lot about ourselves, but I was not confident enough to tell him how old I was and what I was running from. He didn't mention his age either, but I'd say he was right up there with me. He walked me back to the door of the inn and gently kissed me goodnight.

I asked him if he wanted to come up to my room, but he said, "No, not yet."

Right before he turned to leave me, he wrapped his arms around me and buried his head in my neck. I hugged him back and felt a way I hadn't in a very long time, completely safe.

My tablet pinged early this morning, and I expected another email from the government asking where I was. But it wasn't from the government; it was Wilda. I started to open it immediately until I read the subject line: "Where are you?" I wanted so badly to open it and perhaps hear something from my best friend, but I was too afraid that I was being duped. I deleted it unopened.

Steve and I were together again by midmorning. This time he'd brought a picnic to have on the ledge where we'd sat yesterday. Sitting with him quietly, I felt no need to try to force conversation. We spoke to each other as if we'd always known each other. I couldn't believe I was feeling this close to someone after only two days. We sat there for a very long time, only speaking if we saw something we wanted to point out to the other.

By midafternoon and quite a bit of wine, we thought we'd better get off the ledge and head back to town. We walked along the path holding each other's hand. So gently and easily did we touch.

As we walked along, Steve asked me nonchalantly, "Do you like to dance? My Naia was my very favorite dance partner, but do you dance?"

I answered back that I did enjoy dancing, but my Stephen hadn't been a very good dancer, so I never had the chance to be one either.

"Well, madam." He laughed. "We can do everything possible to change you into my second favorite dance partner!"

My feelings were hurt a little bit by that because I didn't want to be anyone's second anything, but I didn't say anything. Later on, I realized I should have.

After a quick bite to eat, Steve went back to where he was staying to bring back his regular sized mensa tablet that had all types of songs recorded on it. I was game to try anything, hoping not to disappoint him. He played song after song, counting the rhythms into my ear. But whatever dance he played, I could not do it as well as his Naia.

He continually stopped me and would tell me how I was doing it wrong. He constantly referenced his Naia and how she would sway here and turn there. I was growing more and more upset with this ignorant behavior as the night wore on. Finally, I'd had enough. I told him my feelings were hurt by his criticisms and his comparison to his dead wife.

He looked at me in astonishment and said gruffly, "I was only trying to teach you to be as good a dancer as my wife was."

I opened the front door and pointed out, "I'm not your wife."

He left without another word. I could not believe any man on earth would be so stupid as to compare me and find me wanting, then be dumb enough say it to me! I went upstairs and cried for a while. Then the good vibes I'd felt since being here started to come back, and I felt exhilarated that I might have just dodged a big old ugly mess! I never saw Steve in town or out on the trails again. That was fine with me.

Chapter 28

November 29, 2525

Days passed so pleasantly, and I felt so wonderful that when the bell pinged with instructions on November 29, I paid little attention. I was still getting emails from friends—actually, every one I'd ever known—asking where I was. Never opened. Deleted.

I had become so attached to the young woman, Jody, who owned the inn, that I stared at her in disbelief when she told me one morning that it was time for me to go. I'd grown to love her and her two children as well.

"Jody, tell me why," I begged. "Have I done something to offend you? Haven't I always paid you in a timely manner? Do you want more money?"

No matter what I asked or how I pleaded, her answer was no.

She expected me to be gone by the next day! I could not believe this! She left me no choice but to level with her. I sat there and told her why I'd been led to her inn. Who was Kentura Bing, and how was he involved with her? I told her about Robin, whose writings had led me here. I begged her again to help me put all the pieces of the puzzle together.

She looked at me with sympathy but then said, "You must be gone by tomorrow."

I looked at her helplessly and then left the inn to retrieve my flight pack from the locker in the square. I spent the rest of the night on my mensa tablet, trying to figure out where I should go. I didn't know why, but something directed me to the deserts of the southwest twenty-ninth quadrant. I had no idea why, but then again, why not?

The government would surely find me now that'd I'd left my safe haven on the mountainside. I knew it would just be a matter of time before they swooped down and captured me. I was determined and desperate enough to stay one step ahead of them for as long as possible. After powering up my flight pack and strapping my few belongings onto my chest, I was ready to take off. I looked around at my beautiful mountains one last time. I doubted if I'd ever get to see them again.

I calculated it should take about five hours to get from the mountains to the desert. At some point during this trip, I will need to set down and find the public facilities again and grab something to eat. I was mystified by my lack of appetite. I was really never hungry anymore, but I knew I had to eat.

The take off was slow and gentle. I had my oxygen plugs with me, but unless I ran into a storm, I planned to stay at an altitude where I wouldn't need them. I wanted to fly down the coastline and see if I could find anything left of a real beach. The ocean had swallowed up most of the land on the western side of the Rockies, but perhaps there was still some beach left as I traveled farther south.

Chapter 29

December 5, 2525

As the Rockies started to be hills, the water reached inland for many miles. I could feel the temperature start to change the further south I went. Flying provided its own wind, of course, but this wind was dry and hot. I saw a small patch of land with a few dwellings below me. I figured this was about the best I could hope for as far as a small village is concerned. The lower I got, the hotter it was.

There were no people out on the street anywhere, but that was perfectly understandable in this intense heat. Then I heard something I hadn't heard in many years—barking. I heard a dog barking! I hadn't seen one since I was a little girl! Pets were very much discouraged and had been for a very long time. Supposedly, they took up too much valuable room and resources, but someone in this place had one!

I walked in the direction of the barking dog. It was a very low bark like it came from a very big dog. The dog was standing in front of a house with no restraint or tether. It did not snarl or growl, just continued its low, "Woof! Woof! Woof!"

As I started talking to it, the barking subsided, and a big long tail started to wag furiously. I stepped closer to it, and it seemed beside itself in happiness. I reached out to let him sniff my hand. Then I petted his head, and he seemed in heaven.

About this time, a door banged open, and out walked a young woman. Something about her seemed very familiar. Suddenly, she stopped short and said, "Mama?"

It was Emmy, my Emmy! I hadn't seen her in almost twenty years. We'd had an argument decades ago, and she'd never forgiven me or answered me when I reached out to her. I ran to her and held her in my arms and felt like I never wanted to let her go! Never again did I want to let my precious Emmy go!

It was hard to fathom how I could have been drawn to the one place in this country where she was. For the first time, I looked to the sky and whispered, "Thank you, God."

We drew apart and looked at each other. To me, she just seemed an older version of the little girl I remembered, "Here, Mama, come on inside," she beckoned. I looked back at the dog.

"Can he come inside out of the heat too?" I asked.

"Of course, he can. Come on, Porter," she said.

When I sat down on her small sofa, Porter jumped up next to me and tried to fit into my lap. I loved this huge dog with aspirations of being a lap dog, settling in as best he could.

Her couple partner was a very nice person who seemed to sense that Emmy and I had so much to catch up on and left to visit friends for the evening. I felt so blessed to see Emmy again. I hid no secrets from her. If this was my last night as a free woman, I could ask for nothing better. I told her about it being my last year because I knew she had not kept up with my birthdays. This saddened her until I told her I was trying to escape my fate. I told her everything. I told her about her father's death three years ago. I told her about the big party on turning sixty-nine. I told her about my friends and how they were forced to stay away from me. I told her about Jack's death and Robin's pregnancy.

I knew I had a very short time with her. I knew that the government would locate me, and she'd be in trouble if I stayed very long. She told me about her life. She'd become a real live daredevil in my eyes. All those things that frightened me wouldn't faze her at all. I told her about my one skydiving adventure, and she laughed and laughed.

"You, Mama? You jumped out of a plane?"

I assured her, "Yes, I did! And I'd do it again if I could!"

We had a grand laugh over that statement! Emmy went on to tell me about the mountain climbing she'd grown to love. She showed me pictures on her mensa tablet of her hanging on the side of a precipice with the ground far below. She told me that she looked for new adventures all the time, sometimes with her couple partner, but mostly by herself.

I asked if she was ever afraid, and she admitted, "Yes, sometimes when I get myself in a sticky situation, I feel afraid, but I never feel more alive than when I conquer that fear and get myself to safety again."

I tremendously admired her for her courage. If only I could be just like her, I might be further along in my fight to safety for myself by now. I would not tell her where I was going. Frankly, I wasn't sure myself. I warned her that government agents would surely come here to look for me. I told her to be absolutely truthful with them.

"Tell them I've been here, but I did not tell you where I was going next."

We talked till the wee hours of the morning. For about the last hour, when we became exhausted and talked out, we sat with her head on my shoulder, me stroking her hair as I used to when she was little. When I could tell that she'd fallen into a deep sleep, I gently lay her down on the couch. It was too hot to cover her. I stood looking down at my little girl for a long time. I would be gone when she awoke.

Donning my flight pack after strapping on my bag, I lifted off as the tears flowed down my face. I almost felt as if this was truly my last year. I didn't care too much anymore, for I'd gotten to see my Emmy. The government had quit sending me messages now. I guessed there would be no more warnings. When they found me, there would be blood.

Chapter 30

December 29, 2525

I decided to head east again. Now it seemed more like a waiting game. How far could I travel? How far could I get before they tracked me down? I set down in a big city, even though I usually avoided them. I needed to recharge my pack and see if I could find a place to stay for a few days and wash my clothes and be still for a while. Looking on my mensa tablet, I saw a small inn in a suburb away from so much of this hubbub. Setting my GPS to the address, I rested my head on the bag strapped to my chest and let the pack lead me there. I was so tired.

This establishment was much like every other one. It was nice enough and would give me a place to lay my head. The owner, Bog DigDo Miller, ran his scanner over my neck and finished the check in process. I was again surprised that he asked me nothing about being on a government list as a missing person. He didn't smile much but was very soft spoken.

"Let me lead you to your room," he said kindly. Something about this young man touched my heart. I was not sure what it was, perhaps because I was dead tired and needed to sleep, but he somehow seemed special to me.

I slept till late the next morning. Washing up, getting dressed I went into the main area of the inn. Bog was there and invited me to join him in a meal. He seemed so humble and quiet. I asked him about becoming an inn owner, and did he enjoy it? He told me his story about his earlier years that broke my heart. He'd had his troubles and addictions and had fought them for many years. During this period, he lost jobs and a wife. They'd had no children.

He'd been sober now for over fifteen years. He was originally from Indian decent; that explained his dark hair and beard. I asked him if he'd ever traveled to India, where he might have family.

"No, I haven't even thought about trying to do that. Maybe that is something to think about." That brought a thought to my mind. *Does India have an Aged Out Law?* I wondered.

I didn't know why I hadn't thought of India. They were certainly overcrowded, but perhaps they hadn't enacted the barbaric ritual of killing off their mothers and fathers. I told Bog how much I appreciated the meal and excused myself to head back to my room to do a bit of research. Searching my mensa tablet for all I could find on India, I was delighted to see that most of India let their elders live! Maybe finding Bog, and him being from a country where older people were allowed to live out their natural life, was providence banging on my door!

At the evening meal, it was just Bog and me. I told him I'd like to stay here with you for as long as I could.

"I like it here," I told him.

"You do?" he asked me in astonishment. "What do you like about it?"

"I like your inn," I answered, "and I like your company, and I like your location."

All this was true. The inn was comfortable enough. The location was not in a big city, but close enough if I wanted to go into the city. Then there were my mysterious feelings for Bog. I could not put my finger on it. It certainly wasn't love like between a man and a woman, but more like between a mother and her child. I felt a great tenderness for him. It might have been because he might have family in a land where I wouldn't have to die, and that was sure a perk. But it seemed far more than that, and that really puzzled me. For now, though, I was very content being here.

Not hearing anything from the government left me confused and constantly looking over my shoulder. As long as they were asking me where I was, they didn't know. Days passed, and I was left alone, so I began to feel more comfortable with my situation and being with Bog. He was always so courteous and kind, and my feelings for him continued to grow. I encouraged him to see if he had any family in India. We spent long hours together looking at his family tree to see if we could find a distant cousin or an aunt or uncle. He sent out emails to many people that could possibly be related to him, but so far no one answered in the affirmative.

Time passed, and we enjoyed each other's company. We liked the same music and read books on our tablets, then discussed them. Occasionally, we went into the city for an evening out. He was a wonderful dining companion, and young men didn't bother me when he was with me. He didn't drink at all, so I curtailed my alcohol use considerably when I was in his company. On his birthday, I wrote out an email and sent it to him. I told him how much his friendship meant to me and how I cherished our time together. I bought him a small cake to celebrate after dinner that night. He was so pleased! I guessed it had been a long time since anyone had made such a fuss over him. He told me the email I sent him had touched his heart and that he felt the same way about me.

As I headed to bed later that night, he gave me a hug. I hugged him back as if I was hugging my son. I was in such a good place now. Days went by, and nothing changed at all! We enjoyed so many good times together. We had a healthy competition on all things trivia, and we'd dance to some of the songs we enjoyed. I grew to love him, and he loved me in return. I had to stop and marvel that in all the places I'd stayed for any length of time, I felt attached to the people who were there. I only hoped and prayed that Bog wouldn't suddenly tell me one day that I had to leave.

Chapter 31

I wondered many times if Bog was lonely for a girl his own age. I was sure he had the same feelings and urges as other young men his age. I hated to bring it up because I really didn't want anything to ever change. But the love I felt for Bog couldn't be that selfish. It wasn't many days later that he came running to me with an email from a man in India. This man said he was distantly related to Bog's father. He also went on to say that he had a daughter who needed to get married. I wondered why she "needed" to marry, but Bog seemed so excited by the email I couldn't be happier for him.

Over the next few days, he and the girl's father exchanged information, and the father seemed eager for Bog to get to know his daughter. The daughter, Alka, seemed just as eager to get to know Bog. This distant courtship took a real toll on the relationship I had with Bog. I tried very hard not to feel resentful; I wanted Bog's happiness. Such a sweet and kind young man deserved all the happiness he could get.

During this courtship phase, I spent much of my time reading and walking the neighborhood. I met some very nice people along the way. Many were about my age. Since none of them knew of my dreadful government status, I was welcomed into their groups and friendships. This was wonderful! I had people to hang out with again! We had dinners together, and I'd laugh at their southern twangs. Many of these women looked like they could be on their last year as I was, but we never spoke of it. Occasionally, one of us would disappear; we'd be sad for a day or so, but then we got back to the very important process of having a good time. Being out with the "girls," I could feel free to imbibe again. We'd get tipsy and laugh till our sides hurt.

One day, we'd gathered at Ava's house, and she opened champagne! I didn't know what we were celebrating, and champagne wasn't my drink of choice, but I was game! As we sat there and got giggly, Ava started to talk.

"I wanted to tell all of you how much your friendship and love have meant to me."

What? I thought. I so hoped that this wasn't going where I was afraid it was! Maybe I could excuse myself and get up and leave. I didn't want to hear this!

She continued, "As some of you know, my time is growing very short."

I felt my throat tighten, and tears come to my eyes.

"I am ready to go," she said. "There is something better than this life after I'm gone, so I feel sure that I'm going to a much better place." Most of the other women were nodding sadly as she spoke.

I had no idea what the hell she was talking about. Where in the world did she think she was going after she died? She was going to be killed and then burned to a crisp! Why was she so accepting, as the other ladies seemed to be too?

I stood quickly and said, "Excuse me, I must go. I'm not feeling well." I ran to the door, threw it open, and was out of there! How had I gotten myself mixed up with these nuts? They seemed so normal until tonight!

"Some place after we are killed?" I scoffed at the idea of such craziness. Unless that someplace was in an urn sitting on someone's kitchen table, what other place could this woman have meant?

Chapter 32

When I got home that night, Bog was sitting at his computer, but I was too disturbed to have much of a conversation anyway. I wiggled my fingers at him as I passed by and headed to my room. I lay in bed, thinking about tonight for a very long time. Did these women know something I didn't? After I'd bolted out of there tonight, I didn't know how welcome I'd be if I tried to contact any of them to explain all this to. I got my mensa tablet and started my games, something I hadn't done in quite a while. I needed to get my mind on other things and hopefully fall fast asleep.

The next morning, when I came downstairs, Bog was very excited to tell me something. He and Alka had set a date to be married!

"Oh, wow!" I exclaimed, "that is wonderful! Come and tell me all about it."

We sat together on his couch, but he was so excited he could barely sit still. I'd never heard him talk so much since I'd known him.

"She's so beautiful and so sweet and kind. She actually reminds me so much of you," he said.

I was very flattered, even though I knew he didn't know her well enough to know much about her at all. I hugged and congratulated him, then asked him the big question. "What are your plans? Is she coming to America, or are you going to India?"

"Oh, I'm going to go to India. She wants to be close to her parents, and they would be aged out if they came here."

"I understand," I said. I was truly happy for Bog but wondered what I'd do now? "I'll certainly miss you and living here," I said. "It's been such a wonderful time being here at your inn."

His face shaded for a moment. "Oh, Naia, I don't want to leave you behind! I can't leave you knowing I'll never see you again!"

I patted his hand. "Yes, dear, you will leave and have a wonderful life with your bride, and you will be a wonderful father to all of your children!" I hugged him tight and assured him I'd be fine.

"No, no, you won't," he exclaimed. "I know how old you are, and what will happen to you if I'm not here to protect you?"

"Bog, darling," I said, pulling him into my arms, "you can't protect me. No one can protect me." As I said this to him, I realized how true this was. No one but I could protect me. The only chance I had was to rely on myself, and that may be a lost cause too.

I helped Bog pack up what he wanted to take to India with him. He was traveling molecularly and would be in India with all his belongings almost instantly. I walked with him to the closest molecular station and bid him farewell. I cried all the way back to the inn. At this point, I had about five months left. The heart of me had been broken, and I really couldn't feel much of anything—no fear, no anger, no nothing. I decided to go back home.

I think I'm done, I thought to myself. *I don't think I can beat them. They've won.*

So depressed was I at this reckoning of my fate that I decided I'd take all the time I wanted on my journey home. I was fairly certain that my last five months would be spent in some sort of locked-down environment and my days of freedom were coming to an end.

I was really quite shocked that they hadn't ended my free reign sooner. I'd heard tales of the people who'd tried to escape. It seemed they were rounded up quickly and not seen again until their ashes were returned to the designated survivor. I first started by walking from Bog's Inn. I had my flight pack strapped to my back and my few belongings strapped to my chest. Both were relatively lightweight, and I didn't tire easily from carrying them. I could take off at any time, but first, I had to walk till I was so weary I couldn't take another step. I knew I'd never sleep again, otherwise.

All my plans, all my ambitions, all the loves I met during this trip were gone now. If I tried to lie down without being totally exhausted, every single thought would come back and haunt me into total despair.

Walk, put one foot in front of the other, I kept telling myself.

No matter how much I longed to sit down, I put one foot in front of the other. Within five hours, I came to a small town in the twenty-first quadrant called Cooperstown. I saw nothing to distinguish it from every other small town I'd passed through, but by now I was so tired and I hungry. I was worn out. I stopped at a small restaurant to eat a bite of food. I couldn't even remember what I ordered. I had no desire for alcohol, and no young men tried to tempt me. If I'd been in better frame of mind, I would have been concerned by all these things happening at the same time, but it never occurred to me to wonder.

I found a small house with a room to rent and stopped there. It seemed as if this little house came my way via a miracle. I had literally taken my last possible step to the point of collapsing, and there it was, right in front of me. I knocked on the door, and a young woman answered it. I told her my business, and she let me in. If I hadn't been so totally exhausted, I would have been shocked that she did not run her scanner over my chip, but she didn't. She showed me to a guest space with a small cot. I sat down, then lay down, and was off into a sublime oblivion of sleep. Some time during the night, I roused enough to realize there were a bunch of people in my room. The little curtain that separated my space from the main room had been pulled back, and all these people were watching me. I tried to focus on who they might be, but my eyes wouldn't cooperate. Later, I had that recurring dream. It was my babies crying for me to come to them. But once again, I could not get myself to my feet to answer their cries.

When I woke up midmorning, I realized that I had been crying in my sleep. My pillow was damp, and my eyes were damp and caked. This did nothing to improve my mood, so I got out my mensa tablet to play a game to try to get my mind in a better place.

Chapter 33

It was close to noon when I got up and cleaned myself up a little. This place had a small bathroom that serviced the entire house. It had no tub or shower. I had to be content to do the best I could in the sink. Then hating to put my filthy clothes back on, I decided to wash out the gray and blacks I'd had on yesterday and hung them on a rack to dry. I scurried back to my room wrapped in a towel and found my other pair of clothes. They had not been cleaned very recently either, but they still felt better than what I'd had on. Walking into the main room, I was greeted by a small boy of about six, I judged. When I said hello, he smiled and giggled at me.

I asked him his name, and he said, "Tobias."

I asked Tobias where his mom was, and he shrugged his shoulders as if he didn't know. I found that odd. But when you were in a stranger's house, it served no purpose to be too curious. I walked into the small kitchen to see if anything was available to eat. Tobias followed me in.

"I'm hungry," I said. "What about you?" He nodded his head vigorously, so I replied, "Let's see what we have to choose from." He watched me intently as I looked to see what supplies there were.

Hmmmm... Not too much to choose from," I thought.

I asked him, "Has your mother ordered your food today?" Again, the shoulder shrug. "What's your mom's name?" I asked him. Again, the shoulder shrug. Then I asked, "Don't you know anything?" Again, the shoulder shrug.

I guess the kid doesn't know! I snickered to myself.

I came upon a package of freeze-dried tuna fish. I rehydrated it for the two of us and made one tuna sandwich. There was very little bread, so I spread it very thick with the tuna and sliced it in two for the both of us. He gobbled the thick dry sandwich as if he hadn't eaten in a week, but my hunger was quickly satisfied, so I gave him the biggest part of mine. It disappeared as quickly as he could chew and swallow.

With no sign of his mother, I began to call out, "Is anyone here? Tobias and I are looking for you."

Still no reply. I began to worry somewhat. This child was too young to be left on his own! How did his mom know that I wasn't some kind of child killer? She had no way of knowing anything about me since she hadn't scanned my chip. If she needed to go out or have some free time, why didn't she take him to the nearest parent R and R? Those centers were everywhere because most parents could not stand to be cooped up all day with their kids. So why was he here alone?

Dog gone it! I thought. *I don't want to be stuck here very long with a kid!*

So I suggested we play a game. I got my mensa tablet and found an age appropriate game for him to play. That occupied him for an hour or so. But since he had my tablet, there was nothing for me to do but sit there. At some point, the boredom was so overwhelming I nodded off with my head lying back on the couch. When I woke up, my tablet was lying there beside me, but no Tobias.

I must have slept a very long time by the angle of the sun, I thought.

Dusk was quickly falling, and there appeared to be no one in the house but me. I called out a few more times, but no one answered. Wandering back to the kitchen, I looked to see if I could find anything else to eat. That one-fourth of a tuna sandwich had been digested long ago. I went into the bathroom and found that my washed-out clothes were dry enough to wear. I went back to my room and put them on and headed out for something to ease my hunger. Tonight I might have to quench my thirst as well. Riding in my ordered car, I found a small little restaurant and ordered a drink before I ordered food. It was a pleasant little place, and I enjoyed looking at the people come and go. A young man, surely barely of legal drinking age, asked if he could by me a drink? I thanked him but said no. He looked at me for a moment as if I'd hurt his feelings.

I found that strange, because these young men get turned down all the time.

Oh, well, I thought. Even if I wanted company tonight, I would not take a man into a stranger's house, not without permission anyway. I sat there for a long time, watching all that was going on around me. I didn't realize how long I'd been there until the proprietor tapped me on the shoulder and told me he was closing for the night. I startled at his tap and then saw I was the only one left in the restaurant. I must have either fallen asleep as I sat there or my mind completely wandered far from me. I had no memory of the last two hours!

It was late by the time I opened the door to the small house. Again no one was there. I thought it too late to yell for someone and assured myself that I would see them in the morning. Again I fell into a sound sleep within minutes. The dream came again. The curtain was pulled back, and a bunch of people were standing there, looking at me. This time, one of them called my name, but I was too tired and sleepy to answer them. Then total darkness enveloped me again.

Chapter 34

When I awoke the next morning, I could hear the sound of children playing.

"So there were more kids here than Tobias today," I reasoned.

I went into the bathroom to wash up before I got dressed. Looking into the mirror, I could hardly believe my eyes. I looked so damned old!

When was the last time I noticed myself? I wondered. How had I aged so much in the few months I'd been away from home?

I saw wrinkles I'd never seen before, and my hair was streaked with gray! I was always so vain. How had I let this happen? Maybe all the worry and angst over the past months had caused what I considered premature aging. All the good times I'd had and all the losses I'd faced in the last few months had surely done this to me! I decided that I needed to move on today. I was feeling more energized than I had in the past few days, even with the shock of my appearance.

Pulling the curtain back and going into the main room, I saw that there were two little girls playing with Tobias today. They were all looking at their own little screens and playing so nicely together. The young woman who'd let me in the first night was also sitting there, staring at a screen of her own. She didn't acknowledge me when I spoke to her, so I walked out the door. No one seemed to notice I was leaving, and that was fine with me. I'd had just about all the goodbyes I wanted for one lifetime.

I had no desire to walk anymore or see anymore small towns. I wondered if I would enjoy going into a big city, but the idea didn't light a fire under me, so I guess that was a no. I had left my flight pack plugged in every place I stayed, so it was fully charged. It was time to go back. I wanted to go home.

I programmed in my address and thought I'd fly low and slowly. I wanted to go home, but I didn't know what might be waiting for me there. I wasn't nearly as scared as I'd been seven months ago, but I still was not ready to welcome my death.

It would take me twelve hours to fly home. I would prepare by eating before I take off, wearing a diaper, and putting my pack into sleep mode if I grow tired. I was also on autopilot, so I didn't have to worry about hitting anything. I put in my oxygen plugs in case I fell asleep and autopilot thought I needed to be at a higher altitude for some reason. I was totally prepared. Since I was flying east this time, dawn appeared to be very near for almost the entire flight.

While I had my flight pack in sleep mode, sleep would not come. Out of curiosity, I decided to do a series of crisscrosses across the quadrants. This would add a few days to my flight, but since this might be my last taste of freedom, I should take advantage and see places I'd only heard about.

The natural wonders of the country were all the politically correct and nonconfrontational touristy places left to see. All the monuments and statues had long since been torn down. I remembered being told there once was a statue in the third quadrant harbor that met many of the immigrants coming into the country long, long ago. It turned out that all art and memories of the country's past had offended one group or another, so when the Equality Law was passed, all that was erased from the country's history and most people's memories. All presidential portraits, all religious artifacts, all memorial statues, or anything that even hinted at this country's past inevitably seemed to offend someone. And the way deemed best to not hurt anyone's feelings was to destroy it all.

Chapter 35

I had already flown across the desert and seen the glaciers of the north country, the Grand Canyon, and flown south following the big river that runs from the north all the way down into the big gulf. It was all very beautiful. Works of art were no longer allowed in public anymore. People could still create as long as it was done in the privacy of one's own home. It was never to be put on public display! That would be against the Equality Law since not everyone could paint or draw or sew or play an instrument as well as someone else.

One needed to be very careful not to offend someone with their knowledge or talent. Individual accomplishment was discouraged and never to be made known to others. Most people were very careful to know and obey all the laws, but breaking the Equality Law was dealt with much more harshly than any other law. Those who broke the law found out the hard way how serious it was to do so. While there were containment centers for those who merely upset and disappoint the government, there were no more prisons anymore. I could barely remember when the last one closed. Now if someone in a family broke that law, they were put into a medically induced coma; it was up to the family to make arrangements for the criminal's care. That was why starting an IV became such a popular class to take. But as I said, I took first aid instead because of my phobia about needles. There were some particularly uncaring families who just let their loved one lie there until they died. Stephen had known how to start an IV, but I was very proud to say no one in our family had ever needed a line started for a crime against equality! Then when Robin came to me, as sick as she was, it would have been a very useful skill to have.

I wondered occasionally about Robin. I didn't know how she managed to disappear like she did and what to make of the cryptic messages she left behind. I thought about how I was so sure I was on some special mission to decipher what she'd written. I still believed that there was something to her reference either to Kentura Bing or 1953 Pearl Street that I really need to uncover. If I was not immediately apprehended when I got home, I would try to find out more about this mystery. Now that I had a renewed purpose, I really needed to get home!

I set down none too gently on arriving back at my house. I was tired, hungry, and dirty. I unlocked all five locks on my door and entered into the space that had been mine for so many years.

"The shower must come first," I commanded myself.

The shower felt marvelous, but my exhaustion had overcome my hunger. I knew I needed to eat something, so I drank a liquid dinner. Lying down in my own bed felt so good, and I fell asleep immediately.

My dreams were haunted again by the same old nightmare. I could hear my children calling out, "Mama, Mama," but I couldn't find them, and I was too weak to search.

Chapter 36

January 1, 2526

Waking the next morning to the ping of my computer, I got up and walked to the machine and hesitantly took a look. I had gotten many emails while I was gone. Very few were personal. Many were from the government demanding to know where I was. I thought that was probably what this missive would be, too, but I was wrong! This was from Wilda begging me to tell her where I was. As I looked back through my old emails, there were many sent from her.

Looking at a few of them, they all asked the same question: "Where are you?"

I immediately responded to this morning's email, telling her I was back home. She responded quickly that she was coming right over. I quickly dressed, rubbed the weeks of accumulated dust from a few flat surfaces, and waited for her arrival.

Within minutes, she was here! She must have flown here, in her hurry. That was exactly what she'd done! When I opened the door, she shoved it shut and threw herself into my arms and cried. Huge wracking sobs shook her body and wet my shoulder. I pulled her to the couch and made her sit down. When she felt relaxed enough to let me go, I pushed her away and stared into my best friend's face. I was horrified! Wilda looked two hundred years old! It hadn't been that long since I'd seen her! What could have happened to cause this? Then I remembered the last time I'd really studied my own face and the shock I felt at how much I'd aged. I attributed mine to stress; I wondered if Wilda's aging was brought on by something similar?

I offered her something to drink, and even though it was early morning, she wanted bourbon. I poured her a good three fingers full and handed it to her. To my amazement, she quickly downed it all! We didn't speak for a little while as the bourbon worked its magic and she began to calm down. When she had her breath again, she demanded to know where I'd been.

Normally, I wouldn't allow anyone to question my movements, but this was Wilda, so I began to talk. "Well," I said, "it started out as my search looking for clues about what Robin wrote about Kentura Bing and the 1953 Pearl Street address." I told her about going to Kentura Bing's house at the Pearl Street address in Bishop Town and how I'd met Kentura Bing's son, who told me that his father had passed away some time ago. He had claimed not to know Robin at all, and I had no reason not to believe him, I explained to Wilda. Then I told her all the places I'd been.

First, I flew to New Falls in the thirty-first quadrant to see what I could find there. That was a very strange experience, I told her. I had been greeted at that place by a woman far too old to still be alive. I told Wilda about having my chip read at check in, but no one had come after me. I left out the part about meeting the second Steve and my namesake, his late wife, Naia. I was still a little embarrassed by that entire episode. I told her about the affection I felt for the manager of the inn, Jody. Then I told her how sad I'd been when I was told I had to leave.

I told Wilda about my great urge to go to the desert. I told her about the miracle of finding Emmy! I told her how the years of distance had fallen away in one evening. My daughter and I had gotten through the anger and hostility to our love for each other again!

I told her about my stay with my Indian friend, Bog Digdo Miller, whom I'd grown to love. I told her about his finding love in India, the land of his ancestors. I told her how happy I'd been for him but how much I missed him and his company. I told her about seeing as many of the natural wonders of the country as I could before coming back last night. After I'd told her everything, we sat there in silence for a long time.

When she spoke, she asked for another bourbon. This time, I joined her. After a big gulp of that throat burning concoction, she asked me a question.

"Do you remember that I'm in my last six weeks?"

Oh, my heavens! How could I have forgotten how close she was? Oh god, she had less than two months to live, and I was rambling on about where I'd been!

"Oh, Wilda!" I exclaimed. "I am so sorry that I deserted you for so many weeks. I really did start out thinking I was going to find a way out of these executions, and if I had, I promise you I would have come back for you." She looked at me quite skeptically, and I didn't blame her at all. When I first started out, I was so eager to try to find my own way out of my scheduled death that I didn't think I was thinking of anyone but myself. I'd like to think I'd have come back, but I just didn't know for sure.

"But, Wilda," I said, "I'm not giving up! I still think something strange has happened, and I'm determined to get to the bottom of it." I motioned for her to come very close. Then I whispered, "When I first started my Chinese lessons, Sally had hinted of a like-minded group who had some sort of plan to continue to live!"

Wilda jerked away from me and looked at me in amazement. Pulling her close to my mouth again, I continued, "A man in my Chinese class was supposed to meet me, but I blew that by my exuberant response when he contacted me."

I told her about DeQuan from class, as well, and his odd behavior and all his questions. Then I told her about what happened at the supposed celebration in my class. I told her about the puff on the marijuana cigarette and how sick it had made me. I told her about waking up in the bathroom and no one else being in the building. I told her about me having to spend the night in the big room where I knew a party had been earlier that evening. Then I told her about realizing my keys to the house were gone, about coming home to my house and finding my door unlocked and the papers I'd gotten in Robin's room gone!

Then I told her about my being pretty sure that there were cameras in the house because no one could have found my hiding place if there weren't. She backed away again, looking entirely freaked out, and then she started turning her head this way and that to see if she could spot one of these cameras. I'd already tried, but I hadn't found one yet either.

I did not tell her about the big beautiful house I was taken to the first time I tried to find Kentura Bing. A few times over the last months, I'd tried to reconstruct the memory of that house in my mind. I could see a blurred image of it, but no sharp details. When I thought about it, though, a great wave of sentimentality enveloped me.

Even though I wasn't acknowledged by the people there, for some reason, I feel a deep affection for them. That was why I was determined to go back to Kentura Bing's house. I didn't care what his son told me. There was more to learn there. I could feel it so strongly. I believed I could find all my answers there and find my peace as well.

I once again whispered to Wilda, "I'm going back to the Bing house. I know I can find answers there."

This time, Wilda didn't say a word to attempt to stop me. As short as her time was, I knew there was no terror greater than the one she was facing in less than six weeks. Not wanting to be alone nor wanting her to be alone, I asked her to spend a few days with me. I knew that her daughter, Michelle, was coming to spend her last days with her quite soon, but she wasn't here yet. We needed each other, just as we always had. Now there were two of us to fight!

Chapter 37

I was absolutely amazed that I had not been picked up by the government yet for my rebellious actions, but so far, so good. After a simple breakfast of dried fruit and tea, I ordered a car to take us for that two-hour drive to Bishop Town. I'd brought along some playing cards for us to pass the time on the trip. We played a number of hands in two hours, and Wilda beat me at all but two. Seeing the steeple of the Bishop Town's government building in the distance was my first observation that we were getting close. We put the cards away in expectation of the journey coming to an end. We both looked at each other, and it was obvious we were both very nervous. The closer I got to 1953 Pearl Street, the faster my heart beat. We really didn't have much of a plan, mainly one of us trying to keep Simon Bing occupied while the other did our best to have a look around. I guessed snooping around would be a more accurate description of what we wanted to do.

Arriving at the doorstep of the brown house I recognized from my last trip, we exited the car and knocked on the door. No answer. We knocked loudly again and again, still no answer. Wilda and I would not be deterred by this; in fact, this might be a good thing! As we cautiously crept around the house, we looked in every window and saw nothing but empty rooms! All the furniture from the house was gone! This house seemed abandoned! Walking around to the very back, we tried to stay out of view of the prying eyes of neighbors.

This was not an easy task since all the homes were only a few feet apart. At the rear of the house, there was a back door, as most houses always had back doors for quick exits in case of fire. I tried the door, but it was locked as I expected it to be. Determined to not let this stop me, I asked Wilda to be a lookout as I picked at the lock to see if I could get it open. No luck! So much for my breaking-and-entering plan! Why hadn't we thought to bring some sort of tool with us? But then again, we never dreamed we'd be trying to break into the house! Sorely disappointed by this development, we had no choice but to get back in the car and return home. This time, we spent the time staring out the windows at the endless rows of brown homes. We had nothing to say.

Back at home, we rested awhile in defeat. We'd accomplished nothing! I sat pondering where in the world Simon Bing had disappeared to. There was something so strange about that house. My first trip to that address, there had been a big white house that seemed out of a fairy tale. The second trip, Simon had invited me in and served me tea in what appeared to be a grander house than most of us had. Now there was nothing; it was empty. I believed with all my heart that there was something sinister going on in that house, but I couldn't imagine what it might be.

"Wilda," I said, "I have an idea." Recalling what I'd done when I came home after my house had been broken into and calling the locksmith for new locks, I said, "What if we call a locksmith from Bishop Town and tell this person we've lost our keys and need the locks changed with new keys?"

"Do you think that would work?" she asked skeptically. Wilda had a very logical mindset, while I could get carried away on flights of fancy that often met with failure.

I answered her, "I don't know if it would or not, but at this point, what've we got to lose?"

Wilda answered, "I have very little left to lose, but you have the last few months of your life that could be spent in confinement if this doesn't work."

That was very true. I could spend my last precious months in government hands, and that would be horrible, I'd been told.

"Give me overnight to think about it," I said. I'd have to figure out if there really was any chance of me escaping my death and whether the attempt was worth it. So far, I'd never heard of anyone managing to do so. I wanted so much to find a way to save Wilda.

She had so little time left. But I'd have to get it done in less than six weeks if she was to be rescued!

That night, I looked up lock changers in Bishop Town. There were only two to choose from. Trades and service providers were becoming increasingly rare. Most people who still did it were older than the average. Younger people found it less and less desirable to practice these trades anymore.

When one was found, you were very good to them. While they couldn't get paid for their services, they enjoyed a piece of cake or a shot of bourbon. I guessed when service people completely disappeared, someone would have to pick up the gauntlet and learn to do what people needed doing. That was probably what would happen. When people couldn't find anyone to do jobs for them anymore, someone would either have to have the gumption to learn, or the government would force certain people into these jobs.

I ordered a car for early the next morning and programmed the car for 1953 Pearl Street in Bishop Town. Wilda and I settled back for the ride once again, but this time, neither of us felt like trying to play anything. We didn't feel like talking either. We had little left to say if this ruse didn't work.

Arriving at the house once more, I knocked on the door again for good measure. It was becoming harder and harder for me to trust what I thought I'd seen anymore. Even with Wilda alongside me as a witness, could I have possibly imagined her too? No one came to the door today either. After a check around the house again, looking in all the windows, we found the house as empty as it had been yesterday. Back on the front stoop, I used my mini mensa tablet to contact the lock changer I'd found on the Pipeline last night. I wrote this person a story about being locked out of my house and how urgent it was for me to be able to get back inside. I got the message back that it was a busy time for the lock changer and perhaps they could get to me in two or three days!

"No! No!" I responded. "My best friend is coming to live with me, and she is about to be aged out! We can't stand here on the street, waiting for the few days she has left! Please come now!" I begged.

Taking pity on us, the locksmith wrote back that the lock changer was coming! Coming now!

Wilda and I had tried to prepare our story last night. We both were wrapped tight in many layers of clothes, and both of us wore a metal brace around our lower backs. I had no idea if this would slow down the lock changer's chip reader, but it was all I could think of. I would do most of the talking, for I was a far better liar than Wilda and a pretty convincing actor when I needed to be. We sat on the stoop waiting.

Within an hour, the lock changer showed up. I was able to bring a few tears to my eyes while exclaiming my thanks for his willingness to come. He nodded his head at Wilda and mumbled a quick "Sorry for your troubles, lady."

I guessed that was about as much sympathy as she was going to get, but he was here, and that was what mattered! Neither of us had worn any makeup and had intentionally done nothing with our hair. We surmised that would make us look old and pitiful. We really needed pity now for what we had in mind. He attempted to run his chip reader over our backs but started cursing when he could not get a good read.

"Please!" I begged. "We really need to get inside." It was then that Wilda began to cough.

That hadn't been in the plans, but it seemed to be working because the man said, "Oh, forget it. Two old women wouldn't try anything shady." When he turned his back, and after a few more really convincing coughs, Wilda looked at me with a gleam in her eye, meeting the same one in mine.

Fortunately for us this house only had three locks on it, so he was finished in just under an hour. He handed me three separate keys, one for each lock. Then he stated that he wanted to try to read our chips one more time. I wondered what happened to the little old lady quip about us not being shady. Once again, he could only get partial numbers on us, and he gave up. This would have been the time where I would have invited him in as a special payment, but since I really didn't live in the house and it appeared empty, I had nothing to offer. Maybe I could have climbed into his work truck and had sex with him, but he didn't seem interested and soon realized that this was all he was gonna get. I thanked him profusely and kissed his cheek as a nice old lady might. Again he mumbled a profanity under his breath, got back in his truck, and drove away. We were in!

Chapter 38

Now what? We hadn't made much of a plan for if we actually got inside. Wilda surprised me by taking out some snacks from her bag.

Why hadn't I thought of that? I wondered.

We sat down on the floor in what had been the living room and slowly ate our cookies, pondering what we should do now. Wilda suggested we take a quick look in all the rooms to make sure we were truly alone here. I agreed that was a good idea.

Walking through empty room after empty room, we saw nothing but dust motes floating in the sun with the air as we passed. The kitchen was a different story. The smell in there was bad, really bad! When I opened the refrigerator, I screamed in shock. There was dried blood all over the inside and what looked like a chip in a bed of gore. We both ran out the back door and vomited. The stench was so bad, but what was worse was what was in there. The refrigerator was not running, so the skin and blood had become rancid! I ran back in and closed the refrigerator door, then back outside with Wilda. She was as pale as a ghost, and I would think my brown skin had lightened considerably as well.

"What was that, and who would do that?" I asked.

At that, Wilda leaned over and vomited again. "I can't go back in there," she said in a very shaky voice. "I'm sorry, I can't stand the smell and know what's in there. I just can't do it."

Feeling every bit as repulsed as she did, I said, "Wilda, we have to. We've come too far to let anything at all stop us. We'll figure out something to do about the smell. I promise." She looked at me with wary eyes, but again I said, "I promise."

I left her sitting on the back steps, then took a deep breath, and ran through the kitchen and up the staircase. This was a bigger home than most, with a second floor. Perhaps that was why Simon was gone; he and his husband might have been booted out because this was too large a house for just two people. That might have been it, but something else had to have gone on in this house for what we found in that refrigerator!

There were two small rooms on the top floor. These rooms were not empty. There were small cots in each room. It was really hard to see in here because both small windows in each room had been covered in a black substance. On further examination, it felt as if black paint had been applied to each window. This made both rooms almost totally dark. I reached into my bag and found a small light that I routinely carried with me.

Turning it on and shining it on a cot, I screamed, "Holy shit, holy shit!"

This bed had big dark spots on it that appeared to be dried blood too! Going to the other room, I shined my light down at the other cot. This one was even more than spotted, saturated in blood. I recoiled and ran down the steps through the kitchen and out the back door. Once again, I vomited what few cookies that hadn't come up before.

"Oh, Wilda," I exclaimed, "something really bad has happened here." I told her the story of what I'd found, and she turned even a whiter shade of pale. Now I had to figure out how to get the stink and gore out of the house. I had nothing with me that would help. I certainly was not going to reach in there and touch anything with my hands! It was getting to be midafternoon now and I had to get this done before the sky turned dark. I had to get it done because I'd promised Wilda I would.

The first thing I did was to hold my breath as long as I could and open every window in the place. I had to run back outside frequently to get some fresh air. I searched on my mensa tablet for the nearest Pharma Depository. Perhaps I could find things there that would help. Calling the car again, I left Wilda sitting on the outside steps while I went in search of some de-stinker stuff! The government owned all the pharmaceutical facilities, so I had to be careful what I got. I was bundled up again with the back brace in hopes it might foul up their chip reader, as it had done with the locksmith. My hopes were dashed the minute I walked through the door. An alarm sounded and got the attention of everyone in the store.

An employee walked up to me and sternly said, "I see that the government has business with you. You will need to wait here."

The tears started running down my face! They'd finally caught up with me! I wondered how far I'd get if I tried to run through the door. But it was already too late. A big black government car had pulled up to the front of the store. A woman exited the car, and her eyes were trained directly on me!

"You need to come with me," the woman said with deadly calmness. While her voice was low, her intentions were coming through loud and clear. Grabbing me by the arm, she pushed me toward the waiting car. After slamming the door behind me, she entered the other side and sat beside me without a word.

"Where are you taking me?" I asked.

Her only response to me was "Don't talk. Don't say another word."

I thought about Wilda sitting at the house on Pearl Street, wondering what had happened to me. I could not send her a message because I was sure that by now every electronic device I owned was being monitored.

Chapter 39

I was taken to a small government building, not very far from where they'd picked me up. I was escorted to a small room and told to sit there until someone came in to talk to me. It was very cold in this small dark room, and my teeth started to chatter from both the cold and my fear. It was almost two hours later before the woman who'd come to get me walked into the room.

"Your name is Naia. Is that correct?"

"Yes," I replied.

To this, she asked, "Did you know that the government has been looking for you for almost six months now?"

I put a puzzled look on my face and answered, "Why, no. Whatever for?" I pretended to be just as dumbfounded as I could be that anyone would be looking for me.

"You disappeared. You didn't answer any of the messages you were sent asking where you were. Can you tell me why that was?"

"You tried to contact me?" I asked. "Why were you looking for me? I never got any messages from you."

The woman's face grew angry, and she said, "You are lying to me. We now have all the details of everywhere you've been, whom you've spoken with, and every contact you've made. All these people have already been questioned, but no one, not even your daughter, knew where you were going or where you'd been."

I tried not to let the woman know how hard my heart was pounding when I answered her in as calm a voice as I could muster. "You know, don't you, that I am to be aged out in a few months?" She nodded her head. I went on, "I had no idea that I could not travel and see some of the sights that I'd always wanted to see." I went on firmly. "If I was supposed to report to someone, I wasn't aware of it.

I believe the government said I could travel and have some pleasure in my last months. Is that not correct?"

"Why are you in Bishop Town?" she asked in a cold voice.

I could not think fast enough to give her a good reason, so I got somewhat belligerent and asked, "Is there a law that I can't travel to Bishop Town?"

She looked at me very suspiciously, asking, "Why are you here?"

All I could think to do was shrug my shoulders and ask again, "Why shouldn't I be here?"

I could usually think my way out of a situation, but this time, I supposed I was too scared to have any original thought come into my head.

"We are going to detain you here for a few days," she spoke again in that calm, deadly voice.

"What?" I exclaimed. "Why would you do that? What do you want from me?"

"We want the truth," she replied. "You've been on our radar for quite some time now. We know who your son was. We know that he had coupled with a woman, and she cannot be found either. You must tell us where she is and all that you've been up to. You have acted in the classic way of someone who will not accept aging out in the right spirit. You appear to be someone trying to avoid the fate of everyone in the country who is euthanized at the age of seventy and one month."

This time, I thought I looked convincing that I did not know what she was talking about because, to my horror, she had the lowdown on me.

"I don't know what you're talking about!" I protested.

She turned and walked out of the room. After she was gone, I tried the door to see if I could get out. It was locked.

A very dim light came on about three hours later. I was so tired and so worried about Wilda. I hoped she'd figured out that something had happened to me and had gotten the hell out of Bishop Town! Soon another woman came into the room and escorted me to another small room. I had a rudimentary physical checkup and was then taken to another holding place. This room was just as bleak but had a small cot, a toilet, and a sink in it.

As I sat down on the cot, this woman searched my bag. She confiscated every electronic item of mine that I had with me and took them with her when she left the room. She'd even taken my small flashlight.

This was the most scared and lonely I'd ever been in my life. I'd been pretty much alone for the last three years, but I'd had my games and books to distract me. Now there was nothing but me and the dim little light that shone from under the door. That was it—that was all.

I lost track of how many days and nights I'd been here. I sat and wondered if I would ever get out or see the light again. No one had hit me or anything like that. I was fed, got the occasional change of clothes. I had a sink and toilet in here with me, so I didn't even get to go out for that. I wondered if the prisons of old felt like this.

Every so often, a person would come by and ask me questions about my activities during my unaccounted-for time, and except for the foray here to Bishop Town with Wilda, I really had done nothing that I could not tell them. The interrogations had become my social life. I tried to drag them out as long as possible, but it had almost become a rote exercise by now. I never had enough time with another person, even if that person was my accuser. I thought about making up some big tale to tell them, to keep them with me longer, but I guessed my last ounce of better judgment won out on that.

A woman entered the room at some point. I never knew if it was day or night, so it could have been any time of day. I hadn't seen this one before, but the same questions were being asked.

"Why were you in Bishop Town? Where were you when you didn't respond to our demands to know where you were? Were you or are you involved in a conspiracy to escape your aging out or to overthrow our kind, benevolent government?"

I guessed I didn't answer everything they asked me. I could not tell them why I was in Bishop Town and what I'd been up to here. I couldn't confess to trying to escape my aging out death sentence. This woman asked all the same questions that I'd been asked over and over. She sat there staring at me. I looked her in the eye, and neither of us said anything.

Finally, in a very quiet voice, she said, "You have friends in high places, don't you?"

"What?" I asked incredulously. "What did you say? I don't know if I have any friends left at all. What are you talking about?"

She shook her head the tiniest little bit, got up, and walked out the door. I sat there a while, trying to make sense of and process what she'd asked me about high-placed friends. I certainly had no clout with anyone! Then something seemed different. I couldn't put my finger on it at first; suddenly, it occurred to me that I hadn't heard the lock in the door click when this woman left the room!

Chapter 40

I stood, walked to the door, and tried the knob. It turned easily.

Wait a minute. Let me think this through!

Was this a trap of some kind? Was I supposed to get caught breaking out? Was I to be punished more severely for the attempt? Slowly I turned the knob until I could see an infinitesimal hint of light on the other side of the door. No alarms went off. I heard no sound of any kind of guards or keepers. I slowly opened it a wee bit more—still nothing. Finally, I opened it enough to stick my head out and look; there were rows and rows of closed doors, but nothing else! I stepped completely out the door but did not close it behind me in case I need to get back in there quickly. I walked close to the wall and saw surveillance cameras every few feet, but no one acknowledged that I was walking down the hallway.

At the end of the hall was a single flight of stairs that went down. I knew I had come up a flight of stairs when I was brought here, and I concentrated as hard as I could to remember the layout of the place from that first day. I thought I walked in, and there was a woman behind a desk who sat me down and asked me my name, address, and chip number.

Oh, please, let me remember, I thought. *Let me see. I was taken to a room and given a series of tests to check my mental cognizance and a quick checkup by a person with a stethoscope around his neck. That room was just down the hall and around a corner from the woman behind the desk. From that office, I was marched down a hall to the right, then up the steps, and was placed in my room. I know. I know that front desk was right by the entrance door!*

I tiptoed back to my room and quietly closed the door. Maybe that might buy me some time before they discovered I was not in there. I retraced my steps until I came to the down staircase again. At the bottom of these steps, there was another closed door.

Shoot. I didn't remember coming through this door. There was no glass in the door, so I could not see what was on the other side! There might be an entire room of guards behind this door, and I would be walking right into the room with them!

I could always go back to my room, I thought. No one would be the wiser about my little trip down the stairs. *What if freedom is outside this door?* I screamed inside my head! With a mighty effort, I slowly pushed through that door. No guards, no keepers, no guns, just another hallway. I walked it quickly but as quietly as I could. *There on the left. That's the testing room!* I was sure that was the testing room! I crept down a little farther until I came to an intersection with another hallway. Turning left, I found myself at the end of the hallway, where a lady sat there at the desk. Beyond the desk was the door to my freedom!

I stood there for a while, trying to catch a quick glimpse of the person working this shift. I heard a chair pushed back, a noise like someone groaning and stretching, and then I heard footsteps. Her shoes made a tapping sound as she walked down the hall in my direction! I quickly jerked myself back around the corner and flattened myself to the wall. It was very dim in this hallway, but if she came around the corner, she would surely see me! It was too late for me to do anything now; I could not get back to my room unnoticed and without making noise, so I stood there, waiting for her to discover me! For a brief second, I wondered if I should attack her and try to overpower her. Once again, common sense kicked in, and I knew I wouldn't be able to subdue her. They'd taken my gun away, so I couldn't kill her, and I didn't know if I'd be able to take that step even if I had the opportunity.

Here she comes! I panicked. *I am about to get caught and be in more trouble than I am now!*

She walked around the corner and looked me straight in the eye. Then the impossible happened! She walked right on by me without a word! I quit thinking at all after this. I walked as quickly as I could, opened that door, and headed out into the night!

From this minute on, I am free! I marveled to myself as I hurriedly walked away.

Now that I had my newfound freedom, what was I to do with it? Where should I go? If I tried to go back to my home, would the government be waiting to recapture me? Would my friends' homes be watched if I turned to one of them for help? I was still in Bishop Town with no mensa tablet. I had no way to order a car, no way to reach out to anyone. My flush of euphoria quickly died because I had nowhere to go that I thought safe. I started walking; the only place I knew in Bishop Town was the Bing house. It was quite a distance from where I was, but I had no choice but to once again put one foot in front of the other.

Chapter 41

About three hours later, as the dawn turned the horizon a rosy pink, I finally reached my destination. One more block, passing house after house, and then I was there! I hoped that the house had not been locked back because I no longer had a key. I walked up to the front door and turned the knob... Locked tight. Just for the heck of it, I knocked on the door, hoping by some chance Wilda might have stayed here.

Wait! Wilda? What day is this? Has her death date come and gone while I was locked up? I have to find out what date it is. Wait! What's that?

I heard footsteps from within the house coming to the door! Could that be Wilda? I'd lost all track of time. Maybe I had been confined for a much shorter time than it felt! I heard locks being turned, and then the door swung open. I almost fainted! Standing there on the other side of the door was Simon Bing! I looked past him, and the house was fully furnished. It appeared that I had woken him from a sound sleep.

"Yes, ma'am?" he said. "How may I help you?" I stood there openmouthed, my head confused beyond reason. When I didn't speak, he looked at me more closely. "You look familiar," he said. "Have we met before?"

"Yes," I answered. I stepped beyond the threshold, and Simon backed up a step. "I was here once before. At that time, I asked you about my friend Robin, who had your father's name and address hidden under her mattress. She was pregnant, and she and I had had a tiff. I came here looking for her. Remember now?"

He hesitated for a time, and I could literally see the light come on behind his eyes with recognition. "Ah, yes, now I remember. Are you all right? It's very early in the morning for a visit. Are you having some sort of trouble?" His voice was low and soothing, and when I nodded, he quickly ushered me on in to his home.

He sat me down and immediately left to make tea for us both. Upon his return, he'd also brought two slices of toasted bread with blackberry jam along with the tea. Neither of us said much as we sat quietly eating. I realized I was famished and could not remember what meal I'd last eaten. When my toasted bread and jam were gone, I felt that I had energy now to talk. I had no idea why I trusted this man. I didn't know him at all, but I had a great need to tell some other person what had happened to me.

When I told him about coming the first time to this house and it being the big beautiful home with people and gardens, I could tell he was wary about all that I was saying. I knew I sounded like a raving lunatic, but I *had* to talk! I needed to confide everything in someone to see if he could help me make sense of it all. Why Simon? I didn't know, but he seemed almost like my Stephen, who could listen to my rants and understand what I needed to make everything right.

I told him of my travels and my coming home. I told him about trying to figure out what seemed to be a conspiracy surrounding my aging-out period and how his father's name and 1953 Pearl Street kept coming around and around again in my consciousness. I told him I had to find the reason why! When I told him about my coming here some days ago to find an empty house and gore and a chip in the refrigerator, I immediately knew I'd said too much. He bowed his head, as if in deep thought, then he looked up at me.

"Do you know how this sounds?" he asked. "Do you know you are telling me things that are impossible? You are saying things that have no logic or plausibility. Ma'am, you do certainly need help, but you need far more help than I can give you."

I sat back on his couch, and my tears rolled down my face. I'd told him almost everything that had happened to me over the past six months, and he didn't believe a word I said!

Wait, I thought. *Maybe that is the answer, and I've gone insane! Could that be the only explanation for all the fantastical things I'd seen?*

I didn't speak again. I sat there in front of him, waiting for what he might do.

He returned to the upstairs room. I was very tempted to follow him to see if all that blood was still on his mattress, but I didn't. I only waited. I could hear him talking to someone. I could hear the other person exclaiming, "What!" Then Simon came back down the steps. He had dressed and following him was whom I assumed was his husband, José.

Simon said to me, "Ma'am, this is my husband, José. He has a medical degree but quit practicing a number of years ago. I've asked him to see you. Is that agreeable to you?"

I nodded my head in the affirmative, and José pulled a chair from the kitchen and sat directly in front of me. He took me through a number of exercises to see if I had the ability to see two fingers, to push and pull his hands, and to look with a tiny bright light into my eyes. He felt my head and neck. Then he turned my head to look into my ears, then back around. He looked into my mouth. Then he asked me what year it was. What year it was!

"Wait, what date is this?" I asked intensely.

He looked at me strangely and then questioned me again, "What year is this?"

I stood quickly and exclaimed, "I don't care what year this is. I need to know the date today!"

To calm me, he answered, "It's February 17."

I jumped up and ran to the door, then turned back. "Can one of you call a car for me? I need to get back home!"

"Perhaps you should stay here with us and let us take you to a health facility," said José.

"No!" I screamed. "I have to get back home. Please call a car for me."

I heard Simon whisper to José, "Call the car. She is past the age of receiving any medical treatment anyway."

A sad look passed between them, but José called a car to take me home. I had to go home! I had to find out about Wilda! She only had three more days, and then the countdown to her death would begin.

The car came. Two hours later, I was at my front door. I had no bag, no keys to get inside, but I went to my front door, and the knob turned effortlessly under my hand. I wasn't scared this time. I did not care if someone was in my house again. I didn't care if I was being watched or listened to. I only cared about finding Wilda!

I turned on my computer and waited for it to start up. In those few seconds, I felt complete panic. "Come on, come on!" I yelled at the screen. Finally, the light came on, and it all opened up. I sent Wilda an immediate email telling her I was back home and wanted to be with her. After what seemed an intolerable amount of time, my computer finally pinged.

Opening her reply, she expressed surprise that I was home and said, "Certainly, come on over."

I quickly ordered another car and was shortly standing at Wilda's front door. When I knocked, her daughter, Michelle, open the door and welcomed me inside. Wilda sat quietly on her couch. I ran to sit beside her and threw my arms around her. Wilda smiled wanly and patted my knee.

Michelle answered my unasked question and said, "Mama has taken a tranquilizer. She is a little loopy right now."

I remembered that Stephen had been given tranquilizers in the weeks before he was taken, but he only took them at night so sleep would come. It didn't seem in Wilda's nature to take anything during the day.

Michelle said, "She has become extremely anxious these past few days, almost to the point of hysteria, and asked for something to help her get through these last days. Where Mama doesn't take much medicine, it has affected her more than most, I think."

I could tell Michelle had been crying. She truly loved her mother, and she'd miss her tremendously after she was taken away. Wilda was in such a daze. We really couldn't have much of a conversation. I made small talk with Michelle for a while and then stood to leave. I could do nothing here. I had so hoped I could find a way to save Wilda, but now I was without hope. I asked Michelle if I could be here when they came for her mom, and she gave me permission.

I held my best friend in a tight embrace for a few moments, then tearfully told her goodbye. I cried all the way home.

I stayed in seclusion at home until Wilda's death day on February 20. I was mourning already. The things the two of us had been through together, the things we could still do together if the damned Aging Out law had never been passed! We could have had many more good years together, and the government was taking those years away from us. I was about as angry as I was sad. Still, I could do nothing!

The day of her execution, I was at Wilda's house by about 6:00 a.m. I knew that they usually arrived promptly at eight when death day arrived. When this law was first enacted, many black limos were arriving every day to take people to their death, but now with our numbers growing fewer and fewer, seeing a death car was now a more unusual occurrence.

Wilda was wide awake this morning. She told me she had opted out of taking any more pills. She wanted to be wide awake when she saw her daughter for the very last time. Michelle and I tried to get her to eat something. We suggested everything that Wilda had always loved to eat, but she was not interested. I noticed Wilda was holding tight to a raggedy old book. On closer inspection, I saw that it was a Bible. I had never known Wilda to have a religious bone in her body.

Today, though, she clutched that old book as if it were her rock in the middle of a flood. At exactly 8:00 a.m., I could see out her window as that wretched car pulled up to her door. Wilda stood. Michelle held out her heavy coat, and Wilda put her arms through the sleeves. Michelle buttoned her up. Then Wilda turned to me.

We held each other for one last embrace, and she whispered, "Read the book, my dearest friend in the world. Read the book!"

Through my tears, I promised her I would. The most painful scene of all was her clutching her daughter for the last time. Michelle held on to her so tightly that Wilda had to pull away from her. They looked into each other's eyes for the very last time. Then Wilda turned and walked out the door with the two men on either side of her. Seeing Michelle's desperation at losing her mother, if I could have taken Wilda's place right now, I would have done so in a heartbeat. The car pulled away, and she was gone.

For days after, I stayed secluded in my small home. I had truly lost all hope of finding a way to survive. I hadn't been able to save Wilda, and my will and hope had left me. I didn't have the strength to fight anymore.

Chapter 42

February 29, 2526

I spent another sleepless night spent tossing and turning, hoping to fall asleep and having those golden dreams as I used to—dreams where Stephen and I had each other, the children were young and there was so much to look forward to. I haven't had a dream like that in such a long time. I was lying in my bed groggily in some state of a fever-pitched attempt to fall asleep.

Almost there…

Then came a sharp knock on my door! That sound startled me, and my eyes flew open. I lay there for a moment and wondered if what I thought I heard might have been in my dream starved mind or a big old snore.

It sounded like a knock! I thought. I glanced up and looked at the time. *It's four in the morning*, I chided myself.

So I let my eyes begin to close. Then they popped open again! It did sound like a quick knock on the door, but there had been no more. Surely if someone wanted in, they would have knocked longer and louder!

Oh shit, I thought. *Instead of lying here questioning myself, get up and open the door!*

I rose from bed, made a quick stop in the bathroom, and then went and opened the front door. No one was there, but I had at least checked. It was just as I thought—nobody at all. As I turned to go back into the house, I saw an envelope stuck to my front door. Peeling it off, I saw it had my name hand printed on its face. I looked around to see if anyone was there who might have put it there, but nothing moved that I could see, nothing beyond the light of my doorway. I looked to my neighbors in front and on either side to see if they had an envelope on their front stoops, but I saw none. Going back inside, I locked all the locks, turned on a light, and opened the envelope. I half thought it might be a government warning about how little time I had left, but I was wrong.

Inside was a message that said, "Something very important for you and others will take place later on today at the government office in the town square. Be there!" This was a very cryptic message, and I couldn't imagine what it could be about and why it was sent to me.

I don't want to go downtown today for whatever this might be about! I thought. *What a bunch of bull!* Now I was wide awake. *What to do? What to do?* I asked myself.

I went and retrieved my big mensa tablet and sat on the couch and played games until I began to nod off. I sat there in an awkward position till the pain in my neck woke me up again. It was about ten thirty by then, and I considered eating something. But once again, my appetite was missing. I was very thirsty, though, so I poured myself a small glass of sweet wine.

"Drinking in the morning." I laughed to myself. "Well, why not? Why not do whatever I want, no matter the time?"

The small glass of wine on an empty stomach made me a little giddy. I picked up that envelope and read the message once more.

Oh, I'll go, I thought. *I have nothing else going on today. I still have plenty of time to clean up and get there.*

I ordered a car for eleven thirty but was told by a dispatching robot, "If you want a pickup at that time, you will have to share the car with others who are headed for the same destination. Do you still want a car?"

I responded, "Yes, I want the car."

I didn't think I'd ever ordered a car and been told I'd have to share it! It appeared that many others might have gotten that same knock on their doors this morning. At almost eleven thirty-five, a car stopped, and a horn blew. I was ready and only had to lock my house. Apparently, it was taking too long because the horn blew a second time. Leaving two of my five locks undone, I grumpily went to the car. There were five other people inside, sitting tightly together. This car looked as if it was made for four passengers, but I squeezed in and made it six.

I laughingly thought to myself, *This makes me glad my appetite has slacked off a little bit. The small amount of weight I've lost is the only way I can fit into this car!*

No one was talking as we rode along, so finally I asked, "Did everyone get an invitation to this?"

A couple of people grudgingly nodded to me, but still no one spoke. This worried me a little. Everyone seemed so grim that I wondered if the government was convening us for a mass assassination! There was one younger person in the car, but everyone else seemed about my age.

I spoke again. "Does anyone know why we are supposed to gather at noon? Has anyone heard what this might be about?"

The gentleman whose lap I was practically sitting in said something that heartened and terrified me at the same time. "I think it has something to do with the Aging Out Law and the birth lottery."

I wanted to ask him more questions, but the car stopped, and we had to get out. We were not downtown yet, but the crowd from there had backed up to where we stopped. I began to inch my way among the crowd to get as close a look to what was going on as I could. The town square and beyond was thick with people.

Oh, my, this doesn't look good! There were armed guards out in front of the government's headquarters! I wondered if this was the last thing that Jack saw before he was shot down. Had there been hoards of people rushing the guards? So far, no one was trying to run anywhere at all, but the crowd had pushed the early arrivals up close to the guards. I could see a few people up front trying to back into the crowd to get out of what potentially could be harm's way.

I wanted to get closer, so as I saw people backing up, I tried to get in front of them. I managed to snake my way to the front of the crowd. I was less than two feet away from the guard. He had no expression whatsoever. He just stood there with his rifle across his chest. The woman next to him was a different story, though. She looked considerably younger than he did, and she was actually pointing her gun and yelling at the crowd to disperse.

Again, many people began to back away, but I didn't. I stood my ground. The guard looked me straight in the eye, but she said nothing directly to me. She didn't point the rifle at me, even though I would have been her easiest shot.

I stood there and began to think, *How many times over the past year have I inexplicably gotten out of situations that normally would have been impossible to escape?*

I didn't know if this was being foolish or me accepting one way or another that my time was growing short and I had nothing left to lose. I was not afraid. Stephen and my children would no longer recognize me! I would not run anymore!

I continued to stare at the young woman holding the rifle. I saw no malice in her eyes. I stared in wonder, and perhaps I was misreading her, but there seemed to be tiny bit of compassion in those eyes. The crowd was so eerily quiet. I didn't know how such a mass of people could remain so silent—no paper rustling, no sound of footsteps, no whispers. I wondered if I might have gone deaf. But there was nothing. I gently snapped my fingers to make sure I could still hear, and that tiny snap drew the attention of every single person in that crowd! When I turned around, every single eye was on me! Some in the back had climbed up higher to see me. Good Lord! What was I supposed to do?

Then this lone person began to scream, the pitch rising higher and higher! This voice reached a mighty crescendo on the single word: "No!"

This started a small ripple of people shouting the same word over and over: "No! No! No!"

Before long, the entire crowd of several thousand was echoing the word. Then it struck me. I was the one who'd started the yelling! That first scream had come from me! It had been my voice that uttered the first "No!"

No one moved. No one rushed the guards. It was as if every person there was glued in place. This kept up for several minutes. Then the ten-foot-tall doors of the government building began to open very slowly. It was so dim inside that the figure standing in the doorway was bathed in shadow. As if on cue, the shouting stopped, and all was quiet once more. The mayor, the highest-ranking official appointed by the congressman of our quadrant, who picked all city officials, stepped out into the sun. She was such a young woman, but she looked fierce and, frankly, quite dangerous. There was no trace of kindness in her stance or reflected in her face. After being handed a microphone, she began to talk.

"Citizens," she intoned in a loud and angry voice, "this gathering or protest—or whatever this may be—will not be allowed to continue! Whoever is responsible for this countrywide effort in disobedience will be severely punished! For your own sake, disperse! No one needs to die today. Go home and calm yourselves. Your benevolent government only wants to bring you the most peaceful and equitable life possible. You are breaking the law by assembling. Go! Leave now! This will be your only warning before I instruct my guards to begin firing!"

She turned and reentered the building. Again no one spoke. People began to turn and walk back to where they'd come from. I could tell that there was a palpable change in the people who'd initially entered this square. This was not a flock of cowed sheep leaving the square. This was a mass of people who realized something big was happening! It was a powerful thought to know that people just like us all over the country were assembling, just as we had. Someone or something very powerful had gathered us in all the squares, in all the hamlets, villages, towns, and cities in every quadrant all over the country! We would never have been aware of this strange commonality if the mayor hadn't uttered the words "all over the country."

On my return home, I turned on the central news system. I couldn't believe I hadn't turned it on since the night of Jack's death. Scrolling to find one in English, I finally found one. It was scratchy and crackly like it was coming from far away, but it was in English. There was no mention on this channel of any unrest or gatherings around the country. Most channels were so extremely biased and politically motivated it was hard to find one that would say anything of substance about what was happening in the country. I imagined these channels were so tightly controlled that they would not mention anything the government did not want reported.

I kept scrolling and trying to find anything at all about what had happened. Then I found a channel that was in Chinese! This was coming all the way from China, and they had no reason not to report what was happening here. I couldn't translate every word because it was spoken too quickly for me to understand it all. I could, though, make out enough of what was said to understand that there was some kind of grass roots effort to make monumental changes in our system of government!

This was very exciting but also very scary! The government has massive volumes of weapons that were not available to civilians. We all had handguns but nothing to compare to the drones that could pinpoint an area to deliver devastating bombs and poisonous gases to land any place they chose. I began to wonder how big this was going to be. What exactly were we fighting for? This morning, all I'd heard, second hand, was that this was about the Aged Out Program and the baby lottery. If there was truly an uprising and a resistance, who in the world could possibly be leading it? How could we all be given information if the leaders could not show themselves?

So things went on exactly as they had before the cryptic note appeared on hundreds of thousands of doors throughout the country. Now what? Either nothing would change, or this might be the beginning of a civil war! That thought was almost too huge and scary to contemplate! So many people would die! I'd wait quietly for a few days to see what, if anything, might happen next.

That night, I had that dream again that there were people standing all around me, watching me sleep. I could hear them murmuring, but nothing was clear enough for me to know what they were saying. Some of the people looked so familiar, but I could not place exactly who they were.

Chapter 43

March 7, 2526

Waking the next morning, I did not feel rested. I felt as if I'd been kept awake all night by a group of weird people keeping a strange watch over me throughout the night. I had experienced this same dream at least a dozen times, and I wondered if it meant anything relevant.

Michelle, Wilda's daughter, sent me an email about midmorning and asked if she could visit today. She had something her mother had wanted me to have. I invited her to lunch, and she accepted. I called and ordered a light lunch for the two of us to arrive about eleven thirty. It arrived at the same time Michelle did. I'd moved Stephen off the table, and we sat down to eat and talk.

I asked her how she was doing without her mother.

Tears welled in her eyes, and she answered, "I miss her so much. I could always tell her everything. She didn't always approve of all that I did, but I never doubted for one second she loved me."

As she was speaking, I rubbed her arm gently. It felt strange to be touching another person in such an intimate way. I hadn't touched or been touched lovingly in a long time. At the end of the meal, Michelle reached into the bag she'd brought with her and handed me the book that Wilda had been clutching before she was taken.

"She wanted me to give this to you," Michelle said.

After seeing what it was, I responded, "Michelle, this looks like a centuries-old family Bible!" Its pages were thin and wrinkled. Someone had painstakingly underlined many of the pages and had recorded birth and death information in its pages. "Oh, Michelle!" I exclaimed. "I can't take this from you. This is a family treasure that you need to hand down to your children and grandchildren!"

Waving a dismissive hand, she replied, "I doubt seriously if I will have children, and if I did, I would not subject them to the gibberish in that book. If Mama hadn't expressly asked me to give it to you, I would have tossed it out when I had to clean out her house."

I was dumbfounded, but I did understand. As far as I'd known, Wilda had never professed any religion, but I would gladly accept it in respect and memory for my friend. Soon after the gifting, Michelle stood to leave. We hugged each other fiercely, and then she was gone. I wondered if I'd ever see her again.

Sitting down with the ancient book, I began to look through it. I started to read from the first page but quickly abandoned the effort. While it was in English, it was written in language that made it difficult to understand. I went from page to page, reading some of the underscored sentences. I understood what it said, but it was more like a bunch of random poems than anything cohesive. Then I glanced through the birth and death records. Michelle's birthday was the last one recorded. No one had written down Wilda's death date. I got a pencil and wrote in "February 20, 2526."

I wondered what else I should do with the book. I decided to lay it on the kitchen table next to Stephen. That way, I'd have two loved ones to share memories and meals. Every time I ate over the next few days, I'd glance into the book. What had Wilda wanted me to get from this?

Perhaps just a memory, but then I remembered her whispering to me emphatically "Read the book" as she was leaving me for the last time. Rising I fetched my mensa tablet and sat upon the couch. I asked Know Everything for a simple, modern-day translation of the Bible. Instantly, it was there. I started from the beginning again, and this time, it was much easier to understand.

Had Wilda believed in the God mentioned of this book? Most of the first few chapters were quite entertaining in a fantastical sort of way. As I continued to read, it became apparent that this God had a very huge love for the Jewish people.

"Way to go, Stephen!" I giggled to myself. There seemed to be page after page of laws and commands that seemed overly harsh and, in most cases, downright ridiculous. Those pages I sort of skimmed through, but eventually, there were more interesting parts.

I started to pick it up frequently when there was nothing else to do. Supposedly, some king would come and take the Jews out of slavery. Everybody in it was waiting and speculating on when this huge event would occur. It had become like a fantasy novel to me. I loved to read weird stuff, so whenever I had a free moment, I picked it up and read more. I did not necessarily read it word for word, but I read enough to get the gist. I skipped over the few parts I found dull and boring.

Everything had been quiet for over a week now. It felt as if I was waiting for *something* to happen. I occasionally went out to dinner, but since I had no one to go out with, I usually ordered delivery food. A few days this week, I'd almost forgotten to eat! I'd always had such a hardy appetite that this lack of one worried me, especially when I managed to realize I couldn't remember the last time I ate. I'd started to lose my thirst for my sweet white wine as well. My clothes were becoming much too loose, so this would probably require another trip to the clothing warehouse. I felt like it was surely repressed stress that I must be feeling because my death day was approaching. I say repressed because I was not particularly feeling anxious or scared. Surely, I was, though. I'd be dead within four months, and for some strange reason, I was remaining very calm about it.

Later on that night, as I was about to fall asleep, I heard that serendipitous short knock upon my door. It was the very same one that I heard when I got the message about meeting in the town square. I quickly jumped up, unlocked my locks, and went out to the stoop to peer through the darkness to see if I could see anyone out there. This time, I heard receding footsteps heading west away from town. I was in my nightgown, but I didn't care. I ran after the shadow going down the street.

When I got closer, I whispered loudly, "Wait!"

The shadow stopped and turned into a person the closer I came to it. To my shock and surprise, it was the same man that had been in my Chinese class who got so upset with me because I blurted out Sally's name with excitement when he first approached me. My heart started pounding! I knew that Sally had hinted at some sort of plan to escape being aged out. Maybe I had been forgiven and would be given a second chance to escape with my life!

"Come home with me and tell me what is happening!" I demanded.

He responded, "I've got more homes to attend to tonight. I have to be on my way." He turned to walk away, but I grabbed his arm.

Looking directly into his eyes, I begged, "Please, please, my time grows so short."

"I can't come tonight, but I will come tomorrow at this same time," he replied.

I still held his arm. "Do you promise?" I asked. "You are telling me the truth, and you really will come and talk to me?"

He slowly nodded his head. Putting his hand over mine on his arm, he said, "Yes, I promise I will come."

With that, I had no choice but to let him go. I stood there in the street watching him until he was completely swallowed up into the shadows.

Chapter 44

I walked home quickly. I saw no one out on the street, but I had left home so quickly that I'd left my front door open and had not taken my pistol with me. Less than two houses down from my house, I heard two women arguing. I stopped right where I was and crouched beside my neighbor's stoop. I wanted no trouble.

As they passed my house, I could hear one of them say to the other, "Hey, look! That house's front door is standing open. Maybe we should take a look!"

Oh no, I thought in terror. *What should I do?*

Without thinking long enough to scare myself into inaction, I stood quickly and barked, "Stop! Stay out of my house!" They both sprang around. Both were armed, pointing their pistols at me! I immediately said, "I want no trouble. Please let me go home."

The smaller of the two women snarled and said, "Sure, old lady. We'll let you go home. Let's all go home now."

I tried to think quickly again, but they both had their weapons pointed directly at me, and I felt they'd shoot me if I shouted out for help. If they shot me and did not kill me, I would not be allowed to have any kind of treatment for my wounds.

All this flashed into my head in a nanosecond. I went with them. They continued to point their weapons and followed me into the house. I purposely did not lock the door, and they did not seem to notice. I wanted nothing to slow me down if I had the opportunity to escape! I stood there as they looked through every room of my home. They seemed to be disappointed that I had little that was worth enough to steal.

Their disappointment made them mean. I begged them not to hurt me, but that was a mistake. This seemed to make them more determined than ever to do just that. The larger woman hauled off and backhanded me across the face. I fell to the floor, and the other woman kicked me in the side! I curled up in a fetal position to protect my head and to make myself a smaller target for their assault. I had made a huge error in leaving my house open for even a second. The government treated Aged Out candidates well during their last year, but we were fodder for younger people's cruel enjoyment.

I'd always been so careful. All my life, I'd been on the watch for people like this, and until tonight, I was always armed. But not tonight. After a while of hitting, their kicking and spitting on me must have lost its appeal. I lay on the floor unmoving because I did not want to do anything to draw their attention back to me. I tried to inch my way toward the wall as they raided my liquor supply. If I hadn't been too injured to stand, I could have made my escape now, but I felt as if I had broken bones, and it hurt just to breathe. They were very pleased with my liquor stash and helped themselves until they fell into a semiconscious stupor. When they both seemed to have passed out, I inched my way toward the door.

My gun had been confiscated upon my government confinement, so I had no personal weapon. Both women had put their pistols into the waistband of their pants. I was afraid to try to remove one from either of these seemingly comatose women. I could possibly be misjudging their level of drunkenness, and I could not be beaten again!

I did manage to slide across the floor and make my way to the door. I was too injured, and it hurt too much to reach and open the door. Tears ran down my face at my helplessness. I was in so much pain! I eventually passed out from my injuries. When I came to, I heard angry voices and cursing. They were fighting with one another again! Noticing me in front of the door, they began to scream at me.

Crouching right down beside me, one of them hollered directly into my ear, "Trying to get away, old lady? Gonna try to get us in trouble, huh?" With that, she kicked me again!

She was drawing back to do it again when the other woman stopped her and said, "Don't kill the old bitch. She can get things for us that we can't get."

They stuck my mensa tablet up into my face. "Get us food and more alcohol!" they demanded.

My face was so swollen and bruised from their assault that the facial recognition on my tablet would not turn it on. This drove them both into a fever pitch. They cursed me and slapped me again and again. This went off and on all day and into the night. I could do no more for them, but they still didn't leave! I started to believe that they were intent on killing me. I had no food or liquor and no way to order any for them. They were planning to have as much fun as they could before torturing me to death!

Many young people had been so ill-treated themselves that they found satisfaction by hurting as many others as possible. It was a game to them, a way to relieve their boredom. So many others had been maimed, tortured, and killed by roaming teenagers at night that, after midnight, you did not go out by yourself, especially unarmed. I screamed in agony as they grabbed me up into a sitting position. I was slapped and hit in the face until my nose was bleeding and my front teeth were loose. I must have passed out again. When I awoke, they were both drinking again.

One of them must have gone out and bought all the rubbing alcohol they had money for. I could smell it in the air. I made no noise nor opened my eyes to alert them to my consciousness. They again drank themselves into oblivion; one lay there on my couch and the other on my bed in an unconscious stupor.

A little after midnight, I was alerted that someone had walked up on my porch. The women had left all the lights on, and I could see a face looking in at me. I recognized the face of the man I'd run after the night before. He could see me on the floor and the condition I was in. He could also see the woman on the couch, but he had no way of knowing about the one in my bedroom. As he watched, I tried to nod my head and point a finger to both the assailants on the couch and then in the other direction into my bedroom. I held two of my swollen fingers into the air, so he could recognize there was more than one.

I saw him remove his pistol from his waistband. It was a big one! It certainly wasn't anything like the small handgun I'd once had.

I nodded my head toward the door, and I could see him silently walking to it. I saw the handle turn and the door quietly open. In the full light, he could see how badly injured I was, and I saw his eyes grow deadly cold. He reached for a small silencer that he had in his bag and attached it to his gun.

I shook my head violently. "No!"

My gesture of protest didn't faze him. He walked up to the drunken woman on my couch and put a bullet through her head! The one in my bedroom slept through the death of her friend, and he went into the room and took her out too! There I was, broken and bleeding with two dead women in my home!

I had never really seen anyone killed right in front of me before. I was so scared I was shaking wildly.

He closed and locked the front door, then knelt down beside me. "Let's see how badly you're hurt," he said. He very gently put his hands on my body and felt for my injuries. "I don't think your arms or legs are broken." But when he touched my sides, I moaned with the pain. "You probably have some cracked ribs," he said in a low kind of voice. "The best we can do for that at the moment is to find something to bind you with."

He yanked the bloody sheet off my bed and began to tear it into long foot-wide strips. He pulled my gown over my head and slowly began to wind the bloody cloth around me. He wound it as tightly as I could stand it and still be able to breathe. I hated the smell and wetness of the blood as it touched my bare skin. I hated that my assailant's blood was mixing with mine.

This man, named Jesse, stayed with me for the next seven days. He tended to my wounds and made sure I had food and water. At night, he lay with me in case I needed anything throughout the night. He was so tender and kind that it didn't seem strange at all that he slept beside me every night in my bed. Under his care, my injuries began to heal. He was so gentle and soft spoken, the total opposite of my Stephen. I began to feel a great deal of gratitude and affection for him. When my pain subsided, we lay in each other's arms. It had been a very long time since I'd been moved by a man to the point that I wanted him to make love to me. I lay in bed, staring into his eyes. I could tell he cared about me. I moved my hand to touch his face. I rubbed the worry lines upon his forehead. I rubbed his chest and moved my hand further down to his lower belly. It was here that he stopped me. Drawing my hand up to his lips, he gently kissed my fingers.

He said softly, "Naia, I'm gay."

I was okay with that, but surely as tenderly as he touched me and closely as he lay with me, there surely must be some physical attraction!

"I'm sorry," he said, "but let me help you."

With that, he began to touch my breasts. He gently rubbed my nipples. He got on top of me and began to kiss my breasts and then the hot skin of my stomach. Finally, he used his tongue to bring me to the most exquisite climax I could remember. I longed for him to enter me, but when I touched his penis, it was limp and flaccid. I asked him if there was any way at all that I could satisfy him.

He gathered me close to him and quietly said, "No."

He had told me many things while he was here with me, and together we planned and strategized. I would be assigned tasks that I must accomplish. I thought that if we were successful with the plan, we would always be together. I knew his being gay would mean he'd find his gratification with other men, but that was no concern to me at all, as long as he came home to me. I fell asleep in his arms, his breath in my hair. When I woke up the next morning, Jesse was gone.

My heart was broken. I cried and grieved for a man who'd only been in my life for a few days. I doubted if I would ever find someone like him again, even if I managed to complete my tasks and save my life. I knew others were counting on me to do my part to help save us all, so I could not quit or give up. But after Jesse left, dying didn't seem so bad.

Chapter 45

I was surprised how quickly my injuries were healing. I rarely needed pain relief anymore. I still required more rest though. I had a lot to do physically for my part of the escape plan, so I was taking it very easy. During the day, I walked. I wanted to keep myself as strong as possible so my body would not fail me. I was always very careful to look all around me in my daytime walks. Men and women like the ones who hurt me could still enjoy hurting me if they chose, but it was less likely during the day. I tried to be as invisible and go as unnoticed as possible when I was out. Even in the last six months, it seemed like so many young people were turning on one another and becoming much more violent!

Parent R and Rs were developed so parents wouldn't be so bothered by their children that they might abuse them. It didn't appear to be working. I didn't know what was going on behind the closed doors of the houses around me. Maybe there was still love and nurturing, but it seemed to disappear when anyone over ten or eleven went out into public. Then they became like vultures, and anyone they considered weak was a prime target. I couldn't believe I'd lived long enough to see so many children turning into these teenaged angry monsters. Yet here I was, trying to keep on living.

There seemed to be a tiny fraction of hope from all the escape participants that we could make changes. I didn't know if we could ever make this country great again; it had been so abused by hatred stirred up from the government for centuries. Could so few of us make any difference at all? Today I felt as if my hope was fading, but I did have to carry on.

I opened the Bible on my mensa for the first time in a few weeks and began to read. I wanted to know if the Jews' king had gotten there yet. The book was talking a lot about a man named Moses. I wondered if he was the king. This was where it really started to be a cool read. Apparently, Moses could do all kinds of magic to make King What's His Name mad. This king kept lying to Moses and telling him he could take the Jews with him so they didn't have to be slaves anymore.

Huh…what about that?

Apparently, it came to a head when Moses got tired of being lied to and told the Jews to put lamb's blood (yuck) on their front stoop. He promised them that the death angel—whatever that was—would not kill their male children. When King What's His Name's own kid was killed, he let them go! What a great story! I read the day away but couldn't remember if I'd eaten anything. I did not feel hungry, so I surmised I had.

I'd ordered a new gun, and it arrived by drone today. I'd been on the lookout for it because I didn't want it stolen off my stoop. All the spare bullets I'd had were still here and were the same caliber as this pistol, so I had plenty of ammunition. Today was the first day I must complete one of the tasks on my list for the escape.

I was to go to the town square and watch the coming and goings of certain government officials. I walked into the town and found a bench I could perch on. I pretended to be reading on my mensa tablet, but I was keeping a close watch and recording the time and direction each official headed. I was to do this for a week or more to see if I could derive a daily pattern that these men and women took. After several days of this, it actually became quite comical. They seemed to be so programmed to doing the same thing at the same time every single day I knew what time it was just by who was coming out and who was going in.

I certainly needed no hour counter with these rigid people. I recorded it all on my mensa tablet, and when the time came, I'd be able to use an app that would immediately give me the data all calculated and ready to give to the next person. I could give this information just from my observations, but they wanted it all on record on their computers.

My focus was the certain staff workers of the government in my town. I was not privy to the entire plan. This was done so no one person would know it all. I guessed the few people who'd conceived the plan knew every step, but they were so hidden in the shadows. No one but a chosen few know who they were. Though no one had told me exactly what others were doing, I had a feeling that there were many versions of me sitting in all the towns across the quadrants, watching.

I had no idea how my fact gathering assignment was to be used. I was rather amazed I'd been able to sit here so many days, feigning reading a mensa book, and not a single person had stopped to ask questions or lingered near for a little chitchat. It was as if I'd become invisible! I was a little tired this afternoon when I returned home. I was not certain if I was still recovering from the beatings or if my soul had just gotten tired—tired of this world. It was hard to remember back more than a year ago. I was willing to do anything to escape my fate, but the fight seemed to have drained out of me.

I turned back to the Bible on my mensa tablet and kept on reading. It was really very intriguing if read in understandable language. It was like a suspense novel, and I was hooked! I wanted to see how it would all turn out in the end. By the time I got through the Old Testament, I'd been reading for weeks. Reading tonight, I started to nod off, so I'd leave the New Testament for another time.

I did not know exactly what my next escape plan assignment was to be. I was to load all I'd input into my tablet and copy it to a jump drive to hand off to someone named Charlie. Charlie was supposed to drop by my house tomorrow. I'd gotten a little wine and some cheese and bread in case Charlie wanted to linger awhile. While I might not have all the vim and vigor I had just a few months ago, it was pleasing to know I was going to have company. I looked forward to it. That happy thought was my last before falling into a profoundly restful sleep.

Chapter 46

March 29, 2526

Waking up the next morning, I felt strange. Somehow I felt as if I were in the wrong place, that home wasn't home anymore. Standing and walking to the bathroom, I took a long hard look into the mirror. Well, pleasantly surprised, I felt that I was looking better than I had in a long time. My skin had a youthful glow, and my hair was a rich and thick ebony wave. Maybe all the forced rest and fresh air I was getting while sitting for hours in the town square were having a positive effect, at least on my appearance. I didn't understand how I could look so well on the outside and be so weary of the world on the inside.

Because I was expecting this stranger Charlie later on, I decided to go all out and put on makeup and fix my hair into a pretty up do. By the time I'd done all my primping, I couldn't remember if I'd had breakfast yet. I walked into the kitchen and saw no signs that I'd prepared any food for myself.

Maybe later, after Charlie left, I'd walk to the clothes warehouse and get some new gray and blacks that would fit me better. I wondered how much weight I had actually lost. I reconstituted some cereal and poured my milk powder into some water to pour over it. I tried to make myself eat as much of it as I could hold, but after a few bites, I could not swallow another mouthful. Food, and my love affair with it, seemed to have broken up.

I started reading the New Testament while I waited for Charlie to show up. I'd only read a few pages when I found myself growing very sleepy. I didn't know what was happening to me. I had a great night's sleep last night, and there I was, before noon, worn out and sleepy again!

"Come on, body!" I snickered to myself. "Perk up!" Apparently, my body wasn't in the mood to cooperate. I soon drifted off to dreamland.

The dream came again, but this time, it was much clearer than before. I could hear my babies crying, and once again, I could not reach them. It became very clear that there were people looking at me and watching me in my sleep! Why didn't these people go get my babies and bring them to me? I grew very agitated!

I jumped with a start to a loud knocking at the door. I sat there for a moment in a daze. What? Where was I? What woke me? Then the knock came again, and my mind started making sense to me again. That must be Charlie. I need to let him in.

When I opened the door, I was greeted by a rugged-looking man. When he spoke, he had the accent of an Irish man, and I was instantly charmed. I invited him in and offered him wine and cookies. He gave a hearty laugh and said, "Wine is all well and good, but do you have any beer, by the grace of God?"

I was not a beer drinker, but there could possibly be a bottle stuck behind other things in the refrigerator. I rooted through the contents, and there behind a shelf of a thousand condiments were two cans of Ling Ling! Charlie's eyes lit up when he saw that! I handed him a can and a glass. He expertly poured the beer down the side of the glass to keep the foam to a minimum.

I said, "You look like you've done this before!"

He laughed a hearty laugh and responded, "Ah, yes, more times than I can count!"

We both laughed at that. I poured myself a small glass of wine, and we sat there and companionably chatted for quite a while. The conversation eventually waned, and we sat there quietly for a few minutes. Then he got down to business.

"I've looked over the data that you provided," he said. "It looks as if you did a very thorough job of getting your part of the plan complete. With the data from you and others doing the very same job all over the country, it appears that our government, for the most part, likes well-trained little robots running things. It is amazing how eight out of ten of these people are so programmed by habit that they rarely vary. It is almost eerie. The next step will be the hardest, I'm afraid," he said half apologetically. "The next step will be starting to exterminate enough of these people so the government finds itself in chaos."

"What?" I exclaimed. "What do you mean *exterminate*? By whom? I didn't know killing was part of the plan!" I asserted in sick terror. I shook my head no and then said, "No, not me. I'm not killing anyone!"

He responded with firm resolve, "No one wants to kill anyone, but this is war. And in a war, people die! Are you quitting, or are you willing to participate in the next phase?"

I asked, "What is the next phase?"

Sadly he shook his head and said, "I can't tell you that unless you are with us and willing to do whatever it takes! Your time is fast approaching, and mine is two months later! If we are going to survive and ensure the survival of others, we must act now! No time for pondering. No time to think about anything. Action must begin now. Today! People are counting on you!"

"Okay," I said shakily. "What am I supposed to do?"

He opened a bag he'd brought in with him and took out a very large gun! He hand it to me and asked, "How well do you shoot?"

"I've never shot anyone, but I had lessons many years ago. I am not sure how accurate I would be shooting at a target," I answered.

"Hmmm…" he murmured. "From the sound of that, you will not need this gun."

As he replaced the large gun back into the bag he took it out of, I felt an overwhelming relief! For once, I was profoundly grateful for not being good at something!

Then he said, "Since we cannot count on you for a long-range kill, you will have to do something far more dangerous, I'm afraid."

"What is that?" I asked in dread.

"You will have to go into situations for close-up kills," he told me.

Incredulously I asked again, "What? What? What are you saying? I can't do that!"

He looked at me with alarm and said, "You have to. You have no other choice now that you know so much. If you don't agree, you won't be alive when I leave today."

Knowing my time was already so limited, I thought, *Should I even want to attempt this? Will it hasten my death if someone's bodyguard kills me first?*

But the look on Charlie's face told me that I would not live another hour if I didn't comply.

Resigned to my choices, I asked, "What am I supposed to do?"

For the next two hours, he told me what I must accomplish. I was shocked and ill over what I would have to do in the coming days!

After he explained my task to me, I asked, "When this is done, will I be finished? Will I have helped enough that I will be saved?"

At this, he shrugged his shoulders and bid me good evening.

My assignment was to begin the very next day. I got my flight pack out of the attic and checked it out so it was all ready to go the next morning. I packed my bag with what I thought I might need. Charlie had left me a small gun, much like the one I used to have. He'd left adequate ammunition as well. Looking over what I'd gathered, I didn't think I'd forgotten anything.

I knew I'd never be able to sleep, so I opened my mensa and brought up the Bible again. Now that I was into the New Testament, things were getting even more exciting! Apparently, there was this engaged couple who'd never screwed around, but the woman became pregnant anyway! The man seemed a good sort and didn't want to embarrass her in front of everyone, but I thought he was going to privately dump her. Then supposedly, an angel came to him, who said she was a virgin and pregnant with God's child!

Wow! This was getting better and better! Maybe there were no hospitals back then because she had this baby out in a barn! Surely this kid was not the one who was supposed to be a king, was he? A lot of weird stuff happened through that night, and other kings were guided by a star, of all things, to the barn where the baby was. This *was* the kid they'd been waiting for! I kept reading. A lot happened to him during his life. Many people believed him to be the long-awaited savior, but many others did not. They decided to kill him because too many people were beginning to believe him to be the Messiah and the king of the land didn't like it one bit.

If I understood this correctly, he was sent by God to take the punishment of all the other sinners in the world then and forever. Wow! What a story! I was beginning to get sleepy. For the heck of it, I talked to this Jesus and to his dad tonight, unsure exactly what I was seeking. But peace overcame me, and I fell fast asleep.

I awoke this morning feeling stronger than I'd felt in a very long time. I felt a renewed sense of purpose. I had a job to do, and many people were depending on me to do it. I put on my flight pack and strapped my "necessities bag" to my chest. I looked around at everything I'd managed to amass over my lifetime. It really wasn't very much, but what little I had meant something to me. I might never see my home again, and most of the memories here were very sweet. My first tear fell. Wiping my eyes with my fist, I quit looking, went outside, set my destination on the GPS, and took off. I deliberately did not look back at my home of many years as it grew smaller and smaller behind me. Perhaps if we were able to pull off what seemed impossible, I might see my home again someday.

Chapter 47

My task was to stop in many towns all around the country and kill a certain person in each town. All of us were leaving our own towns, making a kill in a strange town, then quickly flying away. At least that was the plan.

My first target was in quadrant fifteen. I brought up the data from my mensa on this person to get the lowdown on his habits. Okay, I had a name, a place, and a time. Could I do it when I got there? Other people were doing the same thing all over the country. But could I? I had a picture of the man, and I studied it well. I did not want to take a chance on killing the wrong person! Apparently, this guy left his office every day at eleven thirty sharp to go across the street from the government building for lunch at a café. There was no plan for what point in my attack I was supposed to kill him; that choice was left up to me. I landed, hid my flight pack in the bottom of a trash container near the cafe, and proceeded to set myself up and be ready.

I was really amazed how calm I was feeling and how focused I was on doing what I had to do. At eleven twenty-five, I positioned myself about ten feet from the front door of the government building. At exactly eleven twenty-seven, he approached the café as he did by habit every day. I did not look him in the eye at all. I looked like anyone crossing a street. He appeared not to even notice me. As he neared me, I brought my gun out of my pocket and purposely bumped into him. At that moment, I shot him in an upward slant from his jaw into his brain. I kept walking, pulling a jacket I'd had tied around my waist up and over my bloodstained shirt. As I was pulling my flight pack out of the trash, I heard a commotion starting where he lay dead in the street. I never looked back. Strapping my pack on, I took off for my next kill tomorrow.

That night, sitting in a little bar in my next destination, I sat sipping vodka and recharging my mensa. The talk was everywhere by then. Over three thousand government employees had been assassinated that day. Now the government was on to us, and doing the job would become much harder and more dangerous. When my mensa tablet was fully charged, I looked for a place to spend the night. I did not want to stay in a regular boarding house because my chip would be checked and there would be a record of me being in this town. I found a little hidden nook by someone's brown little house and settled myself in for a night of sleeping outside. Fortunately for me, it was spring, and the weather had warmed.

I was awakened the next morning by a young woman nudging me, asking, "Ma'am, are you okay? Do you need any help?" Shoot, dog gone it! I had been sure that I would wake up and be long gone before anyone saw me!

"Yes, dear, I'm fine," I said as sweetly as possible. "I got tired last night flying to my daughter's for her birthday and set down to nap because my flight pack does not have autopilot."

She glanced over at my pack and looked perplexed. "It looks new enough to have autopilot. Come inside with me and let me check it out. You can have a bite to eat and some coffee while I look it over," she said far too kindly.

I quickly responded, "No, that won't be necessary. You look as if you're dressed to be somewhere. I won't keep you." Before she could say anything else, I was up and walking quickly away.

If I could have, I would have kicked myself in the rear. No one was supposed to notice me in a town where an assassination was scheduled! My instructions for this one was *kill a certain woman on her way home later this afternoon.* I knew her route and schedule. As I waited inconspicuously, nearby at the appointed time, nothing happened. The woman, whoever she was, was not following the script.

An hour after the kill was to take place, I heard two women coming toward me, talking to each other. Now I was in a quandary! If my victim was one of them, should I just kill her and let the other one see me, or should I kill them both? I waited, facing away from their approach, and then glanced around to see if my target was one of them. Yes, there she was! I reached into my pocket to get my gun.

The younger woman with her said, "Well, hello again! Is there something wrong with your flight pack that you couldn't get to your daughter's today?" She turned to my target. "Mom, this is the lady I was telling you about earlier, the one who spent the night next to my house because she has no autopilot."

"How do you do?" my target asked.

I answered, "Quite well, thank you." *Super! Damn! Shoot! What else can go wrong with this kill?*

The mother/target asked me kindly if I'd like to have a bite to eat with them before I left for my daughter's house.

Her daughter echoed, "Oh, yes! Please do! That will give me a chance to check out your flight pack before you take off again."

Okay, this one was over. I could not make myself kill them both! No way, no how!

I responded, "I really appreciate your kindness, but I really need to be on my way."

The younger woman genuinely seemed to be disappointed that I would not accept the invitation, but I really did need to go. I had to contact someone to let them know that this mission was not accomplished. I turned my flight pack on, waved farewell as I lifted off, and got the hell away from there!

It was all the talk that almost another 1,500 government workers were killed yesterday! This time, though, some of the assassins were killed or caught! A jailed assassin was a threat to all the rest of us because we had no doubt that the government-tortured person was gonna talk.

That must be the reason for all the secrecy of the plan. Nobody knew enough to completely shut it down. I was sitting in a little "hole in the wall" restaurant, listening to the talk of those around me. If this continued, it surely would not take long for the few government workers left to figure out that someone had been studying their habits. The kills were not random, and the government would know that this was a masterminded plot. Once they figured out the pattern, they would start to vary their comings and goings. I failed yesterday's assignment, but I didn't think one less kill would stop this movement. I had one more task, one more kill. I truly hated this, but I made promises. People were depending on me.

I checked the picture and data on this subject. She was a relatively young-looking woman, and that really made me sick. This person might have children! I had no appetite for this kill at all! The man I killed on the first day would always haunt me. I was relieved I failed yesterday and that woman got to live. Now I had one more target. I was reading her particular pattern, and the task seemed easy enough. It would be very easy if I was a cold-hearted killer, but I had never killed anyone until now.

That night, I found a rooftop to land on and decided I'd wait out the night there. Waiting for the time to end this woman's life had me numb. I didn't feel anything I thought I should. It seemed to me that if I was going to take a life, I should feel something tonight. Maybe this *was* a completely cold-blooded murder I was going to commit. I must be capable of anything now. I did not sleep at all. When dawn finally broke, I watched the sun rise. I continued to sit on that roof because the kill time wasn't till 10:00 a.m.

I wasn't hungry, but I was so tired. Where had all my energy gone? When I first started out to do my part to save so many lives, I'd felt so invigorated, but now it was all I could do to hold up my head. After completing this task, I would go home. I assumed someone would contact me again with something else I must do to help the cause. But if it was killing, *no*, I was done.

At about nine forty-five, I was in position. I knew that she came out each day to go from one government building to another. I was there to make sure she would not make it to the second building. I sat on a bench overlooking the town square. This was probably the very same place where the person who'd been assigned to collect data on this woman had sat. For the next ten minutes or so, I watched people come and go from the second building. I could hear the voices of children every time the door opened and closed. I could see people bringing children into the building and then leaving without them.

What is this place? I wondered.

Then it occurred to me. This was a parent R and R. This young woman I was about to assassinate probably went there every day at ten to check on and visit her child! I did not know for a fact that this was true, but that was what I imagined. At exactly ten o'clock, I watched my target leave the building, walking toward the second building. I had my gun loaded and my finger on the trigger. As she got closer to me, I stood. She was looking so intently at the second building; she did not seem to notice me at all!

In that second, I thought, *What a dummy!* Hadn't she figured out her colleagues are being killed all around the country? Had she no concern for her own welfare?

I was right on top of her when the door from the second building opened, and a small little girl came running toward her, yelling, "Mama, Mama! Look what I drew for you!"

I had my gun out! It was my task! I was responsible! It was now. I had to do it now! I bumped directly into her, which was my plan. I had my pistol aimed straight at her heart—a piece of cake!

Then she mumbled an "Excuse me" and quickly walked on by me. She scooped up the little girl and carried her back into the building. She would never know how close to death she came. Failure number two. I put my gun back in my pocket, took an elevator to the top of the building where I'd stashed my stuff, and took off for home.

It took me eight hours to finally reach home. I really did have autopilot on my flight pack and thought, as tired as I felt, I'd sleep on the flight home. I tried, but sleep would not come.

I knew that once I returned home without doing the job I was assigned to do, I'd likely get a visit from Charlie, or someone just like him, to dispose of me. I sat there for an hour or so, wondering if I should sit here and wait for my executioner or take off for parts unknown. I was so incredibly tired, and maybe it was my time to leave this earth. Suddenly, there was a sharp knock on the door!

Well, that didn't take long, I thought. If this was my time to go, I hoped it was as pain free as possible. I struggled to rise from the couch and walk to the door to let my killer in.

Chapter 48

"Wait! What?" I was incredulous.

Instead of someone standing there to finish me off, Robin was at my door! For a split second, I wondered if it was Robin to do the deed.

But she said, "Hurry up! We have to get you out of here right now! Bring your flight pack and let's go. We have no time left to get you away from here!"

As startled as I was, I did what she asked. I left my home once again in the attempt to save myself. I followed her and did exactly what she told me too. I was the puppy, and she was my master. I was still so tired. It was hard to imagine that I could move this fast and head out once again, but I did! Robin pulled me into a car and told me to hunker down as she programmed in our destination. Being all squashed down in the floor of the car was very uncomfortable, but somehow I managed to fall asleep almost as soon as we started going. I had so many questions for Robin, but they would not get answered until I woke up.

The car stopped about two hours later. It was hard to move with my joints stiff from being so cramped into such a tight space. When I finally lifted my head, I was completely shocked to see we were in front of Simon Bing's house, 1953 Pearl Street, again! Robin rushed me from the car and hurried me inside the house. I thought I'd explored all the possibilities of the Bing residence before I'd been caught and confined before, but the secret of something had been here all along. I remembered I'd seen an abandoned house here that stank from the gore in the refrigerator. I remembered being here with Wilda before I was taken away.

I was confused and having a hard time believing what I was seeing. A man I didn't recognize let us inside and quickly ushered us through a hidden door that looked like part of a bookcase. When it swung open, I couldn't see a thing. It was so dark I could not see one foot beyond the opening. Robin entered first and pulled me along after her. As soon as I was through the entrance, the faux door closed behind me. Now I could see nothing.

"Here, take my hand," said Robin. "I'll get you through to the light."

She seemed to pull me along for miles. Once again, it was put one foot in front of the other. I did this for what seemed like hours. I was slowing us down because I was having trouble keeping up. When I could not take another step, Robin sat me down. I could feel a cold earthen wall at my back. When I touched the floor upon which I sat, it was packed-down dirt. I should have started asking questions at this point, but I was too exhausted to say anything at all. She had been carrying my flight pack and bag for me, but surely she was tired too.

My eyes were not adjusting to the darkness at all. This was the darkest dark I'd ever experienced! We sat there for about ten minutes. Then she stood and pulled me up behind her.

"We have to keep going," she insisted.

Once again, it was one foot in front of the other. We kept walking and walking. By now I could no longer feel my feet. My shoes felt tight as if my feet were very swollen, but there was no pain—nothing at all. When I tripped over my own numb feet and fell, she let me rest again. I wanted to take my shoes off, but I knew they'd swell and I'd never be able to get them back on again.

She began to whisper, "It won't be long now, I promise. I'm taking you to a place where you'll be safe. When we get there, nothing bad is ever going to happen to you ever again."

I could not imagine a place like she spoke of. Had some secret society been formed somewhere on earth where there was no aging out and people were no longer confined? Was it true? I was not going to die today? I sat there, too tired even to nod my head. Right now she was my savior, and I had no questions. This time, she let me lay my head in her lap, and my body stretched out on the dirt floor. This was the most comfortable place I'd ever laid my head. I never wanted to move again. If I could stay right here in this darkness that felt so wonderful, I would never desire anything else. She stroked my hair as I lay there, as I had stroked hers at the hospital when she'd been so sick.

We were this way for a long time till Robin rose once again and urged me to get back up. "We have to walk again. It really is not much further. Then we can rest for a very long time."

I jumped out of my skin when I heard another loud knock. I was sitting back on my couch again! I must have dreamed everything! It felt so real, but it must have been nothing but a fantasy! I was crushed and so disappointed. The knock came again, and once again I struggled from the couch to the door. When I opened it again, this time it was Charlie. He pushed me back, ordered me to sit down, and slammed the door shut.

In a deadly quiet voice, he asked me, "What the hell happened?"

He seemed as if he might explode with the rage he was trying to control. I looked him directly in the eye and told him everything! I told him about the first successful day and the circumstances of my last two failures. He stood there shaking his head, both hands hanging down by his sides, balled up in fists.

"I should kill you where you sit," he said in his barely controlled anger. "Have you any idea how many people you've gotten killed because of your cowardice?"

I had no idea what he was talking about. How had I gotten anyone else killed by not killing these two women? When I put this into a question to him, I could tell it was all he could do not to hit me.

"You stupid bitch!" he yelled. "Have you no idea at all how things in this government ever get changed?"

By now, I was getting angry myself. I just didn't care anymore what this oaf could do to me. "Apparently, I don't!" I yelled back. "Why don't you tell me how to change this government! Frankly, I don't have a clue."

His rage bubbled over, and he slapped me across the face. My head jerked back with the force of his blow. "We have to take it back!

The only way to take it back is to kill all those who oppose us. We have to bring fear into the lives of all the younger people who follow like sheep until something directly affects them. The only way to make them do anything is to scare them into it! You get rid of the ones who enforce the laws that bring us harm. Then you scare the little snowflakes to death. We will be the ones in charge then! No more aging out! We'll be doling out the rules from now on! Are you really that stupid that you didn't know this? This plan has been so carefully thought out, and then people like you and the fools who managed to get caught bring us all down!" With that, he slapped me across the face again. His screaming and yelling were truly terrifying.

I curled up into a ball there on the couch. *Wait. What am I lying on?* I wondered to myself.

In order to move whatever was poking me so hard in the side, I had to move my hand down to shift whatever it was. I felt it; it was my gun! I'd been too tired to take it out and put it away. Without a second thought, I pulled it out and shot Charlie right between the eyes! For a split second, he had the most puzzled look on his face. Then he collapsed on my floor and died. For the first time, I'd killed with absolutely no guilt, none whatsoever. I sat for a while and watched his blood pool behind his head. I really had no idea how to dispose of his body. I would have to do it all by myself; there was no one left to help me this time.

It occurred to me. Now I was on no one's side. I'd be despised by government entities and also by the people who were supposed to save me. The only person I had left was me, and I was very quickly running out of steam.

I let Charlie lay as I tried to figure out what, if anything, I was going to do next. I got towels from my closet and wrapped them around his head. I didn't want to see his blood all over my floor, and I didn't want to see what I'd done. I wondered if I could drag him out of here and put the body somewhere else. Charlie was a good two hundred pounds, and with all the weight I'd lost, I was barely topping a hundred pounds myself.

That did not seem very promising. Then I had an idea. I'd wait till late at night and use his mensa to call for a car. I'd only have to drag him as far as the car! I might be able to do that! This might work! I'd have to be very careful for the car not to pick up my chip number as I worked, but yes, maybe I could do this! I felt a wobble in my legs, as if all my steam was running out! Again I could not remember the last time I'd eaten.

Surely it hadn't been that long ago, I thought. *I'd be starving if I hadn't eaten recently.*

I had to get down on the floor with Charlie to find his mensa and fish it off his body. It was in his back pocket, and I hoped it hadn't broken when he fell. I also found his charger in another pocket, so I plugged it in. I sat there looking at everything I could find stored on his mensa. Most of it was password protected, but he hadn't turned it off when he stuck it in his pocket, so it was already on when I found it!

It was a great piece of luck that old Charlie had not turned off his tablet! I spent the time before I would call the car searching for as much information as I could find on his tablet. He had passwords for most things, but I was so surprised by the information he'd left unprotected. I did not want to send any information from his tablet to mine that would be traceable. I sat there and meticulously wrote on the precious paper I had left all I could find on his mensa that might come in handy for me to know. By the time I'd gotten all the data I could, it was time to use his tablet to call a car for him.

The chip scanner would be in the door of the car. I wasn't sure at all what I would have to do to get his body in there without my chip being read, but I would do the best I could. By the time the car got here, I had a working theory of what I would do. I gathered up my old stepladder and opened the door of the car. I'd position the ladder like a ramp from the road to the car. I had tied Charlie's body into as tight a bundle as I could with some old rope I found in the attic. I'd almost waited too long to attempt this because rigor mortis was beginning to set in. Once I had him bundled as best I could, I took the towel I used around his head and lay it out beside him. I got on Charlie's other side and pushed and rolled him onto the towel. Grabbing one end of the towel, I slowly began to drag his body out to my stoop. I gave him a push with my foot, and he rolled down my two steps to the ground! This had him at the edge of the ladder on the ground. My plan was to roll him onto the ladder and then roll him on into the car. I managed to get him up on the lip of the ladder. But pushing as hard as I could, I couldn't budge him one inch up the ladder. He was just too heavy.

I rested my back against him and tried to use my legs to push him up. I'd get him a fraction of an inch higher, but when I stepped away to reposition, he'd roll right back down! I could not figure out how to get him in the damn car! I was going to have to get into the car first to try to pull him in, but then my chip would be read! I went back into the house and found the metal back brace that had been difficult for the scanner to read once before. I strapped it on and then put on as many layers of clothing as I could. I entered the other door of the car, and immediately a red warning light started flashing. It was trying to scan my chip but was having difficulty. I knew if I didn't act quickly and get him in the car so his chip could be read, a loud alarm would sound to summon authorities.

I untied the rope I'd used to bundle him, but now rigor had set in even more. I had a hard time unrolling him enough to get his legs onto the floorboard of the car. I pulled until I got him halfway into the car. I still had to get his torso in, and I didn't think I'd be able to pull him the rest of the way in. I was getting so hot with all these clothes on, and the back brace curtailed my ability to move. But I had so little time left I couldn't stop for a second. His hips were halfway into the car. The only thing I knew to try now was to lift his torso up far enough where I could shove him into the car. I got him under the arms and mentally prepared myself to lift. I doubted if I'd have more than one chance to get him all the way in before my back gave way.

Since he was so rigid now, I decided to crouch down on the ground behind him and use my legs instead of my back. That would give me my best shot at some kind of leverage. I got into the position I thought best, then I rose from a squat, pushing so hard I could swear I'd torn a muscle in my thigh. But he was coming up! When I was standing up completely, I pushed forward as hard as possible. He was just about entirely in the car when I used my last bit of strength and shoved him the rest of the way in! As his back passed through the car door, I could hear the ding of his chip being read, and the warning light quit blinking.

I reached inside the car and programmed it for as far as it would go on a single charge. That would get him far enough away from me where I hoped we could not be connected to each other. I knew that whoever would find him would call the authorities, and I hoped they'd find no trace of me in the car.

Almost crawling now to get back into the house, I managed to make it to my bed before my body completely broke down. I took two pain pills and tried to sleep. Fortunately, the pills worked, and I slept.

Chapter 49

It was midmorning when my eyes fluttered open. I had to lie there for a moment to remember what I had done that made me so sore this morning. Then it all came rushing back to me. For a little while, I lay thinking about the night before. I thought I did everything to clean up the mess. I didn't think I made any mistakes getting him into the car except for straining my back.

I rose with my legs dangling over the side of my bed. *Yep*, I thought, *I think I've gotten away with murder.*

I had an evil little smile as I walked into the bathroom. Gazing into the mirror, I was horrified. The last time I remember looking at myself, I'd looked much younger than I did today. My face was drooping, and my hair was almost white! What had happened to me in just a few weeks? I'd planned to lay low for the next few days to see if there were going to be any repercussions from Charlie's murder, but seeing how old I looked, my vanity kicked in. I had to go to the Pharma Depository and get hair dye and makeup. I had to make myself look young!

Stepping out my door, I made my way into the town square. I didn't know why it had not occurred to me, but what had happened in my town while I was away on my own murderous quests? I had watched several people and their comings and goings. If someone had been killed, it was because I'd stalked them and given the information to their killers. Walking past the government building, I knew I was right. Big black wreaths hung from the courthouse doors. I wondered who had been killed. Had it been the mayor or her underlings? I'd see if I could find out while I was out on the town.

Reaching the Pharma Depository, I found what I was looking for. I reached for the color that most matched my hair in my youth, then glanced up at the reds, greens, blues, purples, and pinks that were on display. Should I? Just as a lark, I picked up a tube of the purple. With my preferred makeup, I was soon on my way back home. Before leaving the town square, I stopped in a small restaurant to order a glass of wine and see if I could find out which government person had been killed. I sat at the bar and punched in the number of my wine choice from the menu. I was given a reusable wineglass to hold under a spigot that dispensed the wine I'd ordered. It was good and cold, and I sat there nursing it slowly.

Before long, a gaggle of young women came in and sat at a table near me. They were laughing and talking while trying to decide what food order they wanted. There was discussion about calories and various diets, but soon enough they'd all punched in their orders. An automated voice announced when their orders were ready. They had to get their food from a revolving conveyor belt that came from somewhere behind the wall. After getting their food, they returned to their table and got much quieter as they ate.

I turned to the table and said casually, "I saw black wreaths upon the government building. I've been out of town visiting a friend. Did someone pass away?" They all paused midchew and looked up at me.

One of them asked, "You mean you haven't heard?"

"Heard what?" I asked innocently.

"Our mayor and her husband were murdered right outside the door of the building," one told me.

Oh, my gosh! I thought to myself. *Why had her husband been killed too?*

Out loud I said, "Please tell me about it. I'm so shocked!"

Another young woman started recounting the entire event. Apparently, it had happened quickly in front of many witnesses. The mayor left the courthouse, and her husband was waiting for her to go to lunch. The assassin approached the mayor with gun drawn. When the husband saw this, he jumped in front of his wife and was shot through the heart. In shock and terror, the mayor just stood there and was quickly dispatched right along with her husband.

"Did they catch the person who did this?" I asked.

"Not yet," I was told. "But many people saw this man and have described him to the authorities," one of the girls said.

"Have they shared this picture with the public?" I questioned again.

"Oh, yes," said the young woman. "The picture was sent out to everyone's mensa tablet to see if anyone recognized him."

"Oh, really?" I replied. "I wonder why I didn't see the picture on mine."

One young woman pulled out her mensa and brought up the picture for me to see.

Oh my god! I recoiled in horror, trying desperately to appear calm on the outside. "Hmmm," I said in as calm of a voice as I could muster. "I wonder who that might be."

I stood, then thanked the ladies for the information, and left the restaurant. Once outside, I felt as if I might faint. Whoever this man was, he looked like a carbon copy of my son Jack! Making my way blindly back home, I was so lightheaded and confused that I kept tripping over my own feet and bumping into people and objects. The walk back home that I'd traversed so easily on my way into town now seemed a trek of many miles. Time seemed to lose all meaning to me. By the time I reached home, it was late in the evening. Where had the time gone, and what had I done all day? I left home early this morning, heading to the Pharma Depository. I wasn't in the restaurant all that long. I realized that I'd lost hours out of my day, and it really scared me. Was this still anxiety from the looming arrival of my death day, or were other things going on around me? Was someone plotting against me? Something was wrong, and I didn't know what it was. I sat in the dark in my house for a long time this night. I was waiting for something; I just wasn't sure what it might be.

Since sleep refused to come, I went into the bathroom with all my hair products to dye my hair. I stood there for a long time, looking in the mirror. Walking into the kitchen, I retrieved my kitchen scissors and walked back into the bathroom with them in my hand. My hair had been almost to my waist my entire life, and I'd always kept it trimmed. Without a second thought, I started cutting my hair, big long hunks at a time!

When all my hair lay at my feet, it was if I woke up and wondered, *What in the hell have I done? I've cut off all my hair!*

I'd never even considered short hair! How could I have done this? In tears, I reached down and started to pick up the long hanks of hair I'd just cut off. I only have a couple of months left. It would never grow back in time!

Then I started to really take a good look at it. I'd really done a hack job of it, but I could see the potential of something I might like. I didn't try to cut it anymore. Tomorrow I would have to get it done robotically so it would have some style. There were no hair stylists anymore. There was a menu of hairstyles to choose from; you picked the one you wanted and inserted your head in a hood-like apparatus. The style picked was the way the hair would be cut.

By golly, I've gone this far! I thought to myself in excitement. *I might as well go all the way.*

I did not get out my usual color; I pulled out the tube of purple I'd gotten for fun. I never intended to do my entire head in purple, but now I was gonna do it! I was having a ball with this stuff. I put it in, waited the required time, and then rinsed it off. Toweling it dry, I was hesitant to take the towel off to see what I'd done. Slowly, I removed the towel. It wasn't a royal purple like I'd thought it might be but buoyant lavender! I stood looking for a moment. I had lavender hair. I had lavender hair! I loved it! What a great idea! What a change! After my hair trim tomorrow, it would look beautiful!

I began to dry my hair. What used to take at least an hour now took less than ten minutes! My head felt so light! Why hadn't I done this half a century ago? This was great! Now I could sleep!

In the morning, I lay there for a few moments, trying to remember if I'd done something unusual last night. I was sure I did, but for the life of me, I could not remember what it was. I washed up and brushed my teeth. When I looked into the mirror, my waist-length hair was really in a tangle. I spent a good twenty minutes brushing the tangles out of it. I got my dark hair dye and did my hair. I'd use my new makeup the next time I went out. I decided to let my hair air dry, knowing it would take most of the day.

AGED OUT

    I ate a little something—some toast or yogurt or something. I really wasn't very hungry. Looking around the house for something to do, I got my mensa tablet out and clicked on the Bible app. I sat for the next few hours, reading more about what was to happen in this world. The ending was really scary!

Chapter 50

In the afternoon, there was a knock on my door. Was I expecting someone? Like a ton of bricks, it hit me that this might be someone to question me about Charlie's murder or to assign me a new task! I opened up the door and a middle-aged woman stood there.

"Yes?" I asked of the stranger.

"Mom, don't you recognize me?" said the woman.

I looked her over carefully. "René! Is that you, René?" I asked in bewilderment.

"Yes, Mama, it's me."

I rushed to embrace my daughter. I held her, rocking back and forth as if she were still a baby! "Oh, sweetheart," I exclaimed. "It's been such a long time since you last visited!"

René walked in and sat down. "How have you been, Mom?" she asked.

I sat there in a trance, just looking at her. She was my René, but what had happened to her? Where was my young and vibrant René? This woman looked like an older version of her, but René was only in her twenties! What had she been through to have aged her so much?

I didn't want to hurt her feelings about how her looks had deteriorated, so hoping to learn of some reason for her condition, I said, "I've been fine for the most part, did a little traveling in the last few months, and now I'm just waiting." René's face fell when I said I was waiting. She knew exactly what I was waiting for.

"Oh, Mama," she said, gathering me up into her arms. "I'm sorry all this time has passed and we haven't spent any time together. Old wounds heal slowly."

I wondered what she meant by *old wounds*. I remembered we'd had words and she quit talking to me, but that seemed so long ago I didn't remember what we were at odds over.

I rested my head on her shoulder and said, "We are together now. That is what matters. What has happened to you the past few years?"

She proceeded to tell me a long story about her and her couple partner, Amber. They'd been together for a very long time, at least ten years, I thought. "We have an anniversary coming up," she announced. "Soon we will have been together for twenty-five years!"

I sat there in shock! How could this be? René hadn't coupled until she was almost twenty-five herself! Was René almost fifty? How could that be? Then I remembered I'd been about twenty when she was born. The math added up, but the logic didn't. René should still be so young! What had happened to all the years in between? If this were real, then maybe René looked very well for a fifty-year-old.

"Do you plan on staying for a while?" I asked.

She responded, "Only for a few days. My main reason for coming was to see how you are doing and see if you would consider coming back with me to celebrate my anniversary with Amber and all our friends."

"Really?" I asked. I thought about getting away from here for a little bit. But what if someone came with a new task I was required to do? In the end, I answered, "Let me think about it for a little while. I really do want to come."

"Then nothing should stop you, Mom!" she exclaimed. She knew nothing about my mission to stay alive or the other lives that might depend on my actions. I could tell her nothing.

I went into the guest space and began putting sheets on the cot. This bed hadn't been made up since Robin was here—I meant when Robin was really here and not the dream of her I'd had the other night. I hardly ever thought of Robin anymore. If she was still alive, she surely must have had the baby by now. I wondered if it was a girl or a boy. I wondered if I'd ever find out.

I ordered in some food for René and me for a little later on. She ate heartily, but eating just a few morsels filled me up. René seemed apprehensive about how little I'd eaten.

"Mom," she said, "aren't you hungry? You ate so little, and you seem to have lost a lot of weight!"

I replied, "Don't worry about me, sweetie. I need to lose a few pounds."

She looked at me skeptically but said nothing else about it. We talked for a little longer, then went our separate ways to bed. I fell asleep with my mensa on my lap playing my game. Sometime later on in the night, I heard a sharp rap at my door. I ran to answer it because whoever it was, I didn't want them to wake René. If this was about the plan, I wanted René to have no part in it. It could be very dangerous for her if she knew about any of it and was later found not to have turned me in. She'd be in a lot of trouble, and I did not want that for her.

To my exquisite surprise, there stood Jesse at my door! I motioned for his silence and pointed to the guest space. I pulled him into my bedroom and told him of René's visit. I was so happy to see him. I held his hand to my face for a very long time.

He began, "I've needed to talk to you for a very long time. You know that one of us was found murdered, don't you?"

I started to lie and pretend I knew nothing. But I could not lie to Jesse. I told him, "Yes, I know."

He whispered in my ear, "I'll bet you know a lot more than that, but at this point, what difference does it make?"

He looked very tired, and I invited him to lie down with me. He wrapped his arms around me, and very soon we fell asleep entwined together. I could relax completely lying next to Jesse. Jesse left very early the next morning so René wouldn't be too curious. Midmorning Jesse again knocked on my door.

René looked up and asked, "Are you expecting company?"

I answered, "I have an old friend who said he might drop by."

Opening the door, I welcomed Jesse into the house and gushed over him as if I hadn't seen him in months. After introducing Jesse to René, we sat around the kitchen table and ate some fresh muffins that René had baked.

"How do the two of you know each other?" questioned René.

Jesse answered that we'd known each other since we'd taken a class together last fall. "Is that the Chinese language class you took?" René queried.

"That's the one," Jesse said. "Your mom was much better at it than I was, though. She really did well and picked it up quite easily."

René looked at me quizzically. "Why on earth were you trying to learn Chinese anyway, Mom?"

I shrugged my shoulders. "It got me out of the house, and I wanted to see if this old brain still worked," I said jokingly.

She shook her head in wonder at me and told us she had some friends she wanted to visit while she was in town. She excused herself, and soon Jesse and I were alone. Now we could talk. I wondered about the listening devices I was sure were hidden in my house, then began to remember all the conversations I'd had recently that certainly could be viewed as suspicious in nature. No one had come from the government for me yet. Perhaps I wasn't being as closely monitored as I'd feared. When I wrote a note to Jesse, worrying about this, he waved his hand in dismissal and said we were okay.

I trusted him with my life; he'd saved my life once before, and I knew he'd never harm me. He began to talk and explain things to me. He let me know that the killing of government officials had been reasonably successful, but now that the first round of murders had been completed, officials were wising up and taking precautionary measures. Their intelligence people had figured out that particular plan, and now it was on to plan 2.

I grimaced at the thought. "Oh, Jesse," I said. "Please don't send me out to kill more people. I'm not good at it."

He looked at me slyly. "You can be good at it if you have to be."

I knew he was talking about Charlie, and I wondered who else knew. I asked him, "Am I in trouble with everyone now? He was hitting me, and I made him stop. I made him stop for all time, but I was not going to let him kill me!"

"I thought as much when I heard he'd been killed," Jesse said. "I knew he was your handler, and I also knew he was not a man fond of second chances. You do have a chance to redeem yourself, though, and no one will have to be killed in order for you to complete your next task."

I was somewhat relieved that I didn't have to kill this time, but I was so tired of this, tired with every cell in my body. "Okay," I finally said. "Tell me what I must do."

"I'm really not sure," Jesse answered. "I was sent here to tell you there was more to be done, but I was not given the information of what the task was to be. I do know it doesn't involve killing anyone. It was noted that you weren't very good at that."

He handed me a piece of paper. On it was a name and an address. I could not believe what I was seeing! The name on the paper was Kentura Bing at 1953 Pearl Street in Bishop Town!

I jumped up and shouted at Jesse, "What is this? I have been to this house multiple times before! I've never been able to get any information or make much sense of this place. Kentura Bing is dead. He died over ten years ago! His son, Simon, knows nothing that has ever helped me! Why am I being sent back? What can be gained by my going there again?"

Jesse didn't seem shocked or surprised by anything I was telling him. Again he pleaded ignorance and said, "That was the message I was to give you. That is all I know."

"Is there something particular I am to find out or ask about there?" I demanded.

"I just don't know," he answered. "Hopefully, you'll figure it out when you get there."

"When am I to go?" I asked in resignation.

"Tomorrow afternoon," he answered, "a car will come for you at 2:00 p.m."

"Must I go alone?" I asked plaintively.

Jesse nodded. "Yes, this is a task only you can do." With that, he stood, I stood after him, and we embraced.

"Will I ever see you again?" I asked longingly.

"I don't think so," he said sadly. With that, he turned and walked out of my life forever.

When René returned home, I told her about my planned trip tomorrow. She was surprised that I had planned a trip while she was here, visiting me.

"I'm sorry, sweetheart, but this is something I must do while I still have time."

We hadn't spoken yet of my last months, but we both knew that the subject would have to be talked about soon. I still had to make arrangements for my house to be emptied out and a few simple repairs and updates made. But I still had a little time left for that—or at least I hoped I did.

We sat up quite late talking. It really felt wonderful being able to talk to my daughter like a friend. We finally were able to find out that we not only loved each other but that we liked each other just as much. This was a joy that I never thought would happen. It was such a wonderful night!

I woke the next morning to the smell of breakfast being prepared. René must have gone out early this morning to buy what she was cooking. There certainly had been nothing that smelled so good here in the house before she came. I pulled on some old gray and blacks and went into the kitchen. She'd moved her daddy off the kitchen table onto the shelf. I felt a little offended by this because I had never let anyone touch him since his death but me. I quickly calmed myself down when I realized that René had no idea how special to me that urn of ashes was.

"This looks delicious, sweetie," I commented when she sat my plate down in front of me. There were square egg patties! I thought to myself, *I haven't eaten eggs in quite a long time.* I normally used the freeze-dried powdered ones. She'd also chopped up some peppers and onions and added some cheese on top! "Wow!" I exclaimed. "I haven't had anything this tasty in a long time."

"Eat up, Mom," she insisted. "I don't think you've been taking very good care of yourself. You are so thin and pale."

"I just don't have the appetite I used to," I said, defending myself. "I'm pale because I don't have any makeup on yet. I bought new makeup the other day, but I haven't tried it out yet. I will today, before I leave on my trip."

She sat there looking at me like she wasn't satisfied with my explanation. "After you leave today, I'm going to head back home to plan for the party," she informed me.

"Oh, I thought you were gonna stay for a few days longer." I pouted.

"Well, you are leaving on a trip, and there is no point in me just sitting here," she said, trying to make feel guilty. "Besides, I'll be seeing you next week for the party, right?"

"Yes," I said, "I'll see you at the party."

We talked for a little while longer. Then I had to excuse myself to begin to get ready to head out to Bishop Town once again.

I was almost finished applying my makeup when René hollered out, "I'm on my way out, Mom."

"Wait a second," I replied. I hurried into the living room to give René one last hug before she left. "I am really looking forward to your anniversary party next weekend," I said.

She hugged me one last time and said, "Me, too, Mom. See you next weekend."

I closed and locked the door behind her and went back into the bathroom to finish applying my makeup.

Chapter 51

The car arrived precisely at 2:00 p.m. to pick me up. I locked the door behind me and entered the car. I had the next two hours to think up something to ask or a reason for showing back up at the Bing house today. The last time I'd seen Simon and his husband, José, they'd thought me on the brink of insanity. Maybe my visit today would answer that question accurately for them. Riding down the highway, I tried to think of some plausible reason I could use to explain why I was back at their house. But nothin'! I got nothin'!

Pulling up to their door, I climbed out of the car, pushed the return to lot button, and watched the car drive away. Stoking my courage as best I could, I walked up to the door and knocked. Before long, I heard footsteps coming toward me, then the sound of locks being opened. This time, it was José who answered the door. He didn't seem to recognize me at first, but then I could see the light of recognition come into his eyes when he realized it was me.

He didn't invite me in at first but asked, "Ma'am, is there something I can do for you?"

"Yes, you can let me in," I replied.

"I don't understand why you are here again," he said. "We were unable to help you last time."

I replied, "Yes, you are absolutely correct, José, but I was told to come here, so I've come. Please, may I come in?"

He looked at me for a moment, then stood back, and ushered me into the house. After closing the door behind us, he turned and offered me food and drink. I accepted the drink as long as it was something cold and alcoholic. He smiled a little when I said that and went to fetch both of us a drink. When he returned, he handed me the drink and sat down opposite me in the chair.

"Who exactly told you to come here?" José asked.

I replied, "I really don't know who told me. It was given to me in a note."

"Hmmm, in a note, you say? By any chance, did you bring this note with you, and if so, may I see it?" he inquired.

"I did bring it with me," I replied. "But the only thing on it is the name Kentura Bing and this address." I handed him the paper, and he sat studying it for a moment. He looked a combination of puzzled and shocked.

"Is there something wrong?" I asked.

He answered with a question of his own, "When did you receive this?"

"Just yesterday," I answered. "Is there something that is puzzling you about the note?" I asked.

"Well," he said, "yes. Yes, there is. He's been dead for a long time, but this looks so much like my late father-in-law's handwriting. But that seems impossible. Simon is out until later on tonight, and I would like for him to see this. Would it be possible for you to stay until his return?"

"Yes, of course, I can," I said in return. "I would like nothing better than to resolve why I am always being drawn to this house from so many different directions." He nodded. "Is there some place I can lie down?" I asked. "I am suddenly so tired I can barely hold up my head."

"Yes, certainly, come with me."

He started up the stairs, but I was very hesitant to follow him. I remembered with all too much clarity what I'd seen the last time I'd climbed these stairs. I slowly followed him up. He motioned me into the small room on the left.

That had been the bloodiest room, I reminded myself.

He opened the door. There was a lovely small bed, and a nearby window had the sun beaming into the room!

After he left and closed the door behind him, I pulled off the bedspread and sheet to have a closer look at the mattress. It had been soaked in blood the last time I was in this room, and the window had been blacked out. I examined it carefully, and while I found a shadow of a stain, it looked nothing at all like blood-soaked material. It actually was so bright in here I closed the curtain before I lay down. I was so weary I fell instantly to sleep.

I didn't know how much time had passed, but a knock on the door woke me. Opening the curtains, I was surprised that it was almost dark outside.

"Ma'am, are you awake?" I was asked.

I could tell it was José, so I replied that I was. He asked me to come downstairs because Simon had come home. Taking a quick peek in the bathroom mirror before going downstairs, I touched up my makeup and ran a brush through my hair. Then I went downstairs.

Simon stood to greet me as I came down the steps and walked over to take my hand and escort me to a chair. Both he and José sat down across from me.

"May I get you another drink?" asked José.

"Yes, please," I replied.

He soon returned with three drinks on a tray and again sat down next to Simon.

Simon started to talk. "Naia, may I call you Naia?" he asked.

"Of course," I replied.

"Naia, I would like to know how you got this paper. I recognize this is my father's handwriting. I even recognize the paper. I still have a few sheets in my dad's old desk. I don't understand this at all. Did you know him a long time ago? Did he write down this address for you sometime in the past?"

"Simon, I am as perplexed as you are. I never met your father or heard of him at all until I found the scribbled notes my daughter-in-law left behind. I believe I've told you about them before," I answered. "I have been here multiple times, and I'm not sure why. There seems to be some secret or story about your father and this house that I am unable to figure out. I seem to be constantly directed here for something—I just don't know what."

Then a thought occurred to me. "Is there a secret door in that bookcase?" I stood and pointed to the one on the opposite wall. Both Simon and José looked in the direction I was pointing.

Simon said, "No, of course, not. I've lived here all of my life, and I'd know if there were any secret doors or hidden passageways."

"Would you indulge me and check it out?" I asked.

He approached the bookcase and gave it a slight push. Nothing. I walked over to it and looked it over carefully.

"Would you mind if I removed the things on the shelves?" I asked. I could see Simon was starting to look exasperated.

But he finally said, "Okay, fine. Do it if you must."

I carefully began to remove the books and small bird statues from each shelf. I glanced at the titles of some of some of the books as I took them out. There were many topics represented, but quite a few of them were about birds.

"Was your dad a bird enthusiast?" I asked Simon.

"He did enjoy reading and studying pictures of them," he answered. "I can remember as a small child, he would gather me up in his lap, and we'd look through the books, and he'd point out different species of birds to me. I really enjoyed those times when I had his complete attention. He was always so busy. Those times were precious to both of us."

"What did your father do?" I asked.

Simon replied, "Dad was an inventor. He was lauded by many for his achievements in chemistry and the sciences."

"Did he do anything else or have any hobbies?" I questioned.

"He had little spare time," Simon replied. "He was always working in his laboratory, but I suppose if he had a hobby, it would have been woodworking. He seemed to have a real instinct for joinery and how things could come together. He made a few of the pieces here in the house."

"Really? That's very interesting," I said. "Did he, by any chance, build these bookcases?"

It appeared that Simon had an *ah ha* moment. "Yes, he did. I'd almost forgotten about that. He built them when I was a very small boy. I remember him letting me help him 'paint' them."

I thought of something else. "Where was his laboratory located?"

Simon responded, "I really don't know. I was never in his lab. All I remember was that sometimes he was here and sometimes he wasn't. When he wasn't, my mom would tell me he was in his laboratory. It surely wasn't here, or I would have known long before now!"

When the shelves were completely empty, I started studying the shelves and relief work on the sides of the case. I rubbed my hands over all the flat areas in hopes of finding something irregular that might be an opener. I felt nothing at all. Then I carefully touch the decorative swirls and flowers that had been added to the case. I didn't feel anything unusual on the relief work, so then I carefully tried to turn them. Everything was solidly attached until I tried to turn a little fish near the bottom on the right side. It turned forward in my hand, and I could hear a click somewhere in the case.

Simon looked on in disbelief as he watched me. I stood and gently pushed on the bookcase again. This time, it swung open with a creaking sound! We all stood there looking into the darkness before us. There seemed to be a tunnel but nothing else to see at all. No light, no door, just a dark tunnel that seemed to go on forever.

"I'll be damned!" Simon exclaimed. "How did you know about this? You surely have been here in the long ago past. That is the only way you'd know anything about this! My dad must have told you about it!"

"No one told me about it, but someone recently brought me here," I stated. "Robin brought me here. A strange man answered our knock and opened this door through the bookcase so that Robin and I could go through it."

At this, he started yelling, "Are you crazy? I didn't even know this was here, and I've never met anyone named Robin! You are so delusional, or at least I think you are. I have no earthly idea how you knew about this unless you have dementia and don't remember being here in the past!"

"I was never here until this past year," I stated firmly. "I don't remember ever being in Bishop Town in my life until the past year."

"Maybe that's the answer!" he continued to exclaim. "You are ill with dementia and don't remember being here!"

That thought had never occurred to me. Was this true? I was experiencing some really weird stuff lately. *But no*, I told myself. So I replied, "You are free to think whatever you want to, but I don't believe my mind is impaired in any way. Should we consider getting flashlights and seeing where, if anywhere, this tunnel might lead?"

"Hell, no!" Simon shouted. "That just shows me how weak your mind must be. I never knew this to be here. I will not allow anyone in here until I have an engineer check to see if the walls are shored up and won't cave in!"

I pleaded, "When you are assured it's safe, may I go in with you? I think whatever is drawing me here is at the end of this tunnel."

I could see his rage. José placed a restraining hand on his arm and whispered for him to calm down. He quickly turned and walked out the front door.

José said, "He is very upset. I think I should call a car for you to take you home. It would be best if you weren't here when he returns."

"José," I begged, "please let me know what happens here. I have such a short time left, and I have to know why me, why here, and where this tunnel goes. Please, even if Simon never wants to see me again, please let me come back when he isn't home."

José didn't seem to like that idea at all, but he could see how desperate I was. He either felt sorry for me or wanted to get me out of his house because he agreed to get in touch with me soon. When the car arrived to pick me up, I saw Simon standing on the corner, waiting for me to leave. I hoped that José would keep his word to me.

Chapter 52

The man accused of killing the mayor and her husband had not yet been captured. He seemed to be the only suspect witnesses could agree that they saw. The other assassins, including me, had been stealthy enough to get it done and get away without much notice. I pulled his picture up on my computer and studied the drawing very carefully. It was just a drawing that the government had compiled from all the witnesses' statements, but it looked so much like an older and thinner version of Jack! I wondered if my other children had seen it and saw their brother as clearly as I saw my son. Whoever this young man was, he was part of the plan, and someone from the group should know who he was! The problem was that no single person knew all that much—at least those at my level didn't appear to.

Now that I was back at home, having completed the task I was given, I had no idea to whom I was supposed to report that I'd found a tunnel. I didn't know how something I dreamed could turn out to be real! I didn't know who would come to my door next. There was so much I didn't know! I was weary from everything I didn't know, weary to the bone.

In my mind, I knew I should be doing something that could help me avoid my death sentence. I felt as if I should be out there, searching for an answer to save myself. But for the life of me, I had no idea what to search for, and my ambivalence was making me depressed and hopeless. If I had some direction, perhaps I could make myself get up and do whatever I had to, but I was completely out of ideas and motivation.

As I got ready for bed, it occurred to me I could not remember if I'd eaten anything. I thought I remembered eating something at Simon and José's house, but what day was I there? Was it today or the day before? Just to be sure, I got back up and went to the kitchen and rehydrated a bit of steak. After only a few bites, I was full, so I must have eaten recently. Maybe with the stress, my memory and appetite were failing me. I took a handful of vitamins before heading back to bed.

That should do the trick, I thought.

Morning came, but my energy didn't come with it. I made myself eat a bite of toast and then sat with my mensa tablet, going back and forth from game to game. I was tired but was also feeling very restless. The day after tomorrow, I would be going to René and Amber's house to celebrate their anniversary. Maybe I could think of a gift to take them. I searched around the house to see if I could find some sentimental item that they would appreciate. Not much to choose from. I went into the attic and looked through the boxes that had been there for years. I found notes and toys from the kids' childhood, but there was nothing that I could imagine giving to them. I went to my computer and started looking for something that I liked that I thought they might like as well. There really wasn't much to choose from here either. The Equality Law had outlawed jewelry, and clothing items that could make somebody envious. Maybe I could get some exotic food item that could only be gotten in someone's last year, but that might remind everyone that I was in my last year. This was supposed to be a celebration! I couldn't take wine or liquor because René was a recovering addict. It looked as if I might have to go empty-handed. Pooh!

I sat back down on the sofa but immediately hopped back up. I was too restless to sit and do nothing. I decided to clean myself up a little and go out. I didn't know where I was going, but I needed to do something to wear myself out. I didn't understand being so tired and wired at the same time!

When the car came for me, I sat there a moment, trying to decide on a destination to program into the GPS. It was still daylight out, so I programmed in the address for Joyland Park. I hadn't been there in such a long time. It used to be so shady and peaceful. I could find a bench and do a little people-watching before nightfall. When I arrived at the park, there were lots of people walking its trails, so I felt safe to go in alone and sit down on a bench beneath a flowering pear tree. The blossoms were thick and looked like snowflakes heavy on the branches.

Public parks were the only places where it was allowed to have some embellishments. There were flower beds scattered throughout the park. Most were meticulously cared for. I knew the government didn't have workers to take care of the flowers. This was being done by avid gardeners who weren't allowed private gardens anymore. Wilda had always tended a bed in the park nearest her home. I remembered her at times being angry and frustrated because young vandals would tear out the flowers during the night, but she was always resourceful and willing to start all over again. She had such patience and such a love of gardening! How I missed her! When your best friend was taken away, it left a terrible empty spot inside your soul.

I sat there peacefully for about an hour, daydreaming and enjoying being outdoors. I didn't see anyone approaching me until a woman sat down beside me. It startled me a little bit, and she apologized for making me jump.

"Oh, that's okay," I said.

She had a very sweet smile. We sat there companionably for a while, and then she addressed me.

"Your name is Naia, isn't it?"

This really made me jump! In fact, I jumped up off the bench! "Do I know you?" I asked in an agitated voice.

"Please sit back down, and I'll tell you who I am. You have no reason to be fearful or uneasy. I was sent to find you," she replied.

"Why are all these strangers sent to find me?" I demanded to know. I sat back down, but now I was quite wary of why she was "sent" to find me. I sat looking at her without speaking.

"My name is LaToyia. I know you don't know me, but we have friends in common," she said.

"Whom do we have in common?" I asked her.

"Well, actually, we have quite a few friends in common," she responded.

"Who?" I demanded.

"You know all the people we have in common," she continued, "but their names are unimportant right now. Together we have work to do."

"Oh no!" I said. "I am not going to go anywhere with you or do anything with you until you give me names!"

She sat there silently for a moment. Then she quietly asked me if I knew Sally. That shocked me into speechlessness!

Regaining my voice, I asked, "How do you know Sally? Why are you looking for me, and how does Sally enter into anything that you and I would be doing together?"

"Whew!" She smiled. "I was told that you were a feisty one who is very quickly coming into your own, but I wasn't expecting such fire!"

"LaToyia, you don't know what fire is!" I exclaimed. "This is my last year of life, and it has been nothing but sadness, hysteria, and pain. I have had to deal with the loss of a child and losing my best friend. I don't know what this 'coming into my own' is all about, but you'd better not try to trick me or conspire against me because I'll take you out!" I ranted.

Again she softly smiled and said, "I am not here to harm you. I'm here to help you with your problem."

"My problem?" I said. "What problem do I have that you can help me with?"

She laid her hand on mine and looked into my eyes. "I'm here to help you find your safe place, to help you escape your death." After hearing these words, I sat there dumbfounded! "Come," she said, "Let's get into a car and get you home."

After the car arrived, she climbed in beside me. We rode silently back to my house. I unlocked all the locks and reluctantly let her in the door behind me. She walked in as if she owned the place and sat down on my couch. I locked the door and turned to face her.

"Here," she said. "Come here and sit with me." I perched on the edge of the couch and waited for her to start talking. "Have you eaten?" she asked me.

Exasperated, I asked, "Why should that matter?"

"You look emaciated," she said gently with concern in her voice.

This made me mad! "I've lost a few pounds, but I wanted to!" I said rather snidely. "Tell me what you think you can do to 'save' me, or go and leave me alone!"

She began to talk. What she told me over the next few hours horrified me, excited me, and then gave me peace. She answered every question I asked and gave me details of what I would need to do to save myself. I sat there soaking in all she had to say. Then she rose and headed for my kitchen.

"I'm going to fix you something to eat," she insisted. "For what's ahead of you, you will need all your strength." She looked into my pantry and refrigerator and sighed. "There isn't much here. Have you been ordering your meals in?" she queried.

I couldn't remember doing that in a while, so she asked for my mensa tablet. I sat and watched her as she ordered my meals for the next few days. I remembered about the anniversary party and told her I would not need delivered meals over the weekend.

After she'd made all the arrangements, she turned to me and said, "I've told you what needs to be done. Will you remember it all? Everything must occur in the order I told you. I will contact you again when the time comes closer for you to act. We'll go over it again. You must eat the meals I've ordered because your last task will be very hard and you must be prepared by being well nourished and ready to run if necessary. Do you understand?"

"Yes," I answered quietly.

At this, she turned to leave. As she walked through the door, the first ordered meal came, and she made me promise I would eat it all. For the foreseeable future, there was nothing I had to do but wait—wait until the time came. And then I'd have to act quickly. I was determined to eat enough to be stronger and exercise enough to get my endurance back. I sat down to eat with new resolve. I managed to eat at least half of everything on my plate!

The next morning, I got up early. My breakfast was scheduled to arrive at nine. That gave me over an hour to get some exercise. I strapped my bag to my chest. I made sure I had my hydrogen tablets with me in case I got thirsty. I always had oxygen in my bag, and it was much easier to carry water in gas form. I had my mini mensa tablet in case of emergency and my set of house keys. Maybe I should have changed my locks long ago to eye or thumb print recognition, but I just felt safer manually locking my door with a key.

My kids said I was wrong about the newer technology, but both Stephen and I had always used keys. I started off walking with a smooth pace, but it wasn't long before I started losing my breath struggling up the hills. I had to slow down. I tried not to get too down on myself. I hadn't exercised regularly in a long time. A lot had happened in the past year that wore me down both mentally and physically. I walked a mile or so, then turned around and headed back home.

I promised myself, "Tomorrow I'll try to go a little farther than I did today. I'll grow stronger if I keep this up."

I got into the shower and washed the sweat of my exertion away. I towel dried my hair and dressed just a few moments before my breakfast arrived. I had to reheat it, but I did my best to eat the scrambled-egg patty, bacon product, and toast. I celebrated with a very good cup of coffee. I didn't remember the last time I'd bothered to make coffee. I couldn't get it all down, but I put a pretty good dent into this big plate of food! I felt so at peace now. For a while, everything was out of my hands. Someone else was working behind the scenes, and by the time I had to do my last task, I would be ready to tackle it head-on.

Chapter 53

I still hadn't found any sort of gift to take to the girls' anniversary party. I was so worried about offending them by offering them any of my "last-year perks," but then I wondered, *Why not? I know it will be hard for them to have much in the way of food since they only get a weekly allotment for two. Chances are they'd been hoarding their food for weeks to have enough for their celebration.*

Stephen and I had done it many times for the children's birthdays after they'd moved out and we didn't receive food for six anymore. Weeks before a birthday, we'd start eating two meals a day, and if it was a big enough occasion, we'd spread one meal a day out in portions. Then we'd have enough for our guests! I got my mensa tablet and sent a message to René. I offered to bring special food and drink that she could not get.

I heard back from her immediately, and she seemed thrilled that I could make the celebration really special. I ordered food to be delivered to her house the day of the party. I ordered plant-based preformed steaks and lobsters, lots of preformed vegetables, and cakes and pies. I ordered three cases of assorted drinks and hoped there would be enough left to last them for a while. This would probably be the last thing I could ever do for them, and I really did wanted it to be special!

The next day, I did everything I could to get myself looking my best. I had called the clothing warehouse and asked for dressy grays and blacks to be brought to me. I would have to return them after the party, but I was determined to go all out for this occasion. I dyed my hair again and found a tube of purple dye in the bathroom linen drawer.

Where in the world did that come from? I wondered to myself.

I read the instructions on the tube and wondered how fast it would fade if I used a little for the fun of it. After dying my hair my usual dark color, the instructions said I could make as many vibrant streaks of color as I wanted. I took a small section of my hair and, using rubber gloves, applied a streak down the side of my head. I turned this way and that, looking in the mirror, giving my reflection a very big grin. I decided I really liked it! I put up all my hair except for a layer underneath my dark hair. I added purple to this and let my dark hair cascade over the top of it. I made a few more streaks on the outside layer, and I was done.

When I finished the arduous task of drying my long hair, I stood back to take a good look. Swirling my head made the purple underneath visible. I loved the effect. It was a little bright, but I still loved it! I laid out my makeup to apply the next day before I left for the party. I planned on staying the entire weekend, so I packed an extra everyday black and gray into my body bag.

I was so excited by the thought of a party! When my lunch arrived, I really wasn't hungry, but I managed to get some of it down. I spent the afternoon playing games on my mensa and must have dozed off. The toot of a horn woke me, and I was surprised that so much time had passed that my dinner had arrived! It tasted very good, but I still had little appetite. I made myself eat until I felt as if I might be sick.

I managed to eat almost half the meal. After dinner, I did a few more exercises here in the house. It was getting dark now, and it was not safe for me to go outside to walk. After my indoor exertion, I was tired and ready for bed. I had my tummy full. I'd gotten my exercise in today and quickly fell into a sound sleep.

I had that dream again… I could hear my children calling me, and there were people standing around my bed, watching me sleep!

What is up with this dream? I asked myself. *Why do I keep having the same one over and over again?*

The faces, while a wee bit clearer, were still blurry enough that I really couldn't recognize anyone, but I was very upset that no one in this group would go and see to my children.

Are they deaf? Do they not hear them?

I woke suddenly, but the people weren't here anymore, and no one was calling for me. Just as I thought, this was just a dream. But it recurred regularly, and that was very weird! I wished I could dream of happier stuff. I was able to fall back to sleep. For the remainder of the night, if I dreamed at all, there was nothing I could remember.

I got up early the next morning to get my walk in and be back when my breakfast arrived. After eating and getting a shower, I blew my hair dry once again. I really, really liked the purple! I bet I'd get a huge reaction to it because older people rarely did such things. I couldn't wait to see their faces! I carefully applied my makeup. Looking at my makeover in my mirror, I was very pleased by my appearance. I was rocking it! Now I waited for my car to arrive so I could be on my way!

I was so happy I was able to provide the food for this party! It would have been an okay party without my contributions, but this made the party spectacular! I was also very pleased that no one could complain about the unequally luscious food served because it was provided by someone who was being aged out. That was one of the perks of the last year. You could order as much of anything that you wanted, and no bitter townsfolk could complain!

I was never taught much about the history of all the quadrants, but from what little I'd learned, ancient history started being recorded in the twentieth century, in the 1960s. I had no earthly idea what happened before that time, if there was a "before that time." Apparently, we had to thank a great group of pioneers called the Hippies for the greatness of the country today. Whatever came before them, if anything at all, they preached peace and love. They preached never trusting anyone over forty, but the people of today had upped that age to seventy, thank goodness. If there was any history at all before this ancient recorded time, it was not spoken of nor taught.

It seemed there came a time when the dominant people of the country were made to apologize for all the errors and sins of everyone who came before them. There were reparations made to all the people who claimed to be victims, and it was tweaked and tinkered with until the Great Equality Law was passed. My family wasn't here during these dark days of punishment and the eventual growth our sins had provided for the quadrants. But the dawn of daylight fixed everything; at least that was what I'd been told. My mom and dad got sick and were not treated, so they died before getting to live long enough to get the perks of aging out. I'd take the perks okay, but I would refuse the end process. Now that I had a plan, I could enjoy my last few months under the government's power. I was very content!

Chapter 54

When I arrived at René's and Amanda's, the party was just beginning. Some songsters that had volunteered performed a few old songs that had been around through the ages. This surprised me a bit. Maybe it was because this was inside and private; none of these singers would get in trouble for displaying a talent that some others did not have. I hoped to goodness that no one would complain or turn these people in. They were such a joy to listen to, and I couldn't remember the last time I heard live singing. The beauty of these voices was something I could only dream about, and I wondered how René and Amanda had found the talent and someone willing to sing when it could be so easily misconstrued.

We danced, ate, drank, and talked long into the next morning. There were so few things that warranted a celebration anymore that we usually dragged it out for days! We'd stop long enough for a nap, then rise to party again. This usually lasted until no one had the energy to party one second longer.

It took two and a half days for this to occur here at this party! People were lying everywhere around their small home, exhausted by the good times we'd enjoyed. I finally woke up around 9:00 p.m. on the third day. I was one of the oldest people here, so that was probably why it took me a little longer to recuperate than some of the younger people. There were still a few people left, though, lying in the living room floor and one out on the stoop in front of the door! I could honestly say this was the best party I'd ever been to! Now I needed to make my farewells and return home. My preordered food was to start back up again tomorrow morning, so I needed to get home tonight.

I arrived home about four thirty in the morning. All was quiet on my street, so I hurriedly got out of the car, unlocked my door, and got inside. That was always a tricky little scary moment—getting from the car and inside safe and sound. I'd always been very lucky until that night I ran after Jesse and left my door open. I would not let that happen to me again! I climbed into my bed around 5:00 a.m. for a few hours' sleep. I had no concrete plans for tomorrow, but one never knew what might happen to change that.

Rising at the ping of my computer, I saw another missive from the government. After the mass assassinations of government officials, the emails had ceased for a week or so. Apparently, others had stepped in to send the gloom and doom messages. I read it but paid little heed.

"Your time is at the two month period now. Please make solid arrangements to have your home cleaned out and home repairs done. This must be accomplished by the month before your death day. We haven't received confirmation that you have planned this step yet. Please confirm which cremation establishment you've chosen for these tasks. Please do not wait until the last few weeks. You may encounter a backlog and have to spend your last few days dealing with all this confusion and havoc. Please make arrangements now!"

Okay, I thought to myself. *I'll take care of all this today.*

Little did anyone in the establishment know that I would not be using the cremation services, but I could appear to be playing along with all the requirements. It was such a pleasant day! I thought I might walk from cremation establishment to cremation establishment. I had not done my walking while partying at René's, but I needed to quickly get back in the habit! Strength was essential for what lay ahead of me.

I first stopped off at the place that had cremated Stephen's body. They seemed just as efficient as they'd been before, but for the sake of exercise, I'd walk to two or three more. The people at the second cremation home were just creepy, so I did not linger long there. The third one was very welcoming and gladly showed me their cremation room. It had all pertinent forms ready for my children to fill in the blanks and be done with me. I hadn't decided what I wanted done with Stephen's and my ashes. I knew the kids would not relish having them sitting around their houses, and I knew that we'd never be spoken to the way I talked to Stephen. They presented me with the choices I could lawfully use to dispose of our ashes. They seemed somewhat horrified that I still had Stephen's ashes. I decided to take all the information I'd gotten today, take it home, and mull it all over.

I'll talk it over with Stephen. I chuckled to myself.

I arrived home to find my preordered lunch sitting on my stoop. After sitting in the sun for a few hours, it was not fit for eating anymore, so I would need to dispose of the wasted food. I hadn't ordered any compost bags for garbage for a while, so I didn't have one to put this rancid food into. I used my mensa tablet to order a few of them and hoped it would not take too long for them to be delivered. All uneaten foodstuffs must be composted to enrich the chemicals of the food-growing enterprises. No one wanted to live anywhere near one of these places because the stench was horrific, but stench was the blight of all cities anymore. Between garbage and sewage and their treatment methods, there were no completely odor-free areas to live. It was terribly unpleasant in the larger places. That was why I'd try to avoid flying over all the big cities.

I sat for a while, reading through the material the funeral establishments had given me. I decided to go with the one that had taken care of Stephen. I knew I'd be in good hands with them.

Now I needed to decide where to put our ashes. It was not allowed to let them drift into any body of water anymore. With all the ashes of all the dead people, many lakes and rivers would be dried up and severely polluted. Those had to be preserved for drinking water. The oceans, after the big thaw, had grown larger but were off limits for ashes too. After looking at all my options, I decided Stephen and I could be used for industrial purposes as in glue or fertilizer. Yes, that would be fine.

Then it hit me out of the blue. I was not going to be here to worry about any of this! I was going through the motions so that I would arouse no suspicion! It was strange I could let myself get so caught up in the death scenarios that I had forgotten I would not need a single one of these services. I wondered if I'd have a chance to take Stephen with me when the time came for me to leave.

Probably not, I figured.

But we'd been together far too long for me to completely leave him behind. I had never opened his urn before now, but I had to figure out a way to take his essence with me. I thought of the old black and grays I'd worn as a costume to that horrible party with my fellow Chinese learners. I still had it around here somewhere. I looked all over the house and found them up in the attic, where everything I owned seemed to end up. I cleaned them and cut two small squares out of the gray shirt. I hadn't used my hot glue gun in ages, but I got it working and made a small pouch, into which I sprinkled some of Stephen's ashes. I glued all the sides together and attached a string to two sides. This would allow me to wear it around my neck and not encumber my hands at all. I would have Stephen with me when I ran.

Later on that day, before my dinner was scheduled to arrive, I ordered a car to take me to a nearby bar. I hadn't been out drinking by myself in a long time. To my embarrassment, no young man offered to buy me one single drink! I came home to find my dinner waiting with no other choice but to eat it all alone.

After dinner, I went into the bathroom to study myself in the full-length mirror. I wanted to see what had happened to me that I was no longer desirable—even in the dark. I removed my clothes and studied myself from head to toe. I did have some droopy skin from losing weight, but I hadn't realized I'd lost so much. Even my face was sagging where it had been taut and lustrous less than a year ago. My breasts were practically nonexistent, just pendulant skin hanging from my chest. I had no behind anymore. There seemed to be no curves left on my body. My hair had no gray in it, and my makeup had been applied perfectly.

Something besides sag was really off in my face. Looking closely, I knew what it was. My eyes looked empty. There was no sparkle anymore. My eyes looked as if I had already died. It was no wonder no one found me attractive. I looked as if I was already a corpse. I was determined to try and gain a little weight to fill up some of the sag. I also needed to keep up my exercises to increase my stamina and harden my muscles. I'd do it! I'd do it all! I went to bed with that firm resolve in my head and left myself no time to dwell on what I'd seen in the mirror before I fell asleep.

Sleeping so soundly throughout the night, I woke to complete stillness around four in the morning. I lay there in a drowsy state, wondering what had wakened me. I certainly couldn't be awake as a result of having enough rest. If that was the case, I would not feel as tired as I'm feeling. I lay there for a while, trying to discern what woke me. Finally, as the sun was showing its first pink in the eastern sky, I got up and started my day. I did not like to get up so early! With nothing really to do, the days seemed so long already that I would prefer to sleep through them. My breakfast wasn't due for another four hours! I thought about starting my daily walk, but that wouldn't be very smart. As long as the streets held any darkness and no one was up and about, it was just too dangerous to be out yet. I got out my mensa tablet and played my games until I judged it was safe for my walk. Dressing for the warming spring day, I unlocked my door to make my rounds.

When I unlocked and opened my door, there was a note attached to it. Again, I looked around to see if anyone else had a note sticking to their door. To my utter amazement, I could see notes stuck to doors as far as I could see.

Oh, my goodness! I thought. *This must be a drastically important message from the government to show up on everyone's door!*

I took my letter back inside, and after relocking my door, I sat down to see what new and horrific law must be coming for us all. To my shock and amazement, it didn't seem to be all that scary. It seemed that the entire town had been called to meet in the town square in two months' time, at noon on June 28! That was the day before my death day! Would I still be here to attend this meeting?

LaToyia had said nothing in the plan about this! I was very curious as to what this could possibly mean. There were no clues at all! We weren't being threatened or cajoled; it was more of an invitation than a command. It didn't even seem particularly governmental. There was no indication who might be trying to gather the citizens together. Thinking about that, it did become somewhat scary. Who would dare? Who would presume to issue any kind of citizen's notice without the government's backing?

The day before my death day…hmmm.

I did not panic over this because I'd been promised this was not going to happen to me. I would be given one last difficult task before I would make my way to my safe place. Thinking of that, I went out immediately and started my walk. I walked almost five miles today. I am determined to be ready and up for whatever might be thrown at me. I planned on living!

I got back just about the time my breakfast was delivered. This time I managed to get it all down! When lunch came, I did the same thing! I was so determined to be fit and strong enough to do my last task. I ate when I had no hunger and walked when I was tired.

"I'm going to be ready!" I encouraged myself.

Having gotten up so early and done everything I could think to do, the afternoon stretched out in front of me as if it would never end. I went back to Wilda's book on my mensa tablet and started rereading it out of complete boredom. It didn't take long though till I was caught up again in the life of this man whom Stephen's people had been waiting for—this supposed savior named Jesus. When I bothered to look up again, it was almost time for my supper to arrive. I still felt full from my two previous meals, but I was gonna eat it! Come hell or high water, I was gonna eat it!

Groaning I stuffed down the last bite of my supper. Now what? Since I no longer had to worry and planned to avoid being aged out, I had very little to do to occupy my time.

Tomorrow, I thought, *tomorrow, I will start cleaning out the house.*

Chapter 55

April 29, 2526

Earlier this morning, I scheduled the trash truck for a week after my birthday, so I was on top of that! After my walk and my breakfast, I started with the curtained-off second bedroom. It was so tiny; all it had was a cot and a small cubby for guest's belongings. I didn't think I'd find much in there.

I really hadn't been in this room since René's departure. I took the sheets off the cot and repeated what I'd done after Robin left. I put the linens through the lazar cleaner and the mattress outside over a kitchen chair on my small stoop so it could air out. Once again I had to sit by my window to make sure no one stole the mattress. I supposed if anyone tried they'd be very disappointed with it. It was the mattress of my childhood. I'd slept on it all of my life till Stephen and I coupled. When our children came, I retrieved it from my parent's house and used it for my own kids. It was pretty flat and threadbare by now, but it was very unusual to get new mattresses, so someone might want it. I brought it back in after a while, folded the thin mattress into thirds, and left it at the head of the cot for anyone that might get this house after I was gone. They could decide to use it or throw it away. No surprises in that area, nor was I expecting any.

Next, I tackled my bedroom. It was very small too. But if I was to encounter anything that I considered a treasure, it would be here. The shelf in my tiny closet was stuffed full of papers. I pulled them all out and started reading through them one by one. There were formal governmental documents of my marriage and my children's births and their chip numbers. I remembered Stephen and I signing every single one of their birth certificates. I sat and studied all of them. One was July 4, then July 17, August 30, and then Jack on December 25. All were only two or three years apart. It had been a really busy time when the children came. I remembered it being a blissful time as well.

I tucked these official papers in a pouch to leave to one of the kids. Then I continued to look through the rest. Tears gathered at a few of the sweet things Stephen had written to me. When we first were together, paper was still affordable. Now it was more precious than gold! I looked through all of it and cherished every memory of what I'd saved. These few pages held my life. I was pretty sure no one would want or have room for this sentimental stuff. My bathroom was pretty straightforward. I found nothing of import in there. After searching a lifetime worth of my mementoes, I had one small stack. Nothing else was mine. All the furniture, dishes, and linens belonged to the government. I decided to leave the largest cleanup until tomorrow. Then I'd go through the attic.

By the next morning, it seemed as if all hell had broken loose! I could hear loud voices in the street, arguing back and forth! It took little to bring people to violence these days, but I had an idea what this was about. Actually, I was surprised it took twenty-four hours for folks to start questioning the note left on everyone's door the day before.

Nothing like this had ever happened as far as I knew. People seemed angry and afraid, and they wanted answers. I turned on my news channel to see if I could learn anything. To my surprise, there were announcements being made about the note! Usually, if the government wanted to change something or enact a new law, you never heard much about it until it was a done deal. The broadcast seemed to be legitimate. A woman was talking about the note that had been left on every door. She quoted the latest missive:

> Your benevolent government did not authorize any gathering of its citizens! Your government would never risk the health and safety of its townspeople. An unscheduled gathering in the town square on June 28 will not be tolerated.

AGED OUT

Those responsible for posting these notes on the homes of our citizens will be caught and prosecuted to the fullest extent of the law!

There were always talks of government conspiracies. There were so many laws and punishments. People were afraid. And scared people become dangerous! Even though the government disavowed this communication, people would talk to one another in whispers and secrets. The bars and public spaces were occupied by many more people than usual when I went for my morning walk. Some people were carrying the note around in their hands. Loud voices could be heard with every theory imaginable about what this missive could mean!

There was no trust! The more the government proclaimed its lack of involvement with any kind of gathering, the more agitated people became. THEN THE NEWS BROKE THAT THIS SAME NOTE HAD SPREAD TO ALL THE SURROUNDING CITIES! There was a wave of these notes slowly making its way across the country. They were exactly the same notes, only different gathering places! What really got people worked up was that no one delivering these instructions had been caught leaving them. Law enforcement had multiplied throughout the affected areas. But there were not enough people in law enforcement to catch the perpetrators. Everyone knew that someone must have seen something, but nobody was talking.

The members of the government knew this too. Warnings had started being issued about what punishments would follow for not reporting the note senders. Usually, people wanted whatever advantage they could get by kissing the asses of government officials, but this time, no one was reporting it, if they knew anything. That no one was turning anyone in was another huge topic of discussion among uneasy residents. So far, there had been a few riots and murders, but it took so little provocation for something huge to start that everyone seemed very nervous.

I went about my usual day as much as was possible. I tried not to be noticed as I went my own way. I still took my walks through the now much more crowded streets, and I still was trying to eat all that I needed to. What baffled me so much in this situation was that people were not calming down. People weren't taking it as a hoax, no matter how much the government proclaimed it to be! No one even had a clue about anything, but people continued to stay worked up over what they didn't understand as the notes spread farther and farther across the country. The note proliferation felt almost supernatural because no one knew who was spreading them! I was very curious myself, but I felt a sense of glee because I truly thought, for once, that the government was not in control!

So much information was being spread by word of mouth, and no one knew what was to be believed. I tried not to listen because there was really no point. Either people were going to gather on June 28, or they weren't. If I was still here and the plan hadn't gotten me safely out, I thought I'd plan to go. I had nothing to lose.

All the hubbub of the past couple of days had kept me from finally tackling the cleanout of my small attic. I couldn't remember ever really cleaning it out. Usually, stuff was just piled upon other stuff, and I could not guess what might be found under the layers. I took a large basket up with me, sure that there would be much to throw away. All uneatable household garbage was vaporized now, and I didn't think I had ever known anyone who'd seen a dump. As with cemeteries, dumps were now villages and home sites. I climbed up the ladder to the attic, pushed open the overhead door, and ascended until I was able to sit on the attic floor. At its highest peak, I could almost stand up, but the roof slope meant I'd have to scoot on my tummy to reach those far corner areas. I wondered how we'd managed to collect so much stuff that things had gotten pushed into the tiny crevices.

I started emptying the attic piece by piece. There were old toys and old furniture that had seen much better days. I wondered why in the world I kept most of this junk. I could see that some of it were things from my parents' homes. It was entirely likely that there could be stuff from many past generations of our families. There was little for kids to inherit, but it seemed that, generation after generation, the *treasures* (or the few trinkets we had) somehow ended up in my attic!

I was not going to leave all this junk for my kids to store for another generation. If I found anything especially meaningful, I'd keep it for them. But my intent was to junk almost everything here. My basket was getting full quickly with old trinkets that I was sure someone thought very nice for its time. Ugly old broaches that were forbidden to be worn and broken ceramic pieces seemed to be the bulk of what I was finding.

I vaguely remembered a few of the things from my parents' home, but most of it was completely unfamiliar to me. A lot of this could be from Stephen's family. Maybe if anyone had bothered to attach a name and date to all this, it could be resurrected into an involved family "treasure" tree, with pieces coming from many branches of both families. The old jewelry was worthless. Jewelry could not be worn outside of the house, and the pieces here weren't even worth passing on. The little ceramic statues, while not my taste, might be something the kids would want to look at. As long as art was kept out of the public eye, it was allowed to be kept.

There were no old pictures except for the hard drive of my parents and Stephen's mom and dad. I would keep those in case the children were ever curious to look back through them. I hoped those old drives were compatible with today's technology. I was sure there were people with the technical skill to reformat them well enough to be viewed. I halfway considered trying to get them reformatted myself, so I put those in the save pile. I continued on in this way until the attic was almost empty. I had to make numerous trips up and down the ladder to empty the trash basket, but it was almost all gone now. I scooted over to the very farthest eave to retrieve the last thing I could see. It was a real piece of paper with lots of writing on it. I stuck it in my pocket to read later. It had grown very hot up here, and I felt very sweaty and grubby. I carried my last basket for the trash pile downstairs with me.

Almost my entire living room was now stacked with all the things that were in my attic. I would need to call for the vaporizer machine and spend the rest of the day feeding junk into it for disposal. By the time all the attic trash had disappeared into harmless vapor, I was bone-tired. It would still be an hour or so before my supper arrived, and I used the time to shower and wash my hair. Rubbing the water vapor off my bathroom mirror, I was pleasantly surprised by my appearance. It was strange how my looks changed from day to day. On one day, I could be pleased, and the next day, I'd be completely horrified! Maybe this was in some way tied to my mood. I really had no explanation for it. Perhaps how I viewed myself for the day was determined by how I was feeling. I accomplished a lot today, so maybe that was contributing to my good feeling about myself. Who knew?

Chapter 56

Feeling almost human again after my shower, I really would like to have someone to talk to. I'd like to have company, but who? I messaged Keshia and issued an invitation. After Jack's death, everyone had avoided me. I wondered if enough time had passed that I could be considered less tainted.

To my delight, Keshia immediately responded, and she was coming! I called and changed my dinner menu to a more elaborate one and enough for two. I checked that I had enough wine for both of us to get very relaxed. All the trash was gone, but I quickly tidied up a little more and had things looking pretty good by the time she arrived.

I hadn't seen her in so long, and we rushed to embrace each other. She started to apologize for not being responsive after Jack's death, but I stopped her in midsentence. I understood completely why she'd stayed away and told her I might have done the very same thing. We chitchatted for a few minutes, and she gladly accepted my offer of a glass of wine. We left the bottle easily accessible so we could fill our glasses at will.

Around eight thirty, the sound of a horn let me know that dinner had arrived. The robotic arm of the food vehicle allowed me to get it from my front door. I really liked that aspect of the service because you didn't have to step out of the house and leave the door unlocked. Before this invention, it had become dangerous to step out into the street to pick up your food. Any unlocked door could be an invitation for someone to get into your home. People had been killed when the wrong person happened to catch you with an unlocked door. I had almost been killed by those two girls when I'd done that, and I was super vigilant now!

We talked companionably as we ate. Things turned more serious when we began to discuss those friends of ours who'd aged out since the first of the year. Wilda, of course, was gone, and Lynn had been killed in March. I asked Keshia if she'd gotten to be with Lynn much before her death.

"A few times," Keshia replied, "but she was so depressed for so long before she was taken that she had pretty much given up. She wouldn't go anywhere and seemed unable to enjoy anything. I think she was so miserable she was ready for them to take her."

I hated hearing this. Lynn had always been such a joyous person, and I supposed I thought she'd go out the same way. Depression was a death sentence unto itself.

After dinner, we played a couple of rounds of trivia from my mensa tablet. Keshia handily won all the rounds! Around eleven, I called a car to take Keshia home. It had been a really nice evening and one I hoped we could repeat. As she was walking out the door, she hesitated and asked me if I had any idea what had become of Sally.

I hastily pulled her back inside and locked the door again. "What do you mean?" I asked. "I know she ended the friendship with me out of my own stupidity, but did all of you lose touch with her too?"

Keshia looked at me oddly and said, "She disappeared a short time after your son Jack was killed. As far as I know, none of us heard another word from her. You know Sally and her flights of fancy. She could have gone anywhere or done anything! It would have been nice, though, if she'd kept in touch."

My heart was pounding a lot harder now, but I didn't want to arouse any suspicion in Keshia, so I agreed, "Yes, it would have been nice."

When Keshia left and I had relocked the door, I sat down and thought about Sally. Keshia was right; Sally could be anywhere or have done anything. I would love to think that Sally was out there somewhere, having the time of her life, enjoying adventure after adventure. But for some reason, that didn't seem like Sally. She loved a good time as much as anyone, but she also wasn't one to sit around and let a perceived injustice float right past her. I knew Sally had planned to fight getting aged out, but now I started wondering if she was part of the plan. If I knew Sally, she would be a huge part of the plan! While she never spoke to me again after my blunder, I wondered if she was working in my favor behind the scenes. So many situations had gone in my favor for inexplicable reasons; now I wondered if Sally was somehow involved.

I still had not received any news from Simon Bing's husband, José, about the process of exploring the secret tunnel in the house. I wondered if Simon was still upset with me. I would try to contact José tomorrow. Even though he'd promised to contact me with any news, he hadn't yet. I enjoyed a small glass of a sweet dessert wine and then headed to bed.

On my walk this morning, the streets were becoming even more crowded with people over the anxiety of the mysterious note. It appeared to be like a new parlor game that everyone was playing. As far as I knew, the note had been delivered to every home across the country. Other than that, nothing else had happened. That did not stop people from speculating and even betting on what might happen on June 28.

The only reason I could think of for this rush of activity was that people were so bored doing nothing that they'd peculiarly bonded somehow over this mystery. Maybe for many, this was the biggest thing to happen in their lives. While there had become something of a common companionship among many speculators, there was also that fear that kept cropping up and causing many problems.

Returning home and after eating my breakfast, I emailed José for an update on the tunnel at the Bing home. I waited and waited, but he did not respond. I considered taking a car ride to Shepherd Town, but going without an invitation could mean a long ride with no results.

My tiny clothes were becoming tight. I was pleased with my weight gain and my newfound strength! I planned on running the back streets the next day to see if I could do it. I thought I was ready. I'd make sure I was ready when I needed to be.

After three days, and still no answer from the Bing house, I messaged again for them to expect me the following day by 11:00 a.m. I still heard nothing to dissuade me, so I ordered a car for eight thirty the next morning. I wished Stephen and the kids could have known this almost fearless and persistent person I'd become. I didn't know if Stephen would have liked it, but I knew my kids would be proud of me if I could confide in them.

In my mind, I could hear them shouting, "Go, Mom!"

Hearing nothing from the Bings, I climbed into the car the next morning and settled down for the long ride. Instead of empty streets, many were jammed with people standing around, talking, laughing, arguing, and fighting. I had never seen anything like this. It was like this all the way to Shepherd Town, so it took longer than usual to arrive.

Getting there, I dismissed the car. I was not going anywhere until all my questions had answers and my curiosity was satisfied. I knocked very loudly on the front door, but there was no answer. I knocked again and again, and still no one came. Refusing to be discouraged, I walked around to the back of the house as I'd done on previous visits. I tried to look in windows and the back door, but it appeared that every window and door in the house had been painted over in black!

Before I broke in, I considered asking a neighbor if they had any news on the couple, then thought better of that. Chances were their neighbors had no idea who even lived here. You could live beside someone for years, and unless you went out of your way, you probably wouldn't recognize their name or face. Neighbors could possibly be a bit too curious as to why I was there. It would be silly to arouse any questions or suspicions. Walking around to the back door, I took a piece of thick cloth I'd brought with me, just in case, found a fairly good-sized rock, and looked around very carefully. Just because I didn't see anyone watching me didn't mean that someone wasn't. I saw no one and hoped that the status quo of totally ignoring anything that didn't directly involve you would be upheld.

I wrapped the rock in the cloth and gave the glass a hard knock. The glass immediately broke, but I still could not see anything through the broken glass. I gingerly reached into the blackness, taking care not to drag my hand over the shards. My hand immediately met a hard surface that had also been painted black. I knocked on it a few times, but again no answer. I stood there for a moment, trying to figure out what I was up against. My hair stood on end when it came to me that the door had been boarded up!

I went to the side window, not particularly caring if anyone saw me now, and used my rock to break the glass. Again, boarded up and painted black! This house had been abandoned! Where had they gone? I ordered the car to come back for me. While I waited, I put the address 1953 Pearl Street into my query box. To my utter amazement, the return message said there was no such address! I was standing right here in front of it and reading that it did not exist! Something was very wrong here! I still had time to get to the government offices to make my inquiries before they closed.

Trying to enter the offices of the Shepherd Town government, unsurprisingly, was something of a challenge. The data I had to provide at the front entrance was very extensive. When a real person finally came to the door, I was allowed into a little jail cell of a cubicle with bulletproof glass. The guard asked me why I was there. I told him. He asked me if I was armed. I replied that I was. At this point, I was x-rayed to make sure that the gun I claimed was the only one I had. After that check, I was told I would have to leave my gun in a locker just inside the exit of the cubicle. I agreed and put my gun into the locker.

Finally, I was allowed into the building proper. I went straight to the information desk and told the gentleman that I'd come looking for a long-lost friend but that the house at that address looked abandoned. I said nothing about the fact that my mensa had said no such address existed. Surely that was a glitch!

He entered 1953 Pearl Street into his database and stood there looking strangely at what had come up on his screen. "Lady," he said, "I see no listing for that address. Are you sure you are in the right town?"

"Shepherd Town, correct?"

He nodded yes.

"Do you know where Pearl Street is in this town?" I continued my questioning.

"Yes, lady, I know where Pearl Street is," he answered back.

"I was just at that address less than twenty minutes ago, and you tell me it doesn't exist?" I demanded.

"Look, lady," he began to answer me snidely, "I'm just telling you what the record shows. That's all I can say."

I then asked to speak to his supervisor. This did not go over with him well at all. I was directed to take a seat and wait. I waited and waited, and finally, the clerk announced it was time for the offices to close and that I would need to leave. Raging with anger, I had no choice but to go. I had no desire to be arrested today.

I considered staying overnight and coming back tomorrow, but remembering my last overnight stay here, I thought it wise to go back home. I ordered a car and was soon on my way home. It was still daylight when I arrived home, but before I got out of the safety of the car and took the two steps to my door, I had my keys ready and looked around carefully to be sure no one was around who could catch me before I got locked inside. The coast appeared clear, so I jumped out with my gun drawn and stood there only long enough to get in the door. I quickly relocked all five locks.

Chapter 57

The next day, I continued to try to get in touch by email with both Simon and José. I never got an answer from either. I entered the Pearl Street address into every electronic device I owned, and all said there was no such address. Surely I hadn't imagined all the times I'd been there. Hell! I was there yesterday! I broke windows out of the place. It did exist, and no one would convince me otherwise! Going to bed that night, I glanced into my bathroom mirror. I looked as old as the hills.

I was so depressed over yesterday's events I almost talked myself out of my run. I was determined to be able to run two miles today. My goal was five miles, eventually, so I made myself get up and go out. I didn't have too much trouble getting in two miles today, so I would aim higher the next day. After eating every bite of my breakfast, I had the entire rest of the day ahead of me. Why, when I'd been trying so hard to have many more years, did the prospect of one more day seem so daunting?

May 15, 2526

Even though I was promised I wasn't going to die, marking the weeks before my birthday rattled me. Essentially, I had accomplished all that a person who was truly being aged out was supposed to do. The only thing still left undone was having someone come in and see what, if any, small repairs needed to be done for the next occupant of my home.

Jack was the only one of my children who'd ever lived in this house. When it was just Jack, Stephen, and me, we'd been moved from the larger family home to here. He moved out about two years before Stephen was aged out. I was glad he was out of the house before that happened. Stephen wouldn't have liked his children having to see him leave for his death. He probably would have preferred that I hadn't been there either, especially after the way I carried on when they came for him. He was very stoic, not like me at all.

At the beginning of my last year, I had dreamed of finding a way to escape my death while having the most fun I'd ever had. But I found that having no one to have fun with was no fun at all. With the streets so crowded with people these days, I really hesitated to go out to dinner by myself. There were too many people hanging around on the street near my front door for me to feel as if I could get in the house quickly enough to be safe.

The note-on-the-door controversy still continued, and it seemed to be becoming more rabid the closer the date. It was frightening to think what the towns all over the country would be like in the days before June 28. I knew there were famous dates that many of us who were older were taught that someone thought important. I could remember the date, but I couldn't remember actually why the date was sacred. Many of the dates were so many centuries ago that they had become irrelevant. But today I stopped and thought of the dates from so long ago and how only the dates had managed to stay in my head.

Let's see—1963, 1969, 2011, 2087, so many numbers that used to be a memorial to something.

I thought of these because I wondered if 6/28/2526 would become a memorable date. The government would not speak of it. Maybe they hoped that their silence would make all the talk die down. It wasn't, though; that was the strange thing. People were still worked up over this! I couldn't remember a time that something happened and was a huge deal for a week or so, and then people became bored with it and accepted it unchallenged. It took only about two weeks for the baby lottery to become old news, but this was not dying out. Whatever this was, it was growing!

I had scheduled a government-approved handyman to come and look over the house today to see if any repairs needed to be done before I died. He arrived around one in the afternoon and proceeded to search every nook and cranny of my house. He had his mensa tablet out, taking notes as he looked around. When he was ready to leave, I questioned him about the state of my home. He read me off the list he'd made, and it didn't seem like major repairs were needed. That was a relief. I didn't want to spend my last month with the noise of home repairs. The list seemed more of an updating than a repair.

New furniture and appliances were coming the day after I was killed. New house numbers would also be issued because a few new houses had been squeezed into several square feet of empty space that could house small families. I really didn't care what my new house numbers were to be. They would be installed in the days before I died and would mean nothing to me. As the man was leaving, he was kind enough to ask me how I was. He was no spring chicken himself, but that was to be expected. Very few young people bothered to learn a trade. As I said before, when all the people who were ambitious enough to learn anything useful at all were gone, the government would have to make people do it, or robotics would have improved so much that human touch would no longer be required. This had already happened in most professions, but as yet, it still took a human being to tinker with repairs.

The man told me his name was George, and when he asked me how I was, I was very touched. No one cared about feelings anymore, unless they were your own. I told him I was doing well considering and that what I missed most was my friends and having companions to do things with. When I said that, he thoughtfully looked and asked me if I'd like to have dinner with him tonight!

Oh yes! Oh yes! I thought. I wondered if he was asking out of pity. I hoped not, but I wanted to go out with someone so badly my pride was no issue. He promised to pick me up around seven thirty, and I promised to be ready!

I took a great deal of time and effort with my appearance for the night. I'd called and ordered a dressy black and gray, and I carefully applied my makeup and styled my hair. I was all ready to go at least an hour before he was to pick mc up. I poured myself a glass of wine and waited. The first glass made me feel so good I had a second. By the time he arrived, I was downright elated!

He took me to a very nice restaurant, the kind my friends and I used to frequent. There were no robots taking orders or assembly lines of food that we had to retrieve. There was an actual person who brought our drinks, then our food, then after dinner drinks as well. There was piped-in music, and people were dancing! I hadn't danced with a man since I'd danced with that Steve and his obsession with his great dancing first wife. George whirled me around the floor until I was breathless. I was having so much fun I hated to see the evening come to an end. Eventually, it had to end.

We took the car home to my house, and I invited him in. I was surprised when he declined to come in. Both he and I knew that I would thank him with sex. He had told me all evening long how pretty I was and how much he was enjoying himself, and besides all that, it would be dark! He could imagine me to look like anyone he wanted. I did not beg him, though it would have been nice to have someone to give and receive pleasure from. He watched me get inside safely, and then he was gone. I needed to keep reminding myself what a great night I'd had and not take issue with his lack of interest in me. Okay, yes, I needed to remind myself of the fun, but his refusal still hurt my feelings and put a damper on the evening.

"Pooh!" I shouted to no one at all.

I was notified by the government that my floors needed to be refinished. George had said nothing about this. That would mean I'd need to find somewhere else to live for the time it took to refinish and dry. I challenged the order and countered that this could be done after my death. Doing this now would be a hardship on me. I could hardly believe it, but the government okayed my claim! They'd wait till after my death to refinish the damn floors!

After breakfast the next day, I really started to go stir-crazy. I decided to get my flight pack out and cruise around for the day. If I found anything interesting, I could find a place to spend the night. When I cleaned out the attic, I had brought my flight pack down and left it in the corner of my living room beside the couch. It was out of sight and also out of mind. I hadn't plugged it in! It had a little power left in it, but I wouldn't take it out until it was fully charged! I would have to get a later start than I'd planned, but that was no one's fault but my own. I used the time to pack a few indispensables in my chest bag in case I spent the night away from home. The late start I was getting made that much more likely.

I grew so antsy waiting for my flight pack to fully power up. I felt such an almost overwhelming urge to be gone. I had a nagging feeling I was forgetting something or had missed something, but I had no idea what it might be. All I knew was that I was very anxious to take off! I watched the power level on my pack, and it seemed as if it were taking forever to recharge. I tried to play a game on my mensa tablet, but I could not concentrate. I kept crossing the room to check the power gauge. Finally, it was at full power! Putting my mini mensa in my body bag, I strapped it all to my chest. I went outside, started my pack, and took off!

I still marveled at the quietness of my new flight pack! My old one was so loud that earplugs were needed to protect one's hearing. I had my oxygen nose plugs handy, but I didn't have them inserted. My plan was to fly fairly low and just look around. When I planned this trip, I thought I would leisurely fly over wherever my mind took me. But now—and I could swear I didn't know why—I felt this urgency to find something. Where should I start? What was I looking for? Would I recognize it whatever it was?

My takeoff went smoothly, and I was soon soaring away from home. I wished my flight pack was strong enough to fly me across oceans. I was not even sure if any flight pack had that capacity for power storage. Faraway travelers either went by ship or molecular teleportation. I started west, looking at the small towns, and I was low enough to see people. Many, many people were out in the streets, just like in my own town. I supposed they were talking about the note like everyone else seemed to be.

Small town after small town, I spied. Every single one had people milling about in their streets. I smelled something that really stank! In the distance, I could see the beginning of a large sprawling city. I wanted to see if the same things were going on in big cities too. The closer I got, the more horrid the smell became. Finally, I held my nose and started breathing through my mouth. I would do just a quick flyover and check things out. Then I wanted to get away from this awful smell! I wondered how the people who lived there could stand such noxiousness. As I drew closer, I saw a lot of smoke!

Oh no! I thought. *Is the city burning down?*

I tried to fly in under and around the smoke. I'd put my oxygen plugs in so I could get some air. What I saw didn't surprise me, but I thought myself jaded enough that it wouldn't horrify me. People were running around with torches and setting fire to everything around them. These people were burning down their own city! Why would anyone burn down their own homes? Where were they going to live after they'd done this? I was almost sure this started over the note. How things got to this extreme baffled me to no end. I wondered if this started long ago when people quit talking to one another and started hating and arguing with everyone else. I wondered if there was ever a peaceful time. There never had been an era like that in my lifetime.

I was low enough to hear people screaming, "Burn this place down!" I revved my pack up to a faster speed. I had to get away from such idiocy! After the smoke and the stench began to abate, I figured I'd gone as far west as I wanted to. I set my GPS to head north. I gave it no other instructions because I had no particular place in mind. My only destinations were north, south, east, west.

I could feel a barely perceptible change in temperature the farther north I got. The spring season had already started in my area, but it didn't look as if it had the farther north I flew. When I got as far as northern New York, I could still see snow in spots. It never snowed where I lived. I'd heard it used to snow, but I believe that was centuries ago. I couldn't remember anyone in my family ever talking at all about snow. I guided myself toward the snow. I'd never felt it before, and I supposed there was no time like the present. I flew down to the street in the shadow of a medium-sized house. If there had been more snow, it had melted.

I know snow was supposed to be white, but this snow wasn't new snow, and it had gotten dirty as it lay on the ground. It was kind of looked yucky, but I knelt down to touch it. It had a grainy feeling, like it had ice crystals in it. I picked up a handful and squeezed it together. It stuck together like a dirty hard piece of ice. I sat there a moment and tried to imagine what it would be like to be in a snowstorm of white snowflakes drifting down on me. Holding this snow in my hand, I was able to imagine the coldness of each flake. I could almost see the beauty of it all in my mind. Then my eyes flew open, and I was holding a blackened turd of ice in my hand. My fascination with snow was over.

When I looked up, two men were standing close by watching me. I rose slowly as they studied me.

"Whatcha doin', lady?" the taller of the two men asked.

This had every potential to be a dangerous situation for me. I had my gun, but it was packed in my body bag.

Stupid, stupid, stupid! I chastised myself. I rose to my full height and faced them. "I'm not from here, and I've never seen snow before. I am a month away from being aged out, and I wanted to know what it was like," I explained.

This was my most precarious moment. They would either ignore me, be halfway pleasant, or try to hurt me because they knew there would be little consequences of bashing an old woman who already had one foot in the grave. I could see the men relax. Their faces softened, and their rigid posture went limper. The taller man actually smiled at me.

"You should have been here six weeks ago," the man said companionably. "I'll bet we had almost four inches all at one time!"

"Was it pretty?" I asked.

The other gentleman answered, "It sure was when it was comin' down, and it stayed pretty for at least an hour before the dirt from the big city drifted this way."

I knew about this city. It was the biggest one in the country. It was also the poorest one and had the most crime, and more people were murdered there than in any other place in the world. I would avoid that place at all costs! But right now, right here, I was getting to spend a few moments with two seemingly nice men. And I'd gotten to touch snow! All was well. We chatted for a while longer, and then I took off again. I went south again before I headed east. I wanted to avoid the big city completely!

As I was making my turn toward the east, I could see darkness falling in that direction. I wasn't far enough east to see the ocean yet when I realized I'd better find someplace to stay for the night before it got completely dark. I landed on a rooftop of some small town. I got my mensa tablet out and searched for rooms to let. I found one on Mulberry Street. I emailed the proprietor and asked if there was any vacancy. When he emailed me back, he invited me to come on over. I programmed the flight pack to get me there and relaxed on my way to my bed for the night. It was a modest little house and looked not much bigger than my own small home. I knocked on the door, and it was quickly answered by a middle-aged man, who welcomed me inside.

It was cozy but somewhat cluttered. He had to move some of his electronics so I could find a place to sit. He sat down opposite me on the one flat surface in the house that wasn't piled high. He offered me coffee, but I refused. I asked for water instead. He asked me where I was from and what my plans were. I told him my situation and that I had grown anxious and decided that traveling around would be calming. He looked at me now in pity. I didn't like that, but I knew if someone had told me they were weeks away from death, I'd have that same look on my face.

When he asked me if I was hungry, I nodded. "Yes."

"I don't have much food here," he said. "Why don't we go out for dinner?"

I quickly agreed to that. We went to a rather generic restaurant and placed our order into the microphone. They did have a bar here, and I ordered something cold and frothy. The man had introduced himself as Tom but said everyone called him Tommy.

"Tommy?" I asked. "Do you want to have a drink?"

"I'm getting one," he answered.

"I meant an alcoholic drink," I replied.

"I don't drink alcohol," he answered. "My father drank a lot, and it was so hard on my family. It eventually killed him," he said solemnly.

I nodded in understanding, but I enjoyed my drink anyway. I didn't have enough time not to get exactly what I wanted. We talked about the excitement that the note had caused. He had gotten one but, like me, hadn't overreacted to it. He was as curious as I was but had no desire to walk the streets, continually debating the issue. Back home, he showed me the small guest room separated by a curtain from the living room. This was exactly the same configuration as my house. I thanked him and bid him good night. You'd think that, after all that traveling, I'd be bone-tired. But sleep would not come! I still had this nagging feeling that I was leaving something undone. I could only wish I knew what it was.

I got up feeling groggy the next morning. I must have fallen asleep at some point, but I didn't think that I'd slept enough. Tommy again offered me coffee. I normally never drank coffee, but today I felt as if I needed the caffeine. I ate a bowl of rehydrated oatmeal; it was very good. I ended up having a second cup of coffee and felt as if it was finally starting to kick in. Soon thereafter, I announced my intention of getting on my way. Tommy looked a little disappointed but kindly wished me a safe trip and told me to stop by if I was ever around here again. I offered him my hand. He took it and gently brought it to his lips. I left with his kiss on my hand.

I continued on my eastern trek, but this time, I was flying into bright sunlight. About midday, I saw what I'd been on the lookout for. Spread before me was the ocean. It was so pristine and startlingly blue! I had heard stories that long ago, all the oceans had been huge garbage dumps for the trash that human beings produced. Sea life had completely died out. It had taken a very long time to get the trash removed from the waters and vaporized. Many strides had been made to repopulate the oceans. Some types of fish had thrived, but many other species hadn't been as successful yet.

I drifted up and down the coastline. Some of the beaches were crowded, but a few were so isolated that they were empty. I sat down on one of these secluded beaches, removed my pack, and sat down in the sand. I had touched construction sand before but never beach sand in such a large quantity. I took off my shoes and wiggled my toes in the sand; I dug at it with my fingers. I lay down on it and felt the heat from the sun. Then I stood, pulled my clothes off, and walked to the surf. It washed over my feet and cooled my sand-burned feet.

I waded out quite far. Looking back at the shore, I was surprised to see how far from shore I was, and still the water was only up to my thighs. I bent my knees and sunk into the coolness of the waves up to my neck. I hovered there for a while and rose and fell with the waves as they swelled then receded. I was so completely at peace here. There were no thoughts, anxiety, or unrest in my brain. If I knew what a trance felt like, I would think I was in one. Time passed, and I floated there. I believed I would have been content to float in this world forever.

To the point of dozing off in the water, a thought hit me so hard, and I jumped to my feet. All the tension was back in my body now! Why had this idea escaped me? I ran from the water and wasted no time in the sun to dry off before putting my clothes back on. I am gonna hightail it west again. Now I had a theory that could possibly make sense of what I'd been afraid was my insanity!

Before I researched what I thought might have happened, I wanted to go home first. I wanted to be completely prepared with documentation and pertinent questions. It would be dark by the time I made it all the way home, but I would go in the back door and fly low enough to check every shadow that might be a person lurking around my back door. I put my oxygen plugs in and set myself for speed and high altitude, and up I went! I did turn and look back at the ocean and the secluded beach that had been all mine for a little while. I doubted if I would ever see either again.

Chapter 58

I had a tail wind as I flew back toward the west again. I wasn't all that far from home, and at this speed, perhaps there would still be a little daylight left by the time I arrived. The sky was cloudless, and I could see the rooftops as I flew over my neighborhood. I lowered myself to almost rooftop height to see if I could find what I was looking for. Going slowly over the houses, I saw it! Built into a small crevice between two already cramped houses was new construction! Farther on, there were three more of these tiny homes.

I remembered now how inconsequential the house numbers were after George's inspection when the government told me that my house numbers would change to accommodate the new homes on the street. Could this be why 1953 Pearl Street in Shepherd Town was not on any electronic databases? Had there been fill-in construction on Pearl Street too?

Sitting down to my big computer, I entered in my own home address. I was disappointed to see it still there. Then I noticed the asterisk beside my house number.

Clicking on that, I saw words that made my heart pound. It said: "This address will cease to exist when new house numbers are assigned to account for new homes on the block. In the very near future, this home's house number will change."

I looked up several more house addresses from my neighbors. Again there was the asterisk! All the homes from the newest construction on down would change until the block ended.

Perhaps the house on Pearl Street in Shepherd Town had undergone the same transition. I entered site numbers on my mensa and all the questions I should ask to begin to get to the bottom of this. I was tired but was also so excited by my theory I doubted that I'd sleep very much. I was gone the minute I lay down.

I shortened and rushed through my morning walk. Back at home, I gulped down my breakfast and readied myself to be on my way. In my flight pack, I'd be able to get to Shepherd Town much quicker, and I'd be able to fly low over the neighborhood to look for new construction.

I arrived in Shepherd Town in less than twenty minutes. I had set my GPS to get me to Pearl Street, unsure if I could pick it out from the air. I buzzed the rooftops from the beginning to the end. Then I did it two more times. I could not find a splinter that looked like anything new. I landed in the backyard of what I knew to be 1953 Pearl Street. I was glad I had found my new stamina because I planned to walk the length of the entire block. This house was close to the south end of the street, and the only way this house number would change was if there were new houses crammed in north of the house. I walked slowly from the house for the few miles the street continued. I walked until the very beginning of Pearl Street. I hadn't seen any new homes on the way up. But I was determined to start with the house numbers and check for accuracy on the way back. This had to be the answer. It just had to be.

I walked very slowly from the head of the block, studying each border wall and roofline. I counted the house numbers as I went along. By the time I reached the house again, I'd seen nothing that looked like new construction, and the house numbers corresponded with each house. The Bing house was 1953, and there it was! In the flesh! Yet I was being told that it didn't exist!

I checked the house directly south of the Bing house, and its house number read 1953 too! What in the world was going on? How could this be? I stood there looking straight at the house. I walked around to the back, where I'd left my pack. I noticed that someone had repaired the window and door glass I'd broken, but it was still painted out, and nothing penetrated the blackness. I walked to the other 1953 and knocked on the door. Since these were larger family homes, I wasn't surprised when a young woman answered door. I could hear children playing in the background.

"How can I help you?" she asked in a tired voice.

I answered back with my own question, "Why does the house next door"—I pointed at the Bing house—"have the same house number as you do? Why are both houses labeled 1953?"

She looked at me strangely for a moment, "Ma'am," she said, "the house next door is 1951 Pearl. I've lived here almost four years, and this house has always been 1953 Pearl Street!"

I stood looking at her. Then I looked at the Bing house.

"Please look," I said. "Next door, the house belongs to Simon Bing, and it is 1953." I could tell by the way she kept looking over her shoulder as if seeking help that she was completely mystified by what I was claiming. "Look!" I pleaded. "Please come out and look!" This seemed to be the kicker, for she turned and took a step backward and closed the door in my face. I walked back to the front of the Bing house and stood looking at it.

A man from the house next door came out to question me. "What seems to be the trouble?"

As I stood there looking at the Bings' house number, which was 1953, I asked why his house had the same number.

He looked in the same direction I was looking, then said, "I don't understand." He was looking in the direction of the house to the left of the Bing House. "The house number next door is clearly 1951." He was looking at me as oddly as the woman of the house had.

"I'm talking about the house right here in front of us!" I exclaimed. He gave me that blank look again. "Are there any people living in the neighborhood that have been here for a long time?" I asked with exasperation.

He stood there scratching his head as if trying to think. "No one has lived here in forever," he stated. "These are larger family homes, and when children leave, we are downsized."

He saw my face fall, then offered the only suggestion he had. "You can try the house two doors down across the street. As far as I know, they've lived here for a while and have two adult children who can't seem to leave the nest. They may know more about what you are talking about since they've been here longer. Sorry I couldn't be of more help."

I thanked him and crossed the street. I knocked on a door, and a middle-aged woman eventually opened it. She seemed totally disinterested to find out why I was there and didn't say anything until I stated my business.

"Good morning," I began. "I am looking for a friend from my youth. I have been at his home before a long time ago, but it appears he's moved. I wondered if you'd know anything about him. His name was Kentura Bing. He has a son named Simon Bing. Does either name ring a bell?"

She stood there a moment as if trying to remember. "Hmmm... Bing, you say?" I nodded. "It seems as if there might have been a Mr. Bing many years ago. I do think I remember him. I was a very young mother then and didn't have much time for neighbors. But if I remember correctly, a Mr. and Mrs. Bing did live there. I think she died of something at a young age, and he was eventually aged out. I don't remember any son, though. But as I said, I had little to do with neighbors at all. So if it changed hands later on, I wasn't aware of it." She continued, "It sure was a sad day when it burned down about ten years ago. It was really frightening as well. All these homes are connected, and one fire could take out the entire block. We were all very lucky that only one house was destroyed and not the entire neighborhood!"

I stood there stunned. I could not find words to say.

"Are you okay?" she questioned.

I nodded and turned to walk away.

She spoke again before I could completely turn my back. "I remember there was something strange about the fire. Maybe an explosion? I'm sorry. I can't remember anymore."

I mumbled my thanks and walked back to the house that I could so clearly see but no one else did. I came to this house looking for Robin, then asking about Mr. Kentura Bing. Later I came back, and both Simon and José were kind to me. José even looked me over to make sure I was okay. I could remember both of them were worried about me. Then I came here with Wilda and found gruesome blood and gore inside the house. I could still remember how bad the house smelled from the rot. I could remember coming back again and angering Simon by asking about a hidden tunnel; he had refused to let me see where it led. José had promised to call me when Simon thought the tunnel was stabilized enough to be safe to walk through. I also would swear I remember coming here and finding a large white house with men, women, and children enjoying themselves behind the fence of an actual backyard.

All these had happened in the past year. I surely was not completely insane, was I? I walked back behind the Bing house that I clearly see, donned my flight pack, and programmed it to take me back home. While I'd been so anxious to get out of the house a few days ago, now all I wanted was to go home.

I got home and safely back into my house. I flopped down on my couch, completely devoid of any emotion whatsoever. I stared at nothing for what seemed like hours. I was lost. I was insane. I was delusional. Perhaps I was already dead. I couldn't begin to explain this past year and all that had happened to me. I thought things *happened* to me. I was not so sure anymore. I had very distinct memories of this, my last year. I saw them, I heard them, and I lived them! Where was everyone else as I lived through my last year? I had no one to ask for counsel anymore. I had no one to talk to and help me make sense of all this. I was all alone and didn't know how or why this had happened to me. I got through the day. I ate my appointed meals, cleaned up a little, and took a sleeping pill. I did not want to take the chance that I would think of all this throughout the night.

When I woke up the next morning, I debated about getting up and going for my walk. I was up to four miles a day now, and it had been my goal to be able to run for five miles. I was getting closer by the day. I'd gained some much-needed weight, and my weight gain was muscle. I was glad about that, but if everything that I'd lived through in the past year was a figment of my imagination, there really was no point in trying so hard to up my endurance level. I wasn't going to be saved; no one was going to help me. I'd sit here alone and wait for the limo to take me to my death. Apparently, I dreamed up this nightmare of my last year alive. I was heart weary; I saw no reason to keep up with this charade.

I made myself get up out of bed. I did my bathroom essentials but did not get dressed. I would not go out. I didn't love running but had thought it was essential for my survival. But that was just a big lie I'd been telling myself. When my breakfast came, I just picked at it. I was not hungry at all. I paced back and forth in the confines of my small house because I had no reason or will to do anything else. I spent the next three days doing the same thing over and over. On the fourth day, I seemed to perk up a bit and decided I'd take a walk.

I was not planning on running. I just wanted to walk and relax. The streets were still crowded with people still talking about the note and its repercussions. I could not imagine what was left to talk about. The note wasn't that long or detailed to still be a matter of discussion for this long! I had never seen people of all ages talking together, arguing together, or laughing with complete strangers as I had since the infamous note was delivered. I was so used to people adjusting to the most horrible things after a week or two of unrest. This completely baffled me.

Today instead of the small less-crowded back road, I decided to wade into the overcrowded main streets. I decided to jostle my way through the throngs of people and pick up what little snatches of conversation I could. I pushed my way around with a lot of "Excuse me." I paused if I heard a snippet that sounded different and possibly reflective. Most of it was the same old rubbish that had been hashed out weeks ago, but I got in on a few conversations with different perspectives.

One man theorized that it was a government conspiracy to gather as many people in one place as possible, kill them all, and relieve overcrowding. Many were contemplative of this idea.

No one spoke up and said, "The government would never do this to the people!"

This big government entity, which proclaimed such benevolence to its citizens, wasn't trusted at all. All of us who stood here listening had no doubt that this could be a workable theory from those that had our worst interests at heart. I listened. Then I reached over and touched the arm of a man who was close to me. He felt my touch and looked at me in question.

"I am here, aren't I? I am here, and you see me, right? We are standing here in a crowd in the town square, is that correct? You see me, and this is where I am?" He looked at me in frightened puzzlement. "Please just answer my questions," I implored.

He took a step back from me and answered, "We are in the town square, discussing the note that appears to have been delivered to every home in this country. Yes, I see you here, and I saw you listening to our discussions. Does that help you?"

"Yes, thank you!" I exclaimed.

Maybe I have been tricked by someone into doubting myself. Maybe there was a logical reason for what I'd learned this past week. I was giving up much too quickly. I took off running back home. I had a lot of research to do!

I sat down at my big computer and started searching for information on the house fire on Pearl Street ten years ago. I did not expect to learn much since fires at connected houses were quite frequent, and whoever, if anyone, recorded the event, might not have given it much credence. I found nothing and was disappointed. I decided to widen my search and go to the city database and look for structure fires in the town of Shepherds Town. Up came hundreds of accounts of fires that volunteer fire people had worked on. The database went back for decades. Now I entered "Pearl Street," and there were seven entries. When I entered "1953 Pearl Street," there was no report at all. I decided to check on all seven entries and see if I could figure out which had occurred at the Bing house and why no house numbers matched up. There had been a fire twelve years ago at 1951 Pearl Street. I pulled up that report.

This must be it! Twelve years ago, 1951 Pearl Street had burned because of an explosion in the house. Two people had been reported missing and assumed dead from the incident. The report did not mention the name Bing, nor was there any follow-up on the two missing people.

Okay, now I knew there had been a fire a long time ago. Two people were missing, and it was thought that they'd died in the fire.

There was no information about whether any human remains had been recovered. I was convinced that whatever remained of the ravaged house had not been searched at all. Human life was so expendable that a few people might have just shaken their heads in wistfulness, but nobody would have cared enough to do any kind of thorough search for two people. No one would bother. Whatever had burned presumably had been scooped up and vaporized.

This was very interesting, of course, but in no way did this answer my questions about how, in the past year, I'd been to 1953 Pearl Street numerous times and had all the experiences I'd had there but now I'm being told the house that I was in as recently as last week never existed at all. All the people who might have been able to shed some light on this puzzle no longer lived in the family-sized houses or had been aged out. In order to find anyone still alive who might have lived there, I would need chip numbers to track their whereabouts. The history of my chip would show every place I'd lived in, probably every place I'd traveled to, and all the information on my permanent record.

I remembered from my earliest search being baffled by why Kentura Bing seemed to have two chip numbers. I searched the records I'd started last year and found the two different numbers. I was so glad I recorded all this. I would have never remembered these long-involved numbers.

I entered the first number into Know Everything and came back with the name Kentura Bing. I already knew that, so I needed to do a more extensive search. I reentered the search engine and again entered the chip number follow by "all residences." My computer went black as it had the last time I tried to do a follow-up on Mr. Bing. I rebooted and tried it again but got the same results. I needed a much more powerful computer, as in government-owned power. I didn't think I could ask Tracy for help again. She'd gotten in trouble the last time she tried to do me a favor. I had a pretty good hunch she wouldn't do it again.

I was at a standstill and wasn't sure where to turn now. Surely the information was out there somewhere, but I didn't have any idea how to get my hands on it. The mystery of my sanity apparently was going to remain a mystery.

Later on, I had another idea. I turned again to Know Everything and asked for the names and chip numbers of all past and present Pearl Street residents. That did the trick. A long list of names and numbers popped up on my screen. I wondered if I searched each and every name and number on this list, I could find someone who could still remember the people and the fire.

I knew that most of these people had probably been aged out long ago, so I started searching for people who'd been born five years after me and on into this year. I'm sure some former Pearl Street residents were my age and awaiting their deaths this year, as was I. I painstakingly wrote a mass email and sent it to everyone who might still be alive. Now all I could do was wait to see if I got any responses from anyone. I had used the ruse of trying to track down an old friend and hoped someone would be kind enough to answer.

I waited right beside the computer for the next three hours. No responses came. I finally got up to eat, puttered around, played a few games on my mensa tablet, and then went back to check. Still nothing. I had the entire afternoon in front of me with nothing to do. I went back to Know Everything and typed in "fun activities" in my town. Nothing showed up, so maybe there really was nothing fun to do. I checked for emails again—still no responses.

I suppose it was a good thing I was so restless. I thought that meant I was still in the game and not ready to give up quite yet. I spent an hour or so fixing myself up to go out to dinner. Looking into the mirror, I was not entirely pleased by my reflection, but it was better than the last time I'd studied myself. I'd ordered a car and planned on going to the nicest restaurant that I could think of. I wanted one with real people and luscious cocktails, wonderful chem food, and attention to detail. No robots tonight!

My car arrived about six thirty, and I programmed in the address of a highly touted restaurant that I'd never been to before. It took longer than I expected to get there because the streets were still crowded with people. I was surprised when I got to the restaurant that there was a waiting line to eat there. I hadn't seen a line to get into a restaurant, especially a pricey one, in a very long time. I reached the reservation line and was told it would probably be an hour before I could be seated. That was fine with me. I found a seat at the bar and planted myself there until my turn came. I watched the people around me and listened in on snatches of conversation. The note seemed to still be the hot topic.

I sat next to a group who were debating the merits of showing up at the square on the appointed day. Some speculated that some momentous announcement from the government was to be forthcoming. Others still held with the mass-extermination theory. I listened with vague interest. The government had remained very quiet about this; but when they did make a statement, it was to deny government involvement in the gathering, and we are urged not to attend. That denial made people like me just that much more determined to be there on the appointed date. I still had hopes that the note and whoever was responsible for it had plans to topple the government.

After the multiple killings of government officials, the complete domination by the government seemed to ease a little. I believed the deaths scared them. I was not sure who they were. I knew the government officials of my town but had no idea who might really be leading the country. There used to be elected presidents and other law makers who ran the country, but that ended a number of years ago. I might have gotten to vote when I was thirteen or fourteen, but eventually, that stopped happening. I didn't remember anyone objecting to it when politics was abolished. I no longer knew who was actually running the country other than the hometown appointees. Ultimately, whoever made the laws might not even be human beings. Artificial intelligence could possibly have reached the level of human intelligence times a million! I believed everyone was relieved when political parties and elections were no longer an issue. Whatever or whoever was running the show, everyone had accepted it. We went along and did what we were told—until now. Now I thought there was definite dissension and growing pushback.

Chapter 59

I was quite tipsy when I was finally called to dinner. There was recorded music coming from overhead speakers, and some couples were dancing. I ate in silence watching them, wishing I had someone to dance with. No one asked to buy me a drink.

I got home quite late and searched my area thoroughly to make sure no one was hanging around my front door. Seeing no one close enough to cause me any harm, I exited the car but left the door open in case I needed to make a quick getaway. After getting my door unlocked, I checked around again to make sure I was still alone, took a step back to the car, hit the return button, and dashed back to my open door. I slammed the door shut behind me and locked all five locks. I saw the car pulling away as I looked out my window. There I was, late at night and not at all sleepy. It really was no wonder why there was so much crime and mischief committed by people of all ages. There was nothing at all to do!

I looked for a book to read on my tablet, but nothing really appealed to me. I started to reread the Bible that was still stored on my mensa. I had put Wilda's real Bible in a box to keep it safe. My children would find it after my death. I had written a note and placed it inside, telling whichever one of my children found it what it was and, before discarding it, to make sure that Michelle really didn't want to keep it.

I started over from the beginning again and continued to read. It would be wonderful if all this was real. But I didn't believe in fairy tales anymore. I grew drowsy and turned my tablet off. Just for the heck of it, I prayed. I asked God to help me get through the next six weeks of my life. Perhaps I was just talking to myself, but I was able to peacefully fall asleep.

The next morning, I got up and got out of the door quickly. The temperature was heating up, and I wanted to get my run in as early in the day as possible. While there were still people out in the streets, it was not as crowded as it would become a little later on.

I reached my five-mile goal today! Hurrah for me! With no one to help celebrate my accomplishment, I went into the house and waited for my breakfast to arrive. I really hadn't gotten much of an appetite back, but I still continued to make myself eat until all the food was gone.

It was 11:00 a.m. Now what? I went to my computer to check my emails, and to my surprise, I had one! It was from a former Pearl Street resident. I had given up on that, but someone had finally answered me. I read the letter with excitement. It was from a man who'd once lived five doors north of 1953 Pearl Street and remembered the fire. He asked what I wanted to know. Again I wrote that I was looking for a friend or any of his relatives because I'd lost touch with him. I did not want to ask all my questions online and suggested we meet somewhere later today. He suggested a small bar on a main thoroughfare, and that seemed safe enough to me. We agreed to meet at five this afternoon. I hadn't gotten any notifications from the government in at least two weeks. It appeared their harassment and suspicions about me had lessened. That was certainly fine with me!

I worked especially hard on my appearance for tonight. I didn't know why, but I still had that vain streak I'd had all my life. My hair had little gray, and I did my makeup judiciously to highlight my best features and attempt to minimize my flaws. I pulled my hair up into an attractive updo and put on my newest and cleanest black and grays. I was ready far sooner than was necessary, but I was excited and anxious to meet this man who might have answers for me! The last hour seemed to crawl by as I waited for my car to pick me up. I stared out the window, willing the car to pull up to my door. After what seemed like forever, it finally arrived!

On the ride to the restaurant, I was nervous. I thought I had a list of questions I might want to ask, but if the man lived five houses away from 1953 Pearl Street, he might have no knowledge, and from five houses away, it would be very unusual.

AGED OUT

I knew I was looking for a man named Geoffrey. He said he'd be waiting for me outside the bar. When I arrived, there were many people hanging around outside the bar. I was not surprised by that at all since crowds were frequent now. Getting out of the car, I stood for a moment, looking for a face that might be a Geoffrey. It did not take long before a man approached me and said my name.

I answered back, "Geoffrey?"

He nodded, and we shook hands.

Geoffrey said, "I have a reservation for us in about half an hour. Since the note, every place fills up very quickly! I'm amazed by how this summons has changed people so much!"

I could only nod in agreement. "Imagine having to make a reservation to get into a bar!" I commented.

We sat on a bench that must have been new. I was fairly certain that there was never a waiting list before to get into this neighborhood bar. We sat and spoke pleasantries until his name was called. When we were seated, I felt no need to try to lower my voice or hide our conversation. Not so long ago, I would have tried to mask any conversation about things that might attract the government's interest. I didn't know when that feeling stopped, but I was not scared anymore.

It appeared that the government had, for all intents and purposes, gone underground and was leaving people alone. It was also possible that every word we spoke was being recorded for later consequences. I had so little time left that it didn't bother me too much. I sort of wondered if Geoffrey had any such concerns.

When we were seated and had ordered our drinks, he got right down to the subject at hand. "What makes you so curious about the Bing gentleman and the fire that happened so long ago?"

I responded, "I've been searching for the Bing family for the past year. I will be aged out in the next few weeks, and I want to reconnect with my old friends while I still have a chance."

I did not tell him any more of the story about being at the house and the changes I'd seen there. I wanted to hear his story before I told him anything about mine.

"Tell me all about the Bings," I asked him. "I want to know everything since the last time you saw them."

He seemed to be a happy storyteller, which was what I needed right now. He rubbed his chin and got a faraway look as if he were remembering times past.

"I actually knew Dr. Bing quite well," he said.

I had to stop him there. "Mr. Bing was a doctor?" I asked in wonder.

He seemed surprised that I didn't know this. He responded, "Oh yes, he was one of the smartest and most knowledgeable men I've ever known. He was a physicist and worked on many projects in that underground laboratory of his."

I exclaimed, "So the hidden tunnel led to a lab?"

He answered, "It wasn't so hidden the times I was there. There was a door in his living room that led straight to it. I know I was there multiple times. I'm not sure what he was working on, but he was very disciplined with his research and had some great plan for mankind he was trying to perfect. I never really understood very much about his plans, but I respected him enough to sit there and listen while he talked. I remember wild thoughts from him about time travel and having people come back long after they'd died. It sounded a lot like that old-fashioned idea of cryogenics, but he seemed to think he was close to finding an answer to whatever mystery he was trying to solve."

I asked, "So he was working on this until he was aged out? Is that correct? Then no one continued to carry on his work?"

"Oh, hell no," Geoff responded. "He wasn't aged out! He died long before he would have had to age out, or that was the story at the time. One day he was here, and soon thereafter, he wasn't. I really don't know if he came to his end in the explosion and fire at his house or if that was a ruse to disguise his disappearance."

I listened to this in amazement. "What about his son?" I asked. "What about his son, Simon?"

It was his turn to look at me in shock. "Dr. Bing was never married! He never had a son at all. His name was Simon. Simon Kentura Bing."

Now I was confused beyond all measure. I didn't even know what to ask next. Geoffrey was the closest answer I had to the Bing mystery, and I had to keep him talking. I could not let the evening end—this was too important. I asked Geoffrey to come home with me so we could continue talking. He got that look in his eye that I might be trying to seduce him. I didn't care. If I had to sleep with him to get some answers, okay with me.

When we got to my house, I welcomed Geoffrey in. I asked him to tell me everything he knew and could remember about Dr. Bing.

He began his narrative. "I met him when I was about forty-five. He was a few years older than I was, but we got along famously. I was an amateur chemist, and we met at a bar one night and got to talking. I had a very tiny space devoted to my lab, but Kentura had this enormous underground laboratory, where he worked. I often wondered how he was able to stay in such a large house. I asked him once, but he seemed uneasy with my questions. He mumbled around and stated this and that but never really gave me a reason. I figured it really was none of my business and quit asking. He'd sometimes ask about the chemical compositions in the human body. I had studied online for years and had learned so much that I was quite an authority on the subject. He wanted to read the many papers I had written that were filed away on jump drives in my attic. I gladly lent them to him. No one else had ever read them, and he seemed quite excited about my theories. It made me feel really good that someone appreciated my years of dedication and study. After he read everything I'd written, he asked me in confidence if he could tell me what he was working on, and I would promise never to let it leak to the government. That scared me a little bit, not because I was all that afraid of them, but because I was uneasy about what Kentura might be trying to do. I did agree though. Now, before I tell you any more, I want to know the truth about why you are searching for Dr. Bing. Are you with the government? As far and I know, Kentura has been dead for quite a few years now, but when I say that, I have to add I would not be surprised to hear from him again someday."

Amazed by what he'd already told me, I decided to tell him everything that had occurred around me in the past year. I told him of Jack's death and then Robin's stay with me and her sudden disappearance. I told him about finding the name Kentura Bing in some notes she'd left behind and the address 1953 Pearl Street. I told him about my trips to the house, every word and every experience I'd had with Simon Bing and his husband, José. I told him about going there once and seeing a big white house with a yard, trees, and flowers. I told him about the people enjoying themselves in the backyard and how I could not get the attention of anyone to let me in. I told him about the pain in the shoulder I'd felt while I stood there and waking up to find myself in an idling car in front of my house. I told him about my trip with Wilda and the gruesome sights we'd seen in what seemed like an abandoned house. I told him about my dream that Robin had come for me, taken me to 1953 Pearl Street, and a man letting us in. I told Geoffrey about watching the man move a piece of trim on the bookcase and a door opening into a dark and dank tunnel. I told him how dark and long it was. I told him about Robin pulling me through and seeming certain she knew where we were going. I told him of waking the next morning and seemingly having never left my bed. I told him of traveling there recently to be told that the house next door was 1953 Pearl Street and that the house I'd seen that very morning had never existed at all! Then I told him that my aging out was planned in the next few weeks but that I had secretly been working with a group who'd promised me I was not going to die. I ran out of breath telling him everything!

He asked, "Who's in this group?"

Maybe I should have been wary about that question, but since I really didn't know, no one could wheedle or torture the information out of me.

"I don't know," I answered. I got my information from random people who showed up at my door with tasks for me to do to prepare for my escape. I got no last names. It was never the same person twice, and the person who told me what to do knew no more than the person before them. I lied a little bit about never seeing the same person twice. I was not going to tell him of my participation in the murders of government officials. I was never going to mention the name Sally to anyone, ever. She seemed to be the only constant, given the many people who'd approached me.

He listened intently and only interrupted with a question once or twice. When I finished, he slowly stood, stretched, and told me it was late and that he needed to get home.

"What?" I exclaimed. "I thought you'd be here through the night! Why are you leaving?"

He said, "With all you've told me tonight, I know of no way to help you. I've told you everything I know about Dr. Bing, and I cannot explain all that happened to you in the past year."

He started for the door. I begged him to stay and help me figure it all out, but he kept walking. Before he closed the door, he stopped and turned back to me. "You know that what you've described really didn't happen, don't you? Are you that far gone that you imagined this entire last year of your life?"

I felt the unshed tears in my eyes threatening to spill down my cheeks. I said as calmly as I could, "Do you think that what you're telling me hasn't already occurred to me? Many times during this past year, I've questioned my sanity. I promise you—for me, everything I told you tonight is the absolute truth!"

He looked at me with a look that seemed to hold the slightest bit of fear. "Naia, I believe you are mentally ill. Everything you've told me about tonight is not possible! I'm sorry, but you need far more help that I can give you."

"If I am delusional, please stay and help me figure it all out!" I begged. "Why do I know things that I really shouldn't know? I had never heard of Kentura Bing until I found those notes of Robin's. I wish I had someone who could stand up for me and tell you I am not crazy and that I did experience all that I've told you tonight, but I don't have anyone left! Do you understand? They've all been aged out! All the people who might have been able to vouch for me are all dead and gone!"

He shook his head and said, "I'm sorry." Then he was gone.

I stood hurriedly and locked the door behind him. I got a blanket and curled up on my small couch. I spent the rest of the night curled up in fetal position. By dawn, I came to the conclusion that, all alone, I would never be able to solve this puzzle. I decided to give up, hoping that if I were really going to be saved from my execution, all would become clear soon. What if I had imagined it all? What if I was going to be sitting right here, waiting for my executioner one month past my birthday? Now I had no idea what to believe.

The next morning, I did not go out and walk my five miles. When my breakfast came, I could only eat a few bites. I couldn't get in the mood to play a game or read or have any desire to get dressed and go out at all. I sat right there on the couch the entire day, with very few thoughts at all. I only stood when a car tooted to announce the arrival of one of my meals. Most of it went into my own trash laser to be vaporized and released cleanly into the air through a vent to the outside. I actually considered, once again, the idea of taking my own life.

If the next few weeks were going to be as miserable as today, I thought I'd rather go out on my own terms. I wondered if Geoffrey would tell my wild story to his friends. Would he consider telling the government that I was insane and lead them to the conclusion I had a plan to escape? If I got locked up again, it would be impossible to get out as I did last time when I was given the opportunity to walk straight out the door. Maybe I was crazy. When I stopped to think about how I'd gotten through the last ten months and always managed to find my way home and be okay, it was surely the delusions of a crazy person! If I'd really been to all the places I thought I'd been and seen all the people I'd thought I'd seen, I would have been found and confined months ago. I remembered the guard at the confinement facility saying to me that I had friends in high places. But I had no idea what that even meant. I was suddenly moved to pray. I had never really tried it in earnest before, but after reading the version of Wilda's Bible, I felt the need to try.

I sat down on the floor. I didn't know why, but the floor felt like the right place to pray. I tried to imagine this Jesus God sitting across from me and having a conversation with him. From here, I prayed. "Hi, God. It's me—Naia. I feel very confused right now and wonder if there is anything you can do to help me. Is there any way you can bring me peace and comfort? I will resign myself to my fate if that is what you say I should do. Right now I'm lost, and I need you to help me find my way. Thanks, Jesus God. Amen."

After I'd said my prayer, I went into my bedroom to lie down and soon fell fast asleep. I slept through to the next morning. I felt rested and refreshed. I decided to go for my run. Maybe all this preparation was for nothing at all, but I felt compelled to do it. I locked my door behind me. My run went well. I had no trouble now with a five-mile run. When breakfast came, I ate every bite. My mood has brightened considerably.

I sort of giggled to myself. "If I am crazy, I'm gonna go out crazy strong!"

Chapter 60

I called and cancelled my lunch meal because I decided to take myself out for lunch. I went into my bathroom with the small box of belongings I'd been allowed to keep. It had my mouth care products, hairbrushes, and my makeup. I washed my face in the bathroom sink and was very happy at my appearance even without makeup. I looked good. I looked as good as I felt. I had come to the conclusion that my moods were directly projected from my face. I decided that for this morning, I looked very good for a sixty-nine-year-old woman!

I decided not to order a car. I felt okay walking to a restaurant this time of day. The vultures usually never came out until the nighttime. I walked with strong steps! I walked with pride! I walked with confidence! I could feel myself smiling with every step I took. I found myself repeating the cadence of "I am strong, proud, and confident!" to the beat of my own footsteps!

It took me very little time before I was in the heart of town. I looked around to decide what restaurant I wanted. I settled on the local Indian restaurant. I love Indian food, and it reminded me of the meals that Bog Digdo Miller prepared for me. Once inside, I ordered a cocktail and quickly downed the entire thing. I ordered a second and nursed this one along much more slowly. When my food arrived, I ate with relish! I had requested the food be spiced mildly, but even mild Indian food was hot and spicy.

After lunch, I went to the bench where I'd sat and watched the mayor's comings and goings to note and prepare for her murder by her assassin. I didn't particularly feel guilty about that, which surprised me. I couldn't go through with the murder of the woman and her mother, and again I couldn't go through with murdering the mother in front of her little girl. I must have an especially soft spot for mothers and daughters.

The square was full of people again as it had been since the note. I could not believe that people were still talking and speculating about what the note said. I had never seen people so excited, so apprehensive, or so curious about an event in my lifetime! Talking about the note seemed to be everyone's new social life, and those participating were enjoying it!

I sat there for about an hour, then realized the afternoon was slipping away. I would be home long before dark, but as the sun sank into the west, that tiny bit of terror still lingered from my attack. I walked quickly and was home within an hour. The sun, though lower, was still beaming brightly. I let myself in, locked all the locks, and played my game on my mensa tablet. As I sat there, I could hear throngs of people on the street, on their way home for the evening. I bet there were still lots of people out there talking.

This note seemed to change people, though I could not understand why. People were socializing and coming together as never before! While there was still some fighting and killing over differences of opinion, most seemed to accept the differing opinions of others. Accepting that there could be people with different viewpoints would not have been tolerated a few weeks ago; now most people were actually listening to strangers and enjoying the thoughts of others. This was amazing and so strange.

The government had preached for so long that we must be afraid of everyone "out there." People were not only finding what separated them, many were finding out for the first time what they have in common! Tentative friendships were being formed and this is changing everything! I noticed that people are starting to look each other in the eye. They are much more likely to acknowledge a stranger who passes them on the street. They seemed much more likely to offer help if it was needed. All these things were miracles that I'd certainly never seen before! I wonder if the author of the note knew this might happen. So many questions and very few answers, but that did not stop the speculation!

Tonight as I slept, I had two familiar dreams, but this time, I had them both. They seemed to intertwine. I could hear my children calling for me, "Mama! Mama!" I wanted desperately to rise and find them, but my body was just too tired to get me to my feet. Then my bedroom filled up with people. Their faces were getting a little clearer now. I could see people I recognized but could not put a name to a face. I tried to talk and begged someone standing here, looking at me, to please find my children and bring them to me. I tried so hard to talk, but all that came out of me was a throaty growl. The people had been talking among themselves, but when I made the noise, they all grew quiet and looked at me intently. I wished I knew who these people were. I felt if I could see someone I knew, I'd feel so much more at peace with these recurring dreams.

They began to fade away from sight. And when the last trace of them was gone, my eyes popped open, and it was morning! I never felt completely rested after these dreams, especially now that they were connecting themselves together somehow. I made myself get up, but instead of running today, I took a fairly fast-paced walk. I hadn't gotten very far before I was so tired it was hard to put one foot in front of the other. I had no trouble running my five miles yesterday. I wondered if I was getting sick. I immediately turned around to head back home. I usually ran on a back street to avoid the crowds, but today many people were here chatting with one another. There was no yelling, only the calm *exchange* of words.

This feeling of wonderment was even starting to engage me. It hadn't before. But I'd never seen people relate to one another like this! I knew this was happening all over this country. Could it be happening like this all over the world? That thought gave me chills! I tried to tune into some news channel, but there was so much static I could not make any sense of it. I tried to find the Chinese channel; I'd had luck with that before. I did find what I believed was the news in Chinese, but I could not make out a single word of it. Had I already forgotten the language I'd studied so intensely for my class? I certainly hoped not. Maybe this wasn't Chinese at all. Perhaps it was some other Asian tongue that I was not at all familiar with.

AGED OUT

I got on my big computer. The only news we got online was from our government. Perhaps they'd make mention of the phenomena of their people and the new attitudes among them. Looking at the government site, I couldn't believe I thought there would be anything encouraging, pleasant or true!

The government was issuing all kinds of warnings to people. They were warning everyone to stay inside and refrain from talking to strangers, that it was not safe! All kinds of diseases could be spread with all this co-mingling. The government would step in if these dangerous activities continued. This was the first time I'd seen the government reference the note since the very first day of its arrival. In big bold letters it read:

> If you are still conversing about the note, you are making fools of yourselves! This entire note about a meeting is a complete hoax! Whoever is responsible for this should be considered extremely dangerous! Do not gather anywhere on June 28! Stay in your homes with the doors locked. Coming out and doing what this note suggests could get you killed! This warning is from your kind and benevolent government!

Well, well, this little missive made me even more determined to go! That was the day before my appointment with my executioner, so I had nothing to lose if I went a day earlier.

It was midafternoon by now, and I still felt so tired. I slowly sipped on a glass of wine, hoping it would put me to sleep. When it didn't, I had a second glass. I had no memory of how many glasses I consumed, but it eventually had its desired effect. I dozed off right there on the couch, and I didn't rouse again until I heard the toot of the car delivering my supper.

I peeked out my window to see if anyone was lingering around. Many people were lingering around! I stood there and debated about opening the door and attempting to get my meal. Finally, I threw all caution to the wind, unlocked my multiple locks, and flung the door wide open. What happened next shocked me to my core.

A young man noticed me, and he went to the car, retrieved my supper, and brought it to me! He then said, "Enjoy your meal, ma'am."

I stood there so dumbstruck. I could not speak! I finally came to myself enough to say "Thank you!" to his receding figure.

Normally, I would have backed up as quickly as possible into the house to securely lock my door. In my shock, I just stood there and looked all around me. My next-door neighbor, Wanda, was sitting out on her stoop. We had a nodding acquaintance with each other, but I didn't think we'd ever actually spoken. She saw me standing stupidly, holding my plate of food.

She said, "Naia, come on over and sit with me while you eat your food."

As surprised as I was by this neighborly exchange, I was even more surprised to find myself walking over to sit with her. I was not sure how long we'd lived side by side, but I thought it might have been a long time. We sat there chatting companionably for what seemed like hours. I had long since finished my food and realized it was totally dark and that I really needed to go home. Normally, I would have been scared to death, but tonight all the people hanging around did not seem threatening to me. I felt that if anyone tried to harm me, many of these people would come to my aid! I bid Wanda goodnight and went back to my house—but not before she and I made plans to get together again soon.

This was one miraculous evening! I hoped so mightily that this truly was happening all around the world! That night, I said a prayer to Jesus God again, asking for his blessings on all the people that somehow this feeling of amity would continue.

I slept so well this night. No dreams that I remember, No particular worries at all, and I felt hope for the first time in forever! I'm not even sure what this hopeful feeling was about, but I was feeling good right down into my bones!

Still riding the high of yesterday, I planned on running today. I hadn't gotten very far, and I was out of breath! My heart was pounding so quickly and so hard I wondered if it was going to come right out of my chest. This was very discouraging. I had been doing so well. I could only hope when it came time for my escape, I'd be able to physically do what I needed to. By the time I returned home, I was so weary all I could do was go to bed. I messaged my food service and told them not to deliver any breakfast. I was too tired to eat. I fell sound asleep again. I thought I'd gotten so much rest last night, but apparently, it was not enough.

I slept until early afternoon. I looked out my window and saw lunch sitting on my stoop. I thought I'd be up long before now, or I would have canceled lunch too. I brought it inside to see if anything was still edible. Some crackers and an apple looked okay, but the other stuff had sat too long in the warming spring sun. I was glad I wasn't starving, but I did make myself eat the apple and crackers. I wondered if I had been forgoing meals again. Maybe that was why I was feeling so weak. I tried to recall my last meal, but I couldn't remember when I last ate.

I couldn't stand just sitting here, but I could not think of anything to do. I wished there were places to go, but I didn't know where that might be. I considered taking some more classes at the university, but whether I would be saved from my execution or they came for me on the appointed date, I would not be able to finish whatever class I started. I thought more about it. Why did it matter if I could finish the class or not? Having a place to go around other people and having to use my mind for some other purpose besides dread could make my time left so much more pleasant.

I got on my mensa and looked up adult education in the same college I'd taken the Chinese class. I wanted to find a subject that would require intense study. Having another subject I find interesting would fill my days trying to learn the content and would be the best thing that could happen to me. I started to really get excited by the thought of having something left to strive for. I looked at all the course offerings. There really weren't all that many, which surprised me a bit. There were no art or music offerings. There was too much chance of being better than someone else, enough so that just being better could offend. They did still allow dance classes even though there were no live musicians. Maybe it was very good that there was so much music recorded before the Equality Law was enacted! Music and art had to be strictly a homebound hobby now.

Okay, I'm going to take a dance class. I don't have a partner, but the syllabus says it isn't necessary to have one.

I called the college the next day and enrolled in dance class. I chose to take it three times a week; that should keep me busy enough. It would be good exercise for me as well. My morning runs had turned into run/walks. I found I was walking far more than I was running, but I could keep up a pretty good pace. I entered a food schedule on my mensa; that way, there'd be no more missed meals. I couldn't afford to get weaker!

Chapter 61

My first class was tonight, and I was so excited. I hoped I could enjoy every second of it. The only downside was that there would be no intense home study.

I thought to myself, *Dancing is so social. Perhaps I can find friends or a group of people to gather with. That would be wonderful!*

The class started at 7:00 p.m. and lasted for two hours. The first hour was learning the steps; the next hour was practicing with fellow students. I ordered a car to pick me up half an hour before class. I didn't order a return car. I wanted to see if the group wanted to get together after class. I could always get a car as long as I had my mini mensa with me. I made sure my pistol was firmly attached to my ankle. I spent a considerable amount of time on my makeup and hair. There was a sparkle in my eye that I hadn't seen in a while. I knew I looked pretty good that the sparkle came back!

I had ordered my evening meal much earlier than usual. I wanted to make sure I remembered to eat. By six thirty, I was so excited that I willed the car to hurry up! When it arrived, I looked around carefully and saw no one that appeared threatening. After locking my door behind me, I eagerly entered the car. I programmed it to the correct address, and I was off!

As I looked out the window, I saw so many people out communicating and seemingly being friendly with one another. It didn't seem nearly as scary to be out at night. Maybe it was a false sense of security, but I was beginning to believe that if someone tried to harm me, a complete stranger might come to my aid. This sense of community was unlike anything I'd ever encountered before. It had been unthinkable that only a few months ago, everyone feared everyone else. That was what the government had always espoused, that everyone was out to harm everyone else. This note thing had performed a miracle. I only wished it had come along when I was much younger.

The car pulled in directly in front of the door to the building where the class met. I took a quick look around out of habit and then entered the building. The class was in an auditorium with lots of room. I was surprised to see at least thirty other people already there! I introduced myself to the instructor, was warmly greeted, and then turned to face the people who'd watched me come in. Most of them smiled at me and welcomed me into the group. We stood around chatting till everyone who signed up was accounted for.

The teacher began by calling for us to be quiet and then giving us an overview of what we'd be learning over the course of the class. She asked us to pair up. Surprisingly, there were about as many men there as women, so only two couples were composed of female partnered with female. The gentleman who approached me told me his name was Jules, and I introduced myself as Naia. We watched the instructor demonstrate a couple of steps, and then we were to attempt to copy what she did. The steps were to the beat of "one, two, three," "one, two, three" rock step.

She started the music, and we practiced doing that for about ten minutes. Jules and I had no problem with that step, but the next sequence was a little harder. It involved a turn in the "one, two, three" beat sequence, and it was easy to get out of step by turning too quickly or slowly. After practicing that for another ten minutes, she showed us another couple of steps before announcing that these were the steps we would be practicing for the second hour of class. We were encouraged to switch partners frequently and get used to being able to dance with everyone. Jules whispered in a flirty tone that he really didn't want to switch partners. I flirty-toned right back that we'd dance again before the evening was over.

My next partner was a very young man who looked as if he might be in his late twenties. He was a cutie, but he didn't have as strong a lead as Jules had, and it made dancing with him a little more challenging. For the next forty-five minutes, we change partners whenever the instructor said, "Switch!"

AGED OUT

It was getting close to the last switch of the evening when I found myself facing Jules again.

He laughingly said, "I told you I was going to dance with you again."

I smiled up into his face and looked him in the eye. "I told you that I knew we would," I responded.

Jules looked to be in his fifties and was quite handsome. I was really surprised that he was paying so much attention to me. There were much younger women here, but I felt flattered by his attention. As the class came to a close, a gentleman suggested to the group that we all go to Ringer's Bar, where we could continue the evening and practice our dancing. A few people didn't want to do that, but I was certainly game. The thought of extending the evening made me very happy. We decided to walk to the bar, and with this newfound sense of security being in a group, I felt completely comfortable doing so.

The bar was quite crowded, and there was the sound of many voices. What thrilled me to no end was that none of the voices seemed angry or aggressive. There were people talking, discussing, and laughing, but there was no yelling or cursing at all! We waited for a while before being able to get two tables close enough together where we could try to get to know one another. We began by learning one another's first names, and we laughed as we made mistakes and couldn't recall the names on the first try.

We all ordered drinks and rose to our feet to get out on the dance floor. The young twentysomething man had already asked me for the first dance, so we worked our way—*and it was work*—around the room. When that dance came to an end, Jules was waiting for me to come back to the table. Before I could get off the floor, another gentleman swooped me up, and we danced till the next song ended. Jules was standing right behind me when this dance ended. He asked me if I'd like to go back to the table because my drink had been served. That sounded great to me, so we went back and sat down.

Most of the other people were still on the dance floor, so we had no trouble carrying on a conversation. Of course, the first topic of most conversations lately was about the note. I really had no theory about what it could be about, but Jules expanded on all the things he thought it might be. I listen politely but was ready to get back up on the dance floor. I suggested we dance. He looked a little hurt that I didn't want to sit there all night while he gave me all his ideas about what the note might mean. I really didn't want to hurt his feelings, but that gathering was the day before my death day. And while I planned to go, I really didn't care too much about what the note might mean. I was either going to be gone or dead by the next day!

We danced to the next two songs when the twentysomething man, whose name I learned was Mark, tapped Jules on the shoulder to take his place. Jules didn't look as if he liked it all that much, and I didn't like that he was already acting possessive. I suggested he go ask someone else to dance while I danced with Mark. He didn't say anything. I took Mark's hand and turned my back on Jules. I was not looking for anything but a good time, and I didn't want to make any deeper connection than that. Jules walked back to the table and sat there watching me.

Oh, dear, I thought. That look on his face didn't look very positive to me. If I had more time, a chance love affair might have been fun. But I didn't have the luxury of more time. I danced with a few other gentlemen and once with another lady. Jules didn't dance again at all. When I grew tired of dancing and looked toward the table, Jules wasn't there. I glanced around the room; it appeared he had left the bar. He probably decided to go home. I called for a car and was soon inside my home. I changed my clothes and removed all my makeup and got ready for bed. That was when I heard a persistent and loud knock upon my door.

I didn't want company this night. I was tired and wasn't inclined to listen to anyone else tonight. I peeked outside my window, and to my amazement, there stood Jules!

Oh, no! I thought. *What does he want?*

Instead of throwing open my door, I raised my window a crack and said, "Jules, it's late, and I'm tired. Can this wait till our next class?"

He looked at me sternly and commanded, "Let me in."

He was acting very strangely, and I was a little frightened.

I responded, "No, Jules, not tonight!"

I said that just as sternly as he'd commanded me to open the door. It quickly went through my mind that I never knew who might try to contact me with a task or something about my getaway. But Jules? He didn't appear to be one of those people. He said nothing that made me think that he was in any way involved with my escape. Then he started knocking again, harder and harder. He didn't say anything; he just stood there knocking and staring at me through the window.

Much to my surprise, a group of young women had been watching this exchange from across the street and came up on my porch and asked me if I needed any help.

I responded, "I don't know. Do I need help, Jules? Or will you leave me alone?"

He stopped his knocking and looked angrily at the young women who'd come to my aid. This, of course, angered the young women, and they started a mass chant for him to go away. They moved as a group closer to him and appeared quite threatening. He looked harshly at me. Then he turned and stepped off my porch. One of the young women asked me if I was okay. I responded that I was and thanked them for helping me.

After they left, I sat and thought about what in the world could be wrong with Jules that he would show up at my door and act so menacing. I so hoped that whatever this was would not interfere with my classes. I really had enjoyed tonight and didn't want some crazy person ruining it for me.

The next day, I contacted some of my other classmates. Without telling them why, I asked if I could ride to class with them.

One woman immediately answered, "Of course."

So we agreed that her car would pick me up the next night. I felt much more at ease. I considered that Jules might have had far too much to drink, and that could be why he behaved so strangely. I was willing to give him another friendly chance. But at the slightest bit of unease, I would stop him! No matter what that might entail, I wasn't going to be afraid of him and would stop him in his tracks if I had to!

The next morning, I started out for my run. I was very disappointed because again I had no stamina. I tried to walk as quickly as possible, but that soon turned into a saunter. What in hell happened to me? I was okay at dancing the night away the evening before, but now I was as weak as a kitten. My walk was a little more than a mile, but I was worn out! I wondered if, after I laid down to take a nap, I'd wake up feeling more like my strong self.

Luckily, I heard the car horn toot, or I would have forgotten to eat my breakfast. I ate as much as I could hold and lay back down in bed. I must have dozed right off because the dream came quickly. There were a half dozen people standing and staring at me again. I wished I knew what this stupid dream meant! To have it over and over again, it was surely something in my subconscious that made it come back so frequently. I lay there watching the people as they stood there watching me. They looked very solemn, and one even appeared to be in tears. They all had that look of familiarity, but I could not place a single one of them.

They faded away in a while. Then came the voices of my children hollering for me. "Mama, come back. Come back to us, Mama!" I jerked awake and found myself lying right there in my bed. What I'd heard this time seemed so real! I jumped from my bed and looked into my living room. I really expected to see four sweet happy faces because I finally came back to them. The room was empty. I felt a little dizzy. Maybe I'd jumped up too quickly, but boy, that all seemed and felt so real! Maybe I should be more concerned if I had enough time left to delve into the meaning of this dream, but I couldn't muster the energy or the curiosity to do any heavy-duty dream research.

When I looked at the clock, I was surprised to see it was early afternoon. I looked at my porch, and just as I suspected, there sat my lunch. I'd slept through the car signal again. I brought it in and went straight to the trash with it. I was not at all hungry, and looking at it made me a little nauseous. I had class tonight, and I wanted to be ready and able to feel like going. I sat down on my couch with my mensa tablet. I piddled around and thought to look on Ask Everything about dreams. Perhaps I could find some kind of interpretation of what this recurring dream could mean. I read through some of it but soon grew bored. There was just too much information. Whoever wrote this might just be guessing what things meant. Dream interpretation wasn't an exact science as far as I knew.

I played my game for a while, then got up to get ready for tonight. I hadn't realized how long I'd sat there playing, but looking at the clock, I had very little time to get ready. Not long into my grooming ministrations, I heard the car horn announcing my supper had come. I stopped what I was doing and thought to graze on it as I finished my hair and makeup. I looked a little more tired than I had last night, but I still looked pretty damn good! Again, I heard the car toot. This was my classmate with her car to pick me up. I glanced down at my plate of food. I ate very little. I was not all that hungry, though. I slipped on my shoes and looked into the mirror, noticing my clothes were becoming loose on me again.

I'll do better tomorrow, I promised myself.

My classmate Deloris looked very nice tonight too. When I climbed into the car, she looked at me with concern. "Are you feeling okay?" she asked me.

I answered, "I'm okay. I was feeling a little tired earlier, but I'm ready to boogie now!"

We both laughed at that and had a steady conversation all the way to class. I said nothing about Jules's behavior last night. I hoped that things would be back to normal tonight.

Jules was there but appeared to be ignoring me.

That's okay, I thought.

As the instructor showed us new steps, I practiced with a number of partners—none of them Jules. I was kind of curious to know what had caused his aggressive behavior last night but thought it best to leave it alone. In the second hour of class, when we attempted to put the new steps we'd learned tonight into a reasonable resemblance of dance, Jules approached me. I looked at him warily and asked if he had recovered from the prior night.

He answered me back in a monotone voice, "Yes, I feel fine. I don't want to talk about the other night."

I nodded to agree with him. I was surprised that he didn't offer me an apology for what he'd done, but none was forthcoming, so I let it drop. There was no flirting tonight. It almost felt like he was dancing with me as some sort of penance. When the dance ended, I thanked him, and without meeting my eyes, he turned and walked away. That was the only time I danced with him that night. No one suggested we go out tonight and dance. I was sort of disappointed but sort of relieved too. I didn't feel up to a night of dancing. I was content to go back home.

As the car approached my house, I thanked Deloris for fetching me. Then, on a lark, I asked her if she wanted to come in and visit for a while. She agreed with a smile, so both of us got out of the car and entered my home. She was younger than me and seemed a little surprised when she saw my house.

"Do you live all alone here?" she inquired.

"Yes, I'm a widow. All my children are grown and have moved out. When the four of them were smaller, we lived in a much bigger house."

She seemed to understand and said, "I still have my partner and our two teenage children at home. I really appreciate your inviting me. It's so nice to have a little peace and quiet."

I thought back to those days when I had teenage children. I remembered how boisterous they could be, and then there was René's drug problems, which caused both Stephen and me so much distress. Deloris asked me how my husband had died.

"He was aged out almost four years ago," I answered.

"Oh, I am so sorry!" she replied. "So many of us want to do away with this legal extermination. There are very few people I know who aren't willing to care for a parent or spouse, but that choice is taken away from us."

Then I told her I had less than six weeks left.

She looked horrified, and then she seemed angry and replied, "I would never have guessed you were old enough for this…this horror! I can't believe you are calmly taking a dancing class and not out on the run somewhere!"

"What about your parents?" I asked. "Have you had to lose them already?"

She answered back strangely, "Uhhhh, not yet." She seemed reluctant to say anything else, so we changed the subject to our classmates. We laughingly talked about poor young Mark.

"He really has two left feet, doesn't he?" she asked in mirth.

"And Caroline," I added, "she must not be able to count to four because she is always off the beat. It must be hard to lead her. I saw Andy tonight trying to count the beat in her ear: 'Step, quick, quick step.'"

We almost rolled on the floor laughing about poor, sweet Caroline.

Then Deloris started talking about Jules. "I thought you two were going to be an item after the other night, but you didn't dance together at all tonight, did you?"

I felt uncomfortable talking about Jules, but I replied, "We did have a dance, but we were never going to be an item. I don't have enough time left to be an item with anyone."

I shouldn't have said this because she looked very solemn and troubled. "I'm so sorry, Naia," she said.

Now she looked really uncomfortable, and I quickly offered her a glass of my really tasty wine. She declined my offer and said she really needed to get on home. I told her I hoped we could do this again sometime; she nodded, hugged me, and left.

Note to self: Don't tell anyone else who doesn't need to know that I have little time left. It really puts a damper on the conversation.

The next morning, I did get up and made myself walk. I ate all my breakfast, and while sitting in the living room, I heard a ping on my computer. I hadn't had anything from the government in many weeks now, so I thought it might be from them. I walked into the bedroom, where my big computer was, and was shaken to see it was an email from Jules. I opened it and was surprised to see it was an invitation to dinner for tonight! I sat for a while, thinking about whether to accept or not. I didn't want to upset him again, but I didn't want to be exposed and perhaps be in danger from him again. I wrote back to him, thanking him for the invitation but saying that I could not see him tonight. I hesitated for just a second before I pressed Send. Thankfully, I heard nothing else from him. I started to become a little angry. I should not have to feel leery and fearful about attending a dance class! That damned Jules better not ruin this for me!

The weekend went by slowly. Except for the extraordinary amount of people on the street, I saw no one I recognized. I wished I had the courage to just walk around out on the street at night, talking and laughing with random strangers. I'd never seen anything like this before. All my life, I'd been taught that strangers had one purpose, and that was to hurt me! I wished I was young enough to be part of this new friendliness, but I was still too afraid. I remembered the torture those two young girls had put me through, and I never wanted to take that chance again.

Monday was dance class again, and I wished I was looking more forward to it than I was. Jules had made me afraid, and fun and fear were not very compatible. I didn't take nearly as much time on my appearance as I had in the past. I applied a minimum of makeup and pulled my hair up into a bun. Looking at myself in the mirror, I was always stunned when I saw myself looking so old!

I managed to eat most of my supper, and it wasn't long after that when I heard the toot of the horn from the car I'd ordered. I came out, forgetting to look around, but all the people on the street gave me a sense of security. I could get used to that! I climbed into the car and arrived a little early for the class. I could see others hanging around and waiting for the auditorium door to be unlocked, and one of them was Jules. I didn't try to attract any attention to myself, which was really out of character for me. I stood alone in the back of the group and listened enviously as they talked so easily among themselves. I reached down as if to scratch my ankle, just to reassure myself that I had remembered to bring my gun. I felt the outline of it and hoped I'd never have to use it again.

When the door clicked open, I greeted the instructor and said hello to both Deloris and Mark. I didn't see Jules anywhere. Maybe I could relax and enjoy the class. We were about ten minutes into to class when Jules came rushing in. He apologized for being late and asked what he'd missed. She quickly brought him up to speed. When it was time for us to practice with a partner, Jules was immediately in my face.

"Hello, Jules," I tried to say pleasantly, but he said nothing in return and still appeared to be angry with me.

We successfully learned that step and waited uncomfortably to be taught the next one. In the second hour, he claimed my first dance. I didn't want to start anything, but he was making dance class miserable for me.

Finally, I said to him, "I want to talk to you."

At this, he said, "Fine, let's go outside."

I quickly responded, "Oh no, what I want to say can be said right here."

"I don't want to talk to you in front of all these people," he responded angrily.

I replied back just as angrily, "You have made me so uncomfortable and anxious that I will only consider talking to you surrounded by other people! I want you to leave me alone! Dance with other people. Don't ask me again! If you do, I will loudly reject the invitation. Do you understand me? Leave me alone, and I'll do the same with you. You bother me again, and I will make you extremely sorry you did!"

He looked at me in amazement, then said "Bitch!" under his breath and turned and walked away from me.

I chided myself that I'd better be willing to do just what I'd threatened if he approached me aggressively again. I comforted myself that Jules could end up with Charlie if he wasn't very careful!

The next week went better. I attended my classes, and then I came home. There was no more socializing after class, and I felt the loss of that. I began to get very depressed again. By the following week, I didn't want to go back to class. What had seemed so much fun at first now seemed more work than it was worth.

After I missed the first class, a few of my classmates, including Deloris, messaged me to check on me. I wrote a group email and told them all that I was fine but that the dance class was too rigorous for me. I didn't know if any of them believed this, but that was all they were going to get from me. Soon, no one contacted me anymore.

On the next weekend would be my seventieth birthday. I'd heard nothing more from the government, nor have I heard nothing from anyone about any kind of plan for my rescue or much of anything else.

I brightened considerably when my children contacted me and told me they were coming for my birthday. Emmy asked if she could spend the month of June with me. I was very surprised by this, but I told her I'd love nothing better. I thought all my living children would be here on June 29 if I was still here. I felt so happy that I had this last chance to really reconnect with Emmy. I laughed out loud when Emmy asked if she could bring her great big dog, Porter, with her.

"Yes, of course!" I replied. "That would be wonderful!"

Chapter 62

May 29, 2526

The day of my birthday dawned rainy and gray. I knew the rain was good to relieve the drought that my quadrant had been experiencing, but it was not at all cheerful. My children would be arriving separately, and I was a little nervous about the three of them being here together. There was a lot of bad blood between all of them, and it hurt my heart that it took my last birthday for all of us to be together again.

Jack, of course, would be absent. He was my baby, and his not being here would be sad. But I should be grateful that they'd all agreed to be here with me while I was still alive. I never thought that would be possible, but we were all gathering here today!

René was the first to arrive. She brought me wine even though she couldn't drink any. That was as good a gift as she could give me under the circumstances. She didn't bring her wife, Amber, with her. It was silently assumed that my birthday would be only for me and my children. Arvin arrived next, and it had been so long since I'd seen him that I was not sure I would recognize him out on the street! I'd only met his couple partner, Natalie, once. He lived quite a distance away, and I rarely heard from him. I got the occasional email, but that was about it.

I hugged him tight, and he whispered, "I love you, Mama."

That brought tears to my eyes because he never said it very often. He was quiet and much more like his dad than any of my other children. He looked more like me—dark hair and skin—but he had Stephen's blue eyes and certainly his temperament.

The three of us sat down and managed to have a nice conversation. So far, there were no awkward silences, and I was looking forward but also worried about when Emmy arrived. She hadn't spoken to her sister and brother in such a long time. When Jack died, the only one who had acknowledged it at all was a note that René sent me. I hadn't heard a single word from the other two.

Over the years, this caused me much sorrow that my children seemed to be enemies and were very estranged from me. I didn't know what happened to the family I raised, but I must have done something very wrong for them to feel this way about one another and me. I had gotten quite numb in the last few years about the behavior of my children. I couldn't fix it, it was heartbreaking to try, and I finally accepted that I didn't really know these adults at all. But right now, so far, so good.

Late in the afternoon, Emmy arrived with Porter. Porter was a godsend! We all formed a bond around having great big Porter right there in our faces. He was almost too big to fit in my small living room, but we scooted everything around enough so that he could lie down if he wanted to. We laughed at his antics and the stories Emmy told about him. It was so unusual to have a pet anymore, and one that took up as much space as Porter did was almost unheard of!

I had ordered a literal feast to be delivered later on that night. By the time the food arrived, Emmy, Arvin, and I had consumed at least three bottles of wine and were giddy, getting reacquainted. Everything was funny and silly! We didn't address any issues this night, and frankly, I didn't want to resolve anything. I wanted no anger and stress. If they wanted to, they could sort everything out when I was no longer around. I'd cried over the three of them for so many years. I was through with tears. I thought they all showed so much love to me by their restraint. Whether what was going on here was real or not, I was finally getting to enjoy the adult version of my children—something I never thought would happen.

Emmy and Porter shared my bedroom, while Arvin took the couch and René the guest cot. It was not the wildest birthday I'd ever had, but I thought it just might have been the sweetest. I only wished Stephen had lived to see this. They didn't all gather for his last birthday. I felt pretty sure they all regretted that.

Emmy and I curled up together, with Porter taking up the remaining space on the floor. I slept so soundly and well, more so than in a very long time. There were no dreams, no knocks on the door, just me with my three babies under the same roof! If Jack were here, it would have been perfect, but this was such a phenomenon for those of us left to be in the same space that all I could feel was gratefulness for the people here now.

We all woke up around midmorning. I didn't even attempt to take my walk this morning. I didn't want to miss a single moment of what was going on here. I'd ordered every kind of breakfast food I could think of, plus mimosas and Bloody Marys. We feasted and drank the morning away. I knew that Arvin and René had to go back later on this afternoon, and it all seemed we were trying to get in every ounce of all the happiness of being back together again.

Around three, both Arvin and René were leaving. Both promised to be right here by my side on June 29 and stay until I was gone. I hoped the next thirty days would drag by because it felt like I had a lifetime of things I still wanted to do. I don't know why I hadn't been able to think of these things in the past few months while I still had the chance. It is so strange that I can think of many things now that it's too late to do them.

Emmy and I were getting along very well. We were both trying very hard to keep the hurtful feelings at bay. There were a million things that we probably should talk about, but time was too precious to bring up anything painful. While I was still afraid to go out into the world after the sunset without being safely in a car, Emmy had no fear at all. Most nights, after dinner, she would insist that we go out and get involved in something interesting. We always had Porter with us, and that alone made me feel safer. He lumbered along behind Emmy no matter where she went. He was so sweet, but I knew he'd become a killer if anyone threatened Emmy. I enjoyed exploring this new community that seemed to be growing around us.

I questioned Em about it, and she said, "Mama, this is how it was always meant to be. It's too bad that it took the murders of so many government officials and this strange note to bring us together, but it is a new day! The people will only grow stronger together! The people are going to take back the country and make it great again!" she exclaimed.

I certainly didn't know what it would take to make the country great again because I'd never known it any other way but the way it was now. The law of the land had been the same for many centuries, so I didn't know how these young people—whom I'd assumed were lazy and uncaring—had any kind of vision for it to change. I did sit and listen in on many conversations, and I was amazed at the opinions that these young people were spouting and the dreams they had. I didn't know where these radical new ideas were coming from because I'd never been exposed to any talk like this, ever! Emmy held her own and came up with many exciting thoughts as I listened. I was so proud of her. She was warmly received and respected by the small groups she spoke to.

I was always very wary about walking home late at night. But the streets were always full, and I had fearless Emmy and Porter by my side. My death was scheduled for less than three weeks away, and yet I was very calm. I was no longer scared of dying. I had pretty much given up on any plan for escape, and it really didn't worry me so much anymore. If I got away, that would be great. If not, I was having the best month of my life anyway! I couldn't remember the last time I'd felt so content.

Emmy was constantly reminding me to eat. I put on a pretty good show of eating, but I had no appetite at all anymore. My clothes were once again hanging off me, but at this point, that just made them that much more comfortable.

As much as I was enjoying this time, I did feel as if I was getting weaker. I made no attempt at walking anymore. After about two weeks, I quit walking to town with Emmy in the evenings. She reluctantly followed her own path with my blessings and encouragement. I wanted her last memories of me to be good ones and not a vigil for the dying. I'd been sleeping a lot, but so far, I'd had no more disturbing dreams. It seemed that these last few weeks were going so much better than I could have imagined. Emmy and Porter had moved to

AGED OUT

the guest space after her siblings had gone. I was sleeping so soundly I was surprised when, late one night, there was a short staccato knock on the door.

What surprised me even more was that the knock did not wake Emmy or rouse Porter. I peeked out my window and was surprised to see LaToyia there! I'd completely forgotten she'd promised to be back to finalize the plans for my safe departure. I quietly opened the front door to allow her in. I motioned for her to follow me into the bedroom so Emmy and Porter would not be disturbed. It was here that she told me that plans had changed. I was to have a much larger part in this task than I would have thought possible.

On June 28, during the gathering, I was to speak to the crowd!

I protested immediately that I was not a public speaker and that I couldn't do it! I had no idea what was going on, and I would not know what to say. She smiled at me and told me I'd know what to say when the time was right.

"Are you crazy?" I asked in the very loudest whisper I had. "I don't know what the gathering is all about. Why would I know what to say?"

She looked at me sweetly and said, "I promise you that you will know exactly what to say when it's time."

Then she got up from the side of my bed and made way to leave. I didn't want her to leave me yet. I was terrified of what she thought I could do. As she walked to the front door, I asked her if I was to get any kind of script or talking points to prepare.

She answered, "No, you will be just fine with what is in your heart."

I still was so confused, but she walked out the door, closing it behind her. I had nothing particular in my heart that was worth the notion that anyone would listen to me.

This is absolutely ridiculous! I thought to myself. I stood there about five minutes longer, my mouth hanging open in shock.

I *really* had my mouth hanging wide open in puzzlement! I finally came to myself enough to move. I tiptoed into the guest space to check on Emmy. When I peeked in, Porter raised his huge big head, and his tail banged back and forth on the floor. I reached down to pet him and remembered all the times I looked in on Emmy when she was a little girl. I remember when her thumb was ever present in her mouth, one of her stuffed animals tightly hugged in the other arm. We missed out on so much with each other all these years, and it made me very sad to think about the relationship we might have had. I walked back to my room and found sleep impossible to come by for the rest of the night.

The next morning, Emmy was up bright and early. She asked me if I wanted to walk into town for breakfast. I told her I had a few other things to do and to go on without me. I was feeling tortured about what LaToyia told me about speaking before the crowd on June 28. If she'd given me something to read to the gathering, I would feel so much better about this. I knew people were expecting something truly historic or mind-blowing to happen at this event, and they were going to be very disappointed if all that happened was me trying to fumble my way through a speech. I had nothing to say to anyone but to tell them that June 28 was the day before I would die. I might garner a little sympathy, but I felt as if the crowd would expect much more than that.

I sat down at my computer and attempted to write something, but after a sentence or two, I realized I had nothing to say. Being put into this situation was horrible! Since I had the day before me with little to do, I decided to contact all the people that I'd grown close to this past year. My first attempt was to reach Bog DigDo Miller. We'd been in touch a few times since he'd gone to India. He and his new wife seemed very happy, and they would be parents by the end of the year.

I wrote, "Dear Bog, this may be our last correspondence. As well you know my aged out day was June 29. I wanted to let you know again that I treasure the time we spent together. We had so many heartfelt talks, discussed many books, and occasionally danced the night away! I am so happy that things are going well for you, and I know you will be a wonderful papa. I have nothing but the most loving memories of my time spent with you. Have a very happy life!"

I felt the tears on my face as I wrote. This seemed really trite to me, but then again, I was no poet or author. That thought again made me very anxious about what in the world I would say to a group of people who were probably expecting flashing lights and fireworks.

I had to leave the computer for a while to recompose myself. When I returned, I wrote to Jody at the inn. We hadn't interacted in the same way that Bog and I had, but we had grown to love each other. I never could understand why she'd told me I had to leave there so suddenly. Then I remembered that if I hadn't left at that very moment, I might have not had that tremendous urge to go to the desert. I might not have magically found Emmy again! It was almost as if she knew what was in store for me and didn't want me to miss it.

After writing to a few more people, I stopped and thought about all the experiences I'd had over the last year. I was astounded by the love, the trauma, the kindness, the hatred, and the intrigue I'd experienced in the past twelve months! I had a story right here in my own life. I didn't know if anyone else would want to share it, but I wanted people to know!

From that moment on, I started writing as of the occasion of my sixty-ninth birthday. I wrote about my hope for my life to be spared and the odd things I did that I thought might help me save myself. I wrote about jumping out of the airplane and my desire to learn Chinese. I wrote about my experience at the class party and how I woke up in the bathroom the following day, all alone. I wrote about pregnant Robin being here and all I'd experienced after following the lead of a few cryptic notes Robin had left behind.

I wrote about all my experiences at 1953 Pearl Street, from my first visit at the big white house with the amazing gardens and people enjoying themselves on the back terrace and me being unable to get their attention to let me in. I wrote about the horror and gore that Wilda and I had seen when we went by ourselves. I wrote about my time in detention somewhere in a prison after being picked up at the Pharma Depository and my miraculous and absurdly easy escape from confinement.

I wrote of going to the Pearl Street address and seeing that it was clean and whole and meeting with Simon and José there. I told of knowing where a secret tunnel was because I'd had a dream about Robin taking me there. I wrote of Simon's anger when I knew how to open the hidden door to the tunnel that he insisted he knew nothing about. I remembered the promise that José had made to me about letting me know when Simon was certain it was safe. I felt it was so important that I find out what was at the end of the tunnel. I returned again, only to be told that the house I'd been to multiple times no longer existed! I wrote about meeting George and him telling me about an underground laboratory that had belonged to Simon's father, Kentura Bing. I repeated what he'd told me about a big explosion where supposedly Kentura Bing had been killed. But no physical evidence had ever been found to prove that he'd died there.

I wrote about the night I ran after Jesse and returned home to the two girls who had beaten me and almost killed me till Jesse returned and killed them. I told of the plan I was involved in to kill government officials. I told about being sent to scout out the patterns of these people so their assassins could easily anticipate where to kill them. I told them I had not had the stomach to kill all three people on my own list and had invoked the wrath of Charlie, whom I ended up killing by myself and whose body I disposed of.

Then I wrote of the strange things that had happened to me and that I sometimes doubted my sanity. I told of my absentmindedness and how food no longer had any appeal for me. I wrote about all the things I used to keep so hidden in fear that the government would find out I was trying to escape my Aged Out date. I wrote how now, for some reason, I had no fear of that anymore. They had plenty on me if they wanted to prosecute me, but no one had ever come to arrest me.

I wrote of that magic note left on all the doors of all the inhabitants of every town in the country. I told of my amazement that such a short missive that really said nothing much at all had stirred things up so much. People were leaving their homes—not to fight, rape, or steal, but to talk to each other, to offer their own opinions that other people were at least willing to listen to. I spoke about how this amity had yet to end, and now it seemed people were coming out just to enjoy one another.

I wrote of the excitement of watching a young man playing a guitar and singing out in the public square! He wasn't arrested for showing his talent, and when he finished, people clapped and hollered for more. They didn't seem angry that he had a gift they didn't have. They enjoyed what he could do. This made me wonder if more artists and talented individuals might start publicly showing their own gifts and talents too.

The real kicker would be if anyone wanted to buy someone else's work. That was so illegal that anyone should profit from their own hand. It was hard to imagine but not nearly as impossible to imagine as it was six months ago. If no one was arrested doing this, what an impact this would have on everyone! Everyone might want to earn something from their talents. People might be so interested that they might start working for talented people to earn, learn, and get out of the house!

It seemed that I remembered somewhere back in ancient history that this was what this country did. All of us who'd lived by the government's care imagined this to be horrible, but maybe it hadn't been horrible at all! Could there have been people from long ago who actually enjoyed working?

I felt like what I was expressing here was really science fiction, but with new attitudes and enough time passing that the government could be trusted not to arrest and interfere with this free enterprise, it might become something of a trend. I just wouldn't be here to see it.

By the time I'd recorded all my thoughts, I was exhausted. I almost considered letting all my words remain on my hard drive, but then I thought of what might happen if my computer fell into the wrong hands. I'd used real names here, and it could be fatal if any of this were ever found. With a long sigh, I highlighted everything I'd written and then pushed the delete button. All the things I'd thought or experienced in the last year of my life would remain safely in my memory.

I was still apprehensive about what I was supposed to say to the crowd on the 28th, but looking back over this past year, maybe I'd have another miracle. And as LaToyia said, it would all come to me, and it would be the right thing to say.

The next week flew by. Emmy and I went out for dinner many times. Sometimes I'd order in whatever she was in the mood for, and we'd talk until the wee hours of the morning about nothing in particular and then about everything. We laughed, and we cried, but we enjoyed each other's company so much. Gone were those days when we found so much wrong with each other. We were still entirely different, but the most important thing was that we were mother and daughter. I guessed we'd finally grown up enough to appreciate the differences.

It was now June 22. I had one week left. Emmy had asked me several times if there was anything I wanted to do in the time I had left. She suggested we take a short trip to someplace I'd always wanted to see or do something I'd always wanted to do. I explained I had already seen what I wanted and couldn't think of anything I wanted to do that I hadn't already done. She smiled and looked at me, and I could imagine all the things she'd want to do when her time came. I was content with everything now, and I imagined Emmy would never be content until she had completed every sight and sound and adventure she could imagine. But then again, that was Emmy, not me. We were different. Now we could love the difference.

When my children were here on my birthday, I had them look at the few possessions I had to see if there was anything they might want. Just as I guessed, they all took some little token to remember me by, and everything else was to be junked. The trash truck was due on the morning of the 27th, and all the reminders of my life would be taken and evaporated. I had already gotten rid of almost everything myself, all except the furniture and appliances, which technically belonged to the government. Everything here was so old and outdated. I didn't imagine they'd leave much. I knew that there were plans for putting in a new floor. I wondered what else they might change and who would be spending the last years of their lives right here under this small roof.

I had a thought. Perhaps I could hide a small memento someplace in the house. I would find a spot where it would not be apparent that something was there, and maybe who moved in next might never find it. But I'd go to my ashes knowing it was there. I tried to think of something profound, but nothing came to me. In the end, I took Wilda's Bible and put it in the attic under the loose board.

Michelle had said she had no use for it and would burn it, but I would find a better resting place for it. Before I went up the steep stairs to place it there, I wrote a short piece about the woman who'd owned it and what a beautiful person she'd been. I professed how honored I'd been to be her friend. Then I signed and dated it. I lovingly wrapped it in a towel and carried it upstairs. I lay it gently between the rafters and replaced the board on top of it. Now I felt like I'd completed my last gift to this home. I was ready to let it go. I felt so content and serene, and I continued to stay that way until the thought of that speech at the gathering entered my mind. I had a moment of panic, but then it subsided, and I forgot about it—until it popped up to frighten me again. It was an endless cycle.

All my children were planning on coming here on the 28th and spending my last hours with me. Most of the furniture would have been taken by then, but I doubted if we'd try to do much sleeping anyway. I'd ask to keep my bed and my couch; they could take everything else. They could get the rest after this was no longer my home. I'd ordered a lot of different foods and drinks for my last night. I wanted it to be more like a party than a dirge.

By the time Emmy returned home, I was exhausted. She looked concerned about me because I looked and felt so tired. When she expressed it, I tried to console her that if I was going to be aged out anyway, it was time for me to be worn out. She still looked troubled, but there was little either of us could do about it. She made me eat some supper, and then I excused myself and went straight to bed.

Right before I fell asleep I said, "Thank you, Jesus God." I'd been doing that for a few weeks now, and strangely it made me happy just to say the words.

I woke up early because the trash truck was due today. I couldn't imagine they'd send a very big one. My house was tiny, and the street was so narrow. A large truck would not fit between me and the house across the street. Emmy got up early, too, to sit and wait with me. We had some tea and some really sweet and gooey pastries. I didn't have to worry about weight gain anymore, so I ate as many as my shrunken stomach could hold. Finally, we heard the creak of the brakes from the truck. Soon, my lifetime of memories in this home would be gone. I looked around at what remained one last time, and then I opened the door.

There were two young men who said nothing. I told them not to take my bed or my couch, and they left them both. One of them tried to flirt a bit with Emmy, but she was having none of that. He quickly got the message. It didn't take them long to get everything. I had to sign an inventory list, and then my lifetime of stuff was gone. I felt my eyes welling a little bit, and Emmy saw it too.

"Here, Mama, let's go out for a while, maybe get a sandwich and take it to the park for a picnic," she suggested.

I had not been to the park in a while, so I was more than agreeable to go. Since I didn't feel up to all the walking, we ordered a car. First, we stopped at a little stand and spoke into a microphone to tell the robot chef what we'd like on our sandwiches. It took less than a minute for them to drop down into the food shoot. We picked them up, climbed back into the car, and headed to the park.

I had a special place where I wanted to eat, and Emmy followed me as I found my way there. Thankfully, the bench beside where I wanted to eat was empty. It was June now, and the days were getting very warm. This bench sat under a tree, so luckily we were in the shade. We opened our sandwiches and drinks and companionably sat there, quietly eating our lunch.

Finally I said, "That flowerbed right over there, the one that's full of weeds, that was the one that Wilda took care of for years and years. The last time I was here, it was full of the most beautiful flowers and not a weed in sight. Look how quickly things disappear when they are not taken care of."

We sat there for almost an hour, not talking, only thinking our own thoughts. I remembered coming here and helping Wilda pull weeds and then plant flowers. She was here almost every day; me, not nearly so much. Almost in harmony, Emmy and I looked at each other and decided it was time to go. As with many places these past few days, I stood there a moment, giving tribute to a place I'd never see again. With a deep sigh, I turned, and we got in the car to return home. Feeling a wee bit melancholy, I lay down to take a nap. I had to mentally and physically prepare myself for tomorrow so I'd be at my utmost peak when I needed to speak. Emmy didn't know that I was to do this, and I thought it best not to frighten or more likely embarrass her with what I'd been called upon to do.

I didn't need anyone telling me not to do it. I was scared enough already.

Chapter 63

June 28, 2526

The next day dawned sunny and quite warm. I put on my next-to-best black and grays and sat down, trying to make inspiration come to me before it was time to go. Nothing came. I hoped I would not stand up there and make a fool of myself, not on my next-to-last day. I didn't want everyone to think I was some batty old woman babbling nonsense because I was senile. I really did want to leave this earth with at least a smidgen of dignity left intact. But I supposed that it was what it would be. Worrying about it would not make it any easier. I sat still and tried not to think at all. I was pretty good at blank, empty mindlessness.

The street had been busy all morning. I was glad the trash truck had come and gone yesterday. It wouldn't have been able to get down the street if they'd come today for all the people walking toward the town square. By 10:00 a.m., the street was completely blocked by people headed for whatever the day held for them. I felt like Emmy and I needed to get started that way, too, or the town square would back up all the way to my front door!

When I expressed my need to leave, Emmy said, "Why so early, Mama? You know what this is likely to be—some old government action to put us all in our place. I'm in no hurry to hear about some new law or punishment. I don't really care if we go at all. We'll hear all about it before the day is out."

"No," I protested. "I need to get there soon. I want to be right down in the front so that I can hear all that is being said."

"Mama, no, you don't," Emmy said. "If there is going to be any trouble, that is the most likely place it will occur! We need to stay far back!"

"Honey," I said, "I'm leaving right now. You can certainly choose the time when you want to go or if you want to stay home, but I'm going right now!"

This was the closest thing to a disagreement that Emmy and I had had up to this point. I could see some of that Emmy fire come up in her eyes. But just as quickly as it was there, it was gone.

She nodded. "Okay, Mama, we'll go now."

I opened the door, and we pushed our way into the crush that was headed downtown. We tried to hold hands so we wouldn't be separated, but the push and pull of all the people soon ended that. I was ahead of her.

I heard her yell, "I'll meet you back home when it's over!"

It didn't take long for the crowd to come to a standstill. I didn't know that there were this many people in the entire town! I could not get stuck way back here on a side road; I needed to get to the front! I had about an hour before the event was to start to worm and push my way through the throngs of people. If I saw the slightest space, I'd push myself into it. After about forty-five minutes, I could at least see the town square. I felt almost suffocated trying to jam my way into every tiny space I could push my way into. Ahead of me, I saw several people starting to faint from the heat and close quarters. I hoped I would not join them on the ground, but when someone went down, I moved up. By the time there were only about five people ahead of me, I took to the ground and crawled. I got stepped on a few times and might even have broken a finger, but I was almost there.

Finally, a man looked down and saw me. "Here, lady," he said. "Get up off the ground!" He reached down and pulled me up by the arm. "Here, stand in front of me. You're so short I can see over you."

I was now standing directly in the center on the front row! I'd made it!

It seemed we stood there for a long time, and nothing was happening. People began to grow restless, and an attitude came over the crowd that I'd hoped I'd never see again. People were getting angry! They were starting to yell and curse about being here in the heat and nothing happening!

It was about now that the big doors of the government building started to open. The crowd immediately started to calm down, and soon there was no noise at all. The vice mayor came out of the building and stood at a small podium with a microphone. A small platform had been built so everyone could see him. No one made a sound.

Then he began to laugh! A few people nervously started to laugh along with him for a few seconds, then stopped when they realized there was nothing to laugh about.

After his laughter stopped, he cleared his throat and began to speak. "What did you all think was going to happen here today? All of you are stupid fools! How many times did we tell you this was a hoax? But no, you would not listen to your most benevolent government! Haven't we always done what was best for you? Haven't we always taken care of you? Why have you come here? Nothing is going to happen here! Go back to your homes and vow never to be so stupid and foolish again! You all are ridiculous!"

With that, he turned his back on the crowd to return inside to his plush office. For a second, everyone seemed to have no breath at all. We were in such disbelief.

Then the yelling and cursing started again.

"Why were we brought here?"

"Who has pulled such a nasty joke on the whole country?"

The first punch was thrown and chaos broke out.

The only thing I could think of was that this must be my moment! It was time for me to make the most important speech of my life. I climbed up onto that platform with the microphone at its highest level, and I started to speak.

"Stop it! Stop it, everyone! We will not return to the days before we all received this note! We will not!" I guessed that the sight of a little old woman screaming into the microphone was enough to get their attention for the moment. But I really needed to follow up with something that would inspire them, something they would listen to.

"From the day this note was delivered to our doors, we've all been so curious about what it meant. Have you not seen the monumental change in the last few weeks since it arrived? Before we got this note, when was the last time you felt safe enough to go out into the streets and have conversations with one another? When was the last time differing opinions did not start a fight? When was the last time, before the note, that you heard laughter in the street? When was the last time a neighbor felt comfortable talking to another neighbor?"

They were all listening now. No one had tried to stop me or yelled at me to shut up! It was coming to me! My fears had been for naught. Everything I needed to say was coming right out of my mouth!

"We will not go back to the way it was before. We *must never* go back to the way it was before! I don't want to be scared every time I leave my home. I don't want to be afraid of being attacked and my neighbors ignoring my pleas for help. I want to be able to go out and enjoy myself. I'd like someone who can sing being able to sing to me out in public. I don't want to be afraid of my government for not thinking and doing every tiny thing they demand. I don't want to be chipped, I don't want to be spied on, and I don't want to be told when and if I can have a baby and at what age I must die! We have to take this country back! Tomorrow I am being aged out, and it is too late for me. But if we make our own decisions about our lives, no one can tell us when we've lived long enough or if it's okay to share our talents or bear children. NO MORE!"

The crowd started to get somewhat restless again. I could not understand this until I felt his meaty hand upon my shoulder. The vice mayor had come back out and was trying to speak again! He pushed me away, and I almost fell down to the concrete below. This didn't seem to sit well with the crowd. They started to push toward the stage. I was not going to let this jackass take this crowd away from me. I climbed back up on the podium and pushed myself in front of the mayor.

At that second, a huge explosion thundered! I felt a searing pain and a tremendous jolt, felt myself falling, and then everything went black.

It was wildly speculated that I had saved the vice mayor's life by stepping in front of him at the exact moment when an assassin's bullet was aimed straight toward his heart.

Chapter 64

June 29, 2526, 8:00 a.m.

I was trying so hard to find the light again when I realized I was back in my own bed! Had I hallucinated all of this afternoon? I was not hallucinating again, I realized. I was right back home in my own bed. I must be dreaming that same old dream again. I could see all these people standing here, looking at me. They were coming into much clearer focus than they'd ever appeared before.

Oh my god! I could not believe what I was seeing. All my children were there, standing over me! Emmy, René, and Arvin were all there, surrounding my bed! A person behind René came into clearer focus. It was Bog Digdo Miller! Standing beside him was Jody from the inn! I could hear them speaking among themselves.

One said, "Poor Mama. This illness has been so terrible for her. The past few months, I thought many times we were going to lose her. Thank God that Aged Out Law was passed last year, or this could have lasted for many more years."

Another said, "It would have been a lot better if she hadn't had to go through this."

Then I heard "But there were times I thought she was getting better!"

A voice said, "Sometimes she'd call out one of our names. Then sometimes she'd curse at whatever she was seeing in her head."

The first one said, "Look at her poor body. She is nothing but skin and bones."

The last said, "I don't want to lose my mama, but she has suffered enough. Let's get her out of this hell of her own mind."

Emmy turned and said through her tears, "Dr. Bing, I guess we are as ready as we will ever be."

Everyone started to weep. What was going on here?

"I'm waking up! I can see all of you!" I tried to yell to them, but my voice made no noise.

One by one, everyone in the room came to kiss my cheek. Emmy broke down and started to sob! I could feel her tears wetting my cheek.

"Honey, I'm all right!" I wanted to reassure her, but my words could not be heard.

When she pulled back, Simon Bing came to my side and patted my arm. He had a large hypodermic in his hand.

"I'll do it," said Arvin. "I've started a lot of IVs. It will be the last thing I can ever do for my mama."

I felt the pinch in the crook of my elbow. He taped my arm to a hard board. I could tell from the slight tug on the line that he was hooking it up to something else. I felt the heat of the fluid as it started to circulate throughout my body. It didn't hurt, but I lay there puzzled for a second or two.

Then everything started to get dark again.

Chapter 65

When I woke the second time, Robin was there.

She said, "Come on Naia! We must hurry."

I quickly got up. She grabbed my hand, and we started out into the night. She had my jet pack, and she strapped it on me. She hurriedly programmed it and quickly donned one of her own.

"Come on, we don't have much time!"

We took off into the night air. It felt wonderful to be flying. It was so much cooler during the evening! My hair was blowing back behind my head. The wind was luscious. I realized I didn't have oxygen buds in my nose. When I whispered to Robin about it, she promised I didn't need them. I thought this strange because we were very high into the night sky. I felt if I reached just a little higher, I could touch a star!

We flew for about fifteen minutes, and then she motioned for me to land. I knew where we were the moment we touched ground. We were at 1953 Pearl Street in front of the big white house with the beautiful gardens! This time when she knocked on the door, it was answered immediately.

"Ma'am," said a very stately-looking older gentleman, "my name is Kentura Bing, and I'm so glad you're here. We've been waiting for you for a long time. But we must hurry!"

I watched as he moved that now-familiar fish-shaped corbel next to his bookshelf. A door opened into the tunnel. The tunnel wasn't as dark as it had been before when Robin had brought me here. As soon as Robin and I were in, Kentura Bing followed along behind us, closing the door behind him.

That was when we started running! I was surprised I was doing so well. As weak as I'd felt lately, I was really making headway and still had plenty of air! Suddenly, the world shook as a loud boom went off somewhere behind us! I started to stop and look back, but Robin hurried me on. We ran and ran. I didn't need to stop at all! Way off in the distance, I began to see the darkness starting to fade.

"Is that a light up there?" I asked excitedly. "Are we about to get to your laboratory?"

I could imagine that whatever the doctor had been working on all these years had been successful. This was my way to my new life! I couldn't wait to see what he'd invented that would save me.

Finally, at the end of the tunnel, we ran out into the bright sunlight. We'd arrived at a lovely, verdant garden. There were flowers and trees, and it was the loveliest sight I'd ever seen! There was every color imaginable! The rays of the sun were just warm enough as the breeze brushed my face. There were a lot of people milling about, talking and softly laughing with one another. I stood silently for a moment to try to take it all in.

Robin said, "You're safe now, Naia. You have earned your peace."

I looked at her in amazement and then realized where I was. I was on the other side of the fence where I'd begged to be let in once before. I was on the inside now! I stood there in wonder and delight.

Then the crowd parted, and a familiar-looking man came into view.

"Sweetie, I've been waiting for you! You always were running late."

It was Stephen! He was teasing me the way he always had. I ran into his arms! He held me so tightly I finally feel truly safe!

Stephen said, "Look who's with me, Naia."

A very handsome young man approached. "Mama, it's me—Jack!" he said.

I couldn't believe it. I had my baby back! He hadn't died after all. Someone had gotten to him and saved him just as they had me! I held him in my arms for a very long time. Then we stood back and looked at each other. He looked wonderful! He looked happy! This was the best day of my life!

Then he stepped aside, and there stood Robin. She had the sweetest little baby in her arms!

"Mama, this is your grandson, Matthew," he told me. I had been unable to speak until now.

"Oh," I said, "he is so beautiful. He appears to be an angel!"

As I looked around, I was in awe! Wilda, Sally, and Lynn were there, frantically waving at me! I was so grateful that we'd all managed to get to Dr. Bing's incredible invention and be saved! I never thought I'd see all the people that I loved ever again. Both Jack and Robin smiled.

Then Robin spoke, "Come on over here, Naia. Come over here, where you can rest."

I took her hand and crossed over to my family...

Chapter 66

June 29, 2135, 8:15 a.m.

"Let's give her one last kiss and let her go," said René. "Then I'll cover her up so she will never be cold again…"

"Goodbye, dear Mama. We love you." These words were repeated three times by three different voices. Everything was so peaceful and calm.

After one last look, René pulled the sheet up over the face of the woman who'd been their mother. Everyone was quiet as they left the room.

Final Chapter

She needed a hero, so that was what she became

Naia's assassination changed the course of history and started a grassroots revolution. Naia's words to those who gathered in response to an anonymous note were echoed among the throngs of people. Soon, those words reverberated across the entire country:

> We will not return to the days before we all received this note! We will not! From the day that the note was delivered to our doors, we've all been so curious about what it meant. Have you not seen the monumental change in the last few weeks since it arrived? Before we got this note, when was the last time you felt safe enough to go out into the streets and have conversations with one another? When was the last time differing opinions did not start a fight? When was the last time, before the note, that you heard laughter in the street? When was the last time a neighbor felt comfortable talking to their neighbor?
>
> We will not go back to the way it was before. We must *never* go back to the way it was before! I don't want to be scared every time I leave my home. I don't want to be afraid of being attacked

and my neighbors ignoring my pleas for help. I want to be able to go out and enjoy myself. I'd like someone who can sing being able to sing to me out in public. I don't want to be afraid of my government for not thinking and doing every tiny thing they demand. I don't want to be chipped, I don't want to be spied on, and I don't want to be told when and if I can have a baby and at what age I must die!

We have to take this country back! If we make our own decisions about our lives, no one can tell us when we've lived long enough or if it's okay to share our talents or bear children. No MORE!

Those words became the rallying cry for a nation in revolt of its leaders and their attempts to cling to power. Over a period of months, the people ousted government officials across the country and gathered to create a new form of government—a republic—in which individual rights were more important than government's rights. In honor of the woman whose words inspired a revolution and who, according to popular lore, was the last person to be threatened by the Aged Out Law, a memorial statue of Naia was erected in the square of her hometown. It was the first public memorial built in centuries. (Of special note, Naia's three living children and Wilda's daughter, Michelle, lay flowers at the base of the statue that had been propagated from the utility box secret garden that Wilda had so lovingly tended.)

Eleven months later, after deposing all existing government officials, the leaders of this revolution convened on May 29—in honor of what would have been Naia's seventy-first birthday—to create a new guiding document and set of principles to govern the masses.

It began with the words **"We, the People…"**

About the Author

Karen Patrice "Pat" Nussbaum is a sixty-seven-year-old grandma who lives in Nicholasville, Kentucky, with her husband and best friend, Stephen. She is retired from careers in special education, working with the elderly in assisted-living facilities, and long-term care planning. Pat has written opinion columns for her city newspapers, including the Albany (NY) *Times Union* and *Lexington Herald-Leader*. She is well known for her compelling letters to people in power that frequently prove positive for the betterment of her community and those seeking fair treatment. Pat has always been a storyteller, and she finally wrote one down!

Pat is also a political junkie who believes the United States is the greatest country to have ever existed on planet Earth. Her novel, *Aged Out*, is offered as a political thriller that portrays the type of futuristic outcome that could emerge from today's socialistic trends and ideologies. The novel's heroine, Naia Gold, is a reflection of her own efforts as a lone woman to restore sense and sensibility to a culture whose moral compass and overall ethos may be headed toward self-destruction. Pat believes her novel is very timely with regard to current political and social issues.

CPSIA information can be obtained
at www.ICGtesting.com
Printed in the USA
BVHW080227211221
624508BV00006B/95